DESPERATE REMEDIES

THE NEW WESSEX EDITION

THE NEW WESSEX EDITION

THOMAS HARDY

Desperate Remedies

A Novel

Introduction by
C. J. P. Beatty

'Though an unconnected course of adventure is what most frequently
occurs in nature, yet the province of the romance-writer being artificial,
there is more required from him than a mere compliance with the
simplicity of reality.'

Sir W. Scott

PAPERMAC

First edition published elsewhere 1871

New Wessex Edition first published 1975
Reprinted six times
Reissued 1986 by
Macmillan London Limited
4 Little Essex Street London WC2R 3LF
and Basingstoke

Associated companies in Auckland, Delhi, Dublin, Gaborone,
Hamburg, Harare, Hong Kong, Johannesburg, Kuala Lumpur,
Lagos, Manzini, Melbourne, Mexico City, Nairobi, New York,
Singapore and Tokyo

Reprinted 1986, 1988

ISBN 0-333-41749-6

Co-ordinating editors
Caroline Hobhouse
Edward Leeson

Typeset by Filmtype Services Limited, Scarborough
Printed and bound in Great Britain by
Cox & Wyman Ltd

Contents

Biography

1840	Hardy born at Higher Bockhampton, near Dorchester. His father and grandfather were master-stonemasons, also keen performers in the band or 'quire' of the local parish church.
1848	Attended school established by his local patroness Julia Augusta Martin. About this time his mother gave him Dryden's *Virgil*, *Rasselas* and *Paul and Virginia*.
1849	Transferred to school in Dorchester. Played fiddle at local weddings and dances.
1856–61	Articled to Dorchester architect John Hicks. Studied Latin and Greek from five to eight in the morning. Began writing verse. Was introduced to modern thought by his friend Horace Moule, son of the Vicar of Fordington.
1862–7	In London, working for the architect Arthur Blomfield. Read widely; studied paintings in National Gallery; became an agnostic.
1867–70	Returned to Dorset for health reasons and was employed by Hicks, and his successor Crickmay, on church restoration.
1868	Completed draft of first novel, 'The Poor Man and the Lady' (later destroyed).
1870	Sent by Crickmay to St Juliot in Cornwall and met future wife Emma Lavinia Gifford. Writing *Desperate Remedies*, his first published novel.
1873	Invited by Leslie Stephen to contribute serial (*Far from the Madding Crowd*) to *Cornhill*.
1874	Married and took rooms in Surbiton.
1876–8	Living at Sturminster Newton; writing *The Return of the Native*.
1878–81	Living in London. Was becoming well known in literary circles. Had serious illness while writing *A Laodicean*.
1881	Took house at Wimborne Minster.
1883	Went to live in Dorchester.
1885	Moved into the house, Max Gate, in Dorchester, which he had built for himself. He and his wife continued to make long annual visits to London.
1888–91	Writing many short stories. Publication of *Tess of the d'Urbervilles* in 1891 created furore.
1892	His father died.
1892–4	Worsening relations with his wife, the trouble being exacerbated by the writing of *Jude the Obscure*. In 1893 they visited Dublin and met Mrs Henniker, with whom he collaborated on a short story and perhaps fell in love.

1895–6	Publication of *Jude* causes scandal. He resolved to give up novel-writing.
1897–8	Writing and revising poems for his first collection, *Wessex Poems*.
1902	Began *The Dynasts*.
1904	His mother died.
1910	Received the Order of Merit.
1912	Making final revision of the Wessex novels. His wife died in November.
1913	In March made penitential pilgrimage to St Juliot and later to his wife's birthplace, Plymouth. Wrote flood of poems 'in expiation'.
1914	Married Florence Dugdale. At outbreak of war joined group of writers pledged to write for the Allied Cause.
1914–28	Wrote and revised the material for several more collections of verse.
1928	Died. His ashes were buried in Westminster Abbey and his heart in his first wife's grave in Stinsford churchyard.

Hardy's Major Works
with year of book publication

1871 Desperate Remedies
1872 Under the Greenwood Tree
1873 A Pair of Blue Eyes
1874 Far from the Madding Crowd
1876 The Hand of Ethelberta
1878 The Return of the Native
1880 The Trumpet-Major
1881 A Laodicean
1882 Two on a Tower
1886 The Mayor of Casterbridge
1887 The Woodlanders
1888 Wessex Tales
1891 A Group of Noble Dames
1891 Tess of the d'Urbervilles
1894 Life's Little Ironies
1896 [1895] Jude the Obscure

1897 The Well-Beloved
1898 Wessex Poems
1902 Poems of the Past and the Present
1903 The Dynasts, pt 1
1906 The Dynasts, pt 2
1908 The Dynasts, pt 3
1909 Time's Laughingstocks
1913 A Changed Man and Other Tales
1914 Satires of Circumstance
1917 Moments of Vision
1922 Late Lyrics and Earlier
1923 The Famous Tragedy of the
       Queen of Cornwall
1925 Human Shows
1928 Winter Words
1952 Our Exploits at West Poley

Acknowledgments

The General Editor thanks the following for their kind assistance in answering queries: the Librarian of the English Folk Dance and Song Society; Mr John S. Creasey of the Museum of English Rural Life; and the Editor of *Notes and Queries*. He would also like to express a general indebtedness to R. L. Purdy's *Thomas Hardy: a bibliographical study* (Oxford University Press, 1954; reissued 1968); F. B. Pinion's *A Hardy Companion* (Macmillan, 1968); and Denys Kay-Robinson's *Hardy's Wessex Re-appraised* (David & Charles, 1972).

P. N. FURBANK

Introduction

In 1868 Thomas Hardy had completed his first novel, 'The Poor Man and the Lady', and the following year Chapman & Hall 'promised to put the book in hand'.[1] Subsequently, however, he was persuaded to see their reader George Meredith, and it was he who advised the would-be novelist either to rewrite 'The Poor Man and the Lady' or 'what would be much better ... attempt a novel with a purely artistic purpose, giving it a more complicated "plot" than was attempted with *The Poor Man and the Lady*'.[2] Hardy took Meredith's advice, and the result was *Desperate Remedies*, published anonymously in three volumes by Tinsley Brothers in 1871.

At this stage, then, it can be affirmed that Hardy was no novice. He had written one novel, an architectural prize essay, a sketch, 'How I Built Myself a House',[3] and a considerable number of poems rejected at the time but later to be published in different volumes of verse.[4] To judge from the poetry alone, Hardy was a great writer in the making even before 1869. But he had never tried his hand at a mystery story after the style of Wilkie Collins, which was broadly speaking what Meredith had in mind.

In the *Life* (p. 85), we are reminded of the situation as it was in the late 1860s: 'It was a sort of thing he had never contemplated writing, till, finding himself in a corner, it seemed necessary to attract public attention at all hazards.' Although Hardy had been in the architectural profession since 1856 and was highly competent, he could not be called the architect of a single building then in existence. He had never been his own master and was obliged to carry out the commissions of his employer, however distasteful some of these must have been, especially in the field of 'restoration'. Furthermore, he had always wished to be a poet or, if not a poet, then presumably a novelist. The publication of *Desperate Remedies* was the breakthrough, the first of a long series of

---

[1] F. E. Hardy, *The Life of Thomas Hardy 1840–1928* (1962) p. 60.

[2] Ibid. p. 62.

[3] R. L. Purdy, *Thomas Hardy: a bibliographical study* (1954) p. 293.

[4] See *Life*, p. 54.

novels which took him to the forefront of Victorian letters.

The book divides naturally into two parts, the first ending after Cytherea's wedding in Chapter 13, section 4. Indeed, this part could almost be published separately as 'Too Late Beloved', one of the titles Hardy was to think of for his *Tess of the d'Urbervilles*. After the wedding, Cytherea largely disappears from the scene, the men take over, and the last third or so is devoted to the sensational in the best Wilkie Collins manner, though with flashes of the real Hardy here and there. It is with these first thirteen chapters that I shall chiefly concern myself here.

The heroine, Cytherea Graye, is a fascinating young woman, thoroughly honest and carefully educated, and everything seems set fair. Then, quite unexpectedly, there is a reversal; she loses her father who is already a widower, and finds herself alone in the world except for Owen, her elder brother. Just before her father's fatal accident Hardy explains the situation in poetical terms:

It was the last hour of experience she ever enjoyed with a mind entirely free from a knowledge of that *labyrinth* into which she stepped immediately afterwards – to continue a perplexed course along its mazes for the greater portion of twenty-nine subsequent months. (ch. 1, sect. 3; my italics)

This image of the labyrinth lies behind the whole book. Its significance is obvious on the purely sensational, detective level; on the emotional and spiritual level it greatly enriches our concept of the characters and events. As we are reminded in *A Dictionary of Symbols* by J. E. Cirlot (1971), the labyrinth has primitive origins and religious connotations, and can be interpreted as being either good or evil, positive or negative. Perhaps it can even resemble a human mixture of the two. In this particular instance the labyrinth appears to stand for life itself. We are scarcely born until we understand 'the real meaning of Taking Thought', as Hardy puts it (ch. 1, sect. 3). Life only really begins when one enters the labyrinth, and ability to cope with its unexpected twists and turns depends mainly on two things: the particular qualities with which one is endowed and the experience gained in the labyrinth itself.

It is illuminating to put side by side Wilkie Collins's description of Magdalen in his novel *No Name* (1862) and Hardy's description of Cytherea:

... The eyes ... were of that nearly colourless gray, which, though little attractive in itself, possesses the rare compensating merit of interpreting *the finest graduations* of thought, *the gentlest changes* of feeling, the deepest trouble of passion, with a subtle transparency of expression which no darker eyes can rival. ... The whole countenance ... was rendered additionally striking by its extraordinary *mobility*. The large, electric, light-gray eyes were hardly ever in repose; all varieties of expression followed each other over the plastic, ever-changing face, with a giddy rapidity which left sober analysis far behind in the race. ... Her figure ... instinct with such a seductive, serpentine *suppleness*, so lightly and playfully graceful, that its movements suggested, not unnaturally, the movements of a young cat – her figure was so perfectly developed already that no one who saw her could have supposed that she was only eighteen. She bloomed in the full physical maturity of twenty years or more – bloomed naturally and irresistibly, in right of her matchless health and strength. ... Her headlong course down the house stairs; the brisk activity of all her movements; the incessant sparkle of expression in her face; the enticing gaiety which took the hearts of the quietest people by storm ... all sprang alike from the same source; from the overflowing physical health which strengthened every muscle, braced every nerve, and set the warm young blood tingling through her veins. ... (*No Name*, ch. 1; my italics)

Indeed, *motion* was her speciality, whether shown on its *most extended scale* of bodily progression, or *minutely*, as in the uplifting of her eyelids, the bending of her fingers, the pouting of her lip. The carriage of her head – *motion within motion* – *a glide upon a glide* – was as delicate as that of a *magnetic needle*. And this flexibility and elasticity had never been taught her by rule, nor even been acquired by observation, but ... had naturally developed itself with her years. In infancy, a stone or stalk in the way, which had been the inevitable occasion of a fall to her playmates, had usually left her safe and upright on her feet after the narrowest escape by *oscillations* and whirls for the preservation of her balance. ...

But to attempt to gain a view of her – or indeed of any fascinating woman – from a *measured category*, is as difficult as to appreciate the effect of a landscape by exploring it at night with a lantern — or of a full chord of music by piping the notes in succession. Nevertheless it may readily be believed ... that among the many winning phases of her aspect, these were particularly striking: –

During pleasant doubt, when her eyes brightened stealthily and smiled ... as distinctly as her lips, and in the space of a single instant expressed clearly *the whole round of degrees* of expectancy which lie over the wide expanse between Yea and Nay. (*Desperate Remedies*, ch. 1, sect. 3; my italics)

Each author realizes that, as Wilkie Collins says, 'sober analysis' of the heroine's more subtle qualities is an impossible feat. However, there is no doubt that Hardy is determined to make a serious attempt at such an analysis, which will give the reader a chance to assess Cytherea's likely performance in the labyrinth. Indeed, it is this attempt that distinguishes Hardy's description from that of Wilkie Collins. It is clear that Cytherea's special attribute is the ability to skirt round obstacles in her path without losing her balance; but Hardy is at the same time attempting something very different, namely no less than a 'Beaufort scale'[1] of feminine sensibility in which the woman herself is the recording instrument. One emotion soon to be registered is the particular doubt that immediately precedes falling in love, before reflection has set in (ch. 3, sect. 2). This intermediate situation is perhaps the most 'blissful', when the girl is anxious not to 'be misconstrued or under-rated to the breadth of a shadow of a hair' and when the simplest question can give rise to 'a series of minute blushes'. A few moments later her feelings are actually mapped out by the movement of the boat that carries the lovers across the bay. The zigzags representing Cytherea's hesitations or unwillingness to look Edward Springrove in the eye, the semi-circular sweep indicating her embarrassment at being unable to avoid his ardent gaze, graph the course of her emotions.

This love-scene also presents us with the first clear reference to the Classical world in the novel. Not for Cytherea and Edward the shriek of the mandrake from the darker shores of sexuality (ch. 12, sect. 6), but the 'bloom' and the 'purple light' strong on the lineaments of both (ch. 3, sect. 2). Let us look more closely at Hardy's source:

> Thee the voice, the dance, obey,
> Temper'd to thy warbled lay.
>   O'er Idalia's velvet-green
>   The rosy-crownèd Loves are seen
> On Cytherea's day
>   With antic Sports, and blue-eyed Pleasures,
>   Frisking light in frolic measures;
> Now pursuing, now retreating,
>   Now in circling troops they meet:
> To brisk notes in cadence beating
>   Glance their many-twinkling feet.
> Slow melting strains their Queen's approach declare:
>   Where'er she turns the Graces homage pay.
> With arms sublime, that float upon the air,
>   In gliding state she wins her easy way:

---

[1] A scale devised by Admiral Sir Francis Beaufort (1774–1857) for measuring wind velocity by number from 0 to 12.

> O'er her warm cheek, and rising bosom, move
> The bloom of young Desire, and purple light of Love.[1]

As it is 'Cytherea's day' in the poem it would appear that the Queen so honoured must be Aphrodite/Venus herself. The lines quoted are part of a Pindaric ode on 'The Progress of Poesy' by Thomas Gray. Do they not explain why Hardy chose the name Cytherea for his two main female characters (as well as the surname 'Graye' for his heroine), although, of course, he was no doubt already familiar with the name Cytherea from his reading of Virgil? It is indeed she who delivers the god, as Hardy puts it. The bliss of the young lovers is hinted at, too, in the description of what they see beneath the surface of the water where tiny creatures and even weeds seem to partake of the same harmony:

> The breeze had entirely died away, leaving the water of that rare glassy smoothness. . . . Purples and blues of divers shades were reflected from this mirror accordingly as each undulation sloped east or west. They could see the rocky bottom some twenty feet beneath them, luxuriant with weeds of various growths, and dotted pulpy creatures reflecting a silvery and spangled radiance upwards to their eyes. (ch. 3, sect. 2)

However, this ecstasy of love lasts but a few minutes, as Edward feels constrained to make a partial confession of some fault on his side that ruins everything. 'Doubt – indefinite, carking doubt had taken possession of her.' Outwardly Cytherea is as graceful as ever; inwardly she forgets 'herself to marble like Melancholy'. The needle has stopped registering. It is significant that on her wedding day she 'seemed to stand more like a statue than Cytherea Graye' (ch. 13, sect. 3).

In one particular Cytherea is in a comparable plight to the heroine of *No Name*: she finds herself orphaned and practically penniless early in the book, and is obliged to take up some kind of employment. As we know, very little choice was open to Victorian women. Cytherea obtains a post as lady's-maid in the first instance to Miss Aldclyffe of Knapwater House. No sooner is she there than Hardy likens her to the

---

[1] See *Poems of Thomas Gray*, ed. Austin Lane Poole (1948) p. 47. This does not exclude a Virgilian source for 'purple light' – 'aether et lumine vestit/purpureo, solemque suum, sua sidera norunt' (*Æneid*, bk VI, ll. 640–1) – so much as suggest that Virgil may have derived *his* 'purple light' from an earlier poet, perhaps Pindar. Dryden's translation (1697) for the above runs as follows: 'With ether vested, and a purple sky . . . Stars of their own, and their own suns, they know.' See also Donald Davie's 'Hardy's Virgilian Purples', in *Agenda*, Spring–Summer 1972, pp. 138–56. Cf. 'the purple light' in *A Pair of Blue Eyes*, ch. 4, and 'the purple light and bloom of her own passion' in *The Woodlanders*, ch. 24. I am indebted to Prof. H. F. Brooks for the discovery of this most important poetic source.

Blessed Damozel as she leans upon the window sill of her little room and looks out over the garden. In an early Budmouth scene when she was in lodgings with her brother, Cytherea had wondered in an idle moment whom she might marry: gentleman of fashion, soldier, sailor or even 'rather a poor man – noble-minded and affectionate, but still poor—' (ch. 2, sect. 2). Now she is in a grand house but in the position of a servant, and her day-dreaming takes on a melancholy tone, even leading her to the workhouse! The Forest of Arden would be preferable. . . . In Rossetti's poem, the Blessed Damozel is in heaven musing over her lover who has still to join her, and all would appear to be most spiritual and unearthly. But the irony of 'The Blessed Damozel' should not be lost on us: by analogy with the poem, Knapwater House is Cytherea's heaven, although there is little as yet to warrant the description in her eyes. She is depressed and bewildered. It is then that, beyond the lawn and flower beds, she notices some innocent sheep bearing the branded letters 'E.S.' (ch. 5, sect. 2). She is at once taken out of her reverie, and soon verifies that Farmer Edward Springrove, Edward's father, has recommended her for the post. Her lover is, in this way, at hand. Knapwater House is indeed to become their heaven but not until the epilogue, entitled 'Sequel'. If Cytherea herself is hardly conscious of the vivid flowers that are just beneath her window – the Blessed Damozel in the poem has three lilies in her hand, with obvious symbolic significance – the reader should realize that these lush plants of high summer can suggest the passions of another Cytherea which are to declare themselves a few hours later. The knowledge that Edward is near, together with her own independent spirit, enables Cytherea Graye to weather the early encounters with her new mistress.

It is at this stage in the novel that we begin to realize that, although Cytherea Graye is the heroine, the other Cytherea, namely Miss Aldclyffe her employer, is likely to play an important role in the story. Such premonitions are indeed correct as Miss Aldclyffe ultimately directs operations on both the emotional and the economic planes. Her early passionate scenes with her young namesake have been called Lesbian; but a further explanation could be that she is a tragic example of a woman deprived of the filial affection which should have been hers. The scene presented by Hardy is certainly convincing; and one wonders whether the portrait of Miss Aldclyffe does not owe something to his own observations of the lady of the manor when he was barely ten years old. She treated him as a substitute for a child of her own.[1] Miss

[1] See *Life*, pp. 18–19.

Aldclyffe is a powerful figure whose precise equal is difficult to find in the other Wessex novels (though Mrs Charmond in *The Woodlanders* shows some points of similarity).

Now, it must be unique to find two main characters sharing the name Cytherea, which is, appropriately enough, an epithet of Aphrodite/Venus, the goddess of love. Superficially, the same name was chosen for reasons of plot, but in the labyrinth of experience this choice of one name for the two most important characters in the novel is of deeper significance. The innocent young Cytherea thinks she has already tasted some of the agonies of love but the cynical Miss Aldclyffe taunts her with these lines from Shelley:

> Love's passions shall rock thee
> As the storm rocks the ravens on high,
> Bright reason will mock thee
> Like the sun from a wintry sky.

But this is to anticipate. The meeting of the two Cythereas at Knapwater House is not such a coincidence as one might think, for the real tragedy lies in the answer to the question: does each succeeding generation have to make the same irrevocable mistakes in matters of love? Miss Aldclyffe has seen it all before, has experienced all the bitterness of love. On her own admission she is an ill-tempered woman half out of her mind: 'I have met deceit by deceit, till I am weary of it – weary, weary – and I long to be what I shall never be again – artless and innocent, like you . . .' (ch. 6, sect. 1). She is a woman with a past, used to laying false trails, and covering her tracks; yet her new lady's-maid is different. The convergence of these two could mean a change in her for the better. Perhaps after years of wandering in the labyrinth searching for a way out she comes round the same old corner to discover not the usual blank wall and sense of despair, but her other self, her real self – Cytherea. Miss Cytherea Aldclyffe was innocent once: 'I am a lonely woman, and I want the sympathy of a pure girl like you. . . .' She wants to hear Cytherea say her prayers: 'It would seem so like old times to me – when I was young, and nearer – far nearer Heaven than I am now. . . .' So begins her unburdening to her newly acquired child, and their first long meeting has a completely therapeutic effect on the older woman.

It so happens that during the night Miss Aldclyffe's father dies and the whole situation changes. For the first time in her life she is in sole charge of affairs. What will she do now? Will the soothing presence of Cytherea Graye continue to have a good effect or will Miss Aldclyffe's tendency to deceit quickly regain the upper hand? She does not mourn her father's death. They obviously had differences over a certain man, namely, Æneas Manston, whom we still have to meet. Manston means a great deal to Miss Aldclyffe yet she has shown him 'indifference for so many, many years' because of her father. Now that she wishes to contact him again he is not so easy to find. She does not even realize that he has married, and it is clear that he is very reluctant to apply for the post of steward at Knapwater House, a post which he nevertheless obtains over the heads of much better candidates including Edward Springrove. It is equally clear that Miss Aldclyffe must have some special reason for wanting him near, and now she can gratify her desire and install him as steward in the Old Manor House on the estate. Miss Aldclyffe's lawyer, who was instructed to advertise the post of steward on her behalf, describes Manston as 'a voluptuary with activity' – a completely unbiased assessment – so that altogether little harmony can be expected to develop as a result of this idiosyncratic appointment. Once again on the plot level the whole operation is neatly contrived. Manston was moderately happy/unhappy in his own part of the labyrinth and had learnt not to expect anything much from the mysterious Miss Aldclyffe. All of a sudden come overtures from the great lady and he is offered a sinecure which he would be foolish to refuse.

On a deeper level, though, we can see the introduction of Manston at this point as the inevitable expression of the darker side of Miss Aldclyffe's character. She is tired of secrets and continual pretence and now perhaps the volcanic nature of her passions can erupt more freely. However, there is another possible reason for the introduction of Manston: he is the character who completes the quartet. The word 'labyrinth' comes from a Greek word meaning 'a double-bladed axe' and is thereby connected with the Gemini myth. If Edward and Cytherea stand for innocent and youthful love, then Manston and Miss Aldclyffe represent the opposite edge of the axe, namely, passion and intrigue. The four have to converge upon one point if they are to act out their predestined roles – Carriford (from carré, the French for 'a square', I suggest) is their meeting-place in the labyrinth; and all four at one time or other have to come to the Great House (or its estate), which Hardy says 'approximated to a square on the ground plan'. What Cytherea has fathomed about the past history of her older companion was that the 'reckless adventuring of the lady's youth seemed connected with deeds of darkness rather than of light'. Inevitably, darkness is attracted by light; and Manston, like Miss Aldclyffe, is attracted to Cytherea so that Edward Springrove now has two rivals to face, while the young Cytherea has two potential enemies to contend with.

Amid all the dramatic events at Knapwater House the reader – and indeed Cytherea herself – is inclined to forget the existence of Edward Springrove; yet he is clearly meant to be the hero of the love story as he is likened early in the novel to the Great Duke Ferdinand in 'The Statue and the Bust':

> He looked at her as a lover can;
> She looked at him as one who awakes –
> The past was a sleep, and her life began.

This comparison not only adds a sense of dignity to their association but the use of Browning's poem is an earnest of the genuine quality of their love. The poem, too, warns the reader of the likely outcome of the affair. Already we have noticed that something seems to be holding Edward back in spite of their mutual declaration of love. Browning's message is clear: Have the courage of your convictions. Their love was too precious a gift to be frittered away. After her marriage Cytherea pathetically quotes these lines from the poem to a broken Edward Springrove:

> The world and its ways have a certain worth,
> And to press a point where these oppose
> Were a simple policy.

The fact is that Edward Springrove is almost as unschooled in the ways of the world as Cytherea Graye. He, too, wanders into a labyrinth (ch. 11, sect. 4) where he soon discovers that scrupulous honesty alone affords inadequate protection against hidden snares.

Now, the Knapwater estate also comprises a second manor-house, the presence of two being a unique feature in the whole range of the Wessex novels. This is the original Elizabethan manor-house (now dilapidated and only about two-thirds of its original size) which has been hastily adapted for Manston's occupation.

Critics have pointed to quasi-Gothic elements in *Desperate Remedies* and these no doubt exist; but they can be exaggerated. One might see Gothic overtones in the first meeting between Cytherea and Manston at the Old House when the atmosphere was oppressive and full of a sense of foreboding. (Wilkie Collins, too, knew how to use an old building to advantage in *No Name* when he makes old Admiral Bartram sleepwalk through the ancient and neglected banqueting-hall.) But the meeting must also be seen in relation to the labyrinth as a whole and to Cytherea's first outing alone with Edward Springrove in Budmouth Bay discussed above. Hardy uses some of the same shapes to link the two scenes together: zigzags of lightning and balls of fire correspond to the zigzags and semi-circular sweep of the young lovers' cockle-boat. But this time Cytherea is far from being in control of the situation. Then there is the music Manston plays on his organ as a defiant counterpoint to the storm. This, too, is a totally new experience, for Cytherea had never heard such powerful harmonies before.

The power of the music did not show itself so much by attracting her attention to the subject of the piece, as by taking up and developing as its libretto the poem of her own life and soul, shifting her deeds and intentions from the hands of her judgment and holding them in its own. (ch. 8. sect. 4)

One is tempted to interpose here: where is her much vaunted sense of balance which Hardy insisted upon early in the book? It is not forgotten. She is not swept off her feet – 'His influence over her had vanished with the musical chords' – and inwardly she registers that such an experience must not be allowed to occur again. If, later, she reaches the bitter depths of indifferent despair – 'She felt as one in a boat without oars, drifting with closed eyes down a river – she knew not whither' – it is through constant and unrelenting pressure on the part of the powers that be. She does not love Manston and never will.

The setting of the greater part of the story is the village and parish of Carriford. Hardy singles out four buildings for special treatment – the Great House or Knapwater House, the Old House or what is left of the original Elizabethan manor-house, the Three Tranters Inn, and the church – and he introduces them approximately in this order. Knapwater House stands on an eminence and is a handsome example of a country gentleman's ideal residence at the end of the eighteenth century. Some idea of the wealth of its owners can be gathered from the fact that they were able to abandon the Elizabethan house a quarter of a mile away. Its position was too damp and unhealthy for them, but it is now used in part as labourers' cottages. Hardy the antiquarian may well prefer the Old House to its more modern substitute, but he has no illusions as to the inevitability of change. However attractive this building might be architecturally, Miss Aldclyffe was only interested as far as 'its fitness for adaptation to modern requirements' was concerned. The third building is the posting-inn, and it, too, is in a state of neglect. A medieval inn – magnificent in its bustling heyday – it is now slowly dying as a result of the recent arrival of the railway and already has the air of a fossil. Hardy places many scenes in the church, the fourth building. Gradually one can form some impression of it as a whole from the scattered details Hardy gives. It is very much the centre of community life. Mr Raunham, the Rector, is a distant relative of the Aldclyffes. Clearly the main employer in the village is the lord of the manor, that is, Miss Aldclyffe herself after her father's death. Farmer Springrove, as landlord of the Three Tranters, must have been an important member of the community; but following the disappearance of the stage-coach he has felt obliged to eke out 'his attenuated income by increasing the extent of his agricultural business if he would still maintain his social standing'. He has in addition a small cider-making business. Hardy gives us a fairly full picture of the village, from the lord of the manor to the postmistress and Crickett, the parish clerk, a character much applauded by the earliest reviewers. The village is going through a period of transition. The posting-inn has lost its main purpose; the Old House has seen better days. Yet all four buildings belong essentially to the history of the place. The severity of the architecture of Knapwater House and its remoteness from the village (more than a quarter of a mile away) reflect the attitude of the landowners living there. The word 'romantic' is applied to the Elizabethan fragment and to stage-coach travelling, but never to the Great House. This is not just a question of Hardy's preference for Elizabethan or medieval architecture. It is a way of stating that all is not quite as it should be in the countryside, where too much hangs upon the words of the lord of the manor. We only have to think of Strooden, the superintending workman, who is far from reassured by Miss Aldclyffe's remarks on the appointment of a steward over him. There is, too, the unnamed villager who accosts Manston on the night of the fire, 'a small farmer originally, who had drunk himself down to a day-labourer and reputed poacher'. Here it might be illuminating to quote from Michael Millgate:

The situation of the village tradesman . . . was full of potential drama. Not only was this class, as Hardy says, 'better-informed' than the labouring class, it had much greater prospects of mobility, up or down, and much greater opportunity for independent action of every kind.[1]

This unnamed labourer had once belonged to the class Millgate describes. In the same novel, however, there is an excellent example of a farmer's son who is rising in the world. At one point there

[1] *Thomas Hardy: his career as a novelist* (1971) p. 212.

is an interview at Knapwater House between Miss Aldclyffe and Edward Springrove which Hardy describes as follows:

Miss Aldclyffe, like a good many others in her position, had plainly not realized that a son of her tenant and inferior could have become an educated man, who had learnt to feel his individuality, to view society from a Bohemian standpoint, far outside the farming grade in Carriford parish, and that hence he had all a developed man's unorthodox opinion about the subordination of classes. (ch. 11, sect. 4)

As we know, Edward Springrove has become an architect – no small achievement when seen against the background of his humble Carriford origins.

Undoubtedly, the most dramatic event in the whole novel is the fire that burns down the Three Tranters Inn together with dwellings adjoining. A building which had lasted some 400 years is destroyed in a matter of minutes. For Hardy has a Victorian obsession with time. 'The man of measuring eye' ('Heiress and Architect') is able to control space, to assess size and distance and to appreciate the order of the stellar universe; so why not demonstrate his mastery of time? First, draw the reader's attention to the paramount importance of time by including a time measurement in the heading of every chapter and section (except Sequel). (Wilkie Collins attempts the same in *No Name*, less obtrusively, and chiefly in the letter sequences.) The first chapter, for example, covers thirty years and serves as a prologue, while Sequel covers an hour or so and acts as an epilogue. But to return to the fire and its signal importance in Hardy's time-scheme. If we limit the novel's time-span to the twenty-nine months subsequent to Cytherea's stepping into the labyrinth on 12 October 1863 and remember that the inn was burnt down between half-past eleven and midnight on 28 November 1864, we can say that Hardy is working to a time-scale of one half-hour in twenty-nine months. Such is his precision. This half-hour, it could be argued, is also the most decisive in the lives of the chief protagonists. But this is not all. The Great Fire of 1666, which Hardy also mentions, completely changed the face of London. Similarly, the village of Carriford will never be the same again. Hardy, too, makes a point of informing us that the Houses of Parliament were burnt down in the evening of 16 October 1834. Whereas the Houses of Parliament were rebuilt, no rebuilding of the ancient inn is ever mooted, although Edward Springrove is an architect. We may also remind ourselves that the foundation of Rome presupposed the destruction of Troy, which was largely brought about by fire (*Æneid*, bk II).

During the previous autumn Farmer Springrove had been reclaiming a piece of waste land by ploughing, harrowing, cleaning – a thoroughly back-breaking business symbolic of man's immemorial struggle to wrest sustenance from the earth. Now the same man, through his carelessness, is going to cause a fire that will consume not only the ancient inn but several houses besides. The section that leads up to the conflagration itself is headed 'From Ten to Half-past Eleven p.m.' (ch. 10, sect. 2) but, exceptionally, the drama is heightened by Hardy's almost minute-by-minute commentary as the moment approaches for the flames from the heap of couch-grass to take over:

> . . . a quarter past eleven. . . .
> At twenty minutes past eleven. . . .
> Five minutes later. . . .
> A short time subsequent to this. . . .
> . . . in less than thirty seconds. . . .

The inn is no longer 'time-honoured' – Hardy's own ironic description here – but fire-consumed. It is significant that the railway-porter could have prevented the fire: 'But the cottages not being his, he went on his way to the station, where he was about to resume duty for the night.' He is an alien figure and the affairs of the village are none of his business. The villagers are taken completely unawares; they cannot deal with such a catastrophe. Mr Raunham has the village fire-appliance brought to the scene but its hose can only play a few innocuous drops of water on to the roaring flames. The pace of things has become too rapid. The inn cannot be restored. The Industrial Revolution cannot be halted. In the cities, conditions among the poor are much worse. Their sheer inability to understand or cope with the problems of the new industrial age is presented by Hardy in a short scene, of which the following is the most telling detail:

Against the wall a Dutch clock was fixed out of level, and ticked wildly in longs and shorts, its entrails hanging down beneath its white face and wiry hands, like the fæces of a Harpy. . . . (ch. 16, sect. 4)

Through this image of the Harpy/clock Hardy manages to convey not only the squalor, dirt and stench of a tenement in mid-Victorian London – Harpies were notorious for their filthy habits – but also the ever-brooding presence of death, another characteristic function of the Harpies being to snatch away the souls of the dead.

But, to return to Carriford village, as the church clock strikes the hour of midnight with the Three Tranters Inn 'a mere heap of red-hot charcoal', the 'bewildered chimes' begin to run through the air of the Old Hundred-and-Thirteenth Psalm:

Ye saints and servants of the Lord, the triumphs of his Name record[1]

and so forth. What can these words do to help when the earth is on fire? What does the Christian message mean to Victorian England? In the same scene Hardy notes that the white of the labourers' smock-frocks is repeated in the whiteness of the headstones in the churchyard, 'the surface of which, raised by the interments of generations, stood four or five feet above the level of the road'. This brings to mind the shock wisdom of the last sentence in Manston's confession at the end of the novel: 'When we survey the long race of men, it is strange and still more strange to find that they are mainly dead men, who have scarcely ever been otherwise' (ch. 21, sect. 1). We can all say 'Amen' to that.

The vivid scene of the fire, then, which occurs at a critical point nearly half-way through, while essential to the melodramatic plot also reveals something of the human ecology of the countryside. It was not merely that 'all stood still, and gazed silently, awestruck and helpless, in the presence of so irresistible an enemy' and that church, cottage and mansion (Knapwater House does send its fire engine too) were equally powerless in the face of disaster, but also that Farmer Springrove, the lessee of the cottages, might be required by the lessor, Miss Aldclyffe, to have them rebuilt according to the agreement between landlord and tenant. Furthermore, the cottages were not insured, which meant that Springrove alone would be responsible for finding the minimum of £600 necessary to rebuild the houses, should Miss Aldclyffe insist upon her rights. Such uncertainties were hardly conducive to the improvement of the countryman's lot. The whole question of the farm-labourer, his landlord and the depopulation of the countryside is thus broached for the first time in Hardy's published work. This was a problem which he was to touch upon in so many of his subsequent novels and one which lies at the very root of the tragedy in *The Woodlanders*. The problems that now beset Farmer Springrove are similar to those which cause the death – however indirectly – of Giles Winterborne, and contribute to the destitution of the Durbeyfields in *Tess of the d'Urbervilles*.

Indeed, Farmer Springrove resembles – no one more closely –

---

[1] The first line of Psalm CXIII, from N. Tate and N. Brady, *A New Version of the Psalms of David. Fitted to the Tunes Used in Churches* (n.d.).

Farmer Broadford who appears in *An Indiscretion in the Life of an Heiress*, which Hardy published in the *New Quarterly Magazine* in July 1878. This work, indeed, is of special interest to us as, according to Mrs Florence Hardy, who republished it in 1934 in a limited edition, it is 'an adaptation by the author of his first novel, *The Poor Man and the Lady*, which was never published . . .'.[1] Farmer Broadford's family house had lapsed to the squire on the dropping of the lives for which it was held. He was not dispossessed, however, as Winterborne is to be, but 'after his father's death the family had continued as before in the house and farm, but as yearly tenants'. Later the squire decides that he wants to enlarge his park and that Broadford's old house is an encumbrance. Efforts are made to persuade the squire to change his mind; whereupon Farmer Broadford, who is an old man, conveniently dies, partly, one feels, as a result of worrying about the question of the tenure: 'Were the house and farm . . . taken away . . . it would affect his life . . . out of all proportion to the seriousness of the event' (pt I, ch. 3). The house is then pulled down. In fact, the two farmers are virtually interchangeable and deserve an equal share of our commiseration. True, Miss Aldclyffe does not need to have a house or houses pulled down to enlarge her park as the fire has done that for her: 'I don't want them rebuilt; you know it was intended by my father, directly they fell in, to clear the site for a new entrance to the park?' (ch. 11, sect. 1). It serves her purpose later, however, to mask her real intentions and insist, ironically enough, on the rebuilding of the cottages knowing full well that Springrove cannot afford to do so.

Desperate Remedies is very much more than a mystery story. In it Hardy is beginning his life-long study of man's situation on earth and examining the Classical and Judaeo-Christian cultures to see if they furnish any answer to the problems that face mankind in the new industrial age. On the Classical side we have already noted the description of the love between Cytherea and Edward Springrove. Furthermore, the story of Æneas provides a valid term of reference for much of the book. Hardy's mother gave her son a copy of Dryden's *Virgil* before he was ten, and the *Æneid*, 'of which he never wearied' (*Life*, p. 59), is quoted at least six times in *Desperate Remedies*, either in the original Latin or in Dryden's translation. Why, then, did Hardy give the name Æneas to Manston? Was it only because he was manipulated by Miss Aldclyffe to begin with, as Virgil's hero was manipulated by the gods? Miss Cytherea Aldclyffe, as 'the goddess of love', rules her domain

[1] See Purdy, p. 275.

from a Classical building and her estate contains a Grecian temple in which she talks of love to her young neophyte and namesake while swans (birds often associated with Venus) swim 'involuntarily' by. The image of the labyrinth in *Desperate Remedies*, with which first Cytherea and then Edward is associated, has obvious Classical connotations too. The famous Cretan labyrinth is mentioned in books V and VI of the *Æneid*. But, as I suggested at the outset, the labyrinth could stand for life itself which comprises *all* possible cultures, the Christian included.

What of Hardy's presentation of the Judaeo-Christian world? First there is the importance of the village church as the centre of the community, together with the innumerable references to the Bible, many of which fall from the lips of secondary characters like Clerk Crickett and Farmer Springrove. It is clear that the Bible and the church services have long provided a code of living for the simple folk of Carriford village who have scarcely yet realized how the advent of the railway is to affect them. Edward is the only protagonist whose first name is really Christian (Edward the Confessor, Edward the Martyr), while Springrove suggests perhaps a pastoral background, the grove where the goddess of love is worshipped. On the human level, then, it is he who should unite the two worlds through his marriage to Cytherea Graye, a girl with a Classical first name and a Christian upbringing. Twice, however, he is referred to as a ghostly figure, the second time being when he emerges 'spectre-thin' from the chantry of medieval tombs on the day of the wedding (ch. 13, sect. 3). In this connection it is difficult not to think of Swinburne, whom Hardy so much admired, and his 'pale Galilean'.[1] These 'reclining figures of cross-legged knights' are coeval with the inn which has been ruthlessly swept away.

Here we must turn to Cytherea herself, this tragic figure of a heroine caught in a dilemma where the only solution to her problem seems to lie in the Victorian sense of duty. Even Christianity tells her she must marry a man she does not love for the sake of her brother. The theme of time is especially poignant here. In her conversation with Owen after the wedding she imagines the 'Poor girl!' exclamations of sympathizers with her lot, a moving moment indeed:

'. . . "Poor girl!" was a whole life to me; as full of hours, minutes, and peculiar minutes, of hopes and dreads, smiles, whisperings, tears, as theirs. . . .' (ch. 13, sect. 4)

Time is not merely chronological but, measured in Bergsonian or

[1] See 'Hymn to Proserpine', in *Poems and Ballads*, 1st series (1866).

Proustian terms, it records suffering as well as joy and lies within the human heart. Moreover, Cytherea is the first Hardy heroine to be connected with the self-immolating doctrines in the Sermon on the Mount – incidentally Virgil's Dido practised self-immolation also – which we shall see exemplified to the full in *Tess of the d'Urbervilles*.

What is this young woman, who expresses so much dignity in the face of despair, really searching for? An answer may be found in the following lines from her last conversation with Edward in Chapter 13, section 4: '. . . to be a dependent and to have no other spot for the heart to *anchor* upon – O, it is mournful and harassing!' (my italics). The anchor can serve as the binding image of her experience. The anchor of salvation has long been a symbol of Christian hope and faith. It is also appropriate when we recall the opening scenes in Budmouth Bay and Hardy's later description of her plight, as being adrift in a boat without oars. Indeed, the anchor seems to represent man's eternal quest for a permanent home. Looking ahead to *Jude the Obscure* we read:

Jude . . . suddenly grew older. It had been the yearning of his heart to find something to anchor on, to cling to – for some place which he could call admirable. (pt I, ch. 3)

and later:

To an impressionable and lonely young man the consciousness of having at last found anchorage for his thoughts, which promised to supply both social and spiritual possibilities, was like the dew of Hermon, and he remained throughout the service in a sustaining atmosphere of ecstasy. (pt II, ch. 3)

But Jude was destined never to complete his pilgrimage. Æneas, that reluctant sailor, always hoped that each anchorage on his way would be the final one, but he *did* in the end achieve what destiny had in store for him.

Desperate Remedies was the subject of, in all, four important reviews; three were reasonably encouraging, but one was savage. The first appeared in the *Athenaeum* (1 April 1871) and stated that it was 'a powerful novel' and 'an even better notice' appeared in the *Morning Post* (13 April 1871). However, of the review in the *Spectator* (22 April 1871) Hardy wrote:

. . . alas . . . the *Spectator* brought down its heaviest-leaded pastoral staff on the prematurely happy volumes. . . . He remembered, for long years after, how he had read this review as he sat on a stile . . . on his way home to Bockhampton. The bitterness of that moment was never forgotten; at the time he wished that he were dead. (*Life*, p. 84)

The fourth review, almost certainly written by Hardy's friend and patron, H. M. Moule, came out in the *Saturday Review* (30 September 1871).

In his introduction to *Thomas Hardy: the critical heritage* (1970), the editor R. G. Cox writes:

All the reviews [of *Desperate Remedies*] agree in selecting for praise those parts of the novel which point forward to Hardy's most characteristic later work; their censure is directed against sensationalism and an over-complicated plot.

With hindsight the reviewers might have seized on very different points, some of which I have tried to highlight above; but hindsight is not necessarily an advantage to a critic. How many of us can read Hardy today, for example, without thinking of his Wessex? Yet the term 'Wessex' was first introduced by Hardy in *Far from the Madding Crowd*, published in 1874. At least the original readers of *Desperate Remedies* in 1871 were not mesmerized by Hardy's Wessex, as it did not then exist! In the first edition Creston was a 'seaport town and watering-place in the west of England', Carriford was a village half an hour's journey by train from Creston on the line to Southampton. The contemporary reader would have been quite satisfied with these few geographical indications and would hardly have wondered whether any village could possess *two* manor-houses, for example. The point I wish to make here is that in *Desperate Remedies* we already see Hardy the technicist at work, shaping his own world.[1] Knapwater House exists in the pages of *Desperate Remedies* and nowhere else. It is there as a powerful statement of order and symmetry in the Classical tradition. Similarly, the Three Tranters Inn, romantic in character, is there to represent the Middle Ages or the Christian thread in the pattern. One thinks of Chaucer and his pilgrims. The Old House is in a similar category. Certainly very few manor-houses like it survived into the mid-nineteenth century with 'an old arched gateway' even if 'two-thirds of the place . . . was already pulled down, or gone to ruin'. If real, it must have been a large and impressive mansion when complete!

[1] See *A Laodicean*, bk III, ch. 11; also 'The Science of Fiction', in *Thomas Hardy's Personal Writings*, ed. Harold Orel (1967) p. 134; and *The Architectural Notebook of Thomas Hardy*, ed. C. J. P. Beatty (1966) p. 19.

Hardy was obviously partly flattered and partly puzzled at the desire of later readers to identify all the buildings in his works, but he did his best to satisfy their wishes even though this sometimes led to strange compromises and alterations. In the case of Knapwater House he let it be thought that Kingston Maurward House, Stinsford, Dorset, was the original by allowing an illustration of Kingston Maurward to serve as a frontispiece both in the 1896 and 1912 editions of the Wessex novels. We can now perhaps better appreciate Hermann Lea's apparently tentative approach to the problem generally. He writes of Knapwater House that this 'was probably suggested by Kingston Maurward House'.[1] It is significant that the name Carriford was not changed later to conform to Wessex nomenclature and that it occurs nowhere else in Hardy's work.

Such, then, is Hardy's second attempt at the art of fiction. *Desperate Remedies* is undoubtedly a powerful work but it falls between two stools. Hardy was able for only some two-thirds of the book to integrate the truly Hardyan themes of tragic love and Darwinian man's predicament in an industrial society with the melodramatic requirements of the plot. But this is not to say that the last third is a failure on the strictly Wilkie Collins level. It is packed with incident and suspense. Furthermore, melodramatic elements and powers of observation such as might be associated with detection are important ingredients of Hardy's art. Only Hardy, for example, could have thought up the intricacies of the murderer's final efforts to bury the body of his victim watched by no fewer than three pairs of eyes. This technique is used again to brilliant effect on the last day of Mrs Yeobright's life in *The Return of the Native*. Of the four main protagonists the two women are the more fully drawn. Miss Aldclyffe, that imperious female with 'a Roman nose in its purest form, and . . . the round prominent chin with which the Cæsars are represented in ancient marbles', certainly behaves like a Classical goddess in the Victorian world, and Cytherea Graye is so nearly a replica of her younger and better self – at least in her own eyes – that she cannot resist the temptation to live her own life over again in the young girl. Cytherea is an honest young woman of exceptional poise and grace, but her early love-passages with Edward have hardly provided sufficient experience for the trails ahead. She is well able to stand up to Miss Aldclyffe's bullying, but in the special circumstances of the case she finds Manston much more difficult to handle. Edward Springrove strikes one as a fine character, an idealist with

[1] Hermann Lea, *Thomas Hardy's Wessex* (1913) p. 234.

'. . . a keen sense of having been passed in the race by men whose brains are nothing to his own, all through his seeing too far into things . . . thinking o' perfection in things, and then sickened that there's no such thing as perfection. . . .' (ch. 8, sect. 3)

of (as Hardy wrote in a letter to Havelock Ellis)

The Wilhelm Meister and Daniel Deronda class . . . the type to which the great mass of educated modern men of ordinary capacity are assimilating more or less.[1]

He, too, stands up to Miss Aldclyffe, but the plight of his father leaves him little room to manœuvre. Æneas Manston is to some extent enigmatic. How could a man whose passion was of a 'hot voluptuous nature' behave with such restraint, especially in a crucial scene such as the wedding-night? All the forces of society had been ranged on his side to bring about the marriage; now at a stroke these same forces rise against him to deprive him of his bride. Would there, in fact, have been a story at all if society had not exerted strong pressures also on the young Miss Bradleigh and separated her from Ambrose Graye? (In *Tess of the d'Urbervilles* it is the lovers themselves, and no one else, who decide their own fate.) But, whatever may be thought of Manston's behaviour throughout the novel, he undeniably achieves dignity in death.[2] Later, Hardy classified *Desperate Remedies* together with *The Hand of Ethelberta* and *A Laodicean* as a Novel of Ingenuity, an inevitable designation if the novel is to be considered as a whole. Yet for some two-thirds of its length *Desperate Remedies* surely deserves the attention normally given to a Novel of Character and Environment.

I am happy to acknowledge my debt to the Dorset County Museum and the Dorset County Library for access to their respective Hardy collections. Professors Harold Brooks, Michael Millgate, R. L. Purdy and Kathleen Tillotson gladly allowed me to consult them, as also did Jean Brooks, James Gibson, Frank Pinion and the Rev. John Yates. Lastly I am indebted to my Dorset friends John Antell and A. Tilley, and to my wife without whose help the work of editing would have taken far longer.

A star in the text indicates that an explanatory note is to be found at the end of the book, while superior numbers refer to footnotes.

[1] Havelock Ellis, *From Marlowe to Shaw*, ed. J. Gawsworth (1950) p. 7.

[2] I am indebted here to Dr Lennart A. Björk, editor of *The Literary Notes of Thomas Hardy*, vol. I (Gothenburg, 1974).

Prefatory Note

The following novel, the first published by the author, was written nineteen years ago, at a time when he was feeling his way to a method. The principles observed in its composition are, no doubt, too exclusively those in which mystery, entanglement, surprise, and moral obliquity are depended on for exciting interest; but some of the scenes, and at least one or two of the characters, have been deemed not unworthy of a little longer preservation; and as they could hardly be reproduced in a fragmentary form the novel is reissued complete – the more readily that it has for some considerable time been reprinted and widely circulated in America.

January 1889

To the foregoing note I have only to add that, in the present edition of *Desperate Remedies*, some Wessex towns and other places that are common to the scenes of several of this series of stories have been called for the first time by the names under which they appear elsewhere, for the satisfaction of any reader who may care for consistency in such matters.

This is the only material change; for, as it happened that certain characteristics which provoked most discussion in my latest story were present in this my first – published in 1871, when there was no French name for them* – it has seemed best to let them stand unaltered.

February 1896

The reader may discover, when turning over this sensational and strictly conventional narrative, that certain scattered reflections and sentiments therein are the same in substance with some in the *Wessex Poems* and others, published many years later.* The explanation of such tautology is that the poems were written before the novel, but as the author could not get them printed, he incontinently used here whatever of their content came into his head as being apt for the purpose – after dissolving it into prose, never anticipating at that time that the poems would see the light.

August 1912   T.H.

CHAPTER ONE
The Events of Thirty Years

1. December and January, 1835–36

In the long and intricately inwrought chain of circumstance which renders worthy of record some experiences of Cytherea Graye, Edward Springrove, and others, the first event directly influencing the issue was a Christmas visit.

In the above-mentioned year, 1835, Ambrose Graye, a young architect who had just begun the practice of his profession in the midland town of Hocbridge, to the north of Christminster,* went to London to spend the Christmas holidays with a friend who lived in Bloomsbury. They had gone up to Cambridge in the same year, and, after graduating together, Huntway, the friend, had taken orders.

Graye was handsome, frank, and gentle. He had a quality of thought which, exercised on homeliness, was humour; on nature, picturesqueness; on abstractions, poetry. Being, as a rule, broadcast, it was all three.

Of the wickedness of the world he was too forgetful. To discover evil in a new friend is to most people only an additional experience: to him it was ever a surprise.

While in London he became acquainted with a retired officer in the Navy named Bradleigh, who, with his wife and their daughter, lived in Dukery Street,* not far from Russell Square. Though they were in no more than comfortable circumstances, the captain's wife came of an ancient family whose genealogical tree was interlaced with some of the most illustrious and well-known in the kingdom.

The young lady, their daughter, seemed to Graye by far the most beautiful and queenly being he had ever beheld. She was about nineteen or twenty, and her name was Cytherea. In truth she was not so very unlike country girls of that type of beauty, except in one respect. She was perfect in her manner and bearing, and they were not. A mere distinguishing peculiarity, by catching the eye, is often read as the pervading characteristic, and she appeared to him no less than perfection throughout – transcending her rural rivals in very nature. Graye did a thing the blissfulness of which was only eclipsed by its hazardousness. He loved her at first sight.

1

His introductions had led him into contact with Cytherea and her parents two or three times on the first week of his arrival in London, and accident and a lover's contrivance brought them together as frequently the week following. The parents liked young Graye, and having few friends (for their equals in blood were their superiors in position), he was received on very generous terms. His passion for Cytherea grew not only strong, but ineffably exalted: she, without positively encouraging him, tacitly assented to his schemes for being near her. Her father and mother seemed to have lost all confidence in nobility of birth, without money to give effect to its presence, and looked upon the budding consequence of the young people's reciprocal glances with placidity, if not actual favour.

Graye's whole impassioned dream terminated in a sad and unaccountable episode. After passing through three weeks of sweet experience, he had arrived at the last stage – a kind of moral Gaza★ – before plunging into an emotional desert. The second week in January had come round, and it was necessary for the young architect to leave town.

Throughout his acquaintanceship with the lady of his heart there had been this marked peculiarity in her love: she had delighted in his presence as a sweetheart should do, yet from first to last she had repressed all recognition of the true nature of the thread which drew them together, blinding herself to its meaning and only natural tendency, and appearing to dread his announcement of them. The present seemed enough for her without cumulative hope: usually, even if love is in itself an end, it must be regarded as a beginning to be enjoyed.

In spite of evasions as an obstacle, and in consequence of them as a spur, he would put the matter off no longer. It was evening. He took her into a little conservatory on the landing, and there among the evergreens, by the light of a few tiny lamps, infinitely enhancing the freshness and beauty of the leaves, he made the declaration of a love as fresh and beautiful as they.

'My love – my darling, be my wife!'

She seemed like one just awakened.★ 'Ah – we must part now!' she faltered, in a voice of anguish. 'I will write to you.' She loosened her hand and rushed away.

In a wild fever Graye went home and watched for the next morning. Who shall express his misery and wonder when a note containing these words was put into his hand?

'Good-bye; good-bye for ever. As recognized lovers something

2

divides us eternally. Forgive me – I should have told you before; but your love was sweet! Never mention me.'

That very day, and as it seemed, to put an end to a painful condition of things, daughter and parents left London to pay off a promised visit to a relative in a western county. No message or letter of entreaty could wring from her any explanation. She begged him not to follow her, and the most bewildering point was that her father and mother appeared, from the tone of a letter Graye received from them, as vexed and sad as he at this sudden renunciation. One thing was plain: without admitting her reason as valid, they knew what that reason was, and did not intend to reveal it.

A week from that day Ambrose Graye left his friend Huntway's house and saw no more of the Love he mourned. From time to time his friend answered any inquiry Graye made by letter respecting her. But very poor food to a lover is intelligence of a mistress filtered through a friend. Huntway could tell nothing definitely. He said he believed there had been some prior flirtation between Cytherea and her cousin, an officer of the line, two or three years before Graye met her, which had suddenly been terminated by the cousin's departure for India, and the young lady's travelling on the Continent with her parents the whole of the ensuing summer, on account of delicate health. Eventually Huntway said that circumstances had rendered Graye's attachment more hopeless still. Cytherea's mother had unexpectedly inherited a large fortune and estates in the west of England by the rapid fall of some intervening lives. This had caused their removal from the small house in Bloomsbury, and, as it appeared, a renunciation of their old friends in that quarter.

Young Graye concluded that his Cytherea had forgotten him and his love. But he could not forget her.

2. From 1843 to 1861

Eight years later, feeling lonely and depressed – a man without relatives, with many acquaintances but no friends – Ambrose Graye met a young lady of a different kind, fairly endowed with money and good gifts. As to caring very deeply for another woman after the loss of Cytherea, it was an absolute impossibility with him. With all, the beautiful things of the earth become more dear as they elude pursuit; but with some natures utter elusion is the one special event which will make a passing love permanent for ever.

This second young lady and Graye were married. That he did not,

3

first or last, love his wife as he should have done, was known to all; but few knew that his unmanageable heart could never be weaned from useless repining at the loss of its first idol.

His character to some extent deteriorated, as emotional constitutions will under the long sense of disappointment at having missed their imagined destiny. And thus, though naturally of a gentle and pleasant disposition, he grew to be not so tenderly regarded by his acquaintances as it is the lot of some of those persons to be. The winning and sanguine receptivity of his early life developed by degrees a moody nervousness, and when not picturing prospects drawn from baseless hope he was the victim of indescribable depression. The practical issue of such a condition was improvidence, originally almost an unconscious improvidence, for every debt incurred had been mentally paid off with a religious exactness from the treasures of expectation before mentioned. But as years revolved, the same course was continued from the lack of spirit sufficient for shifting out of an old groove when it has been found to lead to disaster.

In the year 1861 his wife died, leaving him a widower with two children. The elder, a son named Owen, now just turned seventeen, was taken from school, and initiated as pupil to the profession of architect in his father's office. The remaining child was a daughter, and Owen's junior by a year.

Her christian name was Cytherea, and it is easy to guess why.

3. October the Twelfth, 1863

We pass over two years in order to reach the next cardinal event of these persons' lives. The scene is still the Grayes' native town of Hocbridge, but as it appeared on a Monday afternoon in the month of October.

The weather was sunny and dry, but the ancient borough was to be seen wearing one of its least attractive aspects. First on account of the time. It was that stagnant hour of the twenty-four when the practical garishness of Day, having escaped from the fresh long shadows and enlivening newness of the morning, has not yet made any perceptible advance towards acquiring those mellow and soothing tones which grace its decline. Next, it was that stage in the progress of the week when business – which, carried on under the gables of an old country place, is not devoid of a romantic sparkle – was wellnigh extinguished. Lastly, the town was intentionally bent upon being attractive by exhibiting to an influx of visitors the local talent for dramatic recitation, and provincial towns trying to be lively are the dullest of dull things.

Little towns are like little children in this respect, that they interest most when they are enacting native peculiarities unconscious of beholders. Discovering themselves to be watched they attempt to be entertaining by putting on antics, and produce disagreeable caricatures which spoil them.

The weather-stained clock-face in the low church tower standing at the intersection of the three chief streets was expressing half-past two to the Town Hall opposite, where the much talked-of reading from Shakespeare was about to begin. The doors were open, and those persons who had already assembled within the building were noticing the entrance of the new-comers – silently criticizing their dress – questioning the genuineness of their teeth and hair – estimating their private means.

Among these later ones came an exceptional young maiden who glowed amid the dulness like a single bright-red poppy in a field of brown stubble. She wore an elegant dark jacket, lavender dress, hat with grey strings and trimmings, and gloves of a colour to harmonize. She lightly walked up the side passage of the room, cast a slight glance around, and entered the seat pointed out to her.

The young girl was Cytherea Graye; her age was now about eighteen. During her entry, and at various times whilst sitting in her seat and listening to the reader on the platform, her personal appearance formed an interesting subject of study for several neighbouring eyes.

Her face was exceedingly attractive, though artistically less perfect than her figure, which approached unusually near to the standard of faultlessness. But even this feature of hers yielded the palm to the gracefulness of her movement, which was fascinating and delightful to an extreme degree.

Indeed, motion was her speciality, whether shown on its most extended scale of bodily progression, or minutely, as in the uplifting of her eyelids, the bending of her fingers, the pouting of her lip. The carriage of her head – motion within motion – a glide upon a glide – was as delicate as that of a magnetic needle. And this flexibility and elasticity had never been taught her by rule, nor even been acquired by observation, but, *nullo cultu*,* had naturally developed itself with her years. In infancy, a stone or stalk in the way, which had been the inevitable occasion of a fall to her playmates, had usually left her safe and upright on her feet after the narrowest escape by oscillations and whirls for the preservation of her balance. At mixed Christmas parties, when she numbered but twelve or thirteen years, and was heartily despised on that account by lads who deemed themselves men, her apt

5

lightness in the dance covered this incompleteness in her womanhood, and compelled the self-same youths in spite of resolutions to seize upon her childish figure as a partner whom they could not afford to contemn. And in later years, when the instincts of her sex had shown her this point as the best and rarest feature in her external self, she was not found wanting in attention to the cultivation of finish in its details.

Her hair rested gaily upon her shoulders in curls, and was of a shining corn yellow in the high lights, deepening to a definite nut-brown as each curl wound round into the shade. She had eyes of a sapphire hue, though rather darker than the gem ordinarily appears; they possessed the affectionate and liquid sparkle of loyalty and good faith as distinguishable from that harder brightness which seems to express faithfulness only to the object confronting them.

But to attempt to gain a view of her – or indeed of any fascinating woman – from a measured category, is as difficult as to appreciate the effect of a landscape by exploring it at night with a lantern – or of a full chord of music by piping the notes in succession. Nevertheless it may readily be believed from the description here ventured, that among the many winning phases of her aspect, these were particularly striking: –

During pleasant doubt, when her eyes brightened stealthily and smiled (as eyes will smile) as distinctly as her lips, and in the space of a single instant expressed clearly the whole round of degrees of expectancy which lie over the wide expanse between Yea and Nay.

During the telling of a secret, which was involuntarily accompanied by a sudden minute start, and ecstatic pressure of the listener's arm, side, or neck, as the position and degree of intimacy dictated.

When anxiously regarding one who possessed her affections.

She suddenly assumed the last-mentioned bearing in the progress of the present entertainment. Her glance was directed out of the window.

Why the particulars of a young lady's presence at a very mediocre performance were prevented from dropping into the oblivion which their intrinsic insignificance would naturally have involved – why they were remembered and individualized by herself and others through after years – was simply that she unknowingly stood, as it were, upon the extreme posterior edge of a tract in her life, in which the real meaning of Taking Thought had never been known. It was the last hour of experience she ever enjoyed with a mind entirely free from a knowledge of that labyrinth into which she stepped immediately afterwards – to continue a perplexed course along its mazes for the greater portion of twenty-nine subsequent months.

The Town Hall,* in which Cytherea sat, was a building of brown

6

stone, and through one of the windows could be seen from the interior of the room the housetops and chimneys of the adjacent street, and also the upper part of a neighbouring church spire, now in course of completion under the superintendence of Miss Graye's father, the architect to the work.

That the top of this spire should be visible from her position in the room was a fact which Cytherea's idling eyes had discovered with some interest, and she was now engaged in watching the scene that was being enacted about its airy summit. Round the conical stonework rose a cage of scaffolding against the blue sky, and upon this stood five men – four in clothes as white as the new erection close beneath their hands, the fifth in the ordinary dark suit of a gentleman.

The four working-men in white were three masons and a mason's labourer. The fifth man was the architect, Mr Graye. He had been giving directions as it seemed, and retiring as far as the narrow footway allowed, stood perfectly still.

The picture thus presented to a spectator in the the Town Hall was curious and striking. It was an illuminated miniature, framed in by the dark margin* of the window, the keen-edged shadiness of which emphasized by contrast the softness of the objects enclosed.

The height of the spire was about one hundred and twenty feet, and the five men engaged thereon seemed entirely removed from the sphere and experiences of ordinary human beings. They appeared little larger than pigeons, and made their tiny movements with a soft, spirit-like silence. One idea above all others was conveyed to the mind of a person on the ground by their aspect, namely, concentration of purpose: that they were indifferent to – even unconscious of – the distracted world beneath them, and all that moved upon it. They never looked off the scaffolding.

Then one of them turned; it was Mr Graye. Again he stood motionless, with attention to the operations of the others. He appeared to be lost in reflection, and had directed his face towards a new stone they were lifting.

'Why does he stand like that?' the young lady thought at length – up to that moment as listless and careless as one of the ancient Tarentines, who, on such an afternoon as this, watched from the Theatre the entry into their Harbour of a power that overturned the State.*

She moved herself uneasily. 'I wish he would come down,' she whispered, still gazing at the sky-backed picture. 'It is so dangerous to be absent-minded up there.'

When she had done murmuring the words her father indecisively laid hold of one of the scaffold-poles, as if to test its strength, then let it go and stepped back. In stepping, his foot slipped. An instant of doubling forward and sideways, and he reeled off into the air, immediately disappearing downwards.

His agonized daughter rose to her feet by a convulsive movement. Her lips parted, and she gasped for breath. She could utter no sound. One by one the people about her, unconscious of what had happened, turned their heads, and inquiry and alarm became visible upon their faces at the sight of the poor child. A moment longer, and she fell to the floor.

The next impression of which Cytherea had any consciousness was of being carried from a strange vehicle across the pavement to the steps of her own house by her brother and an older man. Recollection of what had passed evolved itself an instant later, and just as they entered the door – through which another and sadder burden had been carried but a few instants before – her eyes caught sight of the south-western sky, and, without heeding, saw white sunlight shining in shaft-like lines from a rift in a slaty cloud. Emotions will attach themselves to scenes that are simultaneous – however foreign in essence these scenes may be – as chemical waters will crystallize on twigs and wires. Ever after that time any mental agony brought less vividly to Cytherea's mind the scene from the Town Hall windows than sunlight streaming in shaft-like lines.

4. October the Nineteenth

When death enters a house, an element of sadness and an element of horror accompany it. Sadness, from the death itself: horror, from the clouds of blackness we designedly labour to introduce.

The funeral had taken place. Depressed, yet resolved in his demeanour, Owen Graye sat before his father's private escritoire,* engaged in turning out and unfolding a heterogeneous collection of papers – forbidding and inharmonious to the eye at all times – most of all to one under the influence of a great grief. Laminæ of white paper tied with twine were indiscriminately intermixed with other white papers bounded by black edges – these with blue foolscap wrapped round with crude red tape.

The bulk of these letters, bills, and other documents were submitted to a careful examination, by which the appended particulars were ascertained: –

First, that their father's income from professional sources had been very small, amounting to not more than half their expenditure; and that his own and his wife's property, upon which he had relied for the balance, had been sunk and lost in unwise loans to unscrupulous men, who had traded upon their father's too open-hearted trustfulness.

Second, that finding his mistake, he had endeavoured to regain his standing by the illusory path of speculation. The most notable instance of this was the following. He had been induced, when at Plymouth in the autumn of the previous year, to venture all his spare capital on the bottomry security* of an Italian brig which had put into the harbour in distress. The profit was to be considerable, so was the risk. There turned out to be no security whatever. The circumstances of the case rendered it the most unfortunate speculation that a man like himself – ignorant of all such matters – could possibly engage in. The vessel went down, and all Mr Graye's money with it.

Third, that these failures had left him burdened with debts he knew not how to meet; so that at the time of his death even the few pounds lying to his account at the bank were his only in name.

Fourth, that the loss of his wife two years earlier had awakened him to a keen sense of his blindness, and of his duty by his children. He had then resolved to reinstate by unflagging zeal in the pursuit of his profession, and by no speculation, at least a portion of the little fortune he had let go.

Cytherea was frequently at her brother's elbow during these examinations. She often remarked sadly –

'Poor papa failed to fulfil his good intention for want of time, didn't he, Owen? And there was an excuse for his past, though he never would claim it. I never forget that original disheartening blow, and how that from it sprang all the ills of his life – everything connected with his gloom, and the lassitude in business we used so often to see about him.'

'I remember what he said once,' returned the brother, 'when I sat up late with him. He said, "Owen, don't love too blindly: blindly you will love if you love at all, but a little care is still possible to a well-disciplined heart.* May that heart be yours as it was not mine," father said. "Cultivate the art of renunciation." And I am going to, Cytherea.'

'And once mamma said that an excellent woman was papa's ruin, because he did not know the way to give her up when he lost her. I wonder where she is now, Owen? We were told not to try to find out anything about her. Papa never told us her name, did he?'

'That was by her own request, I believe. But never mind her; she was not our mother.'

The love affair which had been Ambrose Graye's disheartening blow

9

was precisely of that nature which lads take little account of, but girls ponder in their hearts.

5. *From October the Nineteenth to July the Ninth*

Thus Ambrose Graye's good intentions with regard to the reintegration of his property had scarcely taken tangible form when his sudden death put them for ever out of his power.

Heavy bills, showing the extent of his obligations, tumbled in immediately upon the heels of the funeral from quarters previously unheard and unthought of. Thus pressed, a bill was filed in Chancery* to have the assets, such as they were, administered by the Court.

'What will become of us now?' thought Owen continually.

There is in us an unquenchable expectation, which at the gloomiest time persists in inferring that because we are *ourselves*, there must be a special future in store for us, though our nature and antecedents to the remotest particular have been common to thousands. Thus to Cytherea and Owen Graye the question how their lives would end seemed the deepest of possible enigmas. To others who knew their position equally well with themselves the question was the easiest that could be asked – 'Like those of other people similarly circumstanced.'

Then Owen held a consultation with his sister to come to some decision on their future course, and a month was passed in waiting for answers to letters, and in the examination of schemes more or less futile. Sudden hopes that were rainbows to the sight proved but mists to the touch. In the meantime, unpleasant remarks, disguise them as some well-meaning people might, were floating around them every day. The undoubted truth, that they were the children of a dreamer who let slip away every farthing of his money and ran into debt with his neighbours – that the daughter had been brought up to no profession – that the son who had, had made no progress in it, and might come to the dogs – could not from the nature of things be wrapped up in silence in order that it might not hurt their feelings; and as a matter of fact, it greeted their ears in some form or other wherever they went. Their few acquaintances passed them hurriedly. Ancient pot-wallopers,* and thriving shop-keepers, in their intervals of leisure, stood at their shop-doors – their toes hanging over the edge of the step, and their obese waists hanging over their toes – and in discourses with friends on the pavement formulated the course of the improvident, and reduced the children's prospects to a shadow-like attenuation. The sons of these men (who wore breastpins of a sarcastic kind, and smoked humorous pipes) stared at Cytherea with a stare unmitigated by any of the respect that had formerly softened it.

Now it is a noticeable fact that we do not much mind what men think of us, or what humiliating secret they discover of our means, parentage, or object, provided that each thinks and acts thereupon in isolation. It is the exchange of ideas about us that we dread most; and the possession by a hundred acquaintances, severally insulated, of the knowledge of our skeleton-closet's whereabouts, is not so distressing to the nerves as a chat over it by a party of half-a-dozen – exclusive depositaries though these may be.

Perhaps, though Hocbridge watched and whispered, its animus would have been little more than a trifle to persons in thriving circumstances. But unfortunately, poverty, whilst it is new, and before the skin has had time to thicken, makes people susceptible inversely to their opportunities for shielding themselves. In Owen was found, in place of his father's impressibility, a larger share of his father's pride, and a squareness of idea which, if coupled with a little more blindness, would have amounted to positive prejudice. To him humanity, so far as he had thought of it at all, was rather divided into distinct classes than blended from extreme to extreme. Hence by a sequence of ideas which might be traced if it were worth while, he either detested or respected opinion, and instinctively sought to escape a cold shade that mere sensitiveness would have endured. He could have submitted to separation, sickness, exile, drudgery, hunger and thirst, with stoical indifference, but superciliousness was too incisive.

After living on for nine months in attempts to make an income as his father's successor in the profession – attempts which were utterly fruitless by reason of his inexperience – Graye came to a simple and sweeping resolution. They would privately leave that part of England, drop from the sight of acquaintants, gossips, harsh critics, and bitter creditors of whose misfortune he was not the cause, and escape the position which galled him by the only road their great poverty left open to them – that of his obtaining some employment in a distant place by following his profession as a humble under-draughtsman.

He thought over his capabilities with the sensations of a soldier grinding his sword at the opening of a campaign. What with lack of employment, owing to the decrease of his late father's practice, and the absence of direct and uncompromising pressure towards monetary results from a pupil's labour (which seems to be always the case when a professional man's pupil is also his son), Owen's progress in the art and science of architecture* had been very insignificant indeed. Though anything but an idle young man, he had hardly reached the age at which industrious men who lack an external whip to send them on in the world, are induced by their own common sense to whip on themselves. Hence his knowledge of plans, elevations, sections, and specifications, was not greater at the end of two years of probation than might easily have been acquired in six months by a youth of average ability – himself, for instance – amid a bustling London practice.

But at any rate he could make himself handy to one of the profession – some man in a remote town – and there fulfil his indentures. A tangible inducement lay in this direction of survey. He had a slight conception of such a man – a Mr Gradfield – who was in practice in Budmouth Regis, a seaport town and watering-place* in the south of England.

After some doubts, Graye ventured to write to this gentleman, asking the necessary question, shortly alluding to his father's death, and stating that his term of apprenticeship had only half expired. He would be glad to complete his articles at a very low salary for the whole remaining two years, provided payment could begin at once.

The answer from Mr Gradfield stated that he was not in want of a pupil who would serve the remainder of his time on the terms Mr Graye mentioned. But he would just add one remark. He chanced to be in want of some young man in his office – for a short time only, probably about two months – to trace drawings, and attend to other subsidiary work of the kind. If Mr Graye did not object to occupy such an inferior position as these duties would entail, and to accept weekly wages which to one with his expectations would be considered merely nominal, the post would give him an opportunity for learning a few more details of the profession.

'It is a beginning, and, above all, an abiding-place, away from the shadow of the cloud which hangs over us here – I will go,' said Owen.

Cytherea's plan for her future, an intensely simple one, owing to the even greater narrowness of her resources, was already marked out. One advantage had accrued to her through her mother's possession of a fair share of personal property, and perhaps only one. She had been carefully educated. Upon this consideration her plan was based. She was to take up her abode in her brother's lodging at Budmouth, when she would immediately advertise for a situation as governess, having obtained the consent of a lawyer at Aldbrickham who was winding up her father's affairs, and who knew the history of her position, to allow himself to be referred to in the matter of her past life and respectability.

12

Early one morning they departed from their native town, leaving behind them scarcely a trace of their footsteps.

Then the town pitied their want of wisdom in taking such a step. 'Rashness; they would have made a better income in Hocbridge, where they are known! There is no doubt that they would.'

But what is Wisdom really? A steady handling of any means to bring about any end necessary to happiness.

Yet whether one's end be the usual end – a wealthy position in life – or no, the name of wisdom is seldom applied but to the means to that usual end.

CHAPTER TWO
The Events of a Fortnight

1. The Ninth of July

The day of their departure was one of the most glowing that the climax of a long series of summer heats could evolve. The wide expanse of landscape quivered up and down like the flame of a taper, as they steamed along through the midst of it. Placid flocks of sheep reclining under trees a little way off appeared of a pale blue colour. Clover fields were livid with the brightness of the sun upon their deep red flowers. All waggons and carts were moved to the shade by their careful owners; rain-water butts fell to pieces; well-buckets were lowered inside the covers of the well-hole, to preserve them from the fate of the butts, and generally, water seemed scarcer in the country than the beer and cider of the peasantry who toiled or idled there.

To see persons looking with children's eyes at any ordinary scenery is a proof that they possess the charming faculty of drawing new sensations from an old experience – a healthy sign, rare in these feverish days – the mark of an imperishable brightness of nature.

Both brother and sister could do this; Cytherea more noticeably. They watched the undulating cornlands, monotonous to all their companions; the stony and clayey prospect succeeding those, with its angular and abrupt hills. Boggy moors came next, now withered and dry – the spots upon which pools usually spread their waters showing themselves as circles of smooth bare soil, over-run by a net-work of innumerable little fissures. Then arose plantations of firs, abruptly terminating beside meadows cleanly mown, in which high-hipped, rich-coloured cows, with backs horizontal and straight as the ridge of a house, stood motionless or lazily fed. Glimpses of the sea now interested them, which became more and more frequent till the train finally drew up beside the platform at Budmouth Regis.

'The whole town is looking out for us,' had been Graye's impression throughout the day. He called upon Mr Gradfield – the only man who had been directly informed of his coming – and found that Mr Gradfield had forgotten it.

However, arrangements were made with this gentleman – a stout, active, grey-bearded burgher of sixty – by which Owen was to commence work in his office the following week.

The same day Cytherea drew up and sent off the advertisement appended: –

A YOUNG LADY is desirous of meeting with an ENGAGEMENT as GOVERNESS or COMPANION. She is competent to teach English, French, and Music. Satisfactory references. – Address, C.G., Post Office, Budmouth.

It seemed a more material existence than her own that she saw thus delineated on the paper. 'That can't be myself; how odd I look!' she said, and smiled.

2. July the Eleventh

On the Monday subsequent to their arrival in Budmouth, Owen Graye attended at Mr Gradfield's office to enter upon his duties, and his sister was left in their lodgings alone for the first time.

Despite the sad occurrences of the preceding autumn, an unwonted cheerfulness pervaded her spirit throughout the day. Change of scene – and that to untravelled eyes – conjoined with the sensation of freedom from supervision, revived the sparkle of a warm young nature ready enough to take advantage of any adventitious restoratives. Point-blank grief tends rather to seal up happiness for a time than to produce that attrition which results from griefs of anticipation that move onward with the days: these may be said to furrow away the capacity for pleasure.

Her expectations from the advertisement began to be extravagant. A thriving family, who had always sadly needed her, was already definitely pictured in her fancy, which, in its exuberance, led her on to picturing its individual members, their possible peculiarities, virtues,

14

and vices, and obliterated for a time the recollection that she would be separated from her brother.

Thus musing, as she waited for his return in the evening, her eyes fell on her left hand. The contemplation of her own left fourth finger by symbol-loving girlhood of this age is, it seems, very frequently, if not always, followed by a peculiar train of romantic ideas. Cytherea's thoughts, still playing about her future, became directed into this romantic groove. She leant back in her chair, and taking hold of the fourth finger, which had attracted her attention, she lifted it with the tips of the others, and looked at the smooth and tapering member for a long time.

She whispered idly, 'I wonder who and what he will be?

'If he's a gentleman of fashion, he will take my finger so, just with the tips of his own, and with some fluttering of the heart, and the least trembling of his lip, slip the ring so lightly on that I shall hardly know it is there – looking delightfully into my eyes all the time.

'If he's a bold dashing soldier, I expect he will proudly turn round, take the ring as if it equalled her Majesty's crown in value, and desperately set it on my finger thus. He will fix his eyes unflinchingly upon what he is doing – just as if he stood in battle before the enemy (though, in reality, very fond of me, of course), and blush as much as I shall.

'If he's a sailor, he will take my finger and the ring in this way, and deck it out with a housewifely touch and a tenderness of expression about his mouth, as sailors do: kiss it, perhaps, with a simple air, as if we were children playing an idle game, and not at the very height of observation and envy by a great crowd saying, "Ah! they are happy now!"

'If he should be a rather poor man – noble-minded and affectionate, but still poor—'

Owen's footsteps rapidly ascending the stairs interrupted this fancy-free meditation. Reproaching herself, even angry with herself for allowing her mind to stray upon such subjects in the face of their present desperate condition, she rose to meet him, and make tea.

Cytherea's interest to know how her brother had been received at Mr Gradfield's broke forth into words at once. Almost before they had sat down to table, she began cross-examining him in the regular sisterly way.

'Well, Owen, how has it been with you to-day? What is the place like – do you think you will like Mr Gradfield?'

'O yes. But he has not been there to-day; I have only had the head draughtsman with me.'

Young women have a habit, not noticeable in men, of putting on at a moment's notice the drama of whosoever's* life they choose. Cytherea's interest was transferred from Mr Gradfield to his representative.

'What sort of a man is he?'

'He seems a very nice fellow indeed; though of course I can hardly tell to a certainty as yet. But I think he's a very worthy fellow; there's no nonsense in him, and though he is not a public school man he has read widely, and has a sharp appreciation of what's good in books and art. In fact, his knowledge isn't nearly so exclusive as most professional men's.'

'That's a great deal to say of an architect, for of all professional men they are, as a rule, the most professional.'

'Yes; perhaps they are. This man is rather of a melancholy turn of mind, I think.'

'Has the managing clerk any family?' she mildly asked after a while, pouring out some more tea.

'Family; no!'

'Well, dear Owen, how should I know?'

'Why, of course he isn't married. But there happened to be a conversation about women going on in the office, and I heard him say what he should wish his wife to be like.'

'What would he wish his wife to be like?' she said, with great apparent lack of interest.

'O, he says she must be girlish and artless: yet he would be loth to do without a dash of womanly subtlety, 'tis so piquant. Yes, he said, that must be in her; she must have womanly cleverness. "And yet I should like her to blush if only a cock-sparrow were to look at her hard," he said, "which brings me back to the girl again: and so I flit backwards and forwards. I must have what comes, I suppose," he said, "and whatever she may be, thank God she's no worse. However, if he might give a final hint to Providence," he said, "a child among pleasures and a woman among pains was the rough outline of his requirement."'

'Did he say that? What a musing creature he must be.'

'He did, indeed.'

3. From the Twelfth to the Fifteenth of July

As is well known, ideas are so elastic in a human brain that they have no constant measure which may be called their actual bulk. Any important idea may be compressed to a molecule by an unwonted crowding of others; and any small idea will expand to whatever length and breadth

16

of vacuum the mind may be able to make over to it. Cytherea's world was tolerably vacant at this time, and the young architectural designer's image became very pervasive. The next evening this subject was again renewed.

'His name is Springrove,' said Owen, in reply to her. 'He is a thorough artist, but a man of rather humble origin, it seems, who has made himself so far. I think he is the son of a farmer, or something of the kind.'

'Well, he's none the worse for that, I suppose.'

'None the worse. As we come down the hill, we shall be continually meeting people going up.' But Owen had felt that Springrove was a little the worse, nevertheless.

'Of course he's rather old by this time.'

'O no. He's about six-and-twenty – not more.'

'Ah, I see. . . . What is he like, Owen?'

'I can't exactly tell you his appearance: 'tis always such a difficult thing to do.'

'A man you would describe as short? Most men are those we should describe as short, I fancy.'

'I should call him, I think, of the middle height; but as I only see him sitting in the office, of course I am not certain about his form and figure.'

'I wish you were, then.'

'Perhaps you do. But I am not, you see.'

'Of course not, you are always so provoking. Owen, I saw a man in the street to-day whom I fancied was he – and yet, I don't see how it could be either. He had light brown hair, a snub nose, very round face, and a peculiar habit of reducing his eyes to straight lines when he looked narrowly at anything.'

'O no. That was not he, Cytherea.'

'Not a bit like him in all probability.'

'Not a bit. He has dark hair, almost a Grecian nose,* regular teeth, and an intellectual face, as nearly as I can recall to mind.'

'Ah, there now, Owen, you *have* described him! But I suppose he's not generally called pleasing, or—'

'Handsome?'

'I scarcely meant that. But since you have said it, is he handsome?'

'Rather.'

'His *tout ensemble** is striking?'

'Yes – Oh no, no – I forgot: it is not. He is rather untidy in his waistcoat, and neck-ties, and hair.'

17

'How vexing! . . . it must be to himself, poor thing.'

'He's a thorough bookworm – despises the pap-and-daisy school* of verse – knows Shakespeare to the very dregs of the footnotes. Indeed, he's a poet himself in a small way.'

'How delicious!' she said. 'I have never known a poet.'

'And you don't know him,' said Owen drily.

She reddened. 'Of course I don't. I know that.'

'Have you received any answer to your advertisement?' he inquired.

'Ah – no!' she said, and the forgotten disappointment which had showed itself in her face at different times during the day, became visible again.

Another day passed away. On Thursday, without inquiry, she learnt more of the head draughtsman. He and Graye had become very friendly, and he had been tempted to show her brother a copy of some poems of his – some serious and sad – some humorous – which had appeared in the poet's corner of a magazine from time to time. Owen showed them now to Cytherea, who instantly began to read them carefully and to think them very beautiful.

'Yes – Springrove's no fool,' said Owen sententiously.

'No fool! – I should think he isn't, indeed,' said Cytherea, looking up from the paper in quite an excitement: 'to write such verses as these!'

'What logic are you chopping, Cytherea? Well, I don't mean on account of the verses, because I haven't read them; but for what he said when the fellows were talking about falling in love.'

'Which you will tell me?'

'He says that your true lover breathlessly finds himself engaged to a sweetheart, like a man who has caught something in the dark. He doesn't know whether it is a bat or a bird, and takes it to the light when he is cool to learn what it is. He looks to see if she is the right age, but right age or wrong age, he must consider her a prize. Sometime later he ponders whether she is the right kind of prize for him. Right kind or wrong kind – he has called her his, and must abide by it. After a time he asks himself, "Has she the temper, hair, and eyes I meant to have, and was firmly resolved not to do without?" He finds it is all wrong, and then comes the tussle—'

'Do they marry and live happily?'

'Who? O, the supposed pair. I think he said – well, I really forget what he said.'

'That *is* stupid of you!' said the young lady with dismay.

'Yes.'

'But he's a satirist – I don't think I care about him now.'

18

'There you are just wrong. He is not. He is, as I believe, an impulsive fellow who has been made to pay the penalty of his rashness in some love affair.'

Thus ended the dialogue of Thursday, but Cytherea read the verses again in private. On Friday her brother remarked that Springrove had informed him he was going to leave Mr Gradfield's in a fortnight to push his fortunes in London.

· An indescribable feeling of sadness shot through Cytherea's heart. Why should she be sad at such an announcement as that, she thought, concerning a man she had never seen, when her spirits were elastic enough to rebound after hard blows from deep and real troubles as if she had scarcely known them? Though she could not answer this question, she knew one thing, she was saddened by Owen's news.

4. July the Twenty-First

A very popular local excursion by steamboat to Lulwind Cove was announced through the streets of Budmouth one Thursday morning by the weak-voiced town-crier, to start at six o'clock the same day. The weather was lovely, and the opportunity being the first of the kind offered to them, Owen and Cytherea went with the rest.

They had reached the Cove, and had walked landward for nearly an hour over the hill which rose beside the strand, when Graye recollected that two or three miles yet further inland from this spot was an interesting mediæval ruin. He was already familiar with its characteristics through the medium of an archæological work, and now finding himself so close to the reality, felt inclined to verify some theory he had formed respecting it. Concluding that there would be just sufficient time for him to go there and return before the boat had left the shore, he parted from Cytherea on the hill, struck downwards, and then up a heathery valley.

She remained on the summit where he had left her till the time of his expected return, scanning the details of the prospect around. Placidly spread out before her on the south was the open Channel, reflecting a blue intenser by many shades than that of the sky overhead, and dotted in the foreground by half-a-dozen small craft of contrasting rig, their sails graduating in hue from extreme whiteness to reddish brown, the varying actual colours varied again in a double degree by the rays of the declining sun.

Presently the distant bell from the boat was heard, warning the passengers to embark. This was followed by a lively air from the harps and violins on board, their tones, as they arose, becoming intermingled with, though not marred by, the brush of the waves when their crests rolled over – at the point where the check of the shallows was first felt – and then thinned away up the slope of pebbles and sand.

She turned her face landward and strained her eyes to discern, if possible, some sign of Owen's return. Nothing was visible save the strikingly brilliant, still landscape. The wide concave which lay at the back of the hill in this direction was blazing with the western light, adding an orange tint to the vivid purple of the heather, now at the very climax of bloom, and free from the slightest touch of the invidious brown that so soon creeps into its shades. The light so intensified the colours that they seemed to stand above the surface of the earth and float in mid-air like an exhalation of red. In the minor valleys, between the hillocks and ridges which diversified the contour of the basin, but did not disturb its general sweep, she marked brakes of tall, heavy-stemmed ferns, five or six feet high, in a brilliant light-green dress – a broad riband of them with the path in their midst winding like a stream along the little ravine that reached to the foot of the hill, and delivered up the path to its grassy area. Among the ferns grew holly bushes deeper in tint than any shadow about them, whilst the whole surface of the scene was dimpled with small conical pits, and here and there were round ponds, now dry, and half overgrown with rushes.

The last bell of the steamer rang. Cytherea had forgotten herself, and what she was looking for. In a fever of distress lest Owen should be left behind, she gathered up in her hand the corners of her handkerchief, containing specimens of the shells, plants, and fossils which the locality produced, started off to the sands, and mingled with the knots of visitors there congregated from other interesting points around; from the inn, the cottages, and hired conveyances that had returned from short drives inland. They all went aboard by the primitive plan of a narrow plank on two wheels – the women being assisted by a rope. Cytherea lingered to the very last, reluctant to follow, and looking alternately at the boat and the valley behind. Her delay provoked a remark from Captain Jacobs, a thick-set man of hybrid stains, resulting from the mixed effects of fire and water, peculiar to sailors where engines are the propelling power.

'Now then, missy, if you please. I am sorry to tell 'ee our time's up. Who are you looking for, miss?'

'My brother – he has walked a short distance inland; he must be here directly. Could you wait for him – just a minute?'

'Really, I am afraid not, m'm.' Cytherea looked at the stout, round-

20

faced man, and at the vessel, with a light in her eyes so expressive of her own opinion being the same, on reflection, as his, and with such resignation, too, that, from an instinctive feeling of pride at being able to prove himself more humane than he was thought to be – works of supererogation* are the only sacrifices that entice in this way – and that at a very small cost, he delayed the boat till some among the passengers began to murmur.

'There, never mind,' said Cytherea decisively. 'Go on without me – I shall wait for him.'

'Well, 'tis a very awkward thing to leave you here all alone,' said the captain. 'I certainly advise you not to wait.'

'He's gone across to the railway station, for certain,' said another passenger.

'No – here he is!' Cytherea said, regarding, as she spoke, the half-hidden figure of a man who was seen advancing at a headlong pace down the ravine which lay between the heath and the shore.

'He can't get here in less than five minutes,' a passenger said. 'People should know what they are about, and keep time. Really, if—'

'You see, sir,' said the captain, in an apologetic undertone, 'since 'tis her brother, and she's all alone, 'tis only nater to wait a minute, now he's in sight. Suppose, now, you were a young woman, as might be, and had a brother, like this one, and you stood of an evening upon this here wild lonely shore, like her, why you'd want us to wait, too, wouldn't you, sir? I think you would.'

The person so hastily approaching had been lost to view during this remark by reason of a hollow in the ground, and the projecting cliff immediately at hand covered the path in its rise. His footsteps were now heard striking sharply upon the flinty road at a distance of about twenty or thirty yards, but still behind the escarpment. To save time, Cytherea prepared to ascend the plank.

'Let me give you my hand, miss,' said Captain Jacobs.

'No – please don't touch me,' said she, ascending cautiously by sliding one foot forward two or three inches, bringing up the other behind it, and so on alternately – her lips compressed by concentration on the feat, her eyes glued to the plank, her hand to the rope, and her immediate thought to the fact of the distressing narrowness of her footing. Steps now shook the lower end of the board, and in an instant were up to her heels with a bound.

'O, Owen, I am so glad you are come!' she said, without turning. 'Don't, don't shake the plank or touch me, whatever you do. . . . There, I am up. Where have you been so long?' she continued, in a

21

lower tone, turning round to him as she reached the top.

Raising her eyes from her feet, which, standing on the firm deck, demanded her attention no longer, she acquired perceptions of the new-comer in the following order: unknown trousers; unknown waist-coat; unknown face. The man was not her brother, but a total stranger.

Off went the plank; the paddles started, stopped, backed, pattered in confusion, then revolved decisively, and the boat passed out into deep water.

One or two persons had said, 'How d'ye do, Mr Springrove?' and looked at Cytherea, to see how she bore her disappointment. Her ears had but just caught the name of the head draughtsman, when she saw him advancing directly to address her.

'Miss Graye, I believe?' he said, lifting his hat.

'Yes,' said Cytherea, colouring, and trying not to look guilty of a surreptitious knowledge of him.

'I am Mr Springrove. I passed Corvsgate Castle about an hour ago, and soon afterwards met your brother going that way. He had been deceived in the distance, and was about to turn without seeing the ruin, on account of a lameness that had come on in his leg or foot. I proposed that he should go on, since he had got so near; and afterwards, instead of walking back to the boat, get across to Anglebury Station – a shorter walk for him – where he could catch the late train, and go directly home. I could let you know what he had done, and allay any uneasiness.'

'Is the lameness serious, do you know?'

'O no; simply from over-walking himself. Still, it was just as well to ride home.'

Relieved from her apprehensions on Owen's score, she was able slightly to examine the appearance of her informant – Edward Spring-rove – who now removed his hat for a while, to cool himself. He was rather above her brother's height. Although the upper part of his face and head was handsomely formed, and bounded by lines of sufficiently masculine regularity, his brows were somewhat too softly arched and finely pencilled for one of his sex; without prejudice, however, to the belief which the sum total of his features inspired – that though they did not prove that the man who thought inside them would do much in the world, men who had done most of all had had no better ones. Across his forehead, otherwise perfectly smooth, ran one thin line, the healthy freshness of his remaining features expressing that it had come there prematurely.

Though some years short of the age at which the clear spirit bids good-bye to the last infirmity of the noble mind,* and takes to house-

22

hunting and investments, he had reached the period in a young man's life when episodic pasts, with a hopeful birth and a disappointing death, have begun to accumulate, and to bear a fruit of generalities; his glance sometimes seeming to state, 'I have already thought out the issue of such conditions as these we are experiencing.' At other times he wore an abstracted look: 'I seem to have lived through this moment before.'

He was carelessly dressed in dark grey, wearing a rolled-up black kerchief as a neck-cloth; the knot of which was disarranged, and stood obliquely – a deposit of white dust having lodged in the creases.

'I am sorry for your disappointment,' he continued, glancing into her face. Their eyes having met, became, as it were, mutually locked together, and the single instant only which good breeding allows as the length of such a look, became trebled: a clear penetrating ray of intelligence had shot from each into each, giving birth to one of those unaccountable sensations which carry home to the heart before the hand has been touched or the merest compliment passed, by something stronger than mathematical proof, the conviction, 'A tie has begun to unite us.'

Both faces also unconsciously stated that their owners had been much in each other's thoughts of late. Owen had talked to the young architect of his sister as freely as to Cytherea of the young architect.

A conversation began, which was none the less interesting to the parties engaged because it consisted only of the most trivial and commonplace remarks. Then the band of harps and violins struck up a lively melody, and the deck was cleared for dancing; the sun dipping beneath the horizon during the proceeding, and the moon showing herself at their stern. The sea was so calm that the soft hiss produced by the bursting of the innumerable bubbles of foam behind the paddles could be distinctly heard. The passengers who did not dance, including Cytherea and Springrove, lapsed into silence, leaning against the paddle-boxes,* or standing aloof – noticing the trembling of the deck to the steps of the dance – watching the waves from the paddles as they slid thinly and easily under each other's edges.

Night had quite closed in by the time they reached Budmouth harbour, sparkling with its white, red, and green lights in opposition to the shimmering path of the moon's reflection on the other side, which reached away to the horizon till the flecked ripples reduced themselves to sparkles as fine as gold dust.

'I will walk to the station and find out the exact time the train arrives,' said Springrove, rather eagerly, when they had landed.

She thanked him much.

23

'Perhaps we might walk together,' he suggested hesitatingly. She looked as if she did not quite know, and he settled the question by showing the way.

They found, on arriving there, that on the first day of that month the particular train selected for Graye's return had ceased to stop at Anglebury station.

'I am very sorry I misled him,' said Springrove.

'O, I am not alarmed at all,' replied Cytherea.

'Well, it's sure to be all right – he will sleep there, and come by the first in the morning. But what will you do, alone?'

'I am quite easy on that point; the landlady is very friendly. I must go indoors now. Good-night, Mr Springrove.'

'Let me go round to your door with you?' he pleaded.

'No, thank you; we live close by.'

He looked at her as a waiter looks at the change. But she was inexorable.

'Don't – forget me,' he murmured. She did not answer.

'Let me see you sometimes,' he said.

'Perhaps you never will again – I am going away,' she replied in lingering tones; and turning into Cross Street, ran indoors and upstairs.

The sudden withdrawal of what was superfluous at first, is often felt as an essential loss. It was felt now with regard to the maiden. More, too, after a meeting so pleasant and so enkindling, she had seemed to imply that they would never come together again. The young man softly followed her, stood opposite the house and watched her come into the upper room with the light. Presently his gaze was cut short by her approaching the window and pulling down the blind – Edward dwelling upon her vanishing figure with a hopeless sense of loss akin to that which Adam is said by logicians to have felt when he first saw the sun set, and thought, in his inexperience, that it would return no more.*

He waited till her shadow had twice crossed the window, when, finding the charming outline was not to be expected again, he left the street, crossed the harbour-bridge, and entered his own solitary chamber on the other side, vaguely thinking as he went (for undefined reasons),

> One hope is too like despair
> For prudence to smother.*

CHAPTER THREE
The Events of Eight Days

1. From the Twenty-Second to the Twenty-Seventh of July

But things are not what they seem. A responsive love for Edward Springrove had made its appearance in Cytherea's bosom with all the fascinating attributes of a first experience, not succeeding to or displacing other emotions, as in older hearts, but taking up entirely new ground; as when gazing just after sunset at the pale blue sky we see a star come into existence where nothing was before.

His parting words, 'Don't forget me,' she repeated to herself a hundred times, and though she thought their import was probably commonplace, she could not help toying with them, – looking at them from all points, and investing them with meanings of love and faithfulness, – ostensibly entertaining such meanings only as fables wherewith to pass the time, yet in her heart admitting, for detached instants, a possibility of their deeper truth. And thus, for hours after he had left her, her reason flirted with her fancy as a kitten will sport with a dove, pleasantly and smoothly through easy relations, but disclosing its cruel and unyielding nature at crises.

To turn now to the more material media through which this story moves, it so happened that the very next morning brought round a circumstance which, slight in itself, took up a relevant and important position between the past and the future of the persons herein concerned.

At breakfast time, just as Cytherea had again seen the postman pass without bringing her an answer to the advertisement, as she had fully expected he would do, Owen entered the room.

'Well,' he said, kissing her, 'you have not been alarmed, of course. Springrove told you what I had done, and you found there was no train?'

'Yes, it was all clear. But what is the lameness owing to?'

'I don't know – nothing. It has quite gone off now.... Cytherea, I hope you like Springrove. Springrove's a nice fellow, you know.'

'Yes. I think he is, except that—'

'It happened just to the purpose that I should meet him there, didn't it? And when I reached the station and learnt that I could not get on by train my foot seemed better. I started off to walk home, and went about five miles along a path beside the railway. It then struck me that I might not be fit for anything to-day if I walked and aggravated the bothering foot, so I looked for a place to sleep at. There was no available village or inn, and I eventually got the keeper of a gate-house, where a lane crosses the line, to take me in.'

They proceeded with their breakfast. Owen yawned.

'You didn't get much sleep at the gate-house last night, I'm afraid, Owen,' said his sister.

'To tell the truth, I didn't. I was in such very close and narrow quarters. Those gate-houses are such small places, and the man had only his own bed to offer me. Ah, by-the-bye, Cythie, I have such an extraordinary thing to tell you in connection with this man! – by Jove, I had nearly forgotten it! But I'll go straght on. As I was saying, he had only his own bed to offer me, but I could not afford to be fastidious, and as he had a hearty manner, though a very queer one, I agreed to accept it, and he made a rough pallet* for himself on the floor close beside me. Well, I could not sleep for my life, and I wished I had not stayed there, though I was so tired. For one thing, there were the luggage trains* rattling by at my elbow the early part of the night. But worse than this, he talked continually in his sleep, and occasionally struck out with his limbs at something or another, knocking against the post of the bedstead and making it tremble. My condition was altogether so unsatisfactory that at last I woke him, and asked him what he had been dreaming about for the previous hour, for I could get no sleep at all. He begged my pardon for disturbing me, but a name I had casually let fall that evening had led him to think of another stranger he had once had visit him, who had also accidentally mentioned the same name, and some very strange incidents connected with that meeting. The affair had occurred years and years ago; but what I had said had made him think and dream about it as if it were but yesterday. What was the word? I said. "Cytherea," he said. What was the story? I asked then. He then told me that when he was a young man in London he borrowed a few pounds to add to a few he had saved up, and opened a little inn at Hammersmith. One evening, after the inn had been open about a couple of months, every idler in the neighbourhood ran off to Westminster. The Houses of Parliament were on fire.*

'Not a soul remained in his parlour besides himself, and he began picking up the pipes and glasses his customers had hastily relinquished. At length a young lady about seventeen or eighteen came in. She asked if a woman was there waiting for herself – Miss Jane Taylor. He said no; asked the young lady if she would wait, and showed her into the small inner room. There was a glass-pane in the partition dividing this room

26

from the bar to enable the landlord to see if his visitors, who sat there, wanted anything. A curious awkwardness and melancholy about the behaviour of the girl who called, caused my informant to look frequently at her through the partition. She seemed weary of her life, and sat with her face buried in her hands, evidently quite out of her element in such a house. Then a woman much older came in and greeted Miss Taylor by name. The man distinctly heard the following words pass between them:–

'"Why have you not brought him?"'

'"He is ill; he is not likely to live through the night."'

'At this announcement from the elderly woman, the young lady fell to the floor in a swoon, apparently overcome by the news. The landlord ran in and lifted her up. Well, do what they would they could not for a long time bring her back to consciousness and began to be much alarmed. "Who is she?" the innkeeper said to the other woman. "I know her," the other said, with deep meaning in her tone. The elderly and young women seemed allied, and yet strangers.

'She now showed signs of life, and it struck him (he was plainly of an inquisitive turn) that in her half-bewildered state he might get some information from her. He stooped over her, put his mouth to her ear, and said sharply, "What's your name?" "To catch a woman napping is difficult, even when she's half dead; but I did it," says the gatekeeper. When he asked her her name, she said immediately–

'"Cytherea" – and stopped suddenly.'

'My own name!' said Cytherea.

'Yes – your name. Well, the gateman thought at the time it might be equally with Jane a name she had invented for the occasion, that they might not trace her; but I think it was truth unconsciously uttered, for she added directly afterwards: "O, what have I said!" and was quite overcome again – this time with fright. Her vexation that the woman now doubted the genuineness of her other name was very much greater than that the innkeeper did, and it is evident that to blind the woman was her main object. He also learnt from words the elderly woman casually dropped, that meetings of the same kind had been held before, and that the falseness of the *soi-disant** Miss Jane Taylor's name had never been suspected by this dependent or confederate till then.

'She recovered, rested there for an hour, and first sending off her companion peremptorily (which was another odd thing), she left the house, offering the landlord all the money she had to say nothing about the circumstance. He has never seen her since, according to his own account. I said to him again and again, "Did you find any more particulars afterwards?" "Not a syllable," he said. O, he should never hear any more of that! too many years had passed since it happened. "At any rate, you found out her surname?" I said. "Well, well, that's my secret," he went on. "Perhaps I should never have been in this part of the world if it hadn't been for that. I failed as a publican, you know." I imagine the situation of gateman was given him and his debts paid off as a bribe to silence; but I can't say. "Ah, yes!" he said, with a long breath. "I have never heard that name mentioned since that time till to-night, and then there instantly rose to my eyes the vision of that young lady lying in a fainting fit." He then stopped talking and fell asleep. Telling the story must have relieved him as it did the Ancient Mariner,* for he did not move a muscle or make another sound for the remainder of the night. Now isn't that an odd story?'

'It is, indeed,' Cytherea murmured. 'Very, very strange.'

'Why should she have said your most uncommon name?' continued Owen. 'The man was evidently truthful, for there was not motive sufficient for his invention of such a tale, and he could not have done it either.'

Cytherea looked long at her brother. 'Don't you recognize anything else in connection with the story?' she said.

'What?' he asked.

'Do you remember what poor papa once let drop – that Cytherea was the name of his first sweetheart in Bloomsbury, who so mysteriously renounced him? A sort of intuition tells me that this was the same woman.'

'O no – not likely,' said her brother.

'How not likely, Owen? There's not another woman of the name in England. In what year used papa to say the event took place?'

'Eighteen hundred and thirty-five.'

'And when were the Houses of Parliament burnt? – stop, I can tell you.' She searched their little stock of books for a list of dates, and found one in an old school history.

'The Houses of Parliament were burnt down in the evening of the sixteenth of October, eighteen hundred and thirty-four.'

'Nearly a year and a quarter before she met father,' remarked Owen.

They were silent. 'If papa had been alive, what a wonderful absorbing interest this story would have had for him,' said Cytherea by-and-by. 'And how strangely knowledge comes to us. We might have searched for a clue to her secret half the world over, and never found one. If we had really had any motive for trying to discover more of the sad history than papa told us, we should have gone to Bloomsbury; but

28

not caring to do so, we go two hundred miles in the opposite direction, and there find information waiting to be told us. What could have been the secret, Owen?'

'Heaven knows. But our having heard a little more of her in this way (if she is the same woman) is a mere coincidence after all – a family story to tell our friends if we ever have any. But we shall never know any more of the episode now – trust our fates for that.'

Cytherea sat silently thinking.

'There was no answer this morning to your advertisement, Cytherea?' he continued.

'None.'

'I could see that by your looks when I came in.'

'Fancy not getting a single one,' she said sadly. 'Surely there must be people somewhere who want governesses?'

'Yes; but those who want them, and can afford to have them, get them mostly by friends' recommendations; whilst those who want them, and can't afford to have them, make use of their poor relations.'

'What shall I do?'

'Never mind it. Go on living with me. Don't let the difficulty trouble your mind so; you think about it all day. I can keep you, Cythie, in a plain way of living. Twenty-five shillings a week do not amount to much truly; but then many mechanics* have no more, and we live quite as sparingly as journeymen* mechanics. . . . It is a meagre narrow life we are drifting into,' he added gloomily, 'but it is a degree more tolerable than the worrying sensation of all the world being ashamed of you, which we experienced at Hocbridge.'

'I couldn't go back there again,' she said.

'Nor I. O, don't regret our course for a moment. We did quite right in dropping out of the world.' The sneering tones of the remark were almost too laboured to be real. 'Besides,' he continued, 'something better for me is sure to turn up soon. I wish my engagement here was a permanent one instead of for only two months. It may, certainly, be for a longer time, but all is uncertain.'

'I wish I could get something to do; and I must too,' she said firmly. 'Suppose, as is very probable, you are not wanted after the beginning of October – the time Mr Gradfield mentioned – what should we do if I were dependent on you only throughout the winter?'

They pondered on numerous schemes by which a young lady might be supposed to earn a decent livelihood – more or less convenient and feasible in imagination, but relinquished them all until advertising had been once more tried, this time taking lower ground. Cytherea was vexed at her temerity in having represented to the world that so inexperienced a being as herself was a qualified governess; and had a fancy that this presumption of hers might be one reason why no ladies applied. The new and humbler attempt appeared in the following form: –

NURSERY GOVERNESS OR USEFUL COMPANION. A young person wishes to hear of a situation in either of the above capacities. Salary very moderate. She is a good needlewoman. – Address G., 3 Cross Street, Budmouth Regis.

In the evening they went to post the letter, and then walked up and down the Parade for a while. Soon they met Springrove, said a few words to him and passed on. Owen noticed that his sister's face had become crimson. Rather oddly they met Springrove again in a few minutes.

This time the three walked a little way together, Edward ostensibly talking to Owen, though with a single thought to the reception of his words by the maiden at the further side, upon whom his gaze was mostly resting, and who was attentively listening – looking fixedly upon the pavement the while. It has been said than men love with their eyes; women with their ears.

As Owen and himself were little more than acquaintances as yet, and as Springrove was wanting in the assurance of many men of his age, it now became necessary to wish his friends good-evening, or to find a reason for continuing near Cytherea by saying some nice new thing. He thought of a new thing; he proposed a pull across the bay. This was assented to. They went to the pier; stepped into one of the gaily painted boats moored alongside and sheered off. Cytherea sat in the stern steering.

They rowed that evening; the next came, and with it the necessity of rowing again. Then the next, and the next, Cytherea always sitting in the stern with the tiller ropes in her hand. The curves of her figure welded with those of the fragile boat in perfect continuation, as she girlishly yielded herself to its heaving and sinking, seeming to form with it an organic whole.

Then Owen was inclined to test his skill in paddling a canoe. Edward did not like canoes, and the issue was, that, having seen Owen on board, Springrove proposed to pull off after him with a pair of sculls; but not considering himself sufficiently accomplished to do finished rowing before a parade full of promenaders when there was a little swell on, and with the rudder unshipped in addition, he begged that

Cytherea might come with him and steer as before. She stepped in, and they floated along in the wake of her brother. Thus passed the fifth evening on the water.

But the sympathetic pair were thrown into still closer companionship, and much more exclusive connection.

2. July the Twenty-Ninth

It was a sad time for Cytherea – the last day of Springrove's management at Gradfield's, and the last evening before his return from Budmouth to his father's house, previous to his departure for London.

Graye had been requested by the architect to survey a plot of land nearly twenty miles off, which, with the journey to and fro, would occupy him the whole day, and prevent his returning till late in the evening. Cytherea made a companion of her landlady to the extent of sharing meals and sitting with her during the morning of her brother's absence. Midday found her restless and miserable under this arrangement. All the afternoon she sat alone, looking out of the window for she scarcely knew whom, and hoping she scarcely knew what. Half-past five o'clock came – the end of Springrove's official day. Two minutes later Springrove walked by.

She endured her solitude for another half-hour, and then could endure no longer. She had hoped – while affecting to fear – that Edward would have found some reason or other for calling, but it seemed that he had not. Hastily dressing herself she went out, when the farce of an accidental meeting was repeated. Edward came upon her in the street at the first turning, and, like the Great Duke Ferdinand in 'The Statue and the Bust'* –

> He looked at her as a lover can;
> She looked at him as one who awakes –
> The past was a sleep, and her life began.

'Shall we have a boat?' he said impulsively.

How blissful it all is at first. Perhaps, indeed, the only bliss in the course of love which can truly be called Eden-like is that which prevails immediately after doubt has ended and before reflection has set in – at the dawn of the emotion, when it is not recognized by name, and before the consideration of what this love is, has given birth to the consideration of what difficulties it tends to create; when on the man's part, the mistress appears to the mind's eye in picturesque, hazy, and fresh

31

morning lights, and soft morning shadows; when, as yet, she is known only as the wearer of one dress, which shares her own personality; as the stander in one special position, the giver of one bright particular glance, and the speaker of one tender sentence; when, on her part, she is timidly careful over what she says and does, lest she should be misconstrued or under-rated to the breadth of a shadow of a hair.

'Shall we have a boat?' he said again, more softly, seeing that to his first question she had not answered, but looked uncertainly at the ground, then almost, but not quite, in his face, blushed a series of minute blushes, left off in the midst of them, and showed the usual signs of perplexity in a matter of the emotions.

Owen had always been with her before, but there was now a force of habit in the proceeding, and with Arcadian innocence* she assumed that a row on the water was under any circumstances, a natural thing. Without another word being spoken on either side, they went down the steps. He carefully handed her in, took his seat, slid noiselessly off the sand, and away from the shore.

They thus sat facing each other in the graceful yellow cockle-shell,* and his eyes frequently found a resting-place in the depths of hers. The boat was so small that at each return of the sculls, when his hands came forward to begin the pull, they approached so near to her that her vivid imagination began to thrill her with a fancy that he was going to clasp his arms round her. The sensation grew so strong that she could not run the risk of again meeting his eyes at those critical moments, and turned aside to inspect the distant horizon; then she grew weary of looking sideways, and was driven to return to her natural position again. At this instant he again leant forward to begin, and met her glance by an ardent fixed gaze. An involuntary impulse of girlish embarrassment caused her to give a vehement pull at the tiller-rope, which brought the boat's head round till they stood directly for shore.

His eyes, which had dwelt upon her form during the whole time of her look askance, now left her; he perceived the direction in which they were going.

'Why, you have completely turned the boat, Miss Graye,' he said, looking over his shoulder. 'Look at our track on the water – a great semi-circle, preceded by a series of zigzags as far as we can see.'

She looked attentively. 'Is it my fault or yours?' she inquired. 'Mine, I suppose?'

'I can't help saying that it is yours.'

She dropped the ropes decisively, feeling the slightest twinge of vexation at the answer.

'Why do you let go?'

'I do it so badly.'

'O no; you turned about for shore in a masterly way. Do you wish to return?'

'Yes, if you please.'

'Of course, then, I will at once.'

'I fear what the people will think of us – going in such absurd directions, and all through my wretched steering.'

'Never mind what the people think.' A pause. 'You surely are not so weak as to mind what the people think on such a matter as that?'

Those words might almost be called too firm and hard to be given by him to her; but never mind. For almost the first time in her life she felt the charming sensation, although on such an insignificant subject, of being compelled into an opinion by a man she loved. Owen, though less yielding physically, and more practical, would not have had the intellectual independence to answer a woman thus. She replied quietly and honestly – as honestly as when she had stated the contrary fact a minute earlier–

'I don't mind.'

'I'll unship the tiller that you may have nothing to do going back but to hold your parasol,' he continued, and arose to perform the operation, necessarily leaning closely against her, to guard against the risk of capsizing the boat as he reached his hands astern. His warm breath fanned and crept round her face like a caress; but he was apparently only concerned with his task. She looked guilty of something when he re-seated himself. He read in her face what that something was – she had experienced a pleasure from his touch. But he flung a practical glance over his shoulder, seized the oars, and they sped in a straight line towards the shore.

Cytherea saw that he noted in her face what had passed in her heart, and that noting it, he continued as decided as before. She was inwardly distressed. She had not meant him to translate her words about returning home so literally at the first; she had not intended him to learn her secret; but more than all she was not able to endure the perception of his learning it and continuing unmoved.

There was nothing but misery to come now. They would step ashore; he would say good-night, go to London to-morrow, and the miserable She would lose him for ever. She did not quite suppose what was the fact, that a parallel thought was simultaneously passing through his mind.

They were now within ten yards, now within five; he was only now

33

waiting for a 'smooth'* to bring the boat in. Sweet, sweet Love must not be slain thus, was the fair maid's reasoning. She was equal to the occasion – ladies are – and delivered the god –

'Do you want very much to land, Mr Springrove?' she said, letting her young violet eyes pine at him a very, very little.

'I? Not at all,' said he, looking an astonishment at her inquiry which a slight twinkle of his eye half belied. 'But you do?'

'I think that now we have come out, and it is such a pleasant evening,' she said gently and sweetly, 'I should like a little longer row if you don't mind? I'll try to steer better than before if it makes it easier for you. I'll try very hard.'

It was the turn of his face to tell a tale now. He looked, 'We understand each other – ah, we do, darling!' turned the boat, and pulled back into the Bay once more.

'Now steer wherever you will,' he said, in a low voice. 'Never mind the directness of the course – wherever you will.'

'Shall it be Creston Shore?' she said, pointing to a stretch of beach northward from Budmouth Esplanade.

'Creston Shore certainly,' he responded, grasping the sculls. She took the strings daintily, and they wound away to her left.

For a long time nothing was audible in the boat but the regular dip of the oars, and their movement in the rowlocks. Springrove at length spoke.

'I must go away to-morrow,' he said tentatively.

'Yes,' she replied faintly.

'To endeavour to advance a little in my profession in London.'

'Yes,' she said again, with the same preoccupied softness.

'But I shan't advance.'

'Why not? Architecture is a bewitching profession. They say that an architect's work is another man's play.'

'Yes. But worldly advantage from an art doesn't depend upon mastering it. I used to think it did; but it doesn't. Those who get rich need have no skill at all as artists.'

'What need they have?'

'A certain kind of energy which men with any fondness for art possess very seldom indeed – an earnestness in making acquaintances, and a love for using them. They give their whole attention to the art of dining out, after mastering a few rudimentary facts to serve up in conversation. Now after saying that, do I seem a man likely to make a name?'

'You seem a man likely to make a mistake.'

'What's that?'

'To give too much room to the latent feeling which is rather common in these days among the unappreciated, that because some remarkably successful men are fools, all remarkably unsuccessful men are geniuses.'

'Pretty subtle for a young lady,' he said slowly. 'From that remark I should fancy you had bought experience.'

She passed over the idea. 'Do try to succeed,' she said, with wistful thoughtfulness, leaving her glance on him.

Springrove flushed a little at the earnestness of her words, and mused. 'Then, like Cato the Censor, I shall do what I despise, to be in the fashion,'* he said at last. . . . 'Well, when I found all this out that I was speaking of, what ever do you think I did? From having already loved verse passionately, I went on to read it continually; then I went rhyming myself. If anything on earth ruins a man for useful occupation, and for content with reasonable success in a profession or trade, it is the habit of writing verses on emotional subjects, which had much better be left to die from want of nourishment.'

'Do you write poems now?' she said.

'None. Poetical days are getting past with me, according to the usual rule. Writing rhymes is a stage people of my sort pass through, as they pass through the stage of shaving for a beard, or thinking they are ill-used, or saying there's nothing in the world worth living for.'

'Then the difference between a common man and a recognized poet is, that one has been deluded, and cured of his delusion, and the other continues deluded all his days.'

'Well, there's just enough truth in what you say to make the remark unbearable. However, it doesn't matter to me now that I "meditate the thankless Muse" no longer,* but. . . .' He paused, as if endeavouring to think what better thing he did.

Cytherea's mind ran on to the succeeding lines of the poem, and their startling harmony with the present situation suggested the fancy that he was '*sporting*' with her, and brought an awkward contemplativeness to her face.

Springrove guessed her thoughts, and in answer to them simply said 'Yes.' Then they were silent again.

'If I had known an Amaryllis* was coming here, I should not have made arrangements for leaving,' he resumed.

Such levity, superimposed on the notion of *sport*, was intolerable to Cytherea; for a woman seems never to see any but the serious side of her attachment, though the most devoted lover has all the time a vague and dim perception that he is losing his old dignity and frittering away his time.

'But will you not try again to get on in your profession? Try once more; do try once more,' she murmured. 'I am going to try again. I have advertised for something to do.'

'Of course I will,' he said, with an eager gesture and smile. 'But we must remember that the fame of Christopher Wren himself depended upon the accident of a fire in Pudding Lane.* My successes seem to come very slowly. I often think, that before I am ready to live, it will be time for me to die. However, I am trying – not for fame now, but for an easy life of reasonable comfort.'

It is a melancholy truth for the middle classes, that in proportion as they develop, by the study of poetry and art, their capacity for conjugal love of the highest and purest kind, they limit the possibility of their being able to exercise it – the very act putting out of their power the attainment of means sufficient for marriage. The man who works up a good income has had no time to learn love to its solemn extreme; the man who has learnt that has had no time to get rich.

'And if you should fail – utterly fail to get that reasonable wealth,' she said earnestly, 'don't be perturbed. The truly great stand upon no middle ledge; they are either famous or unknown.'*

'Unknown,' he said, 'if their ideas have been allowed to flow with a sympathetic breadth. Famous only if they have been convergent and exclusive.'

'Yes; and I am afraid from that, that my remark was but discouragement wearing the dress of comfort. Perhaps I was not quite right in—'

'It depends entirely upon what is meant by being truly great. But the long and the short of the matter is, that men must stick to a thing if they want to succeed in it – not giving way to over-much admiration for the flowers they see growing in other people's borders; which I am afraid has been my case.' He looked into the far distance and paused.

Adherence to a course with persistence sufficient to ensure success is possible to widely appreciative minds only when there is also found in them a power – commonplace in its nature, but rare in such combination – the power of assuming to conviction that in the outlying paths which appear so much more brilliant than their own, there are bitternesses equally great – unperceived simply on account of their remoteness.

They were opposite Ringsworth Shore. The cliffs here were formed of strata completely contrasting with those of the further side of the Bay, whilst in and beneath the water hard boulders had taken the place of sand and shingle, between which, however, the sea glided noiselessly, without breaking the crest of a single wave, so strikingly calm was the air. The breeze had entirely died away, leaving the water of that rare glassy smoothness which is unmarked even by the small dimples of the least aërial movement. Purples and blues of divers shades were reflected from this mirror accordingly as each undulation sloped east or west. They could see the rocky bottom some twenty feet beneath them, luxuriant with weeds of various growths, and dotted with pulpy creatures reflecting a silvery and spangled radiance upwards to their eyes.

At length she looked at him to learn the effect of her words of encouragement. He had let the oars drift alongside, and the boat had come to a standstill. Everything on earth seemed taking a contemplative rest, as if waiting to hear the avowal of something from his lips. At that instant he appeared to break a resolution hitherto zealously kept. Leaving his seat amidships he came and gently edged himself down beside her upon the narrow seat at the stern.

She breathed more quickly and warmly: he took her right hand in his own right: it was not withdrawn. He put his left hand behind her neck till it came round upon her left cheek: it was not thrust away. Lightly pressing her, he brought her face and mouth towards his own; when, at this the very brink, some unaccountable thought or spell within him suddenly made him halt – even now, and as it seemed as much to himself as to her, he timidly whispered 'May I?'

Her endeavour was to say No, so denuded of its flesh and sinews that its nature would hardly be recognized, or in other words a No from so near the affirmative frontier as to be affected with the Yes accent. It was thus a whispered No, drawn out to nearly a quarter of a minute's length, the O making itself audible as a sound like the spring coo of a pigeon on unusually friendly terms with its mate. Though conscious of her success in producing the kind of word she had wished to produce, she at the same time trembled in suspense as to how it would be taken. But the time available for doubt was so short as to admit of scarcely more than half a pulsation: pressing closer he kissed her. Then he kissed her again with a longer kiss.

It was the supremely happy moment of their experience. The 'bloom' and the 'purple light'* were strong on the lineaments of both. Their hearts could hardly believe the evidence of their lips.

'I love you, and you love me, Cytherea!' he whispered.

She did not deny it; and all seemed well. The gentle sounds around them from the hills, the plains, the distant town, the adjacent shore, the water heaving at their side, the kiss, and the long kiss, were all 'many a voice of one delight',* and in unison with each other.

But his mind flew back to the same unpleasant thought which had been connected with the resolution he had broken a minute or two earlier. 'I could be a slave at my profession to win you, Cytherea; I would work at the meanest honest trade to be near you – much less claim you as mine; I would – anything. But I have not told you all; it is not this; you don't know what there is yet to tell. Could you forgive as you can love?' She was alarmed to see that he had become pale with the question.

'No – do not speak,' he said. 'I have kept something from you, which has now become the cause of a great uneasiness. I had no right – to love you; but I did it. Something forbade—'

'What?' she exclaimed.

'Something forbade me – till the kiss – yes, till the kiss came; and now nothing shall forbid it! We'll hope in spite of all.... I must, however, speak of this love of ours to your brother. Dearest, you had better go indoors whilst I meet him at the station, and explain everything.'

Cytherea's short-lived bliss was dead and gone. O, if she had known of this sequel would she have allowed him to break down the barrier of mere acquaintanceship – never, never!

'Will you not explain to me?' she faintly urged. Doubt – indefinite, carking* doubt had taken possession of her.

'Not now. You alarm yourself unnecessarily,' he said tenderly. 'My only reason for keeping silence is that with my present knowledge I may tell an untrue story. It may be that there is nothing to tell. I am to blame for haste in alluding to any such thing. Forgive me, sweet – forgive me.' Her heart was ready to burst, and she could not answer him. He returned to his place and took to the oars.

They again made for the distant Esplanade, now, with its line of houses, lying like a dark grey band against the light western sky. The sun had set, and a star or two began to peep out. They drew nearer their destination, Edward as he pulled tracing listlessly with his eyes the red stripes upon her scarf, which grew to appear as black ones in the increasing dusk of evening. She surveyed the long line of lamps on the sea-wall of the town, now looking small and yellow, and seeming to send long tap-roots* of fire quivering down deep into the sea. By-and-by they reached the landing-steps. He took her hand as before, and found it as cold as the water about them. It was not relinquished till he reached her door. His assurance had not removed the constraint of her manner: he saw that she blamed him mutely and with her eyes, like a captured sparrow.* Left alone, he went and seated himself in a chair on the Esplanade.

Neither could she go indoors to her solitary room, feeling as she did in such a state of desperate heaviness. When Springrove was out of sight she turned back, and arrived at the corner just in time to see him sit down. Then she glided pensively along the pavement behind him, forgetting herself to marble like Melancholy herself* as she mused in his neighbourhood unseen. She heard, without heeding, the notes of pianos and singing voices from the fashionable houses at her back, from the open windows of which the lamp-light streamed to join that of the orange-hued full moon, newly risen over the Bay in front. Then Edward began to pace up and down, and Cytherea, fearing that he would notice her, hastened homeward, flinging him a last look as she passed out of sight. No promise from him to write: no request that she herself would do so – nothing but an indefinite expression of hope in the face of some fear unknown to her. Alas, alas!

When Owen returned he found she was not in the small sitting-room, and creeping upstairs into her bedroom with a light, he discovered her there lying asleep upon the coverlet of the bed, still with her hat and jacket on. She had flung herself down on entering, and succumbed to the unwonted oppressiveness that ever attends full-blown love. The wet traces of tears were yet visible upon her long drooping lashes.

> Love is a sowre delight, and sugred griefe,
> A living death, and ever-dying life.*

'Cytherea,' he whispered, kissing her. She awoke with a start, and vented an exclamation before recovering her judgment. 'He's gone!' she said.

'He has told me all,' said Graye soothingly. 'He is going off early to-morrow morning. 'Twas a shame of him to win you away from me, and cruel of you to keep the growth of this attachment a secret.'

'We couldn't help it,' she said, and then jumping up – 'Owen, has he told you *all*?'

'All of your love from beginning to end,' he said simply.

Edward then had not told more – as he ought to have done: yet she could not convict him. But she would struggle against his fetters. She tingled to the very soles of her feet at the very possibility that he might be deluding her.

'Owen,' she continued, with dignity, 'what is he to me? Nothing. I must dismiss such weakness as this – believe me, I will. Something far more pressing must drive it away. I have been looking my position steadily in the face, and I must get a living somehow. I mean to advertise once more.'

'Advertising is no use.'

'This one will be.' He looked surprised at the sanguine tone of her answer, till she took a piece of paper from the table and showed it him. 'See what I am going to do,' she said sadly, almost bitterly. This was her third effort: –

LADY'S-MAID. Inexperienced. Age eighteen. – G., 3 Cross Street, Budmouth.

Owen – Owen the respectable – looked blank astonishment. He repeated in a nameless, varying tone, the two words –

'Lady's-maid!'

'Yes; lady's-maid. 'Tis an honest profession,' said Cytherea bravely.

'But *you*, Cytherea?'

'Yes, I – who am I?'

'You will never be a lady's-maid – never, I am quite sure.'

'I shall try to be, at any rate.'

'Such a disgrace—'

'Nonsense! I maintain that it is no disgrace!' she said, rather warmly. 'You know very well—'

'Well, since you will, you must,' he interrupted. 'Why do you put "inexperienced"?'

'Because I am.'

'Never mind that – scratch out "inexperienced". We are poor, Cytherea, aren't we?' he murmured, after a silence, 'and it seems that the two months will close my engagement here.'

'We can put up with being poor,' she said, 'if they only give us work to do. . . . Yes, we desire as a blessing what was given us as a curse, and even that is denied. However, be cheerful, Owen, and never mind!'

In justice to desponding men, it is as well to remember that the brighter endurance of women at these epochs – invaluable, sweet, angelic, as it is – owes more of its origin to a narrower vision that shuts out many of the leaden-eyed despairs* in the van, than to a hopefulness intense enough to quell them.

40

CHAPTER FOUR
The Events of One Day

1. August the Fourth. Till Four o'Clock

The early part of the next week brought an answer to Cytherea's last note of hope in the way of advertisement – not from a distance of hundreds of miles, London, Scotland, Ireland, the Continent – as Cytherea seemed to think it must, to be in keeping with the means adopted for obtaining it, but from a place in the neighbourhood of that in which she was living – a country mansion not twenty miles off. The reply ran thus: –

KNAPWATER HOUSE,*
August 3, 1864

Miss Aldclyffe is in want of a young person as lady's-maid. The duties of the place are light. Miss Aldclyffe will be in Budmouth on Thursday, when, should G. still not have heard of a place, she would like to see her at the Belvedere Hotel, Esplanade, at four o'clock. No answer need be returned to this note.

A little earlier than the time named, Cytherea, clothed in a modest bonnet, and a black silk jacket, turned down to the hotel. Expectation, the fresh air from the water, the bright, far-extending outlook, raised the most delicate of pink colours to her cheeks, and restored to her tread a portion of that elasticity which her past troubles, and thoughts of Edward, had well-nigh taken away.

She entered the vestibule, and went to the window of the bar.

'Is Miss Aldclyffe here?' she said to a nicely-dressed barmaid in the foreground, who was talking to a landlady covered with chains, knobs, and clamps of gold, in the background.

'No, she isn't,' said the barmaid, not very civilly. Cytherea looked a shade too pretty for a plain dresser.

'Miss Aldclyffe is expected here,' the landlady said to a third person, out of sight, in the tone of one who had known for several days the fact newly discovered from Cytherea. 'Get ready her room – be quick.' From the alacrity with which the order was given and taken, it seemed to Cytherea that Miss Aldclyffe must be a woman of considerable importance.

'You are to have an interview with Miss Aldclyffe here?' the landlady inquired.

'Yes.'

'The young person had better wait,' continued the landlady. With a money-taker's intuition she had rightly divined that Cytherea would bring no profit to the house.

Cytherea was shown into a nondescript chamber, on the shady side of the building, which appeared to be either bedroom or dayroom, as occasion necessitated, and was one of a suite at the end of the first-floor corridor. The prevailing colour of the walls, curtains, carpet, and coverings of furniture, was more or less blue, to which the cold light coming from the north-easterly sky, and falling on a wide roof of new slates – the only object the small window commanded – imparted a more striking paleness. But underneath the door, communicating with the next room of the suite, gleamed an infinitesimally small, yet very powerful, fraction of contrast – a very thin line of ruddy light, showing that the sun beamed strongly into this room adjoining. The line of radiance was the only cheering thing visible in the place.

People give way to very infantine thoughts and actions when they wait; the battle-field of life is temporarily fenced off by a hard and fast line – the interview. Cytherea fixed her eyes idly upon the streak, and began picturing a wonderful paradise on the other side as the source of such a beam – reminding her of the well-known good deed in a naughty world.*

Whilst she watched the particles of dust floating before the brilliant chink she heard a carriage and horses stop opposite the front of the house. Afterwards came the rustle of a lady's skirts down the corridor, and into the room communicating with the one Cytherea occupied.

The golden line vanished in parts like the phosphorescent streak caused by the striking of a match; there was the fall of a light footstep on the floor just behind it; then a pause. Then the foot tapped impatiently, and 'There's no one here!' was spoken imperiously by a lady's tongue.

'No, madam; in the next room. I am going to fetch her,' said the attendant.

'That will do – or you needn't go in; I will call her.'

Cytherea had risen, and she advanced to the middle door with the chink under it as the servant retired. She had just laid her hand on the knob, when it slipped round within her fingers, and the door was pulled open from the other side.

2. Four o'Clock

The direct blaze of the afternoon sun, partly refracted through the crimson curtains of the window, and heightened by reflections from the

42

crimson-flock papers which covered the walls, and a carpet on the floor of the same tint, shone with a burning glow round the form of a lady standing close to Cytherea's front with the door in her hand. The stranger appeared to the maiden's eyes – fresh from the blue gloom, and assisted by an imagination fresh from nature – like a tall black figure standing in the midst of fire. It was the figure of a finely-built woman, of spare though not angular proportions.

Cytherea involuntarily shaded her eyes with her hand, retreated a step or two, and then she could for the first time see Miss Aldclyffe's face in addition to her outline, lit up by the secondary and softer light that was reflected from the varnished panels of the door. She was not a very young woman, but could boast of much beauty of the majestic autumnal phase.

'O,' said the lady, 'come this way.' Cytherea followed her to the embrasure* of the window.

Both the women showed off themselves to advantage as they walked forward in the orange light; and each showed too in her face that she had been struck with her companion's appearance. The warm tint added to Cytherea's face a voluptuousness which youth and a simple life had not yet allowed to express itself there ordinarily; whilst in the elder lady's face it reduced the customary expression, which might have been called sternness, if not harshness, to grandeur, and warmed her decaying complexion with much of the youthful richness it plainly had once possessed.

She appeared now no more than five-and-thirty, though she might easily have been ten or a dozen years older. She had clear steady eyes, a Roman nose* in its purest form, and also the round prominent chin with which the Caesars* are represented in ancient marbles; a mouth expressing a capability for and tendency to strong emotion, habitually controlled by pride. There was a severity about the lower outlines of the face which gave a masculine cast to this portion of her countenance. Womanly weakness was nowhere visible save in one part – the curve of her forehead and brows; there it was clear and emphatic. She wore a lace shawl over a brown silk dress, and a net bonnet set with a few blue cornflowers.

'You inserted the advertisement for a situation as lady's-maid giving the address, G., Cross Street?'

'Yes, madam. Graye.'

'Yes. I have heard your name – Mrs Morris, my housekeeper, mentioned you, and pointed out your advertisement.'

This was puzzling intelligence, but there was not time enough to consider it.

'Where did you live last?' continued Miss Aldclyffe.

'I have never been a servant before. I lived at home.'

'Never been out? I thought too at sight of you that you were too girlish-looking to have done much. But why did you advertise with such assurance? It misleads people.'

'I am very sorry: I put "inexperienced" at first, but my brother said it is absurd to trumpet your own weakness to the world, and would not let it remain.'

'But your mother knew what was right, I suppose?'

'I have no mother, madam.'

'Your father, then?'

'I have no father.'

'Well,' she said, more softly, 'your sisters, aunts, or cousins.'

'They didn't think anything about it.'

'You didn't ask them, I suppose?'

'No.'

'You should have done so, then. Why didn't you?'

'Because I haven't any of them, either.'

Miss Aldclyffe showed her surprise. 'You deserve forgiveness then at any rate, child,' she said, in a sort of drily-kind tone. 'However, I am afraid you do not suit me, as I am accustomed to an elderly person. You see, I want an experienced maid who knows all the usual duties of the office.' She was going to add, 'Though I like your appearance', but the words seemed offensive to apply to the ladylike girl before her, and she modified them to, 'though I like you much'.

'I am sorry I misled you, madam,' said Cytherea.

Miss Aldclyffe stood in a reverie, without replying.

'Good afternoon,' continued Cytherea.

'Good-bye, Miss Graye – I hope you will succeed.'

Cytherea turned away towards the door. The movement chanced to be one of her masterpieces. It was precise: it had as much beauty as was compatible with precision, and as little coquettishness as was compatible with beauty.

And she had in turning looked over her shoulder at the other lady with a faint accent of reproach in her face. Those who remember Greuze's 'Head of a Girl',* have an idea of Cytherea's look askance at the turning. It is not for a man to tell fishers of men* how to set out their fascinations so as to bring about the highest possible average of takes within the year: but the action that tugs the hardest of all at an emotional beholder is this sweet method of turning which steals the bosom away and leaves the eyes behind.

Now Miss Aldclyffe herself was no tyro at wheeling. When Cytherea had closed the door upon her she remained for some time in her motionless attitude, listening to the gradually dying sound of the maiden's retreating footsteps. She murmured to herself, 'It is almost worth while to be bored with instructing her in order to have a creature who could glide round my luxurious indolent body in that manner, and look at me in that way – I warrant how light her fingers are upon one's head and neck. . . . What a silly modest young thing she is, to go away so suddenly as that!' She rang the bell.

'Ask the young lady who has just left me to step back again,' she said to the attendant. 'Quick! or she will be gone.'

Cytherea was now in the vestibule, thinking that if she had told her history, Miss Aldclyffe might perhaps have taken her into the household; yet her history she particularly wished to conceal from a stranger. When she was recalled she turned back without feeling much surprise. Something, she knew not what, told her she had not seen the last of Miss Aldclyffe.

'You have somebody to refer me to, of course,' the lady said, when Cytherea had re-entered the room.

'Yes: Mr Thorn, a solicitor at Aldbrickham.'

'And are you a clever needlewoman?'

'I am considered to be.'

'Then I think that at any rate I will write to Mr Thorn,' said Miss Aldclyffe, with a little smile. 'It is true, the whole proceeding is very irregular; but my present maid leaves next Monday, and none of the five I have already seen seem to do for me. . . . Well, I will write to Mr Thorn, and if his reply is satisfactory, you shall hear from me. It will be as well to set yourself in readiness to come on Monday.'

When Cytherea had again been watched out of the room, Miss Aldclyffe asked for writing materials, that she might at once communicate with Mr Thorn. She indecisively played with the pen. 'Suppose Mr Thorn's reply to be in any way disheartening – and even if so from his own imperfect acquaintance with the young creature more than from circumstantial knowledge – I shall feel obliged to give her up. Then I shall regret that I did not give her one trial in spite of other people's prejudices. All her account of herself is reliable enough – yes, I can see that by her face. I like that face of hers.'

Miss Aldclyffe put down the pen and left the hotel without writing to Mr Thorn.

CHAPTER FIVE
The Events of One Day

1. August the Eighth. Morning and Afternoon

At post-time on that following Monday morning, Cytherea watched so anxiously for the postman, that as the interval which must bring him narrowed less and less her vivid expectation had only a degree less tangibility than his presence itself. In another second his form came into view. He brought two letters for Cytherea.

One from Miss Aldclyffe, simply stating that she wished Cytherea to come on trial; that she would require her to be at Knapwater House by Monday evening.

The other was from Edward Springrove. He told her that she was the bright spot of his life: that her existence was far dearer to him than his own: that he had never known what it was to love till he had met her. True, he had felt passing attachments to other faces from time to time; but they all had been weak inclinations towards those faces as they then appeared. He loved her past and future, as well as her present. He pictured her as a child: he loved her. He pictured her of sage years: he loved her. He pictured her in trouble: he loved her. Homely friendship entered into his love for her, without which all love was evanescent.

He would make one depressing statement. Uncontrollable circumstances (a long history, with which it was impossible to acquaint her at present) operated to a certain extent as a drag upon his wishes. He had felt this more strongly at the time of their parting than he did now – and it was the cause of his abrupt behaviour, for which he begged her to forgive him. He saw now an honourable way of freeing himself, and the perception had prompted him to write. In the meantime might he indulge in the hope of possessing her on some bright future day, when by hard labour generated from her own encouraging words, he had placed himself in a position she would think worthy to be shared with him?

Dear little letter; she huddled it up. So much more important a love-letter seems to a girl than to a man. Springrove was unconsciously clever in his letters, and a man with a talent of that kind may write himself up to a hero in the mind of a young woman who loves him without knowing much about him. Springrove already stood a cubit* higher in her imagination than he did in his shoes.

During the day she flitted about the room in an ecstasy of pleasure, packing the things and thinking of an answer which should be worthy of the tender tone of the question, her love bubbling from her involuntarily, like prophesyings from a prophet.

In the afternoon Owen went with her to the railway-station, and put her in the train for Carriford Road, the station nearest to Knapwater House.

Half-an-hour later she stepped out upon the platform, and found nobody there to receive her – though a pony-carriage was waiting outside. In two minutes she saw a melancholy man in cheerful livery running towards her from a public-house close adjoining, who proved to be the servant sent to fetch her. There are two ways of getting rid of sorrows: one by living them down, the other by drowning them. The coachman drowned his.

He informed her that her luggage would be fetched by a spring-waggon* in about half-an-hour; then helped her into the chaise* and drove off.

Her lover's letter, lying snug in her bosom, fortified her against the restless timidity she had previously felt concerning this new undertaking, and completely furnished her with the confident ease of mind which is required for the critical observation of surrounding objects. It was just that stage in the slow decline of the summer days, when the deep, dark, and vacuous hot-weather shadows are beginning to be replaced by blue ones that have a surface and substance to the eye. They trotted along the turnpike road* for a distance of about a mile, which brought them just outside the village of Carriford, and then turned through large lodge-gates, on the heavy stone piers of which stood a pair of bitterns cast in bronze. They then entered the park and wound along a drive shaded by old and drooping lime-trees, not arranged in the form of an avenue, but standing irregularly, sometimes leaving the track completely exposed to the sky, at other times casting a shade over it, which almost approached gloom – the under surface of the lowest boughs hanging at a uniform level of six feet above the grass – the extreme height to which the nibbling mouths of the cattle could reach.

'Is that the house?' said Cytherea expectantly, catching sight of a grey gable between the trees, and losing it again.

'No; that's the old manor-house* – or rather all that's left of it. The Aldclyffes used to let it sometimes, but it was oftener empty. 'Tis now divided into three cottages. Respectable people didn't care to live there.'

'Why didn't they?'

'Well, 'tis so awkward and unhandy. You see so much of it has been

47

pulled down, and the rooms that are left won't do very well for a small residence. 'Tis so dismal, too, and like most old houses stands too low down in the hollow to be healthy.'

'Do they tell any horrid stories about it?'

'No, not a single one.'

'Ah, that's a pity.'

'Yes, that's what I say. 'Tis jest the house for a nice ghastly hair-on-end story, that would make the parish religious. Perhaps it will have one some day to make it complete; but there's not a word of the kind now. There, I wouldn't live there for all that. In fact, I couldn't. O no, I couldn't.'

'Why couldn't you?'

'The sounds.'

'What are they?'

'One is the waterfall, which stands so close by that you can hear that there waterfall in every room of the house, night or day, ill or well. 'Tis enough to drive anybody mad: now hark.'

He stopped the horse. Above the slight common sounds in the air came the unvarying rush of falling water from some spot unseen on account of the thick foliage of the grove.

'There's something awful in the unending o' that sound, ain't there, miss?'

'When you say there is, there really seems to be. You said there were two – what is the other horrid sound?'

'The pumping-engine. That's close by the Old House, and sends water up the hill and all over the Great House. We shall hear that directly. . . . There, now hark again.'

From the same direction down the dell they could now hear the whistling creak of cranks, repeated at intervals of half-a-minute, with a sousing noise between each: a creak, a souse, then another creak, and so on continually.

'Now if anybody could make shift to live through the other sounds, these would finish him off, don't you think so, miss? That machine goes on night and day, summer and winter, and is hardly ever greased or visited. Ah, it tries the nerves at night, especially if you are not very well; though we don't often hear it at the Great House.'

'That sound is certainly very dismal. They might have the wheel greased. Does Miss Aldclyffe take any interest in these things?'

'Well, scarcely; you see her father doesn't attend to that sort of thing as he used to. The engine was once quite his hobby. But now he's getten old and very seldom goes there.'

'How many are there in family?'

'Only her father and herself. He's a' old man of seventy.'

'I had thought that Miss Aldclyffe was sole mistress of the property, and lived here alone.'

'No, m—' The coachman was continually checking himself thus, being about to style her miss involuntarily, and then recollecting that he was only speaking to the new lady's-maid.

'She will soon be mistress, however, I am afraid,' he continued, as if speaking by a spirit of prophecy denied to ordinary humanity. 'The poor old gentleman has decayed very fast lately.' The man then drew a long breath.

'Why did you breathe sadly like that?' said Cytherea.

'Ah! . . . When he's dead peace will be all over with us old servants. I expect to see the whole house turned inside out.'

'She will marry, do you mean?'

'Marry – not she! I wish she would. No, in her soul she's as solitary as Robinson Crusoe, though she has acquaintances in plenty, if not relations. There's the rector, Mr Raunham – he's a relation by marriage – yet she's quite distant towards him. And people say that if she keeps single there will be hardly a life between Mr Raunham and the heirship of the estate. Dang it, she don't care. She's an extraordinary picture of womankind – very extraordinary.'

'In what way besides?'

'You'll know soon enough, miss. She has had seven lady's-maids this last twelvemonth. I assure you 'tis one body's work to fetch 'em from the station and take 'em back again. The Lord must be a neglectful party at heart,* or he'd never permit such overbearen goings on!'

'Does she dismiss them directly they come?'

'Not at all – she never dismisses them – they go theirselves. Ye see 'tis like this. She's got a very quick temper; she flees* in a passion with them for nothing at all; next mornen they come up and say they are going; she's sorry for it and wishes they'd stay, but she's as proud as a lucifer,* and her pride won't let her say, "Stay," and away they go. 'Tis like this in fact. If you say to her about anybody, "Ah, poor thing!" she says, "Pooh! indeed!" If you say, "Pooh, indeed!" "Ah, poor thing!" she says directly. She hangs the chief baker, as mid be, and restores the chief butler, as mid be, though the devil but Pharaoh* herself can see the difference between 'em.'

Cytherea was silent. She feared she might be again a burden to her brother.

'However, you stand a very good chance,' the man went on, 'for I

49

think she likes you more than common. I have never known her send the pony-carriage to meet one before; 'tis always the trap, but this time she said, in a very particular ladylike tone, "Roobert, gaow with the pony-kerriage." . . . There, 'tis true, pony and carriage too are getten rather shabby now,' he added, looking round upon the vehicle as if to keep Cytherea's pride within reasonable limits.

''Tis to be hoped you'll please in dressen her to-night.'

'Why to-night?'

'There's a dinner-party of seventeen; 'tis her father's birthday, and she's very particular about her looks at such times. Now see; this is the house. Livelier up here, isn't it, miss?'

They were now on rising ground, and had just emerged from a clump of limes. Still a little higher than where they stood was situated the mansion, called Knapwater House, the offices* gradually losing themselves among the trees behind.

2. Evening

The house was regularly and substantially built of clean grey free-stone* throughout, in that plainer fashion of classicism which prevailed at the latter end of the eighteenth century, when the copyists called designers had grown weary of fantastic variations in the Roman orders.* The main block approximated to a square on the ground plan, having a projection in the centre of each side, surmounted by a pediment. From each angle of the inferior side ran a line of buildings lower than the rest, turning inwards again at their further end, and forming within them a spacious open court, within which resounded an echo of astonishing clearness. These erections were in their turn backed by ivy-covered ice-houses, laundries, and stables, the whole mass of subsidiary buildings being half buried beneath close-set shrubs and trees.

There was opening sufficient through the foliage on the right hand to enable her on nearer approach to form an idea of the arrangement of the remoter or lawn front also. The natural features and contour of this quarter of the site had evidently dictated the position of the house primarily, and were of the ordinary, and upon the whole, most satisfactory kind, namely, a broad, graceful slope running from the terrace beneath the walls to the margin of a placid lake lying below, upon the surface of which a dozen swans and a green punt floated at leisure. An irregular wooded island stood in the midst of the lake; beyond this and the further margin of the water were plantations and greensward of varied outlines, the trees heightening, by half veiling, the softness of the exquisite landscape stretching behind.

The glimpses she had obtained of this portion were now checked by the angle of the building. In a minute or two they reached the side door, at which Cytherea alighted. She was welcomed by an elderly woman of lengthy smiles and general pleasantness, who announced herself to be Mrs Morris, the housekeeper.

'Mrs Graye,* I believe?' she said.

'I am not – O yes, yes, we are all mistresses,' said Cytherea, smiling, but forcedly. The title accorded her seemed disagreeably like the first slight scar of a brand, and she thought of Owen's prophecy.

Mrs Morris led her into a comfortable parlour called The Room. Here tea was made ready, and Cytherea sat down, looking, whenever occasion allowed, at Mrs Morris with great interest and curiosity, to discover, if possible, something in her which should give a clue to the secret of her knowledge of herself, and the recommendation based upon it. But nothing was to be learnt, at any rate just then. Mrs Morris was perpetually getting up, feeling in her pockets, going to cupboards, leaving the room two or three minutes, and trotting back again.

'You'll excuse me, Mrs Graye,' she said, 'but 'tis the old gentleman's birthday, and they always have a lot of people to dinner on that day, though he's getting up in years now. However, none of them are sleepers – she generally keeps the house pretty clear of lodgers (being a lady with no intimate friends, though many acquaintances), which, though it gives us less to do, makes it all the duller for the younger maids in the house.' Mrs Morris then proceeded to give in fragmentary speeches an outline of the constitution and government of the estate.

'Now, are you sure you have quite done tea? Not a bit or drop more? Why, you've eaten nothing, I'm sure. . . . Well, now, it is rather inconvenient that the other maid is not here to show you the ways of the house a little, but she left last Saturday, and Miss Aldclyffe has been making shift with poor old clumsy me for a maid all yesterday and this morning. She is not come in yet. I expect she will ask for you, Mrs Graye, the first thing. . . . I was going to say that if you have really done tea, I will take you upstairs, and show you through the wardrobes – Miss Aldclyffe's things are not laid out for to-night yet.'

She preceded Cytherea upstairs, pointed out her own room, and then took her into Miss Aldclyffe's dressing-room, on the first floor; where, after explaining the whereabouts of various articles of apparel, the housekeeper left her, telling her that she had an hour yet upon her hands before dressing time. Cytherea laid out upon the bed in the next room all that she had been told would be required that evening, and then went again to the little room which had been appropriated to herself.

Here she sat down by the open window, leant out upon the sill like another Blessed Damozel,* and listlessly looked down upon the brilliant pattern of colours formed by the flower-beds on the lawn – now richly crowded with late summer blossom. But the vivacity of spirit which had hitherto enlivened her was fast ebbing under the pressure of prosaic realities, and the warm scarlet of the geraniums, glowing most conspicuously, and mingling with the vivid cold red and green of the verbenas, the rich depth of the dahlia, and the ripe mellowness of the calceolaria, backed by the pale hue of a flock of meek sheep feeding in the open park, close to the other side of the fence, were, to a great extent, lost upon her eyes. She was thinking that nothing seemed worth while; that it was possible she might die in a workhouse; and what did it matter? The petty, vulgar details of servitude that she had just passed through, her dependence upon the whims of a strange woman, the necessity of quenching all individuality of character in herself, and relinquishing her own peculiar tastes to help on the wheel of this alien establishment, made her sick and sad, and she almost longed to pursue some free, out-of-doors employment, sleep under trees or a hut, and know no enemy but winter and cold weather,* like shepherds and cowkeepers, and birds and animals – ay, like the sheep she saw there under her window. She looked sympathizingly at them for several minutes, imagining their enjoyment of the rich grass.

'Yes – like those sheep,' she said aloud; and her face reddened with surprise at a discovery she made that very instant.

The flock consisted of some ninety or a hundred young stock ewes: the surface of their fleece was as rounded and even as a cushion, and white as milk. Now she had just observed that on the left buttock of every one of them were marked in distinct red letters the initials 'E.S.'

'E.S.' could bring to Cytherea's mind only one thought; but that immediately and for ever – the name of her lover, Edward Springrove.

'O, if it should be—!' She interrupted her words by a resolve. Miss Aldclyffe's carriage at the same moment made its appearance in the drive; but Miss Aldclyffe was not her object now. It was to ascertain to whom the sheep belonged, and to set her surmise at rest one way or the other. She flew downstairs to Mrs Morris.

'Whose sheep are those in the park, Mrs Morris?'

'Farmer Springrove's.'

'What Farmer Springrove is that?' she said quickly.

'Why, surely you know? Your friend, Farmer Springrove, the cider-maker, and who keeps the Three Tranters Inn; who recommended you to me when he came in to see me the other day?'

Cytherea's mother-wit suddenly warned her in the midst of her excitement that it was necessary not to betray the secret of her love. 'O yes,' she said, 'of course.' Her thoughts had run as follows in that short interval: –

'Farmer Springrove is Edward's father, and his name is Edward too.

'Edward knew I was going to advertise for a situation of some kind.

'He watched the *Times*, and saw it, my address being attached.

'He thought it would be excellent for me to be here that we might meet whenever he came home.

'He told his father that I might be recommended as a lady's-maid; and he knew my brother and myself.

'His father told Mrs Morris; Mrs Morris told Miss Aldclyffe.'

The whole chain of incidents that drew her there was plain, and there was no such thing as chance in the matter. It was all Edward's doing.

The sound of a bell was heard. Cytherea did not heed it, and still continued in her reverie.

'That's Miss Aldclyffe's bell,' said Mrs Morris.

'I suppose it is,' said the young woman placidly.

'Well, it means that you must go up to her,' the matron continued, in a tone of surprise.

Cytherea felt a burning heat come over her, mingled with a sudden irritation at Mrs Morris's hint. But the good sense which had recognized stern necessity prevailed over rebellious independence; the flush passed, and she said hastily –

'Yes, yes; of course, I must go to her when she pulls the bell – whether I want to or no.'

However, in spite of this painful reminder of her new position in life, Cytherea left the apartment in a mood far different from the gloomy sadness of ten minutes previous. The place felt like home to her now; she did not mind the pettiness of her occupation, because Edward evidently did not mind it; and this was Edward's own spot. She found time on her way to Miss Aldclyffe's dressing-room to hurriedly glide out by a side door, and look for a moment at the unconscious sheep bearing the friendly initials. She went up to them to try to touch one of the flock, and felt vexed that they all stared sceptically at her kind advances, and then ran pell-mell down the hill. Then, fearing any one should discover her childish movements, she slipped indoors again, and ascended the staircase, catching glimpses, as she passed, of silver-buttoned footmen, who flashed about the passages like lightning.

Miss Aldclyffe's dressing-room was an apartment which, on a casual survey, conveyed an impression that it was available for almost any purpose save the adornment of the feminine person. In its hours of perfect order nothing pertaining to the toilet was visible; even the inevitable mirrors with their accessories were arranged in a roomy recess not noticeable from the door, lighted by a window of its own, called the dressing-window.

The washing-stand figured as a vast oak chest, carved with grotesque Renaissance ornament. The dressing-table was in appearance something between a high altar and a cabinet piano,* the surface being richly worked in the same style of semi-classic decoration, but the extraordinary outline had been arrived at by an ingenious joiner* and decorator from the neighbouring town, after months of painful toil in cutting and fitting, under Miss Aldclyffe's immediate eye; the materials being the substance of two or three old cabinets the lady had found in the lumber-room. About two-thirds of the floor was carpeted, the remaining portion being laid with parquetry of light and dark woods.

Miss Aldclyffe was standing at the larger window, away from the dressing-niche. She bowed, and said pleasantly, 'I am glad you have come. We shall get on capitally, I dare say.'

Her bonnet was off. Cytherea did not think her so handsome as on the earlier day; the queenliness of her beauty was harder and less warm. But a worse discovery than this was that Miss Aldclyffe, with the usual obliviousness of rich people to their dependents' specialities, seemed to have quite forgotten Cytherea's inexperience, and mechanically delivered up her body to her handmaid without a thought of details, and with a mild yawn.

Everything went well at first. The dress was removed, stockings and black boots were taken off, and silk stockings and white shoes were put on. Miss Aldclyffe then retired to bathe her hands and face, and Cytherea drew breath. If she could get through this first evening, all would be right. She felt that it was unfortunate that such a crucial test for her powers as a birthday dinner should have been applied on the threshold of her arrival; but set to again.

Miss Aldclyffe was now arrayed in a white dressing-gown, and dropped languidly into an easy-chair, pushed up before the glass. The instincts of her sex and her own practice told Cytherea the next movement. She let Miss Aldclyffe's hair fall about her shoulders, and began to arrange it. It proved to be all real; a satisfaction.

Miss Aldclyffe was musingly looking on the floor, and the operation went on for some minutes in silence. At length her thoughts seemed to turn to the present, and she lifted her eyes to the glass.

'Why, what on earth are you doing with my head?' she exclaimed, with widely opened eyes. At the words she felt the back of Cytherea's little hand tremble against her neck.

'Perhaps you prefer it done the other fashion, madam?' said the maiden.

'No, no; that's the fashion right enough, but you must make more show of my hair than that, or I shall have to buy some, which God forbid!'

'It is how I do my own,' said Cytherea naively, and with a sweetness of tone that would have pleased the most acrimonious under favourable circumstances; but tyranny was in the ascendant with Miss Aldclyffe at this moment, and she was assured of palatable food for her vice by having felt the trembling of Cytherea's hand.

'Yours, indeed! *Your* hair! Come, go on.' Considering that Cytherea possessed at least five times as much of that valuable auxiliary to woman's beauty as the lady before her, there was at the same time some excuse for Miss Aldclyffe's outburst. She remembered herself, however, and said more quietly, 'Now then, Graye— By-the-bye, what do they call you downstairs?'

'Mrs Graye,' said the handmaid.

'Then tell them not to do any such absurd thing – not but that it is quite according to usage; but you are too young yet.'

This dialogue tided Cytherea safely onward through the hairdressing till the flowers and diamonds were to be placed upon the lady's brow. Cytherea began arranging them tastefully, and to the very best of her judgment.

'That won't do,' said Miss Aldclyffe harshly.

'Why?'

'I look too young – an old dressed doll.'

'Will that, madam?'

'No, I look a fright – a perfect fright!'

'This way, perhaps?'

'Heavens! Don't worry me so.' She shut her lips like a trap.

Having once worked herself up to the belief that her head-dress was to be a failure that evening, no cleverness of Cytherea's in arranging it could please her. She continued in a smouldering passion during the remainder of the performance, keeping her lips firmly closed, and the muscles of her body rigid. Finally, snatching up her gloves, and taking her handkerchief and fan in her hand, she silently sailed out of the room, without betraying the least consciousness of another woman's presence behind her.

Cytherea's fears that at the undressing this suppressed anger would find a vent, kept her on thorns throughout the evening. She tried to read; she could not. She tried to sew; she could not. She tried to muse; she could not do that connectedly. 'If this is the beginning, what will the end be!' she said in a whisper, and felt many misgivings as to the policy of being over-hasty in establishing an independence at the expense of congruity with a cherished past.

3. Midnight

The clock struck twelve. The Aldclyffe state dinner was over. The company had all gone, and Miss Aldclyffe's bell rang loudly and jerkingly.

Cytherea started to her feet at the sound, which broke in upon a fitful sleep that had overtaken her. She had been sitting drearily in her chair waiting minute after minute for the signal, her brain in that state of intentness which takes cognizance of the passage of Time as a real motion – motion without matter – the instants throbbing past in the company of a feverish pulse. She hastened to the room, to find the lady sitting before the dressing shrine, illuminated on both sides, and looking so queenly in her attitude of absolute repose, that the younger woman felt the awfullest sense of responsibility at her Vandalism in having undertaken to demolish so imposing a pile.

The lady's jewelled ornaments were taken off in silence – some by her own listless hands, some by Cytherea's. Then followed the outer stratum of clothing. The dress being removed, Cytherea took it in her hand and went with it to the bedroom adjoining, intending to hang it in the wardrobe. But on second thoughts, in order that she might not keep Miss Aldclyffe waiting a moment longer than necessary, she flung it down on the first resting-place that came to hand, which happened to be the bed, and re-entered the dressing-room with the noiseless footfall of a kitten. She paused in the middle of the room.

She was unnoticed, and her sudden return had plainly not been expected. During the short time of Cytherea's absence, Miss Aldclyffe had pulled off a kind of chemisette of Brussels net,* drawn high above the throat, which she had worn with her evening dress as a semi-opaque covering to her shoulders, and in its place had put her night-gown round her. Her right hand was lifted to her neck, as if engaged in fastening her night-gown.

But on a second glance Miss Aldclyffe's proceeding was clearer to Cytherea. She was not fastening her night-gown; it had been carelessly

56

thrown round her, and Miss Aldclyffe was really occupied in holding up to her eyes some small object that she was keenly scrutinizing. And now on suddenly discovering the presence of Cytherea at the back of the apartment, instead of naturally continuing or concluding her inspection, she desisted hurriedly; the tiny snap of a spring was heard, her hand was removed, and she began adjusting her robes.

Modesty might have directed her hasty action of enwrapping her shoulders, but it was scarcely likely, considering Miss Aldclyffe's temperament, that she had all her life been used to a maid, Cytherea's youth, and the older lady's marked treatment of her as if she were a mere child or plaything. The matter was too slight to reason about, and yet upon the whole it seemed that Miss Aldclyffe must have a practical reason for concealing her neck.

With a timid sense of being an intruder Cytherea was about to step back and out of the room; but at the same moment Miss Aldclyffe turned, saw the impulse, and told her companion to stay, looking into her eyes as if she had half an intention to explain something. Cytherea felt certain it was the little mystery of her late movements. The other withdrew her eyes; Cytherea went to fetch the dressing-gown, and wheeled round again to bring it up to Miss Aldclyffe, who had now partly removed her night-dress to put it on the proper way, and still sat with her back towards Cytherea.

Her neck was again quite open and uncovered, and though hidden from the direct line of Cytherea's vision, she saw it reflected in the glass – the fair white surface, and the inimitable combination of curves between throat and bosom which artists adore, being brightly lit up by the light burning on either side.

And the lady's prior proceedings were now explained in the simplest manner. In the midst of her chest, like an island in a sea of pearl, reclined an exquisite little gold locket, embellished with arabesque work* of blue, red, and white enamel. That was undoubtedly what Miss Aldclyffe had been contemplating; and, moreover, not having been put off with her other ornaments, it was to be retained during the night – a slight departure from the custom of women which Miss Aldclyffe had at first not cared to exhibit to her new assistant, though now, on further thought, she seemed to have become indifferent on the matter.

'My dressing-gown,' she said, quietly fastening her night-dress as she spoke.

Cytherea came forward with it. Miss Aldclyffe did not turn her head, but looked inquiringly at her maid in the glass.

'You saw what I wear on my neck, I suppose?' she said to Cytherea's reflected face.

'Yes, madam, I did,' said Cytherea to Miss Aldclyffe's reflected face.

Miss Aldclyffe again looked at Cytherea's reflection as if she were on the point of explaining. Again she checked her resolve, and said lightly –

'Few of my maids discover that I wear it always. I generally keep it a secret – not that it matters much. But I was careless with you, and seemed to want to tell you. You win me to make confidences that. . . .'

She ceased, took Cytherea's hand in her own, lifted the locket with the other, touched the spring and disclosed a miniature.

'It is a handsome face, is it not?' she whispered mournfully, and even timidly.

'It is.'

But the sight had gone through Cytherea like an electric shock, and there was an instantaneous awakening of perception in her, so thrilling in its presence as to be well-nigh insupportable. The face in the miniature was the face of her own father – younger and fresher than she had ever known him – but her father!

Was this the woman of his wild and unquenchable early love? And was this the woman who had figured in the gate-man's story as answering the name of Cytherea before her judgment was awake? Surely it was. And if so, here was the tangible outcrop of a romantic and hidden stratum of the past hitherto seen only in her imagination; but as far as her scope allowed, clearly defined therein by reason of its strangeness.

Miss Aldclyffe's eyes and thoughts were so intent upon the miniature that she had not been conscious of Cytherea's start of surprise. She went on speaking in a low and abstracted tone.

'Yes, I lost him.' She interrupted her words by a short meditation, and went on again. 'I lost him by excess of honesty as regarded my past. But it was best that it should be so. . . . I was led to think rather more than usual of the circumstances to-night because of your name. It is pronounced the same way, though differently spelt.'

The only means by which Cytherea's surname could have been spelt to Miss Aldclyffe must have been by Mrs Morris or Farmer Springrove. She fancied Farmer Springrove would have spelt it properly if Edward was his informant, which made Miss Aldclyffe's remark obscure.

Women make confidences and then regret them. The impulsive rush of feeling which had led Miss Aldclyffe to indulge in this revelation, trifling as it was, died out immediately her words were beyond recall;

and the turmoil occasioned in her by dwelling upon that chapter of her life, found vent in another kind of emotion – the result of a trivial accident.

Cytherea, after letting down Miss Aldclyffe's hair, adopted some plan with it to which the lady had not been accustomed. A rapid revulsion to irritation ensued. The maiden's mere touch seemed to discharge the pent-up regret of the lady as if she had been a jar of electricity.*

'How strangely you treat my hair!' she exclaimed.

A silence.

'I have told you what I never tell my maids as a rule; of course *nothing* that I say in this room is to be mentioned outside it.' She spoke crossly no less than emphatically.

'It shall not be, madam,' said Cytherea, agitated and vexed that the woman of her romantic wonderings should be so disagreeable to her.

'Why on earth did I tell you of my past!' she went on.

Cytherea made no answer.

The lady's vexation with herself, and the accident which had led to the disclosure swelled little by little till it knew no bounds. But what was done could not be undone, and though Cytherea had shown a most winning responsiveness, quarrel Miss Aldclyffe must. She recurred to the subject of Cytherea's want of expertness like a captious reviewer* who, finding the sentiments of a poet unimpeachable, quarrels with his rhymes.

'Never, never before did I serve myself such a trick as this in engaging a maid!' She waited for an expostulation: none came. Miss Aldclyffe tried again.

'The idea of my taking a girl without asking her more than three questions, or having a single reference, all because of her good l—, the shape of her face and body! It *was* a fool's trick. There, I am served right, quite right – by being deceived in such a way.'

'I didn't deceive you,' said Cytherea. The speech was an unfortunate one, and was the very 'fuel to maintain its fires'* that the other's petulance desired.

'You did,' she said hotly.

'I told you I couldn't promise to be acquainted with every detail of routine just at first.'

'Will you contradict me in this way! You are telling untruths, I say.'

Cytherea's lip quivered. 'I would answer the remark if – if—'

'If what?'

'If it were a lady's!'

'You girl of impudence – what do you say? Leave the room this instant, I tell you.'

'And I tell you that a person who speaks to a lady as you do to me, is no lady herself!'

'To a lady? A lady's-maid speaks in this way. The idea!'

'Don't "lady's-maid" me: nobody is my mistress, I won't have it!'

'Good Heavens!'

'I wouldn't have come – no – I wouldn't! if I had known!'

'What?'

'That you were such an ill-tempered, unjust woman!'

'Possest beyond the Muse's painting,'* Miss Aldclyffe exclaimed –

'A Woman, am I! I'll teach you if I am a Woman!' and lifted her hand as if she would have liked to strike her companion. This stung the maiden into absolute defiance.

'I dare you to touch me!' she cried. 'Strike me if you dare, madam! I am not afraid of you – what do you mean by such an action as that?'

Miss Aldclyffe was disconcerted at this unexpected show of spirit, and ashamed of her unladylike impulse now it was put into words. She sank back in the chair. 'I was not going to strike you – go to your room – I beg you to go to your room!' she repeated in a husky whisper.

Cytherea, red and panting, took up her candlestick and advanced to the table to get a light. As she stood close to them the rays from the candles struck sharply on her face. She usually bore a much stronger likeness to her mother than to her father, but now, looking with a grave, reckless, and angered expression of countenance at the kindling wick as she held it slanting into the other flame, her father's features were distinct in her. It was the first time Miss Aldclyffe had seen her in a passionate mood, and wearing that expression which was invariably its concomitant. It was Miss Aldclyffe's turn to start now; and the remark she made was an instance of that sudden change of tone from high-flown invective to the pettiness of curiosity which so often makes women's quarrels ridiculous. Even Miss Aldclyffe's dignity had not sufficient power to postpone the absorbing desire she now felt to settle the strange suspicion that had entered her head.

'You spell your name the common way, G, R, E, Y, don't you?' she said, with assumed indifference.

'No,' said Cytherea, poised on the side of her foot, and still looking into the flame.

'Yes, surely? The name was spelt that way on your boxes: I looked and saw it myself.'

The enigma of Miss Aldclyffe's mistake was solved. 'O, was it?' said

Cytherea. 'Ah, I remember Mrs Jackson, the lodging-house keeper at Budmouth, labelled them. We spell our name G, R, A, Y, E.'

'What was your father's trade?'

Cytherea thought it would be useless to attempt to conceal facts any longer. 'His was not a trade,' she said. 'He was an architect.'

'The idea of your being an architect's daughter!'

'There's nothing to offend you in that, I hope?'

'O no.'

'Why did you say "the idea"?'

'Leave that alone. Did he ever visit in Dukery Street, Bloomsbury, one Christmas, many years ago? – but you would not know that.'

'I have heard him say that Mr Huntway, a curate somewhere in that part of London, and who died there, was an old college friend of his.'

'What is your Christian name?'

'Cytherea.'

'No! And is it really? And you knew that face I showed you? Yes, I see you did.' Miss Aldclyffe stopped, and closed her lips impassibly. She was a little agitated.

'Do you want me any longer?' said Cytherea, standing candle in hand and looking quietly in Miss Aldclyffe's face.

'Well – no: no longer,' said the other lingeringly.

'With your permission, I will leave the house to-morrow morning, madam.'

'Ah.' Miss Aldclyffe had no notion of what she was saying.

'And I know you will be so good as not to intrude upon me during the short remainder of my stay?'

Saying this Cytherea left the room before her companion had answered. Miss Aldclyffe, then, had recognized her at last, and had been curious about her name from the beginning.

The other members of the household had retired to rest. As Cytherea went along the passage leading to her room her skirts rustled against the partition. A door on her left opened, and Mrs Morris looked out.

'I waited out of bed till you came up,' she said, 'it being your first night, in case you should be at a loss for anything. How have you got on with Miss Aldclyffe?'

'Pretty well – though not so well as I could have wished.'

'Has she been scolding?'

'A little.'

'She's a very odd lady – 'tis all one way or the other with her. She's not bad at heart, but unbearable in close quarters. Those of us who don't have much to do with her personally, stay on for years and years.'

61

'Has Miss Aldclyffe's family always been rich?' said Cytherea.

'O no. The property, with her name, came from her mother's uncle. Her family is a branch of the old Aldclyffe family on the maternal side. Her mother married a Bradleigh – a mere nobody at that time – and was on that account cut by her relations. But very singularly the other branch of the family died out one by one – three of them, and Miss Aldclyffe's great-uncle then left all his property, including this estate, to Captain Bradleigh and his wife – Miss Aldclyffe's father and mother – on condition that they took the old family name as well. There's all about it in the *Landed Gentry*.* 'Tis a thing very often done.'

'O, I see. Thank you. Well, now I am going. Good-night.'

CHAPTER SIX

The Events of Twelve Hours

1. August the Ninth. One to Two o'Clock a.m.

Cytherea entered her bedroom, and flung herself on the bed, bewildered by a whirl of thought. Only one subject was clear in her mind, and it was that, in spite of family discoveries, that day was to be the first and last of her experience as a lady's maid. Starvation itself should not compel her to hold such a humiliating post for another instant. 'Ah,' she thought, with a sigh, at the martyrdom of her last little fragment of self-conceit, 'Owen knows everything better than I.'

She jumped up and began making ready for her departure in the morning, the tears streaming down when she grieved and wondered what practical matter on earth she could turn her hand to next. All these preparations completed, she began to undress, her mind unconsciously drifting away to the contemplation of her late surprises. To look in the glass for an instant at the reflection of her own magnificent resources in face and bosom, and to mark their attractiveness unadorned, was perhaps but the natural action of a young woman who had so lately been chidden whilst passing through the harassing experience of decorating an older beauty of Miss Aldclyffe's temper.

But she directly checked her weakness by sympathizing reflections on the hidden troubles which must have thronged the past years of the solitary lady, to keep her, though so rich and courted, in a mood so repellent and gloomy as that in which Cytherea found her; and then the young girl marvelled again and again, as she had marvelled before, at the strange confluence of circumstances which had brought herself into contact with the one woman in the world whose history was so romantically intertwined with her own. She almost began to wish she were not obliged to go away and leave the lonely being to loneliness still.

In bed and in the dark, Miss Aldclyffe haunted her mind more persistently than ever. Instead of sleeping, she called up staring visions of the possible past of this queenly lady, her mother's rival. Up the long vista of bygone years she saw, behind all, the young girl's flirtation, little or much, with the cousin, that seemed to have been nipped in the bud, or to have terminated hastily in some way. Then the secret meetings between Miss Aldclyffe and the other woman at the little inn at Hammersmith and other places: the commonplace name she adopted: her swoon at some painful news, and the very slight knowledge the elder female had of her partner in mystery. Then, more than a year afterwards, the acquaintanceship of her own father with this his first love; the awakening of the passion, his acts of devotion, the unreasoning heat of his rapture, her tacit acceptance of it, and yet her uneasiness under the delight. Then his declaration amid the evergreens: the utter change produced in her manner thereby, seemingly the result of a rigid determination: and the total concealment of her reason by herself and her parents, whatever it was. Then the lady's course dropped into darkness, and nothing more was visible till she was discovered here at Knapwater, nearly fifty years old, still unmarried and still beautiful, but lonely, embittered, and haughty. Cytherea imagined that her father's image was still warmly cherished in Miss Aldclyffe's heart, and was thankful that she herself had not been betrayed into announcing that she knew many particulars of this page of her father's history, and the chief one, the lady's unaccountable renunciation of him. It would have made her bearing towards the mistress of the mansion more awkward, and would have been no benefit to either.

Thus conjuring up the past, and theorizing on the present, she lay restless, changing her posture from one side to the other and back again. Finally, when courting sleep with all her art, she heard a clock strike two. A minute later, and she fancied she could distinguish a soft rustle in the passage outside her room.

To bury her head in the sheets was her first impulse; then to uncover it, raise herself on her elbow, and stretch her eyes wide open in the darkness; her lips being parted with the intentness of her listening. Whatever the noise was, it had ceased for the time.

It began again and came close to her door, lightly touching the panels. Then there was another stillness; Cytherea made a movement which caused a faint rustling of the bed-clothes.

Before she had time to think another thought a light tap was given. Cytherea breathed: the person outside was evidently bent upon finding her awake, and the rustle she had made had encouraged the hope. The maiden's physical condition shifted from one pole to its opposite. The cold sweat of terror forsook her, and modesty took the alarm. She became hot and red; her door was not locked.

A distinct woman's whisper came to her through the keyhole: 'Cytherea!'

Only one being in the house knew her Christian name, and that was Miss Aldclyffe. Cytherea stepped out of bed, went to the door, and whispered back 'Yes?'

'Let me come in, darling.'

The young woman paused in a conflict between judgment and emotion. It was now mistress and maid no longer; woman and woman only. Yes; she must let her come in, poor thing.

She got a light in an instant, opened the door, and raising her eyes and the candle, saw Miss Aldclyffe standing outside in her dressing-gown.

'Now you see that it is really myself; put out the light,' said the visitor. 'I want to stay here with you, Cythie. I came to ask you to come down into my bed, but it is snugger here. But remember that you are mistress in this room, and that I have no business here, and that you may send me away if you choose. Shall I go?'

'O no; you shan't indeed if you don't want to,' said Cythie generously.

The instant they were in bed Miss Aldclyffe freed herself from the last remnant of restraint. She flung her arms round the young girl, and pressed her gently to her heart.

'Now kiss me,' she said. 'You seem as if you were my own, own child!'

Cytherea, upon the whole, was rather discomposed at this change of treatment; and, discomposed or no, her passions were not so impetuous as Miss Aldclyffe's. She could not bring her soul to her lips for a moment, try how she would.

'Come, kiss me,' repeated Miss Aldclyffe.

Cytherea gave her a very small one, as soft in touch and in sound as the bursting of a bubble.

'More earnestly than that – come.'

She gave another, a little but not much more expressively.

'I don't deserve a more feeling one, I suppose,' said Miss Aldclyffe, with an emphasis of sad bitterness in her tone. 'I am an ill-tempered woman, you think; half out of my mind. Well, perhaps I am; but I have had grief more than you can think or dream of. But I am a lonely woman, and I want the sympathy of a pure girl like you, and so I can't help loving you – your name is the same as mine – isn't it strange?'

Cytherea was inclined to say no, but remained silent.

'Now, don't you think I must love you?' continued the other.

'Yes,' said Cytherea absently. She was still thinking whether duty to Owen and her father, which asked for silence on her knowledge of her father's unfortunate love, or duty to the woman embracing her, which seemed to ask for confidence, ought to predominate. Here was a solution. She would wait till Miss Aldclyffe referred to her acquaintanceship and attachment to Cytherea's father in past times: then she would tell her all she knew: that would be honour.

'Why can't you kiss me as I can kiss you? Why can't you!' She impressed upon Cytherea's lips a warm motherly salute, given as if in the outburst of strong feeling, long checked, and yearning for something to care for and be cared for by in return.

'Do you think badly of me for my behaviour this evening, child? I don't know why I am so foolish as to speak to you in this way. I am a very fool, I believe. Yes. How old are you?'

'Eighteen.'

'Eighteen! . . . Well, why don't you ask me how old I am?'

'Because I don't want to know.'

'Never mind if you don't. I am forty-six; and it gives me greater pleasure to tell you this than it does to you to listen. I have not told my age truly for the last twenty years till now.'

'Why haven't you?'

'I have met deceit by deceit, till I am weary of it – weary, weary – and I long to be what I shall never be again – artless and innocent, like you. But I suppose that you, too, will prove to be not worth a thought, as every new friend does on more intimate knowledge. Come, why don't you talk to me, child? Have you said your prayers?'

'Yes – no! I forgot them to-night.'

'I suppose you say them every night as a rule?'

'Yes.'

'Why do you do that?'

'Because I have always done so, and it would seem strange if I were not to. Do you?'

'I? A wicked old sinner like me! No, I never do. I have thought all such matters humbug for years – thought so so long that I should be glad to think otherwise from very weariness; and yet, such is the code of the polite world, that I subscribe regularly to Missionary Societies and others of the sort. . . . Well, say your prayers, dear – you won't omit them now you recollect it. I should like to hear you very much. Will you?'

'It seems hardly—'

'It would seem so like old times to me – when I was young, and nearer – far nearer Heaven than I am now. Do, sweet one.'

Cytherea was embarrassed, and her embarrassment arose from the following conjuncture of affairs. Since she had loved Edward Springrove, she had linked his name with her brother Owen's in her nightly supplications to the Almighty. She wished to keep her love for him a secret, and, above all, a secret from a woman like Miss Aldclyffe; yet her conscience and the honesty of her love would not for an instant allow her to think of omitting his dear name, and so endanger the efficacy of all her previous prayers for his success by an unworthy shame now: it would be wicked of her, she thought, and a grievous wrong to him. Under any worldly circumstances she might have thought the position justified a little finesse, and have skipped him for once; but prayer was too solemn a thing for such trifling.

'I would rather not say them,' she murmured first. It struck her then that this declining altogether was the same cowardice in another dress, and was delivering her poor Edward over to Satan just as unceremoniously as before. 'Yes; I will say my prayers, and you shall hear me,' she added firmly.

She turned her face to the pillow and repeated in low soft tones the simple words she had used from childhood on such occasions. Owen's name was mentioned without faltering, but in the other case, maidenly shyness was too strong even for religion, and that when supported by excellent intentions. At the name of Edward she stammered, and her voice sank to the faintest whisper in spite of her.

'Thank you, dearest,' said Miss Aldclyffe. 'I have prayed too, I verily believe. You are a good girl, I think.' Then the expected question came.

'"Bless Owen", and whom, did you say?'

There was no help for it now, and out it came. 'Owen and Edward,' said Cytherea.

'Who are Owen and Edward?'

'Owen is my brother, madam,' faltered the maid.

'Ah, I remember. Who is Edward?'

A silence.

'Your brother, too?' continued Miss Aldclyffe.

'No.'

Miss Aldclyffe reflected a moment. 'Don't you want to tell me who Edward is?' she said at last, in a tone of meaning.

'I don't mind telling; only. . . .'

'You would rather not, I suppose?'

'Yes.'

Miss Aldclyffe shifted her ground. 'Were you ever in love?' she inquired suddenly.

Cytherea was surprised to hear how quickly the voice had altered from tenderness to harshness, vexation, and disappointment.

'Yes – I think I was – once,' she murmured.

'Aha! And were you ever kissed by a man?'

A pause.

'Well, were you?' said Miss Aldclyffe, rather sharply.

'Don't press me to tell – I can't – indeed, I won't, madam!'

Miss Aldclyffe removed her arms from Cytherea's neck. ''Tis now with you as it is always with all girls,' she said, in jealous and gloomy accents. 'You are not, after all, the innocent I took you for. No, no.' She then changed her tone with fitful rapidity. 'Cytherea, try to love me more than you love him – do. I love you more sincerely than any man can. Do, Cythie: don't let any man stand between us. O, I can't bear that!' She clasped Cytherea's neck again.

'I must love him now I have begun,' replied the other.

'Must – yes – must,' said the elder lady reproachfully. 'Yes, women are all alike. I thought I had at last found an artless woman who had not been sullied by a man's lips, and who had not practised or been practised upon by the arts which ruin all the truth and sweetness and goodness in us. Find a girl, if you can, whose mouth and ears have not been made a regular highway of by some man or another! Leave the admittedly notorious spots – the drawing-rooms of society – and look in the villages – leave the villages and search in the schools – and you can hardly find a girl whose heart has not been *had* – is not an old thing half worn out by some He or another! If men only knew the staleness of the freshest of us! that nine times out of ten the "first love" they think they are winning from a woman is but the hulk of an old wrecked affection, fitted with new sails and re-used. O Cytherea, can it be that you, too, are like the rest?'

'No, no, no,' urged Cytherea, awed by the storm she had raised in the impetuous woman's mind. 'He only kissed me once – twice I mean.'

'He might have done it a thousand times if he had cared to, there's no doubt about that, whoever his lordship is. You are as bad as I – we are all alike; and I – an old fool – have been sipping at your mouth as if it were honey, because I fancied no wasting lover knew the spot. But a minute ago, and you seemed to me like a fresh spring meadow – now you seem a dusty highway.'

'O no, no!' Cytherea was not weak enough to shed tears except on extraordinary occasions but she was fain to begin sobbing now. She wished Miss Aldclyffe would go to her own room, and leave her and her treasured dreams alone. This vehement imperious affection was in one sense soothing, but yet it was not of the kind that Cytherea's instincts desired. Though it was generous, it seemed somewhat too rank and capricious* for endurance.

'Well,' said the lady in continuation, 'who is he?'

Her companion was desperately determined not to tell his name: she too much feared a taunt when Miss Aldclyffe's fiery mood again ruled her tongue.

'Won't you tell me? not tell me after all the affection I have shown?'

'I will, perhaps, another day.'

'Did you wear a hat and white feather in Budmouth for the week or two previous to your coming here?'

'Yes.'

'Then I have seen you and your lover at a distance! He rowed you round the bay with your brother.'

'Yes.'

'And without your brother – fie! There, there, don't let that little heart beat itself to death: throb, throb: it shakes the bed, you silly thing. I didn't mean that there was any harm in going alone with him. I only saw you from the Esplanade, in common with the rest of the people. I often run down to Budmouth. He was a very good figure: now who was he?'

'I – I won't tell, madam – I cannot indeed!'

'Won't tell – very well, don't. You are very foolish to treasure up his name and image as you do. Why, he has had loves before you, trust him for that, whoever he is, and you are but a temporary link in a long chain of others like you: who only have your little day as they have had theirs.'

''Tisn't true! 'tisn't true! 'tisn't true!' cried Cytherea in an agony of torture. 'He has never loved anybody else, I know – I am sure he hasn't.'

Miss Aldclyffe was as jealous as any man could have been. She continued –

68

'He sees a beautiful face and thinks he will never forget it, but in a few weeks the feeling passes off, and he wonders how he could have cared for anybody so absurdly much.'

'No, no, he doesn't – What does he do when he has thought that – Come, tell me – tell me!'

'You are as hot as fire, and the throbbing of your heart makes me nervous. I can't tell you if you get in that flustered state.'

'Do, do tell – O, it makes me so miserable! but tell – come tell me!'

'Ah – the tables are turned now, dear!' she continued, in a tone which mingled pity with derision –

> 'Love's passions shall rock thee
> As the storm rocks the ravens on high,
> Bright reason will mock thee
> Like the sun from a wintry sky.*

'What does he do next? – Why, this is what he does next: ruminate on what he had heard of women's romantic impulses, and how easily men torture them when they have given way to those feelings, and have resigned everything for their hero. It may be that though he loves you heartily now – that is, as heartily as a man can – and you love him in return, your loves may be impracticable and hopeless and you may be separated for ever. You, as the weary, weary years pass by will fade and fade – bright eyes *will* fade – and you will perhaps then die early – true to him to your latest breath, and believing him to be true to the latest breath also; whilst he, in some gay and busy spot far away from your last quiet nook, will have married some dashing lady, and not purely oblivious of you, will long have ceased to regret you – will chat about you, as you were in long past years – will say, "Ah, little Cytherea used to tie her hair like that – poor innocent trusting thing; it was a pleasant useless idle dream – that dream of mine for the maid with the bright eyes and simple, silly heart; but I was a foolish lad at that time." Then he will tell the tale of all your little Wills and Won'ts, and particular ways, and as he speaks, turn to his wife with a placid smile.'

'It is not true! He can't, he c-can't be s-so cruel – and you are cruel to me – you are, you are!' She was at last driven to desperation: her natural common sense and shrewdness had seen all through the piece how imaginary her emotions were – she felt herself to be weak and foolish in permitting them to rise; but even then she could not control them: be agonized she must. She was only eighteen, and the long day's labour, her weariness, her excitement, had completely unnerved her, and worn her out: she was bent hither and thither by this tyrannical working upon her imagination, as a young rush in the wind. She wept bitterly.

'And now think how much *I* like you,' resumed Miss Aldclyffe, when Cytherea grew calmer. 'I shall never forget you for anybody else, as men do – never. I will be exactly as a mother to you. Now will you promise to live with me always, and always be taken care of, and never deserted?'

'I cannot. I will not be anybody's maid for another day on any consideration.'

'No, no, no. You shan't be a lady's-maid, of course. You shall be my companion. I will get another maid.'

Companion – that was a new idea. Cytherea could not resist the evidently heartfelt desire of the strange-tempered woman for her presence. But she could not trust to the moment's impulse.

'I will stay, I think. But do not ask for a final answer to-night.'

'Never mind now, then. Put your hair round your mamma's neck, and give me one good long kiss, and I won't talk any more in that way about your lover. After all, some young men are not so fickle as others; but even if he's the ficklest, there is consolaton. The love of an inconstant man is ten times more ardent than that of a faithful man – that is, while it lasts.'

Cytherea did as she was told, to escape the punishment of further talk; flung the twining tresses of her long, rich hair over Miss Aldclyffe's shoulders as directed, and the two ceased conversing, making themselves up for sleep. Miss Aldclyffe seemed to give herself over to a luxurious sense of content and quiet, as if the maiden at her side afforded her a protection against dangers which had menaced her for years; she was soon sleeping calmly.

2. Two to Five a.m.

With Cytherea it was otherwise. Unused to the place and circumstances she continued wakeful, ill at ease, and mentally distressed. She withdrew herself from her companion's embrace, turned to the other side, and endeavoured to relieve her busy brain by looking at the window-blind, and noticing the light of the rising moon – now in her last quarter – creep round upon it: it was the light of an old waning moon which had but a few days longer to live.

The sight led her to think again of what had happened under the rays of the same month's moon, a little before its full, the ecstatic evening scene with Edward: the kiss, and the shortness of those happy moments

– maiden imagination bringing about the apotheosis of a *status quo*★ which had had several unpleasantnesses in its earthly reality.

But sounds were in the ascendant that night. Her ears became aware of a strange and gloomy murmur.

She recognized it: it was the gushing of the waterfall, faint and low, brought from its source to the unwonted distance of the House by a faint breeze which made it distinctly perceptible by reason of the utter absence of all disturbing noises. The groom's melancholy representation lent to the sound a more dismal effect than it would have had of its own nature. She began to fancy what the waterfall must be like at that hour, under the trees in the ghostly moonlight. Black at the head, and over the surface of the deep cold hole into which it fell; white and frothy at the fall; black and white, like a pall and its border; sad everywhere.

She was in the mood for sounds of every kind now, and strained her ears to catch the faintest, in wayward enmity to her quiet of mind. Another soon came.

The second was quite different from the first – a kind of intermittent whistle it seemed primarily: no, a creak, a metallic creak, ever and anon, like a plough, or a rusty wheelbarrow, or at least a wheel of some kind. Yes, it was a wheel – the water-wheel in the shrubbery by the old manor-house, which the coachman had said would drive him mad.

She determined not to think any more of these gloomy things; but now that she had once noticed the sound there was no sealing her ears to it. She could not help timing its creaks, and putting on a dread expectancy just before the end of each half-minute that brought them. To imagine the inside of the engine-house, whence these noises proceeded, was now a necessity. No window, but crevices in the door, through which, probably, the moonbeams streamed in the most attenuated and skeleton-like rays, striking sharply upon portions of wet rusty cranks and chains; a glistening wheel, turning incessantly, labouring in the dark like a captive starving in a dungeon; and instead of a floor below, gurgling water, which on account of the darkness could only be heard; water which laboured up dark pipes almost to where she lay.

She shivered. Now she was determined to go to sleep; there could be nothing else left to be heard or to imagine – it was horrid that her imagination should be so restless. Yet just for an instant before going to sleep she would think this – suppose another sound *should* come – just suppose it should! Before the thought had well passed through her brain, a third sound came.

The third was a very soft gurgle or rattle – of a strange and abnormal kind – yet a sound she had heard before at some past period of her life – when, she could not recollect. To make it the more disturbing, it seemed to be almost close to her – either close outside the window, close under the floor, or close above the ceiling. The accidental fact of its coming so immediately upon the heels of her supposition, told so powerfully upon her excited nerves that she jumped up in the bed. The same instant, a little dog in some room near, having probably heard the same noise, set up a low whine. The watch-dog in the yard, hearing the moan of his associate, began to howl loudly and distinctly. His melancholy notes were taken up directly afterwards by the dogs in the kennel a long way off, in every variety of wail.

One logical thought alone was able to enter her flurried brain. The little dog that began the whining must have heard the other two sounds even better than herself. He had taken no notice of them, but he had taken notice of the third. The third, then, was an unusual sound.

It was not like water, it was not like wind; it was not the night-jar, it was not a clock, nor a rat, nor a person snoring.

She crept under the clothes, and flung her arms tightly round Miss Aldclyffe, as if for protection. Cytherea perceived that the lady's late peaceful warmth had given place to a sweat. At the maiden's touch, Miss Aldclyffe awoke with a low scream.

She remembered her position instantly. 'O such a terrible dream!' she cried, in a hurried whisper, holding to Cytherea in her turn; 'and your touch was the end of it. It was dreadful. Time, with his wings, hour-glass, and scythe, coming nearer and nearer to me – grinning and mocking: then he seized me, took a piece of me only. . . . But I can't tell you. I can't bear to think of it. How those dogs howl! People say it means death.'*

The return of Miss Aldclyffe to consciousness was sufficient to dispel the wild fancies which the loneliness of the night had woven in Cytherea's mind. She dismissed the third noise as something which in all likelihood could easily be explained, if trouble were taken to inquire into it: large houses had all kinds of strange sounds floating about them. She was ashamed to tell Miss Aldclyffe her terrors.

A silence of five minutes.

'Are you asleep?' said Miss Aldclyffe.

'No,' said Cytherea, in a long-drawn whisper.

'How those dogs howl, don't they?'

'Yes. A little dog in the house began it.'

'Ah, yes: that was Totsy. He sleeps on the mat outside my father's bedroom door. A nervous creature.'

There was a silent interval of nearly half-an-hour. A clock on the landing struck three.

'Are you asleep, Miss Aldclyffe?' whispered Cytherea.

'No,' said Miss Aldclyffe. 'How wretched it is not to be able to sleep, isn't it?'

'Yes,' replied Cytherea, like a docile child.

Another hour passed, and the clock struck four. Miss Aldclyffe was still awake.

'Cytherea,' she said, very softly.

Cytherea made no answer. She was sleeping soundly.

The first glimmer of dawn was now visible. Miss Aldclyffe arose, put on her dressing-gown, and went softly downstairs to her own room.

'I have not told her who I am after all, or found out the particulars of Ambrose's history,' she murmured. 'But her being in love alters everything.'

3. Half-Past Seven to Ten o'Clock a.m.

Cytherea awoke, quiet in mind and refreshed. A conclusion to remain at Knapwater was already in possession of her.

Finding Miss Aldclyffe gone, she dressed herself and sat down at the window to write an answer to Edward's letter, and an account of her arrival at Knapwater to Owen. The dismal and heart-breaking pictures that Miss Aldclyffe had placed before her the preceding evening, the later terrors of the night, were now but as shadows of shadows, and she smiled in derision at her own excitability.

But writing Edward's letter was the great consoler, the effect of each word upon him being enacted in her own face as she wrote it. She felt how much she would like to share his trouble – how well she could endure poverty with him – and wondered what his trouble was. But all would be explained at last, she knew.

At the appointed time she went to Miss Aldclyffe's room, intending, with the contradictoriness common in people, to perform with pleasure, as a work of supererogation, what as a duty was simply intolerable.

Miss Aldclyffe was already out of bed. The bright penetrating light of morning made a vast difference in the elder lady's behaviour to her dependent; the day, which had restored Cytherea's judgment, had effected the same for Miss Aldclyffe. Though practical reasons forbade her regretting that she had secured such a companionable creature to read, talk, or play to her whenever her whim required, she was inwardly vexed at the extent to which she had indulged in the womanly

73

luxury of making confidences and giving way to emotions. Few would have supposed that the calm lady sitting aristocratically at the toilet table, seeming scarcely conscious of Cytherea's presence in the room, even when greeting her, was the passionate creature who had asked for kisses a few hours before.

It is both painful and satisfactory to think how often these antitheses are to be observed in the individual most open to our observation – ourselves. We pass the evening with faces lit up by some flaring illumination or other: we get up the next morning – the fiery jets have all gone out, and nothing confronts us but a few crinkled pipes and sooty wirework, hardly even recalling the outline of the blazing picture that arrested our eyes before bedtime.

Emotions would be half starved if there were no candle-light. Probably nine-tenths of the gushing letters of indiscreet confession are written after nine or ten o'clock in the evening, and sent off before day returns to leer invidiously upon them. Few that remain open to catch our glance as we rise in the morning, survive the frigid criticism of dressing-time.

The subjects uppermost in the minds of the two women who had thus cooled from their fires, were not the visionary ones of the later hours, but the hard facts of their earlier conversation. After a remark that Cytherea need not assist her in dressing unless she wished to, Miss Aldclyffe said abruptly –

'I can tell that young man's name.' She looked keenly at Cytherea. 'It is Edward Springrove, my tenant's son.'

The inundation of colour upon the younger lady at hearing a name which to her was a world, handled as if it were only an atom, told Miss Aldclyffe that she had divined the truth at last.

'Ah – it is he, is it?' she continued. 'Well, I wanted to know for practical reasons. His example shows that I was not so far wrong in my estimate of men after all, though I only generalized, and had no thought of him.' This was perfectly true.

'What do you mean?' said Cytherea, visibly alarmed.

'Mean? Why that all the world knows him to be engaged to be married, and that the wedding is soon to take place.' She made the remark bluntly and superciliously, as if to obtain absolution at the hands of her family pride for the weak confidences of the night.

But even the frigidity of Miss Aldclyffe's morning mood was overcome by the look of sick and blank despair which the carelessly uttered words had produced upon Cytherea's face. She sank back into a chair, and buried her face in her hands.

'Don't be so foolish,' said Miss Aldclyffe. 'Come, make the best of it. I cannot upset the fact I have told you of, unfortunately. But I believe the match can be broken off.'

'O no, no.'

'Nonsense. I liked him much as a youth, and I like him now. I'll help you to captivate and chain him down. I have got over my absurd feeling of last night in not wanting you ever to go away from me – of course, I could not expect such a thing as that. There, now I have said I'll help you, and that's enough. He's tired of his first choice now he's been away from home for a while. The love that no outer attack can frighten away quails before its idol's own homely ways; it is always so. . . . Come, finish what you are doing if you are going to, and don't be a little goose about such a trumpery affair as that.'

'Who – is he engaged to?' Cytherea inquired by a movement of her lips but no sound of her voice. But Miss Aldclyffe did not answer. It mattered not, Cytherea thought. Another woman – that was enough for her: curiosity was stunned.

She applied herself to the work of dressing, scarcely knowing how. Miss Aldclyffe went on: –

'You were too easily won. I'd have made him or anybody else speak out before he should have kissed my face for his pleasure. But you are one of those precipitately fond things who are yearning to throw away their hearts upon the first worthless fellow who says good-morning. In the first place, you shouldn't have loved him so quickly: in the next, if you must have loved him off-hand, you should have concealed it. It tickled his vanity: "By Jove, that girl's in love with me already!" he thought.'

To hasten away at the end of the toilet, to tell Mrs Morris – who stood waiting in a little room prepared for her, with tea poured out, bread-and-butter cut into diaphanous slices, and eggs arranged – that she wanted no breakfast: then to shut herself alone in her bedroom, was her only thought. She was followed thither by the well-intentioned matron with a cup of tea and one piece of bread-and-butter on a tray, cheerfully insisting that she should eat it.

To those who grieve, innocent cheerfulness seems heartless levity. 'No, thank you, Mrs Morris,' she said, keeping the door closed. Despite the incivility of the action, Cytherea could not bear to let a pleasant person see her face then.

Immediate revocation – even if revocation would be more effective by postponement – is the impulse of young wounded natures. Cytherea went to her blotting-book, took out the long letter so carefully written, so full of gushing remarks and tender hints, and sealed up so neatly with a little seal bearing 'Good Faith' as its motto, tore the missive into fifty pieces, and threw them into the grate. It was then the bitterest of anguishes to look upon some of the words she had so lovingly written, and see them existing only in mutilated forms without meaning – to feel that his eye would never read them, nobody ever know how ardently she had penned them.

Pity for one's self for being wasted is mostly present in these moods of abnegation.

The meaning of all his allusions, his abruptness in telling her of his love, his constraint at first, then his desperate manner of speaking, was clear. They must have been the last flickerings of a conscience not quite dead to all sense of perfidiousness and fickleness. Now he had gone to London: she would be dismissed from his memory, in the same way as Miss Aldclyffe had said. And here she was in Edward's own parish, reminded continually of him by what she saw and heard. The landscape, yesterday so much and so bright to her, was now but as the banquet-hall deserted – all gone but herself.

Miss Aldclyffe had wormed her secret out of her, and would now be continually mocking her for her trusting simplicity in believing him. It was altogether unbearable: she would not stay there.

She went downstairs and found Miss Aldclyffe had gone into the breakfast-room, but that Captain Aldclyffe, who rose later with increasing infirmities, had not yet made his appearance. Cytherea entered. Miss Aldclyffe was looking out of the window, watching a trail of white smoke along the distant landscape – signifying a passing train. At Cytherea's entry she turned and looked inquiry.

'I must tell you now,' began Cytherea, in a tremulous voice.

'Well, what?' Miss Aldclyffe said.

'I am not going to stay with you. I must go away – a very long way. I am very sorry, but indeed I can't remain!'

'Pooh – what shall we hear next?' Miss Aldclyffe surveyed Cytherea's face with leisurely criticism. 'You are breaking your heart again about that worthless young Springrove. I knew how it would be. It is as Hallam says of Juliet* – what little reason you may have possessed originally has all been whirled away by this love. I shan't take this notice, mind.'

'Do let me go!'

Miss Aldclyffe took her new pet's hand, and said with severity, 'As to hindering you, if you are determined to go, of course that's absurd. But you are not now in a state of mind fit for deciding upon any such proceeding, and I shall not listen to what you have to say. Now, Cythie, come with me; we'll let this volcano burst and spend itself, and after that we'll see what had better be done.' She took Cytherea into her workroom, opened a drawer, and drew forth a roll of linen.

'This is some embroidery I began one day, and now I should like it finished.'

She then preceded the maiden upstairs to Cytherea's own room. 'There,' she said, 'now sit down here, go on with this work, and remember one thing – that you are not to leave the room on any pretext whatever for two hours unless I send for you – I insist kindly, dear. Whilst you stitch – you are to stitch, recollect, and not go mooning out of the window – think over the whole matter, and get cooled; don't let the foolish love-affair prevent your thinking as a woman of the world. If at the end of that time you still say you must leave me, you may. I will have no more to say in the matter. Come, sit down, and promise to sit here the time I name.'

To hearts in a despairing mood, compulsion seems a relief; and docility was at all times natural to Cytherea. She promised, and sat down. Miss Aldclyffe shut the door upon her and retreated.

She sewed, stopped to think, shed a tear or two, recollected the articles of the treaty, and sewed again; and at length fell into a reverie which took no account whatever of the lapse of time.

4. Ten to Twelve o'Clock a.m.

A quarter of an hour might have passed when her thoughts became attracted from the past to the present by unwonted movements downstairs. She opened the door and listened.

There were hurryings along passages, opening and shutting of doors, trampling in the stable-yard. She went across into another bedroom, from which a view of the stable-yard could be obtained, and arrived there just in time to see the figure of the man who had driven her from the station vanishing down the coach-road on a black horse – galloping at the top of the animal's speed.

Another man went off in the direction of the village.

Whatever had occurred, it did not seem to be her duty to inquire or meddle with it, stranger and dependent as she was, unless she were requested to, especially after Miss Aldclyffe's strict charge to her. She sat down again, determined to let no idle curiosity influence her movements.

Her window commanded the front of the house; and the next thing she saw was a clergyman walk up and enter the door.

All was silent again till, a long time after the first man had left, he returned again on the same horse, now matted with sweat and trotting behind a carriage in which sat an elderly gentleman driven by a lad in livery. These came to the house, entered, and all was again the same as before.

The whole household – master, mistress, and servants – appeared to have forgotten the very existence of such a being as Cytherea. She almost wished she had not vowed to have no idle curiosity.

Half-an-hour later the carriage drove off with the elderly gentleman, and two or three messengers left the house, speeding in various directions. Rustics in smock-frocks* began to hang about the road opposite the house, or lean against trees, looking idly at the windows and chimneys.

A tap came to Cytherea's door. She opened it to a young maid-servant.

'Miss Aldclyffe wishes to see you, ma'am.' Cytherea hastened down.

Miss Aldclyffe was standing on the hearthrug, her elbow on the mantel, her hand to her temples, her eyes on the ground; perfectly calm, but very pale.

'Cytherea,' she said in a whisper, 'come here.'

Cytherea went close.

'Something very serious has taken place,' she said again, and then paused, with a tremulous movement of her mouth.

'Yes,' said Cytherea.

'My father. He was found dead in his bed this morning.'

'Dead!' echoed the younger woman. It seemed impossible that the announcement could be true; that knowledge of so great a fact could be contained in a statement so small.

'Yes, dead,' murmured Miss Aldclyffe solemnly. 'He died alone, though within a few feet of me. The room we slept in is exactly over his own.'

Cytherea said hurriedly, 'Do they know at what hour?'

'The doctor says it must have been between two and three o'clock this morning.'

'Then I heard him!'

'Heard him?'

'Heard him die!'

'You heard him die? What did you hear?'

'A sound I heard once before in my life – at the deathbed of my mother. I could not identify it – though I recognized it. Then the dog

78

howled: you remarked it. I did not think it worth while to tell you what I had heard a little earlier.' She looked agonized.

'It would have been useless,' said Miss Aldclyffe. 'All was over by that time.' She addressed herself as much as Cytherea when she continued, 'Is it a Providence who sent you here at this juncture that I might not be left entirely alone?'

Till this instant Miss Aldclyffe had forgotten the reason of Cytherea's seclusion in her own room. So had Cytherea herself. The fact now recurred to both in one moment.

'Do you still wish to go?' said Miss Aldclyffe anxiously.

'I don't want to go now,' Cytherea had remarked simultaneously with the other's question. She was pondering on the strange likeness which Miss Aldclyffe's bereavement bore to her own; it had the appearance of being still another call to her not to forsake this woman so linked to her life, for the sake of any trivial vexation.

Miss Aldclyffe held her almost as a lover would have held her, and said musingly –

'We get more and more into one groove. I now am left fatherless and motherless as you were.' Other ties lay behind in her thoughts, but she did not mention them.

'You loved your father, Cytherea, and wept for him?'

'Yes, I did. Poor papa!'

'I was always at variance with mine, and can't weep for him now! But you must stay here always, and make a better woman of me.'

The compact was thus sealed, and Cytherea, in spite of the failure of her advertisements, was installed as a veritable Companion. And, once more in the history of human endeavour, a position which it was impossible to reach by any direct attempt, was come to by the seeker's swerving from the path, and regarding the original object as one of secondary importance.

CHAPTER SEVEN
The Events of Eighteen Days

1. August the Seventeenth

The time of day was four o'clock in the afternoon. The place was the lady's study or boudoir, Knapwater House. The person was Miss Aldclyffe sitting there alone, clothed in deep mourning.

The funeral of the old Captain had taken place, and his will had been read. It was very concise, and had been executed about five years previous to his death. It was attested by his solicitors, Messrs Nyttleton and Tayling, of Lincoln's Inn Fields. The whole of his estate, real and personal, was bequeathed to his daughter Cytherea, for her sole and absolute use, subject only to the payment of a legacy to the rector, their relative, and a few small amounts to the servants.

Miss Aldclyffe had not chosen the easiest chair of her boudoir to sit in, or even a chair of ordinary comfort; but an uncomfortable, high, narrow-backed, oak framed and seated chair, which was allowed to remain in the room only on the ground of being a companion in artistic quaintness to an old coffer beside it, and was never used except to stand in to reach for a book from the highest row of shelves. But she had sat erect in this chair for more than an hour, for the reason that she was utterly unconscious of what her actions and bodily feelings were. The chair had stood nearest her path on entering the room, and she had gone to it in a dream.

She sat in the attitude which denotes unflagging, intense, concentrated thought – as if she were cast in bronze. Her feet were together, her body bent a little forward, and quite unsupported by the back of the chair; her hands on her knees, her eyes fixed intently on the corner of a footstool.

At last she moved and tapped her fingers upon the table at her side. Her pent-up ideas had finally found some channel to advance in. Motions became more frequent as she laboured to carry further and further the problem which occupied her brain. She sat back and drew a long breath: she sat sideways and leant her forehead upon her hand. Later still she arose, walked up and down the room – at first abstractedly, with her features as firmly set as ever; but by degrees her brow relaxed, her footsteps became lighter and more leisurely; her head rode gracefully and was no longer bowed. She preened herself like a swan after exertion.

'Yes,' she said aloud. 'To get *him* here without letting him know that I have any other object than that of getting a useful man – that's the difficulty – and that I think I can master.'

She rang for the new maid, a placid woman of forty, with a few grey hairs.

'Ask Miss Graye if she can come to me.'

Cytherea was not far off, and came in.

'Do you know anything about architects and surveyors?' said Miss Aldclyffe abruptly.

'Know anything?' replied Cytherea, poising herself on her toe to consider the compass of the question.

'Yes – know anything,' said Miss Aldclyffe.

'Owen is an architect and surveyor's draughtsman,' the maiden said, and thought of somebody else who was likewise.

'Yes! that's why I asked you. What are the different kinds of work comprised in an architect's practice? They lay out estates, and super-intend the various works done upon them, I should think, among other things?'

'Those are, more properly, a land or building steward's duties – at least I have always imagined so. Country architects include those things in their practice; city architects don't.'

'I know that, child. But a steward's is an indefinite fast and loose profession, it seems to me. Shouldn't you think that a man who had been brought up as an architect would do for a steward?'

Cytherea had doubts whether an architect pure would do.

The chief pleasure connected with asking an opinion lies in not adopting it. Miss Aldclyffe replied decisively –

'Nonsense; of course he would. Your brother Owen makes plans for country buildings – such as cottages, stables, homesteads,* and so on?'

'Yes; he does.'

'And superintends the building of them?'

'Yes; he will soon.'

'And he surveys land?'

'O yes.'

'And he knows about hedges and ditches – how wide they ought to be, boundaries, levelling, planting trees to keep away the winds, measuring timber, houses for ninety-nine years, and such things?'

'I have never heard him say that; but I think Mr Gradfield does those things. Owen, I am afraid, is inexperienced as yet.'

'Yes; your brother is not old enough for such a post yet, of course. And then there are rent-days, the audit and winding up of tradesmen's accounts. I am afraid, Cytherea, you don't know much more about the matter than I do myself. . . . I am going out just now,' she continued. 'I shall not want you to walk with me to-day. Run away till dinner-time.'

Miss Aldclyffe went out of doors, and down the steps to the lawn: then turning to the left, through a shrubbery, she opened a wicket and passed into a neglected and leafy carriage-drive, leading down the hill. This she followed till she reached the point of its greatest depression, which was also the lowest ground in the whole grove.

The trees here were so interlaced, and hung their branches so near the ground, that a whole summer's day was scarcely long enough to change the air pervading the spot from its normal state of coolness to even a temporary warmth. The unvarying freshness was helped by the nearness of the ground to the level of the springs, and by the presence of a deep, sluggish stream close by, equally well shaded by bushes and a high wall. Following the road, which now ran along at the margin of the stream, she came to an opening in the wall, on the other side of the water, revealing a large rectangular nook from which the stream proceeded, covered with froth, and accompanied by a dull roar. Two more steps, and she was opposite the nook, in full view of the cascade forming its further boundary. Over the top could be seen the bright outer sky in the form of a crescent, caused by the curve of a bridge across the rapids, and the trees above.

Beautiful as was the scene she did not look in that direction. The same standing-ground afforded another prospect, straight in the front, less sombre than the water on the right or the trees all around. The avenue and grove which flanked it abruptly terminated a few yards ahead, where the ground began to rise, and on the remote edge of the greensward thus laid open, stood all that remained of the original manor-house, to which the dark margin-line of the trees in the avenue formed an adequate and well-fitting frame. It was the picture thus presented that was now interesting Miss Aldclyffe – not artistically or historically, but practically – as regarded its fitness for adaptation to modern requirements.

In front, detached from everything else, rose the most ancient portion of the structure – an old arched gateway, flanked by the bases of two small towers, and nearly covered with creepers, which had clambered over the eaves of the sinking roof, and up the gable to the crest of the Aldclyffe family perched on the apex. Behind this, at a distance of ten or twenty yards, came the only portion of the main building that still existed – an Elizabethan fragment, consisting of as much as could be contained under three gables and a cross roof behind.

Against the wall could be seen ragged lines indicating the form of other destroyed gables which had once joined it there. The mullioned and transomed* windows, containing five or six lights, were mostly bricked up to the extent of two or three, and the remaining portion fitted with cottage window-frames carelessly inserted, to suit the purpose to which the old place was now applied, it being partitioned out into small rooms downstairs to form cottages for two labourers and their families; the upper portion was arranged as a storehouse for divers kinds of roots and fruit.

The owner of the picturesque spot, after her survey from this point, went up to the walls and walked into the old court, where the paving-stones were pushed sideways and upwards by the thrust of the grasses between them. Two or three little children, with their fingers in their mouths, came out to look at her, and then ran in to tell their mothers in loud tones of secrecy that Miss Aldclyffe was coming. Miss Aldclyffe, however, did not come in. She concluded her survey of the exterior by making a complete circuit of the building; then turned into a nook a short distance off where round and square timber, a saw-pit, planks, grindstones, heaps of building stone and brick, explained that the spot was the centre of operations for the building work done on the estate.

She paused, and looked around. A man who had seen her from the window of the workshops behind, came out and respectfully lifted his hat to her. It was the first time she had been seen walking outside the house since her father's death.

'Strooden, could the Old House be made a decent residence of, without much trouble?' she inquired.

The mechanic considered, and spoke as each consideration completed itself.

'You don't forget, ma'am, that two-thirds of the place is already pulled down, or gone to ruin?'

'Yes; I know.'

'And that what's left may almost as well be, ma'am.'

'Why may it?'

''Twas so cut up inside when they made it into cottages, that the whole carcase is full of cracks.'

'Still by pulling down the inserted partitions, and adding a little outside, it could be made to answer the purpose of an ordinary six or eight-roomed house?'

'Yes, ma'am.'

'About what would it cost?' was the question which had invariably come next in every communication of this kind to which the super-intending workman had been a party during his whole experience. To his surprise, Miss Aldclyffe did not put it. The man thought her object in altering an old house must have been an unusually absorbing one not to prompt what was so instinctive in owners as hardly to require any prompting at all.

'Thank you: that's sufficient, Strooden,' she said. 'You will understand that it is not unlikely some alteration may be made here in a short time, with reference to the management of the affairs.'

Strooden said 'Yes', in a complex voice, and looked uneasy.

'During the life of Captain Aldclyffe, with you as the foreman of works, and he himself as his own steward, everything worked well. But now it may be necessary to have a steward, whose management will encroach further upon things which have hitherto been left in your hands than did your late master's. What I mean is, that he will directly and in detail superintend all.'

'Then – I shall not be wanted, ma'am?' he faltered.

'O yes; if you like to stay on as foreman in the yard and workshops only. I should be sorry to lose you. However, you had better consider. I will send for you in a few days.'

Leaving him to suspense, and all the ills that came in its train – distracted application to his duties, and an undefined number of sleepless nights and untasted dinners, Miss Aldclyffe looked at her watch and returned to the House. She was about to keep an appointment with her solicitor, Mr Nyttleton, who had been to Budmouth, and was coming to Knapwater on his way back to London.

2. *August the Twentieth*

On the Saturday subsequent to Mr Nyttleton's visit to Knapwater House, the subjoined advertisement appeared in the *Field* and *Builder*★ newspapers: –

LAND STEWARD

A gentleman of integrity and professional skill is required immediately for the MANAGEMENT of an ESTATE, containing about 1000 acres, upon which agricultural improvements and the erection of buildings are contemplated. He must be a man of superior education, unmarried, and not more than thirty years of age. Considerable preference will be shown for one who possesses an artistic as well as a practical knowledge of planning and laying out. The remuneration will consist of a salary of £220, with the old manor-house as a residence. – Address Messrs Nyttleton and Tayling, solicitors, Lincoln's Inn Fields.

A copy of each paper was sent to Miss Aldclyffe on the day of publication. The same evening she told Cytherea that she was advertising for a steward, who would live at the old manor-house, showing her the papers containing the announcement.

What was the drift of that remark? thought the maiden; or was it merely made to her in confidential intercourse, as other arrangements were told her daily. Yet it seemed to have more meaning than common. She remembered the conversation about architects and surveyors, and her brother Owen. Miss Aldclyffe knew that his situation was precarious, that he was well educated and practical, and was applying himself heart and soul to the details of the profession and all connected with it. Miss Aldclyffe might be ready to take him if he could compete successfully with others who would reply. She hazarded a question:

'Would it be desirable for Owen to answer it?'

'Not at all,' said Miss Aldclyffe peremptorily.

A flat answer of this kind had ceased to alarm Cytherea. Miss Aldclyffe's blunt mood was not her worst. Cytherea thought of another man, whose name, in spite of resolves, tears, renunciations and injured pride, lingered in her ears like an old familiar strain. That man was qualified for a stewardship under a king.

'Would it be of any use if Edward Springrove were to answer it?' she said, resolutely enunciating the name.

'None whatever,' replied Miss Aldclyffe, again in the same decided tone.

'You are very unkind to speak in that way.'

'Now don't pout like a goosie, as you are. I don't want men like either of them, for, of course, I must look to the good of the estate rather than to that of any individual. The man I want must have been more specially educated. I have told you that we are going to London next week; it is mostly on this account.'

Cytherea found that she had mistaken the drift of Miss Aldclyffe's peculiar explicitness on the subject of advertising, and wrote to tell her brother that if he saw the notice it would be useless to reply.

3. August the Twenty-Fifth

Five days after the above-mentioned dialogue took place they went to London, and, with scarcely a minute's pause, to the solicitors' offices in Lincoln's Inn Fields.

They alighted opposite one of the characteristic entrances about the place – a gate which was never, and could never be, closed, flanked by lamp-standards carrying no lamp. Rust was the only active agent to be seen there at this time of the day and year. The palings along the front were rusted away at their base to the thinness of wires, and the successive coats of paint, with which they were overlaid in bygone days, had been completely undermined by the same insidious canker, which lifted off the paint in flakes, leaving the raw surface of the iron on palings, standards, and gate hinges, of a staring blood-red.

But once inside the railings the picture changed. The court and offices were a complete contrast to the grand ruin of the outwork which enclosed them. Well-painted respectability extended over, within, and around the doorstep; and in the carefully swept yard not a particle of dust was visible.

Mr Nyttleton, who had just come up from Margate, where he was staying with his family, was standing at the top of his own staircase as the pair ascended. He politely took them inside.

'Is there a comfortable room in which this young lady can sit during our interview?' said Miss Aldclyffe.

It was rather a favourite habit of hers to make much of Cytherea when they were out, and snub her for it afterwards when they got home.

'Certainly – Mr Tayling's.' Cytherea was shown into an inner room.

Social definitions are all made relatively: an absolute datum is only imagined. The small gentry about Knapwater seemed unpractised to Miss Aldclyffe, Miss Aldclyffe herself seemed unpractised to Mr Nyttleton's experienced old eyes.

'Now then,' the lady said, when she was alone with the lawyer; 'what is the result of our advertisement?'

It was late summer; the estate-agency, building, engineering, and surveying worlds were dull. There were forty-five replies to the advertisement.

Mr Nyttleton spread them one by one before Miss Aldclyffe. 'You will probably like to read some of them yourself, madam?' he said.

'Yes, certainly,' said she.

'I will not trouble you with those which are from persons manifestly unfit at first sight,' he continued; and began selecting from the heap twos and threes which he had marked, collecting others into his hand. 'The man we want lies among these, if my judgment doesn't deceive me, and from them it would be advisable to select a certain number to be communicated with.'

'I should like to see every one – only just to glance them over – exactly as they came,' she said suasively.

He looked as if he thought this a waste of his time, but dismissing his sentiment unfolded each singly and laid it before her. As he laid them out, it struck him that she studied them quite as rapidly as he could spread them. He slyly glanced up from the outer corner of his eye to hers, and noticed that all she did was look at the name at the bottom of the letter, and then put the enclosure aside without further ceremony. He thought this an odd way of inquiring into the merits of forty-five men who at considerable trouble gave in detail reasons why they believed themselves well qualified for a certain post. She came to the final one, and put it down with the rest.

Then the lady said that in her opinion it would be best to get as many replies as they possibly could before selecting – 'to give us a wider choice. What do you think, Mr Nyttleton?'

It seemed to him, he said, that a greater number than those they already had would scarcely be necessary, and if they waited for more, there would be this disadvantage attending it, that some of those they now could command would possibly not be available.

'Never mind, we will run that risk,' said Miss Aldclyffe. 'Let the advertisement be inserted once more, and then we will certainly settle the matter.'

Mr Nyttleton bowed, and seemed to think Miss Aldclyffe, for a single woman, and one who till so very recently had never concerned herself with business of any kind, a very meddlesome client. But she was rich, and handsome still. 'She's a new broom in estate-management as yet,' he thought. 'She will soon get tired of this,' and he parted from her without a sentiment which could mar his habitual blandness.

The two ladies then proceeded westward. Dismissing the cab in Waterloo Place, they went along Pall Mall on foot, where in place of the usual well-dressed clubbists – rubicund with alcohol – were to be seen, in linen pinafores, flocks of house-painters pallid from white lead. When they had reached the Green Park, Cytherea proposed that they should sit down awhile under the young elms at the brow of the hill. This they did – the growl of Piccadilly on their left hand – the monastic seclusion of the Palace on their right; before them, the clock tower of the Houses of Parliament, standing forth with a metallic lustre against a livid Lambeth sky.

Miss Aldclyffe still carried in her hand a copy of the newspaper, and while Cytherea had been interesting herself in the picture around, glanced again at the advertisement.

She heaved a slight sigh, and began to fold it up again. In the action her eye caught sight of two consecutive advertisements on the cover, one relating to some lecture on Art, and addressed to members of the Institute of Architects. The other emanated from the same source, but was addressed to the public, and stated that the exhibition of drawings at the Institute's rooms would close at the end of that week.

Her eye lighted up. She sent Cytherea back to the hotel in a cab, then turned round by Piccadilly into Bond Street, and proceeded to the rooms of the Institute. The secretary was sitting in the lobby. After making her payment, and looking at a few of the drawings on the walls, in the company of three gentlemen, the only other visitors to the exhibition, she turned back and asked if she might be allowed to see a list of the members. She was a little connected with the architectural world, she said, with a smile, and was interested in some of the names.

'Here it is, madam,' he replied, politely handing her a pamphlet containing the names.

Miss Aldclyffe turned the leaves till she came to the letter M. The name she hoped to find there was there, with the address appended, as was the case with all the rest.

The address was at some chambers in a street not far from Charing Cross. 'Chambers', as a residence, had always been assumed by the lady to imply the condition of a bachelor. She murmured two words, 'There still.'

Another request had yet to be made, but it was of a more noticeable kind than the first, and might compromise the secrecy with which she wished to act throughout this episode. Her object was to get one of the envelopes lying on the secretary's table, stamped with the die of the Institute; and in order to get it she was about to ask if she might write a note.

But the secretary's back chanced to be turned, and he now went towards one of the men at the other end of the room, who had called him to ask some question relating to an etching on the wall. Quick as thought, Miss Aldclyffe stood before the table, slipped her hand behind her, took one of the envelopes and put it in her pocket.

She sauntered round the rooms for two or three minutes longer, then withdrew and returned to her hotel.

Here she cut the Knapwater advertisement from the paper, put it into the envelope she had stolen, embossed with the society's stamp, and directed it in a round clerkly hand to the address she had seen in the list of members' names submitted to her: –

ÆNEAS MANSTON, ESQ.,
WYKEHAM CHAMBERS,
SPRING GARDENS

This ended her first day's work in London.

The two Cythereas continued at the Westminster Hotel,* Miss Aldclyffe informing her companion that business would detain them in London another week. The days passed as slowly and quietly as days can pass in a city at that time of the year, the shuttered windows about the squares and terraces confronting their eyes like the white and sightless orbs of blind men. On Thursday Mr Nyttleton called, bringing the whole number of replies to the advertisement. Cytherea was present at the interview, by Miss Aldclyffe's request – either from whim or design.

Ten additional letters were the result of the second week's insertion, making fifty-five in all. Miss Aldclyffe looked them over as before. One was signed –

ÆNEAS MANSTON,
133, TURNGATE STREET,
LIVERPOOL

'Now, then, Mr Nyttleton, will you make a selection, and I will add one or two,' Miss Aldclyffe said.

Mr Nyttleton scanned the whole heap of letters, testimonials, and references, sorting them into two heaps. Manston's missive, after a mere glance, was thrown amongst the summarily rejected ones.

Miss Aldclyffe read, or pretended to read after the lawyer. When he had finished, five lay in the group he had selected. 'Would you like to add to the number?' he said, turning to the lady.

'No,' she said carelessly. 'Well, two or three additional ones rather took my fancy,' she added, searching for some in the larger collection.

She drew out three. One was Manston's.

'These eight, then, shall be communicated with,' said the lawyer, taking up the eight letters and placing them by themselves.

They stood up. 'If I myself, Miss Aldclyffe, were only concerned personally,' he said, in an off-hand way, and holding up a letter singly, 'I should choose this man unhesitatingly. He writes honestly, is not afraid to name what he does not consider himself well acquainted with – a rare thing to find in answers to advertisements; he is well recommended, and possesses some qualities rarely found in combination. Oddly enough, he is not really a steward. He was bred a farmer, studied building affairs, served on an estate for some time, then went with an architect, and is now well qualified as architect, estate agent, and surveyor. That man is sure to have a fine head for a manor like yours.' He tapped the letter as he spoke. 'Yes, I should choose him without hesitation – speaking personally.'

'And I think,' she said artificially, 'I should choose this one as a matter of mere personal whim, which, of course, can't be given way to when practical questions have to be considered.'

Cytherea, after looking out of the window, and then at the news-papers, had become interested in the proceedings between the clever Miss Aldclyffe and the keen old lawyer, which reminded her of a game of cards. She looked inquiringly at the two letters – one in Miss Aldclyffe's hand, the other in Mr Nyttleton's.

'What is the name of your man?' said Miss Aldclyffe.

'His name—' said the lawyer, looking down the page; 'what is his name? – it is Edward Springrove.'

Miss Aldclyffe glanced towards Cytherea, who was getting red and pale by turns. She looked imploringly at Miss Aldclyffe.

'The name of my man,' said Miss Aldclyffe, looking at her letter in turn; 'is, I think – yes – Æneas Manston.'

5. September the Third

The next morning but one was appointed for the interviews, which were to be at the lawyers' offices. Mr Nyttleton and Mr Tayling were both in town for the day, and the candidates were admitted one by one into a private room. In the window recess was seated Miss Aldclyffe, wearing her veil down.

The lawyer had, in his letters to the selected number, timed each candidate at an interval of ten or fifteen minutes from those preceding and following. They were shown in as they arrived, and had short conversations with Mr Nyttleton – terse, and to the point. Miss Aldclyffe neither moved nor spoke during this proceeding; it might have been supposed that she was quite unmindful of it, had it not been for what was revealed by a keen penetration of the veil covering her countenance – the rays from two bright black eyes, directed towards the lawyer and his interlocutor.

Springrove came fifth; Manston seventh. When the examination of all was ended, and the last man had retired, Nyttleton, again as at the former time, blandly asked his client which of the eight she personally preferred. 'I still think the fifth we spoke to, Springrove, the man whose letter I pounced upon at first, to be by far the best qualified; in short, most suitable generally.'

'I am sorry to say that I differ from you; I lean to my first notion still – that Mr – Mr Manston is most desirable in tone and bearing, and even specifically; I think he would suit me best in the long-run.'

Mr Nyttleton looked out of the window at the whitened wall of the court.

'Of course, madam, your opinion may be perfectly sound and reliable; a sort of instinct, I know, often leads ladies by a short cut to conclusions truer than those come to by men after laborious round-about calculations, based on long experience. I must say I shouldn't recommend him.'

'Why, pray?'

'Well, let us look first at his letter of answer to the advertisement. He didn't reply till the last insertion; that's one thing. His letter is bold and frank in tone, so bold and frank that the second thought after reading it is that not honesty, but unscrupulousness of conscience dictated it. It is written in an indifferent mood, as if he felt that he was humbugging us in his statement that he was the right man for such an office, that he tried hard to get it only as a matter of form which required that he should neglect no opportunity that came in his way.'

'You may be right, Mr Nyttleton, but I don't quite see the grounds of your reasoning.'

'He has been, as you perceive, almost entirely used to the office duties of a city architect, the experience we don't want. You want a man whose acquaintance with rural landed properties is more practical and closer – somebody who, if he has not filled exactly such an office before, has lived a country life, knows the ins and outs of country tenancies, building, farming, and so on.'

'He's by far the most intellectual looking of them all.'

'Yes; he may be – your opinion, Miss Aldclyffe, is worth more than mine in that matter. And more than you say, he is a man of parts – his brain power would soon enable him to master details and fit him for the post, I don't much doubt that. But to speak clearly' (here his words started off at a jog-trot) 'I wouldn't run the risk of placing the management of an estate of mine in his hands on any account whatever. There, that's flat and plain, madam.'

'But, definitely,' she said, with a show of impatience, 'what is your reason?'

'He is a voluptuary with activity; which is a very bad form of man – as bad as it is rare.'

91

'Oh. Thank you for your explicit statement, Mr Nyttleton,' said Miss Aldclyffe, starting a little and flushing with displeasure.

Mr Nyttleton nodded slightly, as a sort of neutral motion, simply signifying a receipt of the information, good or bad.

'And I really think it is hardly worth while to trouble you further in this,' continued the lady. 'He's quite good enough for a little insignificant place like mine at Knapwater; and I know that I could not get on with one of the others for a single month. We'll try him.'

'Certainly, Miss Aldclyffe,' said the lawyer. And Mr Manston was written to, to the effect that he was the successful competitor.

'Did you see how unmistakably her temper was getting the better of her, that minute you were in the room?' said Nyttleton to Tayling, when their client had left the house. Nyttleton was a man who surveyed everybody's character in a sunless and shadowless northern light. A culpable slyness, which marked him as a boy, had been moulded by Time, the Improver, into honourable circumspection.

We frequently find that the quality which, conjoined with the simplicity of the child, is vice, is virtue when it pervades the knowledge of the man.

'She was as near as damn-it to boiling over when I added up her man,' continued Nyttleton. 'His handsome face is his qualification in her eyes. They have met before; I saw that.'

'He didn't seem conscious of it,' said the junior.

'He didn't. That was rather puzzling to me. But still, if ever a woman's face spoke out plainly that she was in love with a man, hers did that she was with him. Poor old maid, she's almost old enough to be his mother. If that Manston's a schemer he'll marry her, as sure as I am Nyttleton. Let's hope he's honest, however.'

'I don't think she's in love with him,' said Tayling. He had seen but little of the pair, and yet he could not reconcile what he had noticed in Miss Aldclyffe's behaviour with the idea that it was the bearing of a woman towards her lover.

'Well, your experience of the fiery phenomenon is more recent than mine,' rejoined Nyttleton carelessly. 'And you may remember the nature of it best.'

CHAPTER EIGHT
The Events of Eighteen Days

1. *From the Third to the Nineteenth of September*

Miss Aldclyffe's tenderness towards Cytherea, between the hours of her irascibility, increased till it became no less than doting fondness. Like Nature in the tropics, with her hurricanes and the subsequent luxuriant vegetation effacing their ravages, Miss Aldclyffe compensated for her outbursts by excess of generosity afterwards. She seemed to be completely won out of herself by close contact with a young woman whose modesty was absolutely unimpaired, and whose artlessness was as perfect as was compatible with the complexity necessary to produce the due charm of womanhood. Cytherea, on her part, perceived with honest satisfaction that her influence for good over Miss Aldclyffe was considerable. Ideas and habits peculiar to the younger, which the elder lady had originally imitated as a mere whim, she grew in course of time to take a positive delight in. Among others were evening and morning prayers, dreaming over out-door scenes, learning a verse from some poem whilst dressing.

Yet try to force her sympathies as much as she would, Cytherea could feel no more than thankful for this, even if she always felt as much as thankful. The mysterious cloud hanging over the past life of her companion, of which the uncertain light already thrown upon it only seemed to render still darker the unpenetrated remainder, nourished in her a feeling which was scarcely too light to be called dread. She would have infinitely preferred to be treated distantly, as the mere dependent, by such a changeable nature – like a fountain, always herself, yet always another. That a crime of any deep dye had ever been perpetrated or participated in by her namesake, she would not believe; but the reckless adventuring of the lady's youth seemed connected with deeds of darkness rather than of light.

Sometimes Miss Aldclyffe appeared to be on the point of making some absorbing confidence, but reflection invariably restrained her. Cytherea hoped that such a confidence would come with time, and that she might thus be a means of soothing a mind which had obviously known extreme suffering.

But Miss Aldclyffe's reticence concerning her past was not imitated by Cytherea. Though she never disclosed the one fact of her knowledge that the love-suit between Miss Aldclyffe and her father terminated abnormally, the maiden's natural ingenuousness on subjects not set down for special guard had enabled Miss Aldclyffe to worm from her, fragment by fragment, every detail of her father's history. Cytherea saw how deeply Miss Aldclyffe sympathized – and it compensated her, to some extent, for the hasty resentments of other times.

Thus uncertainly she lived on. It was perceived by the servants of the House that some secret bond of connection existed between Miss Aldclyffe and her companion. But they were woman and woman, not woman and man, the facts were ethereal and refined, and so they could not be worked up into a taking story. Whether, as old critics disputed, a supernatural machinery be necessary to an epic or no, an ungodly machinery* is decidedly necessary to a scandal.

Another letter had come to her from Edward – very short, but full of entreaty, asking why she would not write just one line – just one line of cold friendship at least? She then allowed herself to think, little by little, whether she had not perhaps been too harsh with him; and at last wondered if he were really much to blame for being engaged to another woman. 'Ah, Brain, there is one in me stronger than you!' she said. The young maiden continually pulled out his letter, read it and re-read it, almost crying with pity the while, to think what wretched suspense he must be enduring at her silence, till her heart chid her for her cruelty. She felt that she must send him a line – one little line – just a wee line to keep him alive, poor thing; sighing like Donna Clara* –

> Ah, were he now before me,
>   In spite of injured pride,
> I fear my eyes would pardon
>   Before my tongue could chide.

2. September the Twentieth. Three to Four p.m.

It was the third week in September, about five weeks after Cytherea's arrival, when Miss Aldclyffe requested her one day to go through the village of Carriford and assist herself in collecting the subscriptions made by some of the inhabitants of the parish to a religious society she patronized. Miss Aldclyffe formed one of what was called a Ladies' Association, each member of which collected tributary streams of shillings from her inferiors, to add to her own pound at the end.

Miss Aldclyffe took particular interest in Cytherea's appearance that afternoon, and the object of her attention was, indeed, gratifying to look at. The sight of the lithe girl, set off by an airy dress, coquettish jacket, flexible hat, a ray of starlight in each eye and a war of lilies and roses in each cheek, was a palpable pleasure to the mistress of the mansion, yet a pleasure which appeared to partake less of the nature of affectionate satisfaction than of mental gratification.

Eight names were printed in the report as belonging to Miss Aldclyffe's list, with the amount of subscription-money attached to each.

'I will collect the first four, whilst you do the same with the last four,' said Miss Aldclyffe.

The names of two tradespeople stood first in Cytherea's share: then came a Miss Hinton: last of all in the printed list was Mr Springrove the elder. Underneath his name was pencilled, in Miss Aldclyffe's handwriting, 'Mr Manston'.

Manston had arrived on the estate, in the capacity of steward, three or four days previously, and occupied the old manor-house, which had been altered and repaired for his reception.

'Call on Mr Manston,' said the lady impressively, looking at the name written under Cytherea's portion of the list.

'But he does not subscribe yet?'

'I know it; but call and leave him a report. Don't forget it.'

'Say you would be pleased if he would subscribe?'

'Yes – say I should be pleased if he would,' repeated Miss Aldclyffe, smiling. 'Good-bye. Don't hurry in your walk. If you can't get easily through your task to-day put off some of it till to-morrow.'

Each then started on her rounds: Cytherea going in the first place to the old manor-house. Mr Manston was not indoors, which was a relief to her. She called then on the two gentleman-farmers' wives, who soon transacted their business with her, frigidly indifferent to her personality. A person who socially is nothing is thought less of by people who are not much than by those who are a great deal.

She then turned towards Peakhill Cottage, the residence of Miss Hinton, who lived there happily enough, with an elderly servant and a house-dog as companions. Her father, and last remaining parent, had retired hither four years before his time, after having filled the post of editor to the *Casterbridge Chronicle* for eighteen or twenty years. There he died soon after, and though comparatively a poor man, he left his daughter sufficiently well provided for as a modest fundholder and claimant of sundry small sums in dividends to maintain herself as mistress at Peakhill.

At Cytherea's knock an inner door was heard to open and close, and footsteps crossed the passage hesitatingly. The next minute Cytherea stood face to face with the lady herself.

Adelaide Hinton was about nine-and-twenty years of age. Her hair was plentiful, like Cytherea's own; her teeth equalled Cytherea's in regularity and whiteness. But she was much paler, and had features too transparent to be in place among household surroundings. Her mouth expressed love less forcibly than Cytherea's, and, as a natural result of her greater maturity, her tread was less elastic, and she was more self-possessed.

She had been a girl of that kind which mothers praise as not forward, by way of contrast, when disparaging those warmer ones with whom loving is an end and not a means. Men of forty, too, said of her, 'a good sensible wife for any man, if she cares to marry', the caring to marry being thrown in as the vaguest hypothesis, because she was so practical. Yet it would be singular if, in such cases, the important subject of marriage should be excluded from manipulation by hands that are ready for practical performance in every domestic concern besides.

Cytherea was an acquisition, and the greeting was hearty.

'Good afternoon! O yes – Miss Graye, from Miss Aldclyffe's. I have seen you at church, and I am so glad you have called! Come in. I wonder if I have change enough to pay my subscription.' She spoke girlishly.

Adelaide, when in the company of a younger woman, always levelled herself down to that younger woman's age from a sense of justice to herself – as if, though not her own age at common law, it was in equity.

'It doesn't matter. I'll come again.'

'Yes, do at any time; not only on this errand. But you must step in for a minute. Do.'

'I have been wanting to come for several weeks.'

'That's right. Now you must see my house – lonely, isn't it, for a single person? People said it was odd for a young woman like me to keep on a house; but what did I care? If you knew the pleasure of locking up your own door, with the sensation that you reigned supreme inside it, you would say it was worth the risk of being called odd. Mr Springrove attends to my gardening, the dog attends to robbers, and whenever there is a snake or toad to kill, Jane does it.'

'How nice! It is better than living in a town.'

'Far better. A town makes a cynic of me.'

The remark recalled, somewhat startlingly, to Cytherea's mind, that Edward had used those very words to herself one evening at Budmouth.

Miss Hinton opened an interior door and led her visitor into a small drawing-room commanding a view of the country for miles.

The missionary business was soon settled; but the chat continued.

'How lonely it must be here at night!' said Cytherea. 'Aren't you afraid?'

'At first I was, slightly. But I got used to the solitude. And you know a sort of common-sense will creep even into timidity. I say to myself sometimes at night, "If I were anybody but a harmless woman, not worth the trouble of a worm's ghost to appear to me, I should think that every sound I hear was a spirit." But you must see all over my house.'

Cytherea was highly interested in seeing.

'I say you *must* do this, and you *must* do that, as if you were a child,' remarked Adelaide. 'A privileged friend of mine tells me this use of the imperative comes of being so constantly in nobody's society but my own.'

'Ah, yes. I suppose she is right.'

Cytherea called the friend 'she' by rule of lady-like practice; for a woman's 'friend' is delicately assumed by another friend to be of their own sex in the absence of knowledge to the contrary; just as cats are called she's until they prove themselves he's.

Miss Hinton laughed mysteriously.

'I get a humorous reproof for it now and then, I assure you,' she continued.

'"Humorous reproof": that's not from a woman: who can reprove humorously but a man?' was the groove of Cytherea's thought at the remark. 'Your brother reproves you, I expect,' said that innocent young lady.

'No,' said Miss Hinton, with a candid air. '"Tis only a professional man I am acquainted with.' She looked out of the window.

Women are persistently imitative. No sooner did a thought flash through Cytherea's mind that the man was a lover than she became a Miss Aldclyffe in a mild form.

'I imagine he's a lover,' she said.

Miss Hinton smiled a smile of experience in that line.

Few women, if taxed with having an admirer, are so free from vanity as to deny the impeachment, even if it is utterly untrue. When it does happen to be true, they look pityingly away from the person who is so benighted as to have got no further than suspecting it.

'There now – Miss Hinton; you are engaged to be married!' said Cytherea accusingly.

Adelaide nodded her head practically. 'Well, yes, I am,' she said.

The word 'engaged' had no sooner passed Cytherea's lips than the sound of it – the mere sound of her own lips – carried her mind to the time and circumstances under which Miss Aldclyffe had used it

towards herself. A sickening thought followed – based but on mere surmise; yet its presence took every other idea away from Cytherea's mind.
Miss Hinton had used Edward's words about towns; she mentioned Mr
Springrove was attending to her garden. It could not be that Edward was
the man! that Miss Aldclyffe had planned to reveal her rival thus!

'Are you going to be married soon?' she inquired, with a steadiness
the result of a sort of fascination, but apparently of indifference.

'Not very soon – still, soon.'

'Ah – ha! In less than three months?' said Cytherea.

'Two.'

Now that the subject was well in hand, Adelaide wanted no more
prompting. 'You won't tell anybody if I show you something?' she said,
with eager mystery.

'O no, nobody. But does he live in this parish?'

'No.'

Nothing proved yet.

'What's his name?' said Cytherea flatly. Her breath and heart had
begun their old tricks, and came and went hotly. Miss Hinton could not
see her face.

'What do you think?' said Miss Hinton.

'George?' said Cytherea, with deceitful agony.

'No,' said Adelaide. 'But now, you shall see him first; come here';
and she led the way upstairs into her bedroom. There, standing on the
dressing-table in a little frame, was the unconscious portrait of Edward
Springrove.

'There he is,' Miss Hinton said, and a silence ensued.

'Are you very fond of him?' continued the miserable Cytherea at
length.

'Yes, of course I am,' her companion replied, but in the tone of one
who 'lived in Abraham's bosom all the year',* and was therefore
untouched by solemn thought at the fact. 'He's my cousin – a native of
this village. We were engaged before my father's death left me so
lonely. I was only twenty, and a much greater belle than I am now. We
know each other thoroughly, as you may imagine. I give him a little
sermonizing now and then.'

'Why?'

'O, it's only in fun. He's very naughty sometimes – not really, you
know – but he will look at any pretty face when he sees it.'

Storing up this statement of his susceptibility as another item to be
miserable upon when she had time, 'How do you know that?' Cytherea
asked, with a swelling heart.

'Well, you know how things do come to women's ears. He used to live at Budmouth as an assistant-architect, and I found out that a young giddy thing of a girl who lives there somewhere took his fancy for a day or two. But I don't feel jealous at all – our engagement is so matter-of-fact that neither of us can be jealous. And it was a mere flirtation – she was too silly for him. He's fond of rowing, and kindly gave her an airing for an evening or two. I'll warrant they talked the most unmitigated rubbish under the sun – all shallowness and pastime, just as everything is at watering-places – neither of them caring a bit for the other – she giggling like a goose all the time—'

Concentrated essence of woman pervaded the room rather than air. 'She *didn't*! and it *wasn't* shallowness!' Cytherea burst out, with brimming eyes. ''Twas deep deceit on one side, and entire confidence on the other – yes, it was!' The pent-up emotion had swollen and swollen inside the young thing till the dam could no longer embay it. The instant the words were out she would have given worlds to have been able to recall them.

'Do you know her – or him?' said Miss Hinton, starting with suspicion at the warmth shown.

The two rivals had now lost their personality quite. There was the same keen brightness of eye, the same movement of the mouth, the same mind in both, as they looked doubtingly and excitedly at each other. As is invariably the case with women when a man they care for is the subject of an excitement among them, the situation abstracted the differences which distinguished them as individuals, and left only the properties common to them as atoms of a sex.

Cytherea caught at the chance afforded her of not betraying herself. 'Yes, I know her,' she said.

'Well,' said Miss Hinton, 'I am really vexed if my speaking so lightly of any friend of yours has hurt your feelings, but—'

'O, never mind,' Cytherea returned; 'it doesn't matter, Miss Hinton. I think I must leave you now. I have to call at other places. Yes – I must go.'

Miss Hinton, in a perplexed state of mind, showed her visitor politely downstairs to the door. Here Cytherea bade her a hurried adieu, and flitted down the garden into the lane.

She persevered in her duties with a wayward pleasure in giving herself misery, as was her wont. Mr Springrove's name was next on the list, and she turned towards his dwelling, the Three Tranters Inn.

The cottages along Carriford village street were not so close but that on one side or other of the road was always a hedge of hawthorn or privet, over or through which could be seen gardens or orchards rich with produce. It was about the middle of the early apple-harvest, and the laden trees were shaken at intervals by the gatherers; the soft pattering of the falling crop upon the grassy ground being diversified by the loud rattle of vagrant ones upon a rail, hencoop, basket, or lean-to roof, or upon the rounded and stooping backs of the collectors – mostly children, who would have cried bitterly at receiving such a smart blow from any other quarter, but smilingly assumed it to be but fun in apples.

The Three Tranters Inn, a many-gabled, mediæval building, constructed almost entirely of timber, plaster, and thatch, stood close to the line of the roadside, almost opposite the churchyard, and was connected with a row of cottages on the left by thatched outbuildings. It was an uncommonly characteristic and handsome specimen of the genuine roadside inn of bygone times; and standing on one of the great highways in this part of England, had in its time been the scene of as much of what is now looked upon as the romantic and genial experience of stage-coach travelling as any halting-place in the country. The railway had absorbed* the whole stream of traffic which formerly flowed through the village and along by the ancient door of the inn, reducing the empty-handed landlord, who used only to farm a few fields at the back of the house, to the necessity of eking out his attenuated income by increasing the extent of his agricultural business if he would still maintain his social standing. Next to the general stillness pervading the spot, the long line of outbuildings adjoining the house was the most striking and saddening witness to the passed-away fortunes of the Three Tranters Inn. It was the bulk of the original stabling, and where once the hoofs of two-score horses had daily rattled over the stony yard, to and from the coaches without, thick grass now grew, whilst the line of roofs – once so straight – over the decayed stalls, had sunk into vast hollows till they seemed like the cheeks of toothless age.

On a green plot at the other end of the building grew two or three large, wide-spreading elm-trees, from which the sign was suspended representing the three men called tranters (irregular carriers), standing side by side, and exactly alike to a hair's breadth, the grain of the wood and joints of the boards being visible through the thin paint depicting their forms, which were still further disfigured by red stains running downwards from the rusty nails above.

Under the trees now stood a cider-mill and press, and upon the spot sheltered by the boughs were gathered Mr Springrove himself, his men, the parish clerk, two or three other men, grinders and supernumeraries, a woman with an infant in her arms, a flock of pigeons, and some little boys with straws in their mouths, endeavouring, whenever the men's backs were turned, to get a sip of the sweet juice issuing from the vat.

Edward Springrove the elder, the landlord, now more particularly a farmer, and for two months in the year a cider-maker, was an employer of labour of the old school, who worked himself among his men. He was now engaged in packing the pomace* into horsehair bags with a rammer, and Gad Weedy, his man, was occupied in shovelling up more from a tub at his side. The shovel shone like silver from the action of the juice, and ever and anon, in its motion to and fro, caught the rays of the declining sun and reflected them in bristling stars of light.

Mr Springrove had been too young a man when the pristine days of the Three Tranters had departed for ever to have much of the host left in him now. He was a poet with a rough skin: one whose sturdiness was more the result of external circumstances than of intrinsic nature. Too kindly constituted to be very provident, he was yet not imprudent. He had a quiet humorousness of disposition, not out of keeping with a frequent melancholy, the general expression of his countenance being one of abstraction. Like Walt Whitman he felt as his years increased –

I foresee too much; it means more than I thought.*

On the present occasion he wore gaiters and a leathern apron, and worked with his shirt-sleeves rolled up beyond his elbows, disclosing solid and fleshy rather than muscular arms. They were stained by the cider, and two or three brown apple-pips from the pomace he was handling were to be seen sticking on them here and there.

The other prominent figure was that of Richard Crickett, the parish clerk,* a kind of Bowdlerized* rake, who ate only as much as a woman, and had the rheumatism in his left hand. The remainder of the group, brown-faced peasants, wore smock-frocks embroidered on the shoulders with hearts and diamonds, and were girt round their middle with a strap, another being worn round the right wrist.

'And have you seen the steward, Mr Springrove?' said the clerk.

'Just a glimpse of him; but 'twas just enough to show me that he's not here for long.'

'Why mid that be?'

'He'll never stand the vagaries of the female figure holden the reins – not he.'

'She pays en well,' said a grinder; 'and money's money.'

'Ah – 'tis: very much so,' the clerk replied.

'Yes, yes, neighbour Crickett,' said Springrove, 'but she'll vlee* in a passion – all the fat will be in the fire – and there's an end o't. . . . Yes, she is a one,' continued the farmer, resting, raising his eyes, and reading the features of a distant apple.

'She is,' said Gad, resting too (it is wonderful how prompt a journeyman is in following his master's initiative to rest) and reflectively regarding the ground in front of him.

'True: a one is she,' the clerk chimed in, shaking his head ominously.

'She has such a temper,' said the farmer, 'and is so wilful too. You may as well try to stop a footpath as stop her when she has taken anything into her head. I'd as soon grind little green crabs* all day as live wi' her.'

''Tis a temper she have,' the clerk replied, 'though I be a servant of the Church that say it. But she isn't goen to flee in a passion this time.'

The audience waited for the continuation of the speech, as if they knew from experience the exact distance off it lay in the future.

The clerk swallowed nothing as if it were a great deal, and then went on, 'There's some'at between 'em: mark my words, neighbours – there's some'at between 'em.'

'D'ye mean it?'

'I know it. He came last Saturday, didn't he?'

''A did, truly,' said Gad Weedy, at the same time taking an apple from the hopper* of the mill, eating a piece, and flinging back the remainder to be ground up for cider.

'He went to church a-Sunday,' said the clerk again.

'He did.'

'And she kept her eye upon en all the service, her face flickeren between red and white, but never stoppen at either.'

Mr Springrove nodded, and went to the press.

'Well,' said the clerk, 'you don't call her the kind o' woman to make mistakes in just trotting through the weekly service o' God? Why, as a rule she's as right as I be myself.'

Mr Springrove nodded again, and gave a twist to the screw of the press, followed in the movement by Gad at the other side; the two grinders expressing by looks that, if Miss Aldclyffe were as right at church as the clerk, she must be right indeed.

'Yes, as right in the service o' God as I be myself,' repeated the clerk. 'But last Sunday, when we were in the tenth commandment, says she, "Incline our hearts to keep this law,"* when 'twas "Laws in our hearts, we beseech Thee," all the church through. Her eye was upon *him* – she was quite lost – "Hearts to keep this law," says she; she was no more than a mere shadder at that tenth time – a mere shadder. You might have mouthed across to her "Laws in our hearts we beseech Thee", fifty times over – she'd never ha' noticed 'ee. She's in love wi' the man, that's what she is.'

'Then she's a bigger stunpoll* than I took her for,' said Mr Spring-rove. 'Why, she's old enough to be his mother.'

'The row will be between her and that young Curly-wig, you'll see. She won't run the risk of that pretty face being near.'

'Clerk Crickett, I fancy you know everything about everybody,' said Gad.

'Well so's,'* said the clerk modestly. 'I do know a little. It comes to me.'

'And I know where from.'

'Ah.'

'That wife o' thine. She's an entertainen woman, not to speak disrespectful.'

'She is: and a winnen one. Look at the husbands she've had – God bless her!'

'I wonder you could stand third in that list, Clerk Crickett,' said Mr Springrove.

'Well, 't has been a power o' marvel to myself oftentimes. Yes, matrimony do begin wi' "Dearly beloved", and ends wi' "Amaze-ment", as the prayer-book says.* But what could I do, neighbour Springrove? 'Twas ordained to be. Well do I call to mind what your poor lady said to me when I had just married. "Ah, Mr Crickett," says she, "your wife will soon settle you as she did her other two: here's a glass o' rum, for I shan't see your poor face this time next year." I swallered the rum, called again next year, and said, "Mrs Springrove, you gave me a glass o' rum last year because I was going to die – here I be alive still, you see." "Well thought of, clerk! Here's two glasses for you now, then," says she. "Thank you, mem," I said, and swallered the rum. Well, dang my old sides, next year I thought I'd call again and get three. And call I did. But she wouldn't give me a drop o' the commonest. "No, clerk," says she, "you are too tough for a woman's

103

pity." ... Ah, poor soul, 'twas true enough! Here be I, that was expected to die, alive and hard as a nail, you see, and there's she moulderen in her grave.'

'I used to think 'twas your wife's fate not to have a liven husband when I zid* 'em die off so,' said Gad.

'Fate? Bless thy simplicity, so 'twas her fate; but she struggled to have one, and would, and did. Fate's nothing beside a woman's schemen!'

'I suppose, then, that Fate is a He, like us, and the Lord, and the rest o' 'em up above there,' said Gad, lifting his eyes to the sky.

'Hullo! Here's the young woman comen that we were a-talken about by-now,' said a grinder, suddenly interrupting. 'She's comen up here, as I be alive!'

The two grinders stood and regarded Cytherea as if she had been a ship tacking into a harbour, nearly stopping the mill in their new interest.

'Stylish accoutrements about the head and shoulders, to my thinken,' said the clerk. 'Sheenen curls, and plenty o' 'em.'

'If there's one kind of pride more excusable than another in a young woman, 'tis being proud of her hair,' said Mr Springrove.

'Dear man! – the pride there is only a small piece o' the whole. I warrant now, though she can show such a figure, she ha'n't a stick o' furniture to call her own.'

'Come, Clerk Crickett, let the maid be a maid while she is a maid,' said Farmer Springrove chivalrously.

'O,' replied the servant of the Church; 'I've nothing to say against it – O no:

> "The chimney-sweeper's daughter Sue
>   As I have heard declare, O
> Although she's neither sock nor shoe
>   Will curl and deck her hair, O."'

Cytherea was rather disconcerted at finding that the gradual cessation of the chopping of the mill was on her account, and still more when she saw all the cider-makers' eyes fixed upon her except Mr Springrove's, whose natural delicacy restrained him. She neared the plot of grass, but instead of advancing further, hesitated on its border.

Mr Springrove perceived her embarrassment, which was relieved when she saw his old-established figure coming across to her, wiping his hands in his apron.

'I know your errand, missie,' he said, 'and am glad to see you, and attend to it. I'll step indoors.'

'If you are busy I am in no hurry for a minute or two,' said Cytherea.

'Then if so be you really wouldn't mind, we'll wring down this last filling to let it drain all night?'

'Not at all. I like to see you.'

'We are only just grinding down the rathe-ripes and griffins,'* continued the farmer, in a half apologetic tone for detaining by his cider-making any well-dressed woman. 'They rot as black as a chimney-crook if we keep 'em till the regulars turn in.' As he spoke he went back to the press, Cytherea keeping at his elbow. 'I'm later than I should have been by rights,' he continued, taking up a lever for propelling the screw, and beckoning to the men to come forward. 'The truth is, my son Edward had promised to come to-day, and I made preparations; but instead of him comes a letter: "London, September the eighteenth, Dear Father," says he, and went on to tell me he couldn't. It threw me out a bit.'

'Of course,' said Cytherea.

'He's got a place 'a b'lieve?' said the clerk, drawing near.

'No, poor mortal fellow, no. He tried for this one here, you know, but couldn't manage to get it. I don't know the rights o' the matter, but willy-nilly they wouldn't have him for steward. Now mates, form in line.'

Springrove, the clerk, the grinders, and Gad, all ranged themselves behind the lever of the screw, and walked round like soldiers wheeling.

'The man that the old quean* have got is a man you can hardly get upon your tongue to gainsay, by the look o' en,' rejoined Clerk Crickett.

'One o' them people that can contrive to be thought no worse of for stealen a horse than another man for looken over hedge at en,' said a grinder.

'Well, he's all there as steward, and is quite the gentleman – no doubt about that.'

'So would my Ted ha' been, for the matter o' that,' the farmer said.

'That's true: 'a would, sir.'

'I said, I'll give Ted a good education if it cost me my eyes, and I would have done it.'

'Ay, that you would so,' said the chorus of assistants solemnly.

'But he took to books and drawing naturally, and cost very little; and as a wind-up the women folk hatched up a match between him and his cousin.'

'When's the wedden to be, Mr Springrove?'

'Uncertain – but soon, I suppose. Edward, you see, can do anything pretty nearly, and yet can't get a straightforward living. I wish sometimes I had kept him here, and let professions go. But he was such a one for the pencil.'

He dropped the lever in the hedge, and turned to his visitor.

'Now then, missie, if you'll come indoors, please.'

Gad Weedy looked with a placid criticism at Cytherea as she withdrew with the farmer.

'I could tell by the tongue of her that she didn't take her degrees in our county,' he said in an undertone.

'The railways have left you lonely here,' she observed, when they were indoors.

Save the withered old flies, which were quite tame from the solitude, not a being was in the house. Nobody seemed to have entered it since the last passenger had been called out to mount the last stage-coach that had run by.

'Yes, the Inn and I seem almost a pair of fossils,' the farmer replied, looking at the room and then at himself.

'O, Mr Springrove,' said Cytherea, suddenly recollecting herself; 'I am much obliged to you for recommending me to Miss Aldclyffe.' She began to warm towards the old man; there was in him a gentleness of disposition which reminded her of her own father.

'Recommending? Not at all, miss. Ted – that's my son – Ted said a fellow-draughtsman of his had a sister who wanted to be doing something in the world, and I mentioned it to the housekeeper, that's all. Ay, I miss my son very much.'

She kept her back to the window that he might not see her rising colour.

'Yes,' he continued, 'sometimes I can't help feeling uneasy about him. You know, he seems not made for a town life exactly: he gets very queer over it sometimes, I think. Perhaps he'll be better when he's married to Adelaide.'

A half-impatient feeling arose in her, like that which possesses a sick person when he hears a recently-struck hour struck again by a slow clock. She had lived further on.

'Everything depends upon whether he loves her,' she said tremulously.

'He used to – he doesn't show it so much now; but that's because he's older. You see, it was several years ago they first walked together as young man and young woman. She's altered too from what she was when he first courted her.'

106

'How, sir?'

'O, she's more sensible by half. When he used to write to her she'd creep up the lane and look back over her shoulder, and slide out the letter, and read a word and stand in thought looking at the hills and seeing none. Then the cuckoo would cry – away the letter would slip, and she'd start wi' fright at the mere bird, and have a red skin before the quickest man among ye could say, "Blood rush up."'

He came forward with the money and dropped it into her hand. His thoughts were still with Edward, and he absently took her little fingers in his as he said, earnestly and ingenuously –

''Tis so seldom I get a gentlewoman to speak to that I can't help speaking to you, Miss Graye, on my fears for Edward; I sometimes am afraid that he'll never get on – that he'll die poor and despised under the worst condition o' mind, a keen sense of having been passed in the race by men whose brains are nothing to his own, all through his seeing too far into things – being discontented with make-shifts – thinking o' perfection in things, and then sickened that there's no such thing as perfection. I shan't be sorry to see him marry, since it may settle him down and do him good. . . . Ay, we'll hope for the best.'

He let go her hand and accompanied her to the door saying, 'If you should care to walk this way and talk to an old man once now and then, it will be a great delight to him, Miss Graye. Good evening to ye. . . . Ah look! a thunderstorm is brewing – be quick home. Or shall I step up with you?'

'No, thank you, Mr Springrove. Good evening,' she said in a low voice, and hurried away. One thought still possessed her; Edward had trifled with her love.

4. Five to Six p.m.

She followed the road into a bower of trees, overhanging it so densely that the pass appeared like a rabbit's burrow, and presently reached a side entrance to the park. The clouds rose more rapidly than the farmer had anticipated: the sheep moved in a trail, and complained incoherently. Livid grey shades, like those of the modern French painters,* made a mystery of the remote and dark parts of the vista, and seemed to insist upon a suspension of breath. Before she was half-way across the park the thunder rumbled distinctly.

The direction in which she had to go would take her close by the old manor-house. The air was perfectly still, and between each low rumble of the thunder behind she could hear the roar of the waterfall before her, and the creak of the engine among the bushes hard by it. Hurrying on, with a growing dread of the gloom and of the approaching storm, she drew near the Old House, now rising before her against the dark foliage and sky in tones of strange whiteness.

On the flight of steps, which descended from a terrace in front to the level of the park, stood a man. He appeared, partly from the relief the position gave to his figure, and partly from fact, to be of towering height. He was dark in outline, and was looking at the sky, with his hands behind him.

It was necessary for Cytherea to pass directly across the line of his front. She felt so reluctant to do this, that she was about to turn under the trees out of the path and enter it again at a point beyond the Old House; but he had seen her, and she came on mechanically, unconsciously averting her face a little, and dropping her glance to the ground.

Her eyes unswervingly lingered along the path until they fell upon another path branching in a right line from the path she was pursuing. It came from the steps of the Old House. 'I am exactly opposite him now,' she thought, 'and his eyes are going through me.'

A clear masculine voice said, at the same instant –

'Are you afraid?'

She, interpreting his question by her feelings at the moment, assumed himself to be the object of fear, if any. 'I don't think I am,' she stammered.

He seemed to know that she thought in that sense.

'Of the thunder, I mean,' he said; 'not of myself.'

She must turn to him now. 'I think it is going to rain,' she remarked for the sake of saying something.

He could not conceal his surprise and admiration of her face and bearing. He said courteously, 'It may possibly not rain before you reach the House, if you are going there?'

'Yes, I am.'

'May I walk up with you? It is lonely under the trees.'

'No.' Fearing his courtesy arose from a belief he was addressing a woman of higher station than was hers, she added, 'I am Miss Aldclyffe's companion. I don't mind the loneliness.'

'O, Miss Aldclyffe's companion. Then will you be kind enough to take a subscription to her? She sent to me this afternoon to ask me to become a subscriber to her Society, and I was out. Of course I'll subscribe if she wishes it. I take a great interest in the Society.'

'Miss Aldclyffe will be glad to hear that, I know.'

108

'Yes; let me see – what Society did she say it was? I am afraid I haven't enough money in my pocket, and yet it would be a satisfaction to her to have practical proof of my willingness. I'll get it, and be out in one minute.'

He entered the house and was at her side again within the time he had named. 'This is it,' he said pleasantly.

She held up her hand. The soft tips of his fingers brushed the palm of her glove as he placed the money within it. She wondered why his fingers should have touched her.

'I think after all,' he continued, 'that the rain is upon us, and will drench you before you reach the House. Yes: see there.'

He pointed to a round wet spot as large as a nasturtium leaf, which had suddenly appeared upon the white surface of the step.

'You had better come into the porch. It is not nearly night yet. The clouds make it seem later than it really is.'

Heavy drops of rain, followed immediately by a forked flash of lightning and sharp rattling thunder, compelled her, willingly or no, to accept his invitation. She ascended the steps, stood beside him just within the porch, and for the first time obtained a series of short views of his person, as they waited there in silence.

He was an extremely handsome man, well-formed, and well-dressed, of an age which seemed to be two or three years less than thirty. The most striking point in his appearance was the wonderful, almost preternatural, clearness of his complexion. There was not a blemish or speck of any kind to mar the smoothness of its surface or the beauty of its hue. Next, his forehead was square and broad, his brows straight and firm, his eyes penetrating and clear. By collecting the round of expressions they gave forth, a person who theorized on such matters would have imbibed the notion that their owner was of a nature to kick against the pricks; the last man in the world to put up with a position because it seemed to be his destiny to do so; one who took upon himself to resist fate with the vindictive determination of a Theomachist.* Eyes and forehead both would have expressed keenness of intellect too severely to be pleasing, had their force not been counteracted by the lines and tone of the lips. These were full and luscious to a surprising degree, possessing a woman-like softness of curve, and a ruby redness so intense as to testify strongly to much susceptibility of heart where feminine beauty was concerned – a susceptibility that might require all the ballast of brain with which he had previously been credited to confine within reasonable channels.

His manner was rather elegant than good: his speech well-finished and unconstrained.

The pause in their discourse, which had been caused by the peal of thunder, was unbroken by either for a minute or two, during which the ears of both seemed to be absently following the low roar of the waterfall as it became gradually rivalled by the increasing rush of rain upon the trees and herbage of the grove. After her short looks at him, Cytherea had turned her head towards the avenue for a while, and now, glancing back again for an instant, she discovered that his eyes were engaged in a steady, though delicate, regard of her face and form.

At this moment, by reason of the narrowness of the porch, their clothing touched, and remained in contact.

His clothes are something exterior to every man; but to a woman her dress is part of her body. Its motions are all present to her intelligence if not to her eyes; no man knows how his coat-tails swing. By the slightest hyperbole it may be said that her dress has sensation. Crease but the very Ultima Thule* of fringe or flounce, and it hurts her as much as pinching her. Delicate antennae, or feelers, bristle on every outlying frill. Go to the uppermost: she is there: tread on the lowest: the fair creature is there almost before you.

Thus the touch of clothes, which was nothing to Manston, sent a thrill through Cytherea, seeing, moreover, that he was of the nature of a mysterious stranger. She looked out again at the storm, but still felt him. At last to escape the sensation she moved away, though by so doing it was necessary to advance a little into the rain.

'Look, the rain is coming into the porch upon you,' he said. 'Step inside the door.'

Cytherea hesitated.

'Perfectly safe, I assure you,' he added, laughing, and holding the door open. 'You shall see what a state of disorganization I am in – boxes on boxes, furniture, straw, crockery, in every form of transposition. An old woman is in the back quarters somewhere, beginning to put things to rights. . . . You know the inside of the house, I dare say?'

'I have never been in.'

'O well, come along. Here, you see, they have made a door through; here, they have put a partition dividing the old hall into two, one part is now my parlour; there they have put a plaster ceiling, hiding the old chestnut-carved roof because it was too high and would have been chilly for me; you see, being the original hall, it was open right up to the top, and the lord of the manor and his retainers used to meet and be merry by the light from the monstrous fire which shone out from that monstrous fire-place, now narrowed to a mere nothing for my grate, though you can see the old outline still. I almost wish I could have had it in its original state.'

'With more romance and less comfort.'

'Yes, exactly. Well, perhaps the wish is not deep-seated. You will see how the things are tumbled in anyhow, packing-cases and all. The only piece of ornamental furniture yet unpacked is this one.'

'An organ?'

'Yes, an organ. I made it myself, except the pipes. I opened the case this afternoon to commence soothing myself at once. It is not a very large one, but quite big enough for a private house. You play, I dare say?'

'The piano. I am not at all used to an organ.'

'You would soon acquire the touch for an organ, though it would spoil your touch for the piano. Not that that matters a great deal. A piano isn't much as an instrument.'

'It is the fashion to say so now. I think it is quite good enough.'

'That isn't altogether a right sentiment about things being good enough.'

'No – no. What I mean is, that the men who despise pianos do it as a rule from their teeth,* merely for fashion's sake, because cleverer men have said it before them – not from the experience of their ears.'

Now Cytherea all at once broke into a blush at the consciousness of a great snub she had been guilty of in her eagerness to explain herself. He charitably expressed by a look that he did not in the least mind her blunder, if it were one; and this attitude forced him into a position of mental superiority which vexed her.

'I play for my private amusement only,' he said. 'I have never learned scientifically. All I know is what I taught myself.'

The thunder, lightning, and rain had now increased to a terrific force. The clouds, from which darts, forks, zigzags, and balls of fire continually sprang, did not appear to be more than a hundred yards above their heads, and every now and then a flash and a peal made gaps in the steward's descriptions. He went towards the organ, in the midst of a volley which seemed to shake the aged house from foundations to chimney.

'You are not going to play now, are you?' said Cytherea uneasily.

'O yes. Why not now?' he said. 'You can't go home, and therefore we may as well be amused, if you don't mind sitting on this box. The few chairs I have unpacked are in the other room.'

Without waiting to see whether she sat down or not, he turned to the organ and began extemporizing a harmony which meandered through every variety of expression of which the instrument was capable. Presently he ceased and began searching for some music-book.

'What a splendid flash!' he said, as the lightning again shone in through the mullioned window, which, of a proportion to suit the whole extent of the original hall, was much too large for the present room. The thunder pealed again. Cytherea, in spite of herself, was frightened, not only at the weather, but at the general unearthly weirdness which seemed to surround her there.

'I wish I – the lightning wasn't so bright. Do you think it will last long?' she said timidly.

'It can't last much longer,' he murmured, without turning, running his fingers again over the keys. 'But this is nothing,' he continued, suddenly stopping and regarding her. 'It seems brighter because of the deep shadow under those trees yonder. Don't mind it; now look at me – look in my face – now.'

He had faced the window, looking fixedly at the sky with his dark strong eyes. She seemed compelled to do as she was bidden, and looked in the too-delicately beautiful face.

The flash came; but he did not turn or blink,* keeping his eyes fixed as firmly as before. 'There,' he said, turning to her, 'that's the way to look at lightning.'

'O, it might have blinded you!' she exclaimed.

'Nonsense – not lightning of this sort – I shouldn't have stared at it if there had been danger. It is only sheet-lightning now. Now, will you have another piece? Something from an oratorio this time?'

'No, thank you – I don't want to hear it whilst it thunders so.' But he had begun without heeding her answer, and she stood motionless again, marvelling at the wonderful indifference to all external circumstance which now evinced by his complete absorption in the music before him.

'Why do you play such saddening chords?' she said, when he next paused.

'H'm – because I like them, I suppose,' he said lightly. 'Don't you like sad impressions sometimes?'

'Yes, sometimes, perhaps.'

'When you are full of trouble.'

'Yes.'

'Well, why shouldn't I when I am full of trouble?'

'Are you troubled?'

'I am troubled.' He said this thoughtfully and abruptly – so abruptly that she did not push the dialogue further.

He now played more powerfully. Cytherea had never heard music in the completeness of a full orchestral power, and the tones of the organ, which reverberated with considerable effect in the comparatively small space of the room, heightened by the elemental strife of light and sound outside, moved her to a degree out of proportion to the actual power of the mere notes, practised as was the hand that produced them. The varying strains – now loud, now soft; simple, complicated, weird, touching, grand, boisterous, subdued; each phase distinct, yet modulating into the next with a graceful and easy flow – shook and bent her to themselves, as a gushing brook shakes and bends a shadow cast across its surface. The power of the music did not show itself so much by attracting her attention to the subject of the piece, as by taking up and developing as its libretto the poem of her own life and soul,* shifting her deeds and intentions from the hands of her judgement and holding them in its own.

She was swayed into emotional opinions concerning the strange man before her; now impulses of thought came with new harmonies, and entered into her with a gnawing thrill. A dreadful flash of lightning then, and the thunder close upon it. She found herself involuntarily shrinking up beside him, and looking with parted lips at his face.

He turned his eyes and saw her emotion, which greatly increased the ideal element in her expressive face. She was in the state in which woman's instinct to conceal has lost its power over her impulse to tell; and he saw it. Bending his handsome face over her till his lips almost touched her ear, he murmured, without breaking the harmonies –

'Do you very much like this piece?'

'Very much indeed,' she said.

'I could see you were affected by it. I will copy it for you.'

'Thank you much.'

'I will bring it to the House to you to-morrow. Who shall I ask for?'

'O, not for me. Don't bring it,' she said hastily. 'I shouldn't like you to.'

'Let me see – to-morrow evening at seven or a few minutes past I shall be passing the waterfall on my way home. I could conveniently give it you there, and I should like you to have it.'

He modulated into the Pastoral Symphony,* still looking in her eyes.

'Very well,' she said, to get rid of the look.

The storm had by this time considerably decreased in violence, and in seven or ten minutes the sky partially cleared, the clouds around the western horizon becoming lighted up with the rays of the sinking sun.

Cytherea drew a long breath of relief, and prepared to go away. She was full of a distressing sense that her detention in the old manor-house, and the acquaintanceship it had set on foot, was not a thing she wished. It was such a foolish thing to have been excited and dragged into frankness by the wiles of a stranger.

'Allow me to come with you,' he said, accompanying her to the door, and again showing by his behaviour how much he was impressed with her. His influence over her had vanished with the musical chords, and she turned her back upon him. 'May I come?' he repeated.

'No, no. The distance is not a quarter of a mile – it is really not necessary, thank you,' she said quietly. And wishing him good-evening, without meeting his eyes, she went down the steps, leaving him standing at the door.

'O, how is it that man has so fascinated me?' was all she could think. Her own self, as she had sat spell-bound before him, was all she could see. Her gait was constrained, from the knowledge that his eyes were upon her until she had passed the hollow by the waterfall, and by ascending the rise had become hidden from his view by the boughs of the overhanging trees.

5. Six to Seven p.m.

The wet shining road threw the western glare into her eyes with an invidious lustre which rendered the restlessness of her mood more wearying. Her thoughts flew from idea to idea without asking for the slightest link of connection between one and another. One moment she was full of the wild music and stirring scene with Manston – the next, Edward's image rose before her like a shadowy ghost. Then Manston's black eyes seemed piercing her again, and the reckless voluptuous mouth appeared bending to the curves of his special words. What could be those troubles to which he had alluded? Perhaps Miss Aldclyffe was at the bottom of them. Sad at heart she paced on: her life was bewildering her.

On coming into Miss Aldclyffe's presence Cytherea told her of the incident, not without a fear that she would burst into one of her ungovernable fits of temper at learning of Cytherea's slight departure from the programme. But, strangely to Cytherea, Miss Aldclyffe looked delighted. The usual cross-examination followed.

'And so you were with him all that time?' said the lady, with assumed severity.

'Yes, I was.'

114

'I did not tell you to call at the Old House twice.'

'I didn't call, as I have said. He made me come into the porch.'

'What remarks did he make, do you say?'

'That the lightning was not so bad as I thought.'

'A very important remark, that. Did he—' she turned her glance full upon the girl, and eyeing her searchingly, said –

'Did he say anything about *me*?'

'Nothing,' said Cytherea, returning her gaze calmly, 'except that I was to give you the subscription.'

'You are quite sure?'

'Quite.'

'I believe you. Did he say anything striking or strange about himself?'

'Only one thing – that he was troubled.'

'Troubled!'

After saying the word, Miss Aldclyffe relapsed into silence. Such behaviour as this had ended, on most previous occasions, by her making a confession, and Cytherea expected one now. But for once she was mistaken, nothing more was said.

When she had returned to her room she sat down and penned a farewell letter to Edward Springrove, as little able as any other excitable and brimming young woman of nineteen to feel that the wisest and only dignified course at that juncture was to do nothing at all. She told him that, to her painful surprise, she had learnt that his engagement to another woman was a matter of notoriety. She insisted that all honour bade him marry his early love – a woman far better than her unworthy self, who only deserved to be forgotten, and begged him to remember that he was not to see her face again. She upbraided him for levity and cruelty in meeting her so frequently in Budmouth, and above all in stealing the kiss from her lips on the last evening of the water excursions. 'I never, never can forget it!' she said, and then felt a sensation of having done her duty, ostensibly persuading herself that her reproaches and commands were of such a force that no man to whom they were uttered could ever approach her more.

Yet it was all unconsciously said in words which betrayed a lingering tenderness of love at every unguarded turn. Like Beatrice accusing Dante from the chariot,* try as she might to play the superior being who contemned such mere eye-sensuousness, she betrayed at every point a pretty woman's jealousy of a rival, and covertly gave her old lover hints for excusing himself at each fresh indictment.

This done, Cytherea, still in a practical mood, upbraided herself with weakness in allowing a stranger like Mr Manston to influence her as he had done that evening. What right on earth had he to suggest so suddenly that she might meet him at the waterfall to receive his music? She would have given much to be able to annihilate the ascendancy he had obtained over her during that extraordinary interval of melodious sound. Not being able to endure the notion of his living a minute longer in the belief he was then holding, she took her pen and wrote to him also: –

KNAPWATER HOUSE,
September 20th

I find I cannot meet you at seven o'clock by the waterfall as I promised. The emotion I felt made me forgetful of realities.

C. GRAYE

A great statesman thinks several times, and acts; a young lady acts, and thinks several times. When, a few minutes later, she saw the postman carry off the bag containing one of the letters, and a messenger with the other, she, for the first time, asked herself the question whether she had acted very wisely in writing to either of the two men who had so influenced her.

CHAPTER NINE
The Events of Ten Weeks

1. From September the Twenty-First to the Middle of November

The foremost figure within Cytherea's horizon, exclusive of the inmates of Knapwater House, was now the steward, Mr Manston. It was impossible that they should live within a quarter of a mile of each other, be engaged in the same service, and attend the same church, without meeting at some spot or another, twice or thrice a week. On Sundays, in her pew, when by chance she turned her head, Cytherea found his eyes waiting desirously for a glimpse of hers, and, at first more strangely, the eyes of Miss Aldclyffe furtively resting on him. On coming out of church he frequently walked beside Cytherea till she reached the gate at which residents in the House turned into the shrubbery. By degrees a conjecture grew to a certainty. She knew that he loved her.

But a strange fact was connected with the development of his love.

116

He was palpably making the strongest efforts to subdue, or at least to hide, the weakness, and as it sometimes seemed, rather from his own conscience than from surrounding eyes. Hence she found that not one of his encounters with her was anything more than the result of pure accident. He made no advances whatever: without avoiding her, he never sought her: the words he had whispered at their first interview now proved themselves to be quite as much the result of unguarded impulse as was her answer. Something held him back, bound his impulse down, but she saw that it was neither pride of his person, nor fear that she would refuse him – a course she unhesitatingly resolved to take should he think fit to declare himself. She was interested in him and his marvellous beauty, as she might have been in some fascinating panther or leopard – for some undefinable reason she shrank from him, even whilst she admired. The keynote of her nature, a warm, 'precipitance of soul', as Coleridge happily writes it, which Manston had so directly pounced upon at their very first interview, gave her now a tremulous sense of being in some way in his power.

The state of mind was, on the whole, a dangerous one for a young and inexperienced woman; and perhaps the circumstance which, more than any other, led her to cherish Edward's image now, was that he had taken no notice of the receipt of her letter, stating that she discarded him. It was plain then, she said, that he did not care deeply for her, and she thereupon could not quite leave off caring deeply for him: –

Ingenium mulierum,
Nolunt ubi velis, ubi nolis cupiunt ultro.*

The month of October passed, and November began its course. The inhabitants of the village of Carriford grew weary of supposing that Miss Aldclyffe was going to marry her steward. New whispers arose and became very distinct (though they did not reach Miss Aldclyffe's ears) to the effect that the steward was deeply in love with Cytherea Graye. Indeed, the fact became so obvious that there was nothing left to say about it except that their marriage would be an excellent one for both; – for her in point of comfort – and for him in point of love.

As circles in a pond grow wider and wider, the next fact, which at first had been patent only to Cytherea herself, in due time spread to her neighbours, and they, too, wondered that he made no overt advances. By the middle of November, a theory made up of a combination of the other two was received with general favour: its substance being that a guilty intrigue had been commenced between Manston and Miss

Aldclyffe, some years before, when he was a very young man, and she still in the enjoyment of some womanly beauty, but now that her seniority began to grow emphatic she was becoming distasteful to him. His fear of the effect of the lady's jealousy would, they said, thus lead him to conceal from her his new attachment to Cytherea. Almost the only woman who did not believe this was Cytherea herself, on unmistakable grounds, which were hidden from all besides. It was not only in public, but even more markedly in secluded places, on occasions when gallantry would have been safe from all discovery, that this guarded course of action was pursued, all the strength of a consuming passion burning in his eyes the while.

2. November the Eighteenth

It was on a Friday in this month of November that Owen Graye paid a visit to his sister.

His zealous integrity still retained for him the situation at Budmouth, and in order that there should be as little interruption as possible to his duties there, he had decided not to come to Knapwater till late in the afternoon, and to return to Budmouth by the first train the next morning, Miss Aldclyffe having made a point of frequently offering him lodging for an unlimited period, to the great pleasure of Cytherea.

He reached the house about four o'clock, and ringing the bell, asked of the page who answered it for Miss Graye.

When Graye spoke the name of his sister, Manston, who was just coming out from an interview with Miss Aldclyffe, passed him in the vestibule and heard the question. The steward's face grew hot, and he secretly clenched his hands. He half crossed the court, then turned his head and saw that the lad still stood at the door, though Owen had been shown into the house. Manston went back to him.

'Who was that man?' he said.

'I don't know, sir.'

'Has he ever been here before?'

'Yes, sir.'

'How many times?'

'Three.'

'You are sure you don't know him?'

'I think he is Miss Graye's brother, sir.'

'Then, why the devil didn't you say so before!' Manston exclaimed, and again went on his way.

'Of course, that was not the man of my dreams – of course, it couldn't be!' he said to himself. 'That I should be such a fool – such an utter fool. Good God! to allow a girl to influence me like this, day after day, till I am jealous of her very brother. A lady's dependent, a waif, a helpless thing entirely at the mercy of the world; yes, curse it; that is just why it is; that fact of her being so helpless against the blows of circumstances which renders her so deliciously sweet!'

He paused opposite his house. Should he get his horse saddled? No.

He went down the drive and out of the park, having started to proceed to an outlying spot on the estate concerning some draining, and to call at the potter's yard to make an arrangement for the supply of pipes. But a remark which Miss Aldclyffe had dropped in relation to Cytherea was what still occupied his mind, and had been the immediate cause of his excitement at the sight of her brother. Miss Aldclyffe had meaningly remarked during their intercourse, that Cytherea was wildly in love with Edward Springrove, in spite of his engagement to his cousin Adelaide.

'How I am harassed!' he said aloud, after deep thought for half-an-hour, while still continuing his walk with the greatest vehemence. 'How I am harassed by these emotions of mine!' He calmed himself by an effort. 'Well, duty after all it shall be, as nearly as I can effect it. "Honesty is the best policy"'; with which vigorously uttered resolve he once more attempted to turn his attention to the prosy object of his journey.

The evening had closed in to a dark and dreary night when the steward came from the potter's door to proceed homewards again. The gloom did not tend to raise his spirits, and in the total lack of objects to attract his eye he soon fell to introspection as before. It was along the margin of turnip fields that his path lay, and the large leaves of the crop struck flatly against his feet at every step, pouring upon them the rolling drops of moisture gathered upon their broad surfaces; but the annoyance was unheeded. Next reaching a fir plantation, he mounted the stile and followed the path into the midst of the darkness produced by the overhanging trees.

After walking under the dense shade of the inky boughs for a few minutes, he fancied he had mistaken the path, which as yet was scarcely familiar to him. This was proved directly afterwards by his coming at right angles upon some obstruction, which careful feeling with out-stretched hands soon told him to be a rail fence. However, as the wood was not large, he experienced no alarm about finding the path again, and with some sense of pleasure halted awhile against the rails, to listen to the intensely melancholy yet musical wail of the fir-tops, and as the wind passed on, the prompt moan of an adjacent plantation in reply. He could just dimly discern the airy summits of the two or three trees nearest him waving restlessly backwards and forwards, and stretching out their boughs like hairy arms into the dull sky. The scene, from its striking and emphatic loneliness, began to grow congenial to his mood; all of human kind seemed at the antipodes.

A sudden rattle on his right hand caused him to start from his reverie, and turn in that direction. There, before him, he saw rise up from among the trees a fountain of sparks and smoke, then a red glare of light coming forward towards him; then a flashing panorama of illuminated oblong pictures; then the old darkness, more impressive than ever.

The surprise, which had owed its origin to his imperfect acquaintance with the topographical features of that end of the estate, had been but momentary; the disturbance, a well-known one to dwellers by a railway, being caused by the 6.50 down-train passing along a shallow cutting in the midst of the wood immediately below where he stood, the driver having the fire-door of the engine open at the minute of going by. The train had, when passing him, already considerably slackened speed, and now a whistle was heard, announcing that Carriford Road Station was not far in its van.

But contrary to the natural order of things, the discovery that it was only a commonplace train had not caused Manston to stir from his position of facing the railway.

If the 6.50 down-train had been a flash of forked lightning transfixing him to the earth, he could scarcely have remained in a more trance-like state. He still leant against the railings, his right hand still continued pressing on his walking-stick, his weight on one foot, his other heel raised, his eyes wide open towards the blackness of the cutting. The only movement in him was a slight dropping of the lower jaw, separating his previously closed lips a little way, as when a strange conviction rushes home suddenly upon a man. A new surprise, not nearly so trivial as the first, had taken possession of him.

It was on this account. At one of the illuminated windows of a second-class carriage in the series gone by, he had seen a pale face, reclining upon one hand, the light from the lamp falling full upon it. The face was a woman's.

At last Manston moved; gave a whispering kind of whistle, adjusted his hat, and walked on again, cross-questioning himself in every direction as to how a piece of knowledge he had carefully concealed had found its way to another person's intelligence. 'How can my address have become known?' he said at length, audibly. 'Well, it is a blessing I have been circumspect and honourable, in relation to that – yes, I will say it, for once, even if the words choke me, that darling of mine, Cytherea, never to be my own, never. I suppose all will come out now. All!' The great sadness of his utterance proved that no mean force had been exercised upon himself to sustain the circumspection he had just claimed.

He wheeled to the left, pursued the ditch beside the railway fence, and presently emerged from the wood, stepping into a road which crossed the railway by a bridge.

As he neared home, the anxiety lately written in his face, merged by degrees into a grimly humorous smile, which hung long upon his lips, and he quoted aloud a line from the book of Jeremiah –

A woman shall compass a man.*

3. November the Nineteenth. Daybreak

Before it was light the next morning, two little naked feet pattered along the passage in Knapwater House from which Owen Graye's bedroom opened, and a tap was given upon his door.

'Owen, Owen, are you awake?' said Cytherea in a whisper through the keyhole. 'You must get up directly, or you'll miss the train.'

When he descended to his sister's little room he found her there already waiting with a cup of cocoa and a grilled rasher on the table for him. A hasty meal was despatched in the intervals of putting on his overcoat and finding his hat, and they then went softly through the long deserted passages, the kitchen-maid who had prepared their breakfast walking before them with a lamp held high above her head, which cast long wheeling shadows down corridors intersecting the one they followed, their remoter ends being lost in darkness. The door was unbolted and they stepped out.

Owen had preferred walking to the station to accepting the pony-carriage which Miss Aldclyffe had placed at his disposal, having a morbid horror of giving trouble to people richer than himself, and especially to their men-servants, who looked down upon him as a hybrid monster in social position. Cytherea proposed to walk a little way with him.

'I want to talk to you as long as I can,' she said tenderly.

Brother and sister then emerged by the heavy door into the drive. The feeling and aspect of the hour were precisely similar to those under

121

which the steward had left the house the evening previous, excepting that apparently unearthly reversal of natural sequence, which is caused by the world getting lighter instead of darker. 'The tearful glimmer of the languid dawn'* was just sufficient to reveal to them the melancholy red leaves, lying thickly in the channels by the roadside, ever and anon loudly tapped on by heavy drops of water, which the boughs above had collected from the foggy air.

They passed the Old House, engaged in a deep conversation, and had proceeded about twenty yards by a cross route, in the direction of the turnpike road, when the form of a woman emerged from the porch of the building.

She was wrapped in a grey waterproof cloak, the hood of which was drawn over her head and closely round her face – so closely that her eyes were the sole features uncovered.

With this one exception of her appearance there, the most perfect stillness and silence pervaded the steward's residence from basement to chimney. Not a shutter was open; not a twine of smoke came forth.

Underneath the ivy-covered gateway she stood still and listened for two, or possibly three minutes, till she became conscious of others in the park. Seeing the pair she stepped back, with the apparent intention of letting them pass out of sight, and evidently wishing to avoid observation. But looking at her watch, and returning it rapidly to her pocket, as if surprised at the lateness of the hour, she hurried out again, and across the park by a still more oblique line than that traced by Owen and his sister.

These in the meantime had got into the road, and were walking along it as the woman came up on the other side of the boundary hedge, looking for a gate or stile, by which she, too, might get off the grass upon the hard ground.

Their conversation, of which every word was clear and distinct, in the still air of the dawn, to the distance of a quarter of a mile, reached her ears, and withdrew her attention from all other matters and sights whatsoever. Thus arrested she stood for an instant as precisely in the attitude of Imogen by the cave Belarius,* as if she had studied the position from the play. When they had advanced a few steps, she followed them in some doubt, still screened by the hedge.

'Do you believe in such odd coincidences?' said Cytherea.

'How do you mean, believe in them? They occur sometimes.'

'Yes, one will occur often enough – that is, two disconnected events will fall strangely together by chance, and people scarcely notice the fact beyond saying, "Oddly enough it happened that so and so were the same," and so on. But when three such events coincide without any apparent reason for the coincidence, it seems as if there must be invisible means at work. You see three things falling together in that manner are ten times as singular as two cases of coincidence which are distinct.'

'Well, of course: what a mathematical head you have, Cytherea! But I don't see so much to marvel at in our case. That the man who kept the public-house in which Miss Aldclyffe fainted, and who found out her name and position, lives in this neighbourhood, is accounted for by the fact that she got him the berth to stop his tongue. That you came here was simply owing to Springrove.'

'Ah, but look at this. Miss Aldclyffe is the woman our father first loved, and I have come to Miss Aldclyffe's; you can't get over that.'

From these premises, she proceeded to argue like an elderly divine on the designs of Providence which were apparent in such conjunctures, and went into a variety of details connected with Miss Aldclyffe's history.

'Had I better tell Miss Aldclyffe that I know all this?' she inquired at last.

'What's the use?' he said. 'Your possessing the knowledge does no harm; you are at any rate comfortable here, and a confession to Miss Aldclyffe might only irritate her. No, hold your tongue, Cytherea.'

'I fancy I should have been tempted to tell her too,' Cytherea went on, 'had I not found out that there exists a very odd, almost imperceptible, and yet real connection of some kind between her and Mr Manston, which is more than that of a mutual interest in the estate.'

'She is in love with him!' exclaimed Owen; 'fancy that!'

'Ah – that's what everybody says who has been keen enough to notice anything. I said so at first. And yet now I cannot persuade myself that she is in love with him at all.'

'Why can't you?'

'She doesn't act as if she were. She isn't – you will know I don't say it from any vanity, Owen – she isn't the least jealous of me.'

'Perhaps she is in some way in his power.'

'No – she is not. He was openly advertised for, and chosen from forty or fifty who answered the advertisement, without knowing whose it was. And since he has been here, she has certainly done nothing to compromise herself in any way. Besides, why should she have brought an enemy here at all?'

'Then she must have fallen in love with him. You know as well as I do, Cyth, that with women there's nothing between the two poles of emotion towards an interesting male acquaintance. 'Tis either love or aversion.'

They walked for a few minutes in silence, when Cytherea's eyes accidentally fell upon her brother's feet.

'Owen,' she said, 'do you know that there is something unusual in your manner of walking?'

'What is it like?' he asked.

'I can't quite say, except that you don't walk so regularly as you used to.'

The woman behind the hedge, who had still continued to dog their footsteps, made an impatient movement at this change in their conversation, and looked at her watch again. Yet she seemed reluctant to give over listening to them.

'Yes,' Owen returned with assumed carelessness, 'I do know it. I think the cause of it is that mysterious pain which comes just above my ankle sometimes. You remember the first time I had it? That day we went by steam-packet to Lulwind Cove, when it hindered me from coming back to you, and compelled me to sleep with the gateman we have been talking about.'

'But is it anything serious, dear Owen?' Cytherea exclaimed, with some alarm.

'O, nothing at all. It is sure to go off again. I never find a sign of it when I sit in the office.'

Again their unperceived companion made a gesture of vexation, and looked at her watch as if time were precious. But the dialogue still flowed on upon this new subject, and showed no sign of returning to its old channel.

Gathering up her skirt decisively she renounced all further hope, and hurried along the ditch till she had dropped into a valley, and came to a gate which was beyond the view of those coming behind. This she softly opened, and came out upon the road, following it in the direction of the railway station.

Presently she heard Owen Graye's footsteps in her rear, his quickened pace implying that he had parted from his sister. The woman thereupon increased her rapid walk to a run, and in a few minutes safely distanced her fellow-traveller.

The railway at Carriford Road consisted only of a single line of rails; and the short local down-train by which Owen was going to Budmouth was shunted on to a siding whilst the first up-train passed. Graye entered the waiting-room, and the door being open he listlessly observed the movements of a woman wearing a long grey cloak, and closely hooded, who had asked for a ticket for London.

He followed her with his eyes on to the platform, saw her waiting there and afterwards stepping into the train: his recollection of her ceasing with the perception.

4. Eight to Ten o'Clock a.m.

Mrs Crickett, twice a widow, and now the parish clerk's wife, a fine-framed, scandal-loving woman, with a peculiar corner to her eye by which, without turning her head, she could see what people were doing almost behind her, lived in a cottage standing nearer to the old manor-house than any other in the village of Carriford, and she had on that account been temporarily engaged by the steward, as a respectable kind of charwoman and general servant, until a settled arrangement could be made with some person as permanent domestic.

Every morning, therefore, Mrs Crickett, immediately she had lighted the fire in her own cottage and prepared the breakfast for herself and husband, paced her way to the Old House to do the same for Mr Manston. Then she went home to breakfast; and when the steward had eaten his, and gone out on his rounds, she returned again to clear away, make his bed, and put the house in order for the day.

On the morning of Owen Graye's departure she went through the operations of her first visit as usual – proceeded home to breakfast, and went back again to perform those of the second.

Entering Manston's empty bedroom with her hands on her hips, she indifferently cast her eyes upon the bed, previously to dismantling it.

Whilst she looked she thought in an inattentive manner, 'What a remarkably quiet sleeper Mr Manston must be!' The upper bed-clothes were flung back, certainly, but the bed was scarcely dis-arranged. 'Anybody would almost fancy,' she thought, 'that he had made it himself after rising.'

But these evanescent thoughts vanished as they had come, and Mrs Crickett set to work; she dragged off the counterpane, blankets and sheets, and stooped to lift the pillows. Thus stooping, something arrested her attention; she looked closely – more closely – very closely. 'Well, to be sure!' was all she could say. The clerk's wife stood as if the air had suddenly set to amber, and held her fixed like a fly in it.

The object of her wonder was a trailing brown hair, very little less than a yard long, which proved it clearly to be a hair from some woman's head. She drew it off the pillow, and took it to the window; there holding it out she looked fixedly at it, and became utterly lost in meditation: her gaze, which had at first actively settled on the hair, involuntarily dropped past its object by degrees and was lost on the floor, as the inner vision obscured the outer one.

She at length moistened her lips, returned her eyes to the hair, wound it round her fingers, put it in some paper, and secreted the whole in her pocket. Mrs Crickett's thoughts were with her work no more that morning.

She searched the house from roof-tree to cellar, for some other trace of feminine existence or appurtenance; but none was to be found.

She went out into the yard, coal-hole, stable, hay-loft, green-house, fowl-house, and piggery, and still there was no sign. Coming in again, she saw a bonnet, eagerly pounced upon it; and found it to be her own.

Hastily completing her arrangements in the other rooms, she entered the village again, and called at once on the postmistress, Elizabeth Leat, an intimate friend of hers, and a female who sported several unique diseases and afflictions.

Mrs Crickett unfolded the paper, took out the hair, and waved it on high before the perplexed eyes of Elizabeth, which immediately mooned and wandered after it like a cat's.

'What is it?' said Mrs Leat, contracting her eyelids, and stretching out towards the invisible object a narrow bony hand that would have been an unmitigated delight to the pencil of Carlo Crivelli.*

'You shall hear,' said Mrs Crickett, complacently gathering up the treasure into her own fat hand; and the secret was then solemnly imparted, together with the accident of its discovery.

A shaving-glass was taken down from a nail, laid on its back in the middle of a table by the window, and the hair spread carefully out upon it. The pair then bent over the table from opposite sides, their elbows on the edge, their hands supporting their heads, their foreheads nearly touching, and their eyes upon the hair.

'He's been mad after my lady Cytherea,' said Mrs Crickett, 'and 'tis my very belief the hair is—'

'No 'tidn'. Hers idn' so dark as that,' said Elizabeth.

'Elizabeth, you know that as the faithful wife of an officer of the Church I should be glad to think as you do about the girl. Mind I don't wish to say anything against Miss Graye, but this I do say, that I believe her to be a nameless thing,* and she's no right to stick a moral clock in her face, and deceive the country in such a way. If she wasn't of a bad stock at the outset she was bad in the planten, and if she wasn't bad in the planten, she was in the growen, and if not in the growen, she's made bad by what she's gone through since.'

'But I have another reason for knowing it idn' hers,' said Mrs Leat.

'Ah! I know whose it is then – Miss Aldclyffe's, upon my song!'

''Tis the colour of hers, but I don't believe it to be hers either.'

'Don't you believe what they say about her and him?'

'I say nothing about that; but you don't know what I know about his letters.'

'What about 'em?'

'He posts all his letters here except those for one person, and they he takes to Budmouth. My son is in Budmouth Post Office, as you know, and as he sits at desk he can see over the blind of the window all the people who post letters. Mr Manston unvariably goes there wi' letters for that person; my boy knows 'em by sight well enough now.'

'Is it a she?'

''Tis a she.'

'What's her name?'

'The little stunpoll of a fellow couldn't call to mind more than that 'tis Miss Somebody, of London. However, that's the woman who's been here, depend upon't – a wicked one – some poor street-wench escaped from Sodom, I warrant 'ee.'

'Only to find herself in Gomorrah, seemingly.'

'That may be.'

'No, no, Mrs Leat, this is clear to me. 'Tis no miss who came here to see our steward last night – whenever she came or wherever she vanished. Do you think he would ha' let a miss get here how she could, go away how she would, without breakfast or help of any kind?'

Elizabeth shook her head – Mrs Crickett looked at her solemnly.

'I say I know she had no help of any kind; I know it was so, for the grate was quite cold when I touched it this morning with these fingers, and he was still in bed. No, he wouldn't take the trouble to write letters to a girl and then treat her so off-hand as that. There's a tie between 'em stronger than feeling. She's his wife.'

'He married! The Lord so's, what shall we hear next? Do he look married now? His are not the abashed eyes and lips of a married man.'

'Perhaps she's a tame one – but she's his wife still.'

'No, no: he's not a married man.'

'Yes, yes, he is. I've had three, and I ought to know.'

'Well, well,' said Mrs Leat, giving way. 'Whatever may be the truth on't I trust the Lord will settle it all for the best, as He always do.'

'Ay, ay, Elizabeth,' rejoined Mrs Crickett with a satirical sigh, as she turned on her foot to go home, 'good people like you may say so, but I have always found the Lord a different sort of feller.'

127

5. November the Twentieth

It was Miss Aldclyffe's custom, a custom originated by her father, and nourished by her own exclusiveness, to unlock the post-bag herself every morning, instead of allowing the duty to devolve on the butler, as was the case in most of the neighbouring county families. The bag was brought upstairs each morning to her dressing-room, where she took out the contents, mostly in the presence of her maid and Cytherea, who had the entrée of the chamber at all hours, and attended there in the morning at a kind of reception on a small scale, which was held by Miss Aldclyffe of her namesake only.

Here she read her letters before the glass, whilst undergoing the operation of being brushed and dressed.

'What woman can this be, I wonder?' she said on the morning succeeding that of the last section. '"London, N."! It is the first time in my life I ever had a letter from that outlandish place, the North side of London.'

Cytherea had just come into her presence to learn if there was anything for herself; and on being thus addressed, walked up to Miss Aldclyffe's corner of the room to look at the curiosity which had raised such an exclamation. But the lady, having opened the envelope and read a few lines, put it quickly in her pocket, before Cytherea could reach her side.

'O, 'tis nothing,' she said. She proceeded to make general remarks in a noticeably forced tone of *sang-froid*,* from which she soon lapsed into silence. Not another word was said about the letter: she seemed very anxious to get her dressing done, and the room cleared. Thereupon Cytherea went away to the other window, and a few minutes later left the room to follow her own pursuits.

It was late when Miss Aldclyffe descended to the breakfast-table, and then she seemed there to no purpose; tea, coffee, eggs, cutlets, and all their accessories, were left absolutely untasted. The next that was seen of her was when walking up and down the south terrace, and round the flower-beds; her face was pale, and her tread was fitful, and she crumpled a letter in her hand.

Dinner-time came round as usual; she did not speak ten words, or indeed seem conscious of the meal; for all that Miss Aldclyffe did in the way of eating, dinner might have been taken out as intact as it was taken in.

In her own private apartment Miss Aldclyffe again pulled out the letter of the morning. One passage in it ran thus: –

Of course, being his wife, I could publish the fact, and compel him to acknowledge me at any moment, notwithstanding his threats, and reasonings that it will be better to wait. I have waited, and waited again, and the time for such acknowledgment seems no nearer than at first. To show you how patiently I have waited I can tell you that not till a fortnight ago, when by stress of circumstances I had been driven to new lodgings, have I ever assumed my married name, solely on account of its having been his request all along that I should not do it. This writing to you, madam, is my first disobedience, and I am justified in it. A woman who is driven to visit her husband like a thief in the night and then sent away like a street dog – left to get up, unbolt, unbar, and find her way out of the house as she best may – is justified in doing anything.

But should I demand of him a restitution of rights, there would be involved a publicity which I could not endure, and a noisy scandal flinging my name the length and breadth of the country.

What I still prefer to any such violent means is that you reason with him privately, and compel him to bring me home to your parish in a decent and careful manner, in the way that would be adopted by any respectable man, whose wife had been living away from him for some time, by reason, say, of peculiar family circumstances which had caused disunion, but not enmity, and who at length was enabled to reinstate her in his house.

You will, I know, oblige me in this, especially as knowledge of a peculiar transaction of your own, which took place some years ago, has lately come to me in a singular way. I will not at present trouble you by describing how. It is enough, that I alone, of all people living, know *all the sides of the story*, those from whom I collected it having each only a partial knowledge which confuses them and points to nothing. One person knows of your early engagement and its sudden termination; another, of the reason of those strange meetings at inns and coffee-houses; another, of what was sufficient to cause all this, and so on. I know what fits one and all the circumstances like a key, and shows them to be the natural outcrop of a rational (though rather rash) line of conduct for a young lady. You will at once perceive how it was that some at least of these things were revealed to me.

This knowledge then, common to, and secretly treasured by us both, is the ground upon which I beg for your friendship and help, with a feeling that you will be too generous to refuse it to me.

I may add that, as yet, my husband knows nothing of this, neither need he if you remember my request.

'A threat – a flat stinging threat! as delicately wrapped up in words as the woman could do it; a threat from a miserable unknown creature to an Aldclyffe, and not the least proud member of the family either! A threat on his account – O, O! shall it be?'

Presently this humour of defiance vanished, and the members of her body became supple again, her proceedings proving that it was absolutely necessary to give way, Aldclyffe as she was. She wrote a short answer to Mrs Manston, saying civilly that Mr Manston's possession of such a near relation was a fact quite new to herself, and that she would see what could be done in such an unfortunate affair.

6. *November the Twenty-First*

Manston received a message the next day requesting his attendance at the House punctually at eight o'clock the ensuing evening. Miss Aldclyffe was brave and imperious, but with the purpose she had in view she could not look him in the face whilst daylight shone upon her.

The steward was shown into the library. On entering it, he was immediately struck with the unusual gloom which pervaded the apartment. The fire was dead and dull, one lamp, and that a comparatively small one, was burning at the extreme end, leaving the main proportion of the lofty and sombre room in an artificial twilight, scarcely powerful enough to render visible the titles of the folio and quarto volumes which were jammed into the lower tiers of the bookshelves.

After keeping him waiting for more than twenty minutes (Miss Aldclyffe knew that excellent recipe for taking the stiffness out of human flesh, and for extracting all pre-arrangement from human speech) she entered the room.

Manston sought her eye directly. The hue of her features was not discernible, but the calm glance she flung at him, from which all attempt at returning his scrutiny was absent, awoke him to the perception that probably his secret was by some means or other known to her; how it had become known he could not tell.

She drew forth the letter, unfolded it, and held it up to him, letting it hang by one corner from between her finger and thumb, so that the light from the lamp, though remote, fell directly upon its surface.

'You know whose writing this is?' she said.

He saw the strokes plainly, instantly resolving to burn his ships and hazard all on an advance.

'My wife's,' he said calmly.

His quiet answer threw her off her balance. She had no more expected an answer than does a preacher when he exclaims from the pulpit, 'Do you feel your sin?' She had clearly expected a sudden alarm.

'And why all this concealment?' she said again, her voice rising, as she vainly endeavoured to control her feelings whatever they were.

'It doesn't follow that, because a man is married, he must tell every stranger of it, madam,' he answered, just as calmly as before.

'Stranger! well, perhaps not; but Mr Manston, why did you choose to conceal it, I ask again? I have a perfect right to ask this question, as you will perceive, if you consider the terms of my advertisement.'

'I will tell you. There were two simple reasons. The first was this practical one; you advertised for an unmarried man, if you remember?'

'Of course I remember.'

'Well, an incident suggested to me that I should try for the situation. I was married; but, knowing that in getting an office where there is a restriction of this kind, leaving one's wife behind is always accepted as a fulfilment of the condition, I left her behind for awhile. The other reason is, that these terms of yours afforded me a plausible excuse for escaping (for a short time) the company of a woman I had been mistaken in marrying.'

'Mistaken! what was she?' the lady inquired.

'A third-rate actress, whom I met with during my stay in Liverpool last summer, where I had gone to fulfil a short engagement with an architect.'

'Where did she come from?'

'She is an American by birth, and I grew to dislike her when we had been married a week.'

'She was ugly, I imagine?'

'She is not an ugly woman by any means.'

'Up to the ordinary standard?'

'Quite up to the ordinary standard – indeed, handsome. After a while we quarrelled and separated.'

'You did not ill-use her, of course?' said Miss Aldclyffe, with a little sarcasm.

'I did not.'

'But at any rate, you got thoroughly tired of her.'

Manston looked as if he began to think her questions out of place; however, he said quietly, 'I did get tired of her. I never told her so, but we separated; I to come here, bringing her with me as far as London and leaving her there in perfectly comfortable quarters; and though your advertisement expressed a single man, I have always intended to tell you the whole truth; and this was when I was going to tell it, when your satisfaction with my careful management of your affairs should have proved the risk to be a safe one to run.'

She bowed.

'Then I saw that you were good enough to be interested in my welfare to a greater extent than I could have anticipated or hoped, judging you by the frigidity of other employers, and this caused me to hesitate. I was vexed at the complication of affairs. So matters stood till three nights ago; I was then walking home from the pottery, and came up to the railway. The down-train came along close to me, and there, sitting at a carriage window, I saw my wife: she had found out my address, and had thereupon determined to follow me here. I had not been home many minutes before she came in. Next morning early she left again—'

'Because you treated her so cavalierly?'

'And as I suppose, wrote to you directly. That's the whole story of her, madam.' Whatever were Manston's real feelings towards the lady who had received his explanation in these supercilious tones, they remained locked within him as within a casket of steel.

'Did your friends know of your marriage, Mr Manston?' she continued.

'Nobody at all; we kept it a secret for various reasons.'

'It is true then that, as your wife tells me in this letter, she has not passed as Mrs Manston till within these last few days?'

'It is quite true; I was in receipt of a very small and uncertain income when we married; and so she continued playing at the theatre as before our marriage, and in her maiden name.'

'Has she any friends?'

'I have never heard that she has any in England. She came over here on some theatrical speculation, as one of a company who were going to do much, but who never did anything; and here she has remained.'

A pause ensued, which was terminated by Miss Aldclyffe.

'I understand,' she said. 'Now, though I have no direct right to concern myself with your private affairs (beyond those which arise from your misleading me and getting the office you hold)—'

'As to that, madam,' he interrupted, rather hotly, 'as to coming here I am vexed as much as you. Somebody, a member of the Institute of Architects – who, I could never tell – sent to my old address in London your advertisement cut from the paper; it was forwarded to me; I wanted to get away from Liverpool, and it seemed as if this was put in my way on purpose, by some old friend or other. I answered the advertisement certainly, but I was not particularly anxious to come here, nor am I anxious to stay.'

Miss Aldclyffe descended from haughty superiority to womanly persuasion with a haste which was almost ludicrous. Indeed, the *Quos ego*⋆ of the whole lecture had been less the genuine menace of the imperious ruler of Knapwater than an artificial utterance to hide a failing heart.

132

'Now, now, Mr Manston, you wrong me; don't suppose I wish to be overbearing, or anything of the kind; and you will allow me to say this much, at any rate, that I have become interested in your wife, as well as in yourself.'

'Certainly, madam,' he said, slowly, like a man feeling his way in the dark. Manston was utterly at fault now. His previous experience of the effect of his form and features upon womankind *en masse*, had taught him to flatter himself that he could account by the same law of natural selection* for the extraordinary interest Miss Aldclyffe had hitherto taken in him, as an unmarried man; an interest he did not at all object to, seeing that it kept him near Cytherea, and enabled him, a man of no wealth, to rule on the estate as if he were its lawful owner. Like Curius at his Sabine farm,* he had counted it his glory not to possess gold himself, but to have power over her who did. But at this hint of the lady's wish to take his wife under her wing also, he was perplexed: could she have any sinister motive in doing so? But he did not allow himself to be troubled with these doubts, which only concerned his wife's happiness.

'She tells me,' continued Miss Aldclyffe, 'how utterly alone in the world she stands, and that is an additional reason why I should sympathize with her. Instead, then, of requesting the favour of your retirement from the post, and dismissing your interests altogether, I will retain you as my steward still, on condition that you bring home your wife, and live with her respectably, in short, as if you loved her; you understand. I *wish* you to stay here if you grant that everything shall flow smoothly between yourself and her.'

The breast and shoulders of the steward rose, as if an expression of defiance was about to be poured forth; before it took form, he controlled himself and said, in his natural voice –

'My part of the performance shall be carried out, madam.'

'And her anxiety to obtain a standing in the world ensures that hers will,' replied Miss Aldclyffe. 'That will be satisfactory, then.'

After a few additional remarks, she gently signified that she wished to put an end to the interview. The steward took the hint and retired.

He felt vexed and mortified; yet in walking homeward he was convinced that telling the whole truth as he had done, with the single exception of his love for Cytherea (which he tried to hide even from himself), had never served him in better stead than it had done that night.

Manston went to his desk and thought of Cytherea's beauty with the bitterest, wildest regret. After the lapse of a few minutes he calmed himself by a stoical effort, and wrote the subjoined letter to his wife: –

KNAPWATER,
November 21, 1864

DEAR EUNICE, – I hope you reached London safely after your flighty visit to me.

As I promised, I have thought over our conversation that night, and your wish that your coming here should be no longer delayed. After all, it was perfectly natural that you should have spoken unkindly as you did, ignorant as you were of the circumstances which bound me.

So I have made arrangements to fetch you home at once. It is hardly worth while for you to attempt to bring with you any luggage you may have gathered about you (beyond mere clothing). Dispose of superfluous things at a broker's; your bringing them would only make a talk in this parish, and lead people to believe we had long been keeping house separately.

Will next Monday suit you for coming? You have nothing to do that can occupy you for more than a day or two, as far as I can see, and the remainder of this week will afford ample time. I can be in London the night before and we will come down together by the mid-day-train. – Your very affectionate husband,

ÆNEAS MANSTON

Now, of course, I shall no longer write to you as Mrs Rondley.

The address on the envelope was –

MRS MANSTON,
41 CHARLES SQUARE,
HOXTON,
LONDON, N.

He took the letter to the House, and it being too late for the country post, sent one of the stablemen with it to Casterbridge, instead of troubling to go to Budmouth with it himself as heretofore. He had no longer any necessity to keep his condition a secret.

7. *From the Twenty-Second to the Twenty-Seventh of November*

But the next morning Manston found that he had been forgetful of another matter, in naming the following Monday to his wife for the journey.

The fact was this. A letter had just come, reminding him that he had left the whole of the succeeding week open for an important business engagement with a neighbouring land-agent, at that gentleman's residence thirteen miles off. The particular day he had suggested to his wife, had, in the interim, been appropriated by his correspondent. The meeting could not now be put off.

So he wrote again to his wife, stating that business, which could not be postponed, called him away from home on Monday, and would entirely prevent him coming all the way on Sunday to fetch her as he had intended, but that he would meet her at the Carriford Road Station with a conveyance when she arrived there in the evening.

The next day came his wife's answer to his first letter, in which she said that she would be ready to be fetched at the time named. Having already written his second letter, which was by that time in her hands, he made no further reply.

The week passed away. The steward had, in the meantime, let it become generally known in the village that he was a married man, and by a little judicious management, sound family reasons for his past secrecy upon the subject, which were floated as adjuncts to the story, were placidly received; they seemed so natural and justifiable to the unsophisticated minds of nine-tenths of his neighbours, that curiosity in the matter, beyond a strong curiosity to see the lady's face, was well-nigh extinguished.

CHAPTER TEN

The Events of a Day and Night

1. November the Twenty-Eighth. Until Ten p.m.

Monday came, the day named for Mrs Manston's journey from London to her husband's house; a day of singular and great events, influencing the present and future of nearly all the personages whose actions in a complex drama form the subject of this record.

The proceedings of the steward demand the first notice. Whilst taking his breakfast on this particular morning, the clock pointing to eight, the horse-and-gig that was to take him to Chettlewood waiting ready at the door, Manston hurriedly cast his eyes down the column of *Bradshaw** which showed the details and duration of the selected train's journey.

The inspection was carelessly made, the leaf being kept open by the aid of one hand, whilst the other still held his cup of coffee; much more carelessly than would have been the case had the expected newcomer been Cytherea Graye, instead of his lawful wife.

He did not perceive, branching from the column down which his finger ran, a small twist,* called a shunting-line, inserted at a particular place, to imply that at that point the train was divided into two. By this oversight he understood that the arrival of his wife at Carriford Road Station would not be till late in the evening: by the second half of the train, containing the third-class passengers, and passing two hours and three-quarters later than the previous one, by which the lady, as a second-class passenger, would really be brought.

He then considered that there would be plenty of time for him to return from his day's engagement to meet this train. He finished his breakfast, gave proper and precise directions to his servant on the preparations that were to be made for his wife's reception, jumped into his gig, and drove off to Lord Claydonfield's, at Chettlewood.

He went along by the front of Knapwater House. He could not help turning to look at what he knew to be the window of Cytherea's room. Whilst he looked, a hopeless expression of passionate love and sensuous anguish came upon his face and lingered there for a few seconds; then, as on previous occasions, it was resolutely repressed, and he trotted along the smooth white road, again endeavouring to banish all thought of the young girl whose beauty and grace had so enslaved him.

Thus it was that when, in the evening of the same day, Mrs Manston reached Carriford Road Station, her husband was still at Chettlewood, ignorant of her arrival, and on looking up and down the platform, dreary with autumn gloom and wind, she could see no sign that any preparation whatever had been made for her reception and conduct home.

The train went on. She waited, fidgeted with the handle of her umbrella, walked about, strained her eyes into the gloom of the chilly night, listened for wheels, tapped with her foot, and showed all the usual signs of annoyance and irritation: she was the more irritated in that this seemed a second and culminating instance of her husband's neglect – the first having been shown in his not fetching her.

Reflecting awhile upon the course it would be best to take, in order to secure a passage to Knapwater, she decided to leave all her luggage, except a dressing-bag, in the cloak-room, and walk to her husband's house, as she had done on her first visit. She asked one of the porters if he could find a lad to go with her and carry her bag: he offered to do it himself.

The porter was a good-tempered, shallow-minded, ignorant man. Mrs Manston, being apparently in very gloomy spirits, would probably have preferred walking beside him without saying a word: but her companion would not allow silence to continue between them for a longer period than two or three minutes together.

He had volunteered several remarks upon her arrival, chiefly to the effect that it was very unfortunate Mr Manston had not come to the station for her, when she suddenly asked him concerning the inhabitants of the parish.

He told her categorically the names of the chief – first the chief possessors of property; then of brains; then of good looks. As first among the latter he mentioned Miss Cytherea Graye.

After getting him to describe her appearance as completely as lay in his power, she wormed out of him the statement that everybody had been saying – before Mrs Manston's existence was heard of – how well the handsome Mr Manston and the beautiful Miss Graye were suited for each other as man and wife, and that Miss Aldclyffe was the only one in the parish who took no interest in bringing about the match.

'He rather liked her you think?'

The porter began to think he had been too explicit, and hastened to correct the error.

'O no, he don't care a bit about her, ma'am,' he said solemnly.

'Not more than he does about me?'

'Not a bit.'

'Then that must be little indeed,' Mrs Manston murmured. She stood still, as if reflecting upon the painful neglect her words had recalled to her mind; then, with a sudden impulse, turned round, and walked petulantly a few steps back again in the direction of the station.

The porter stood still and looked surprised.

'I'll go back again; yes, indeed, I'll go back again!' she said plaintively. Then she paused and looked anxiously up and down the deserted road.

'No, I mustn't go back now,' she continued, in a tone of resignation. Seeing that the porter was watching her, she turned about and came on as before, giving vent to a slight laugh.

It was a laugh full of character; the low forced laugh which seeks to hide the painful perception of a humiliating position under the mask of indifference.

Altogether her conduct had shown her to be what in fact she was, a weak, though a calculatiⁿg woman, one clever to conceive, weak to execute: one whose best-laid schemes were for ever liable to be frustrated by the ineradicable blight of vacillation at the critical hour of action.

'O, if I had only known that all this was going to happen!' she murmured again, as they paced along upon the rustling leaves.

'What did you say, ma'am?' said the porter.

'O, nothing particular; we are getting near the old manor-house by this time, I imagine?'

'Very near now, ma'am.'

They soon reached Manston's residence, round which the wind blew mournfully and chill.

Passing under the detached gateway, they entered the porch. The porter stepped forward, knocked heavily, and waited.

Nobody came.

Mrs Manston then advanced to the door and gave a different series of rappings – less forcible, but more sustained.

There was not a movement of any kind inside, not a ray of light visible; nothing but the echo of her own knocks through the passages, and the dry scratching of the withered leaves blown about her feet upon the floor of the porch.

The steward, of course, was not at home. Mrs Crickett, not expecting that anybody would arrive till the time of the later train, had set the place in order, laid the supper-table, and then locked the door, to go into the village and converse with her friends.

'Is there an inn in the village?' said Mrs Manston, after the fourth and loudest rapping upon the iron-studded old door had resulted only in the fourth and loudest echo from the passages inside.

'Yes, ma'am.'

'Who keeps it?'

'Farmer Springrove.'

'I will go there to-night,' she said decisively. 'It is too cold, and altogether too bad, for a woman to wait in the open road on anybody's account, gentle or simple.'

They went down the park and through the gate, into the village of Carriford. By the time they reached the Three Tranters it was verging upon ten o'clock. There, on the spot where two months earlier in the season the sunny and lively group of villagers making cider under the trees had greeted Cytherea's eyes, was nothing now intelligible but a vast cloak of darkness, from which came the low sough of the elms, and the occasional creak of the swinging sign.

They went to the door, Mrs Manston shivering; but less from the cold than from the dreariness of her emotions. Neglect is the coldest of winter winds.

It so happened that Edward Springrove was expected to arrive from London either on that evening or the next, and at the sound of voices his father came to the door fully expecting to see him. A picture of disappointment seldom witnessed in a man's face was visible in old Mr Springrove's, when he saw that the comer was a stranger.

Mrs Manston asked for a room, and one that had been prepared for Edward was immediately named as being ready for her, another being adaptable for Edward, should he come in.

Without taking any refreshment, or entering any room downstairs, or even lifting her veil, she walked straight along the passage and up to her apartment, the chambermaid preceding her.

'If Mr Manston comes to-night,' she said, sitting on the bed as she had come in, and addressing the woman, 'tell him Mrs Manston cannot see him.'

'Yes, ma'am.'

The woman left the room, and Mrs Manston locked the door. Before the servant had gone down more than two or three stairs Mrs Manston unfastened the door again, and held it ajar.

'Bring me some brandy,' she said.

The chambermaid went down to the bar and brought up the spirit in a tumbler. When she came into the room, Mrs Manston had not removed a single article of apparel, and was walking up and down, as if still quite undecided upon the course it was best to adopt.

Outside the door, when it was closed upon her, the maid paused to listen for an instant. She heard Mrs Manston talking to herself.

'This is welcome home!' she said.

2. From Ten to Half-Past Eleven p.m.

A strange concurrence of phenomena now confronts us.

During the autumn in which the past scenes were enacted, Mr Springrove had ploughed, harrowed, and cleaned a narrow and shaded piece of ground, lying at the back of his house, which for many years had been looked upon as irreclaimable waste.

The couch-grass* extracted from the soil had been left to wither in the sun; afterwards it was raked together, lighted in the customary way, and now lay smouldering in a large heap in the middle of the plot.

It had been kindled three days previous to Mrs Manston's arrival, and one or two villagers, of a more cautious and less sanguine temperament than Springrove, had suggested that the fire was almost too near the back of the house for its continuance to be unattended with risk; for though no danger could be apprehended whilst the air remained moderately still, a brisk breeze blowing towards the house might possibly carry a spark across.

'Ay, that's true enough,' said Springrove. 'I must look round before going to bed and see that everything's safe; but to tell the truth I am anxious to get the rubbish burnt up before the rain comes to wash it into ground again. As to carrying the couch into the further field to burn, and bringing the ashes back, why, 'tis more than the ashes would be worth.'

'Well, that's very true,' said the neighbours, and passed on.

Two or three times during the first evening after the heap was lit, he went to the back door to take a survey. Before bolting and barring up for the night, he made a final and more careful examination. The slowly-smoking pile showed not the slightest signs of activity. Springrove's perfectly sound conclusion was, that as long as the heap was not stirred, and the wind continued in the quarter it blew from then, the couch would not flame, and that there could be no shadow of danger to anything, even a combustible substance, though it were no more than a yard off.

The next morning the burning couch was discovered in precisely the same state as when he had gone to bed the preceding night. The heap smoked in the same manner the whole of that day: at bed-time the farmer looked towards it, but less carefully than on the first night.

The morning and the whole of the third day still saw the heap in its old smouldering condition; indeed, the smoke was less, and there seemed a probability that it might have to be rekindled on the morrow.

After admitting Mrs Manston to his house in the evening, and hearing her retire, Mr Springrove returned to the front door to listen for a sound of his son, and inquired concerning him of the railway-porter, who sat for a while in the kitchen. The porter had not noticed young Mr Springrove get out of the train, at which intelligence the old man concluded that he would probably not see his son till the next day, as Edward had hitherto made a point of coming by the train which had brought Mrs Manston.

Half-an-hour later the porter left the inn, Springrove at the same time going to the door to listen again for an instant; then he walked round and in at the back of the house.

The farmer glanced at the heap casually and indifferently in passing; two nights of safety seemed to ensure the third; and he was about to bolt and bar as usual, when the idea struck him that there was just a possibility of his son's return by the latest train, unlikely as it was that he would be so delayed. The old man thereupon left the door unfastened, looked to his usual matters indoors, and went to bed, it being then half-past ten o'clock.

Farmers and horticulturists well know that it is in the nature of a heap of couch-grass, when kindled in calm weather, to smoulder for many days, and even weeks, until the whole mass is reduced to a powdery charcoal ash, displaying the while scarcely a sign of combustion beyond the volcano-like smoke from its summit; but the continuance of this quiet process is throughout its length at the mercy of one particular whim of Nature: that is, a sudden breeze, by which the heap is liable to be fanned into a flame so brisk as to consume the whole in an hour or two.

Had the farmer narrowly watched the pile when he went to close the door, he would have seen, besides the familiar twine of smoke from its summit, a quivering of the air around the mass, showing that a considerable heat had arisen inside.

As the railway-porter turned the corner of the row of houses adjoining the Three Tranters, a brisk new wind greeted his face, and spread past him into the village. He walked along the high-road till he came to a gate, about three hundred yards from the inn. Over the gate could be discerned the situation of the building he had just quitted. He carelessly turned his head in passing, and saw behind him a clear red glow indicating the position of the couch-heap: a glow without a flame, increasing and diminishing in brightness as the breeze quickened or fell, like the coal of a newly-lighted cigar. If those cottages had been his, he thought, he should not care to have a fire so near them as that – and the wind rising. But the cottages not being his, he went on his way to the station, where he was about to resume duty for the night. The road was now quite deserted: till four o'clock the next morning, when the carters would go by to the stables, there was little probability of any human being passing the Three Tranters Inn.

By eleven, everybody in the house was asleep. It truly seemed as if the treacherous element knew there had arisen a grand opportunity for devastation.

At a quarter past eleven a slight stealthy crackle made itself heard amid the increasing moans of the night wind; the heap glowed brighter still, and burst into a flame; the flame sank, another breeze entered it, sustained it, and it grew to be first continuous and weak, then continuous and strong.

At twenty minutes past eleven a blast of wind carried an airy bit of ignited fern several yards forward, in a direction parallel to the houses and inn, and there deposited it on the ground.

Five minutes later another puff of wind carried a similar piece to a distance of five-and-twenty yards, where it also was dropped softly on the ground.

Still the wind did not blow in the direction of the houses, and even now to a casual observer they would have appeared safe. But Nature does few things directly. A minute later yet, an ignited fragment fell upon the straw covering of a long thatched heap or 'grave' of mangel-wurzel, lying in a direction at right angles to the house, and down toward the hedge. There the fragment faded to darkness.

A short time subsequent to this, after many intermediate deposits and seemingly baffled attempts, another fragment fell on the mangel-wurzel grave, and continued to glow; the glow was increased by the wind; the straw caught fire and burst into flame. It was inevitable that the flame should run along the ridge of the thatch towards a piggery at the end. Yet had the piggery been tiled, the time-honoured hostel would even now at this last moment have been safe; but it was constructed as piggeries are mostly constructed, of wood and thatch. The hurdles and straw roof of the frail erection became ignited in their turn, and abutting as the shed did on the back of the inn, flamed up to the eaves of the main roof in less than thirty seconds.

3. Half-Past Eleven to Twelve p.m.

A hazardous length of time elapsed before the inmates of the Three Tranters knew of their danger. When at length the discovery was made, the rush was a rush for bare life.

A man's voice calling, then screams, then loud stamping and shouts were heard.

Mr Springrove ran out first. Two minutes later appeared the ostler and chambermaid, who were man and wife. The inn, as has been stated, was a quaint old building, and as inflammable as a bee-hive; it overhung the base at the level of the first floor, and again overhung at the eaves, which were finished with heavy oak barge-boards;* every atom in its substance, every feature in its construction, favoured the fire.

The forked flames, lurid and smoky, became nearly lost to view, bursting forth again with a bound and loud crackle, increased tenfold in power and brightness. The crackling grew sharper. Long quivering shadows began to be flung from the stately trees at the end of the house; the square outline of the church tower, on the other side of the way, which had hitherto been a dark mass against a sky comparatively light, now began to appear as a light object against a sky of darkness; and even the narrow surface of the flag-staff at the top could be seen in its dark surrounding, brought out from its obscurity by the rays from the dancing light.

Shouts and other noises increased in loudness and frequency. The lapse of ten minutes brought most of the inhabitants of that end of the village into the street, followed in a short time by the rector, Mr Raunham.

Casting a hasty glance up and down, he beckoned to one or two of the men, and vanished again. In a short time wheels were heard, and Mr Raunham and the men reappeared with the garden engine,* the only one in the village, except that at Knapwater House. After some little trouble the hose was connected with a tank in the old stable-yard, and the puny instrument began to play.

Several seemed paralyzed at first, and stood transfixed, their rigid faces looking like red-hot iron in the glaring light. In the confusion a woman cried, 'Ring the bells backwards!'* and three or four of the old and superstitious entered the belfry and jangled them indescribably. Some were only half dressed, and, to add to the horror, among them was Clerk Crickett, running up and down with a face streaming with blood, ghastly and pitiful to see, his excitement being so great that he had not the slightest conception of how, when, or where he came by the wound.

The crowd was now busy at work, and tried to save a little of the furniture of the inn. The only room they could enter was the parlour, from which they managed to bring out the bureau, a few chairs, some old silver candlesticks, and half-a-dozen light articles; but these were all.

Fiery mats of thatch slid off the roof and fell into the road with a deadened thud, whilst white flakes of straw and wood-ash were flying in the wind like feathers. At the same time two of the cottages adjoining, upon which a little water had been brought to play from the rector's engine, were seen to be on fire. The attenuated spirit of water was as nothing upon the heated and dry surface of the thatched roof; the fire prevailed without a minute's hindrance, and dived through to the rafters.

Suddenly arose a cry, 'Where's Mr Springrove?'

He had vanished from the spot by the churchyard-wall, where he had been standing a few minutes earlier.

'I fancy he's gone inside,' said a voice.

'Madness and folly! what can he save?' said another. 'Good God, find him! Help here!'

A wild rush was made at the door, which had fallen to, and in defiance of the scorching flame that burst forth, three men forced themselves through it. Immediately inside the threshold they found the object of their search lying senseless on the floor of the passage.

To bring him out and lay him on a bank was the work of an instant; a basin of cold water was dashed in his face, and he began to recover consciousness, but very slowly. He had been saved by a miracle. No sooner were his preservers out of the building than the window-frames lit up as if by magic with deep and waving fringes of flames. Simultaneously, the joints of the boards forming the front door started into view as glowing bars of fire: a star of red light penetrated the centre, gradually increasing in size till the flames rushed forth.

Then the staircase fell.

'Everybody is out safe,' said a voice.

'Yes, thank God!' said three or four others.

'O, we forgot that a stranger came! I think she is safe.'

'I hope she is,' said the weak voice of some one coming up from behind. It was the chambermaid's.

Springrove at that moment aroused himself; he staggered to his feet, and threw his hands up wildly.

'Everybody, no! no! The lady who came by train, Mrs Manston! I tried to fetch her out, but I fell.'

An exclamation of horror burst from the crowd; it was caused partly by this disclosure of Springrove, more by the added perception which followed his words.

An average interval of about three minutes had elapsed between one intensely fierce gust of wind and the next, and now another poured over them; the roof swayed, and a moment afterwards fell in with a crash, pulling the gable after it, and thrusting outwards the front wall of wood-work, which fell into the road with a rumbling echo; a cloud of black dust, myriads of sparks, and a great outburst of flame followed the uproar of the fall.

'Who is she? what is she?' burst from every lip again and again, incoherently, and without leaving a sufficient pause for a reply, had a reply been volunteered.

The autumn wind, tameless, and swift, and proud,* still blew upon the dying old house, which was constructed so entirely of combustible materials that it burnt almost as fiercely as a corn-rick. The heat in the road increased, and now for an instant at the height of the conflagration all stood still, and gazed silently, awestruck and helpless, in the presence of so irresistible an enemy. Then, with minds full of the tragedy unfolded to them, they rushed forward again with the obtuse directness of waves, to their labour of saving goods from the houses adjoining, which it was evident were all doomed to destruction.

The minutes passed by. The Three Tranters Inn sank into a mere heap of red-hot charcoal: the fire pushed its way down the row as the church clock opposite slowly struck the hour of midnight, and the bewildered chimes,* scarcely heard amid the crackling of the flames, wandered through the wayward air of the Old Hundred-and-Thirteenth Psalm.*

4. Nine to Eleven p.m.

Manston mounted his gig and set out from Chettlewood that evening in no very enviable frame of mind. The thought of domestic life in Knapwater Old House, with the now eclipsed wife of the past, was more than disagreeable, was positively distasteful to him.

Yet he knew that the influential position, which, from whatever fortunate cause, he held on Miss Aldclyffe's manor, would never again fall to his lot on any other; and he tacitly assented to this dilemma, hoping that some consolation or other would soon suggest itself to him; married as he was, he was near Cytherea.

He occasionally looked at his watch as he drove along the lanes, timing the pace of his horse by the hour, that he might reach Carriford Road Station just soon enough to meet the last London train.

He soon began to notice in the sky a slight yellow halo, near the horizon. It rapidly increased; it changed colour, and grew redder; then the glare visibly brightened and dimmed at intervals, showing that its origin was affected by the strong wind prevailing.

Manston reined in his horse on the summit of a hill, and considered. 'It is a rick-yard on fire,' he thought; 'no house could produce such a raging flame so suddenly.'

He trotted on again, attempting to particularize the local features in the neighbourhood of the fire; but this it was too dark to do, and the excessive winding of the roads misled him as to its direction, not being an old inhabitant of the district, or a countryman used to forming such judgments; whilst the brilliancy of the light shortened its real remoteness to an apparent distance of not more than half: it seemed so near that he again stopped his horse, this time to listen; but he could hear no sound.

Entering now a narrow valley, the sides of which obscured the sky to an angle of perhaps thirty or forty degrees above the mathematical horizon,* he was obliged to suspend his judgment till he was in possession of further knowledge, having however assumed in the interim, that the fire was somewhere between Carriford Road Station and the village.

The self-same glare had just arrested the eyes of another man. He was that minute gliding along several miles to the east of the steward's position, but nearing the same point as that to which Manston tended. The younger Edward Springrove was returning from London to his father's house by the identical train which the steward was expecting to bring his wife, the truth being that Edward's lateness was owing to the simplest of all causes, his temporary want of money, which led him to make a slow journey for the sake of travelling at third-class fare.

Springrove had received Cytherea's bitter and admonitory letter, and he was clearly awakened to a perception of the false position in which he had placed himself, by keeping silence at Budmouth on his long engagement. An increasing reluctance to put an end to those few days of ecstasy with Cytherea had over-ruled his conscience, and tied his tongue till speaking was too late.

'Why did I do it? how could I dream of loving her?' he asked himself as he walked by day, as he tossed on his bed by night: 'miserable folly!'

An impressionable heart had for years – perhaps as many as six or seven years – been distracting him, by unconsciously setting itself to yearn for somebody wanting, he scarcely knew whom. Echoes of himself, though rarely, he now and then found. Sometimes they were men, sometimes women, his cousin Adelaide being one of these; for in spite of a fashion which pervades the whole community at the present day – the habit of exclaiming that woman is not undeveloped man, but diverse, the fact remains that, after all, women are Mankind, and that in many of the sentiments of life the difference of sex is but a difference of degree.

But the indefinable helpmate to the remoter sides of himself still continued invisible. He grew older, and concluded that the ideas, or rather emotions, which possessed him on the subject, were probably too unreal ever to be found embodied in the flesh of a woman. Thereupon, he developed a plan of satisfying his dreams by wandering away to the heroines of poetical imagination, and took no further thought on the earthly realisation of his formless desire, in more homely matters satisfying himself with his cousin.

Cytherea appeared in the sky: his heart started up and spoke:

> ''Tis She, and here
> Lo! I unclothe and clear
> My wishes' cloudy character.'*

Some women kindle emotion so rapidly in a man's heart that the judgment cannot keep pace with its rise, and finds, on comprehending the situation, that faithfulness to the old love is already treachery to the new. Such women are not necessarily the greatest of their sex, but there are very few of them. Cytherea was one.

On receiving the letter from her he had taken to thinking over these things, and had not answered it at all. But 'hungry generations' soon tread down the muser in a city.* At length he thought of the strong necessity of living. After a dreary search, the negligence of which was ultimately overcome by mere conscientiousness, he obtained a situation as assistant to an architect in the neighbourhood of Charing Cross: the duties would not begin till after the lapse of a month.

He could not at first decide whither he should go to spend the intervening time; but in the midst of his reasonings he found himself on the road homeward, impelled by a secret and unowned hope of getting a last glimpse of Cytherea there.

5. Midnight

It was a quarter to twelve when Manston drove into the station-yard. The train was punctual, and the bell announcing its arrival rang as he crossed the booking-office to go out upon the platform.

The porter who had accompanied Mrs Manston to Carriford, and had returned to the station on his night duty, recognized the steward as he entered, and immediately came towards him.

'Mrs Manston came by the nine o'clock train, sir,' he said.

The steward gave vent to an expression of vexation.

'Her luggage is here, sir,' the porter said.

'Put it up behind me in the gig if it is not too much,' said Manston.

'Directly this train is in and gone, sir.'

The man vanished and crossed the line to meet the entering train.

'Where is that fire?' Manston said to the booking-clerk.

Before the clerk could speak, another man ran in and answered the question without having heard it.

'Half Carriford is burnt down, or will be!' he exclaimed. 'You can't see the flames from this station on account of the trees, but step on the bridge – 'tis tremendous!'

He also crossed the line to assist at the entry of the train, which came in the next minute.

The steward stood in the office. One passenger alighted, gave up his ticket, and crossed the room in front of Manston: a young man with a black bag and umbrella in his hand. He passed out

147

of the door, down the steps, and struck out into the darkness.

'Who was that young man?' said Manston, when the porter had returned. The young man, by a kind of magnetism, had drawn the steward's thoughts after him.

'He's an architect.'

'My own old profession. I could have sworn it by the cut of him,' Manston murmured. 'What's his name?' he said again.

'Springrove – Farmer Springrove's son, Edward.'

'Farmer Springrove's son, Edward,' the steward repeated to himself, and considered a matter to which the words had painfully recalled his mind.

The matter was Miss Aldclyffe's mention of the young man as Cytherea's lover, which, indeed, had scarcely ever been absent from his thoughts.

'But for the existence of my wife that man might have been my rival,' he pondered, following the porter, who had now come back to him, into the luggage-room. And whilst the man was carrying out and putting in one box, which was sufficiently portable for the gig, Manston still thought, as his eyes watched the process –

'But for my wife, Springrove might have been my rival.'

He examined the lamps of his gig, carefully laid out the reins, mounted the seat and drove along the turnpike road towards Knapwater Park.

The exact locality of the fire was plain to him as he neared home. He soon could hear the shout of men, the flapping of the flames, the crackling of burning wood, and could smell the smoke from the conflagration.

Of a sudden, a few yards ahead, within the compass of the rays from the right-hand lamp, burst forward the figure of a man. Having been walking in darkness the newcomer raised his hands to his eyes, on approaching nearer, to screen them from the glare of the reflector.

Manston saw that he was one of the villagers: a small farmer originally, who had drunk himself down to a day-labourer and reputed poacher.

'Hoy!' cried Manston, aloud, that the man might step aside out of the way.

'Is that Mr Manston?' said the man.

'Yes.'

'Somebody ha' come to Carriford: and the rest of it may concern you, sir.'

'Well, well.'

'Did you expect Mrs Manston to-night, sir?'

'Yes, unfortunately she's come, I know, and asleep long before this time, I suppose.'

The labourer leant his elbow upon the shaft of the gig and turned his face, pale and sweating from his late work at the fire, up to Manston's.

'Yes, she did come,' he said. . . . 'I beg pardon, sir, but I should be glad of – of—'

'What?'

'Glad of a trifle for bringen ye the news.'

'Not a farthing! I didn't want your news, I knew she was come.'

'Won't you give me a shillen, sir?'

'Certainly not.'

'Then will you lend me a shillen, sir? I be tired out, and don't know what to do. If I don't pay you back some day I'll be d—d.'

'The devil is so cheated that perdition isn't worth a penny as a security.'

'Oh!'

'Let me go on,' said Manston.

'Thy wife is *dead*; that's the rest o' the news,' said the labourer slowly. He waited for a reply; none came.

'She went to the Three Tranters, because she couldn't get into thy house, the burnen roof fell in upon her before she could be called up, and she's a cinder, as thou'lt be some day.'

'That will do, let me drive on,' said the steward calmly.

Expectation of concussion may be so intense that its failure strikes the brain with more force that its fulfilment. The labourer sank back into the ditch. Such a Cushi could not realise the possibility of such an unmoved David* as this.

Manston drove hastily to the turning of the road, tied his horse, and ran on foot to the site of the fire.

The stagnation caused by the awful accident had been passed through, and all hands were helping to remove from the remaining cottages what furniture they could lay hold of; the thatch of the roofs being already on fire. The Knapwater fire-engine had arrived on the spot, but it was small, and ineffectual. A group was collected round the rector, who in a coat which had become bespattered, scorched, and torn in his exertions, was directing on one hand the proceedings relative to the removal of goods into the church, and with the other was pointing out the spot on which it was most desirable that the puny engines at their disposal should be made to play. Every tongue was instantly silent at the sight of Manston's pale and clear countenance, which contrasted strangely with the grimy and streaming faces of the toiling villagers.

'Was she burnt?' he said in a firm though husky voice, and stepping into the illuminated area. The rector came to him, and took him aside. 'Is she burnt?' repeated Manston.

'She is dead: but thank God, she was spared the horrid agony of burning,' the rector said solemnly; 'the roof and gable fell in upon her, and crushed her. Instant death must have followed.'

'Why was she here?' said Manston.

'From what we can hurriedly collect, it seems that she found the door of your house locked, and concluded that you had retired, the fact being that your servant, Mrs Crickett, had gone out to supper. She then came back to the inn and went to bed.'

'Where's the landlord?' said Manston.

Mr Springrove came up, walking feebly, and wrapped in a cloak, and corroborated the evidence given by the rector.

'Did she look ill, or annoyed, when she came?' said the steward.

'I can't say. I didn't see; but I think—'

'What do you think?'

'She was much put out about something.'

'My not meeting her, naturally,' murmured the other, lost in reverie. He turned his back on Springrove and the rector, and retired from the shining light.

Everything had been done that could be done with the limited means at their disposal. The whole row of houses was destroyed, and each presented itself as one stage of a series, progressing from smoking ruins at the end where the inn had stood, to a partly flaming mass – glowing as none but wood embers will glow – at the the other.

A feature in the decline of town fires was noticeably absent here – steam. There was present what is not observable in towns – incandescence.

The heat, and the smarting effect upon their eyes of the strong smoke from the burning oak and deal, had at last driven the villagers back from the road in front of the houses, and they now stood in groups in the churchyard, the surface of which, raised by the interments of generations, stood four or five feet above the level of the road, and almost even with the top of the low wall dividing one from the other. The headstones stood forth whitely against the dark grass and yews, their brightness being repeated on the white smock-frocks of some of the labourers, and in a mellower, ruddier form on their faces and hands, on those of the grinning gargoyles, and on other salient stonework of the weather-beaten church in the background.

The rector had decided that, in the distressing circumstances of the case, there would be no sacrilege in placing in the church,* for the night, the pieces of furniture and utensils which had been saved from the several houses. There was no other place of safety for them, and they accordingly were gathered there.

6. Half-Past Twelve to One a.m.

Manston, when he retired to meditate, had walked round the church-yard, and now entered the opened door of the building.

He mechanically pursued his way round the piers into his own seat in the north aisle. The lower atmosphere of this spot was shaded by its own wall from the shine which streamed in over the window-sills on the same side. The only light burning inside the church was a small tallow candle, standing in the font, in the opposite aisle of the building to that in which Manston had sat down, and near where the furniture was piled. The candle's mild rays were overpowered by the ruddier light from the ruins, making the weak flame to appear like the moon by day.

Sitting there he saw Farmer Springrove enter the door, followed by his son Edward, still carrying his travelling-bag in his hand. They were speaking of the sad death of Mrs Manston, but the subject was relinquished for that of the houses burnt.

This row of houses, running from the inn eastward, had been built under the following circumstances: —

Fifty years before this date, the spot upon which the cottages afterwards stood was a blank strip, along the side of the village street, difficult to cultivate, on account of the outcrop thereon of a large bed of flints called locally a 'lanch' or 'lanchet'.*

The Aldclyffe then in possession of the estate conceived the idea that a row of cottages would be an improvement to the spot, and accordingly granted leases of portions to several respectable inhabitants. Each lessee was to be subject to the payment of a merely nominal rent for the whole term of lives,* on condition that he built his own cottage, and delivered it up intact at the end of the term.

Those who had built had, one by one, relinquished their indentures, either by sale or barter, to Farmer Springrove's father. New lives were added in some cases, by payment of a sum to the lord of the manor, &c., and all the leases were now held by the farmer himself, as one of the chief provisions for his old age.

The steward had become interested in the following conversation: —

'Try not to be so depressed, father; they are all insured.'

The words came from Edward in an anxious tone.

'You mistake, Edward; they are not insured,' returned the old man gloomily.

'Not?' the son asked.

'Not one!' said the farmer.

'In the Helmet Fire Office, surely?'

'They were insured there every one. Six months ago the office, which had been raising the premiums on thatched premises higher for some years, gave up insuring them altogether, as two or three other fire-offices had done previously, on account, they said, of the uncertainty and greatness of the risk of thatch undetached. Ever since then I have been continually intending to go to another office, but have never gone. Who expects a fire?'

'Do you remember the terms of the leases?' said Edward, still more uneasily.

'No, not particularly,' said his father absently.

'Where are they?'

'In the bureau there; that's why I tried to save it first, among other things.'

'Well, we must see to that at once.'

'What do you want?'

'The key.'

They went into the south aisle, took the candle from the font, and then proceeded to open the bureau, which had been placed in a corner under the gallery. Both leant over upon the flap; Edward holding the candle, whilst his father took the pieces of parchment from one of the drawers, and spread the first out before him.

'You read it, Ted. I can't see without my glasses. This one will be sufficient. The terms of all are the same.'

Edward took the parchment, and read quickly and indistinctly for some time; then aloud and slowly as follows: –

And *the said John Springrove for himself his heirs executors and administrators doth covenant and agree with the said Gerald Fellcourt Aldclyffe his heirs and assigns that he the said John Springrove his heirs and assigns during the said term shall pay unto the said Gerald Fellcourt Aldclyffe his heirs and assigns the clear yearly rent of ten shillings and sixpence . . . at the several times hereinbefore appointed for the payment thereof respectively.* And also *shall and at all times during the said term well and sufficiently repair and keep the said Cottage or Dwelling-house and all other the premises*

and all houses or buildings erected or to be erected thereupon in good and
proper repair in every respect without exception and the said premises in such
good repair upon the determination of this demise shall yield up unto the*
said Gerald Fellcourt Aldclyffe his heirs and assigns.

They closed the bureau and turned towards the door of the church
without speaking.

Manston also had come forward out of the gloom. Notwithstanding
the farmer's own troubles, an instinctive respect and generous sense of
sympathy with the steward for his awful loss caused the old man to step
aside, that Manston might pass out without speaking to them if he
chose to do so.

'Who is he?' whispered Edward to his father, as Manston
approached.

'Mr Manston, the steward.'

Manston came near, and passed down the aisle on the side of the
younger man. Their faces came almost close together: one large flame,
which still lingered upon the ruins outside, threw long dancing
shadows of each across the nave till they bent upwards against the aisle
wall, and also illuminated their eyes, as each met those of the other.
Edward had learnt, by a letter from home, of the steward's passion for
Cytherea, and his mysterious repression of it, afterwards explained by
his marriage. That marriage was now nought. Edward realized the
man's newly acquired freedom, and felt an instinctive enmity towards
him – he would hardly own to himself why. The steward, too, knew of
Cytherea's attachment to Edward, and looked keenly and inscrutably
at him.

7. One to Two a.m.

Manston went homeward alone, his heart full of strange emotions.
Entering the house, and dismissing the woman to her own home, he at
once proceeded upstairs to his bedroom.

Reasoning worldliness, especially when allied with sensuousness,
cannot repress on some extreme occasions the human instinct to pour
out the soul to some Being or Personality, who in frigid moments is
dismissed with the title of Chance, or at most Law. Manston was
selfishly and inhumanly, but honestly and unutterably, thankful for
the recent catastrophe. Beside his bed, for that first time during a
period of nearly twenty years, he fell down upon his knees in a
passionate outburst of feeling.

Many minutes passed before he arose. He walked to the window, and then seemed to remember for the first time that some action on his part was necessary in connection with the sad circumstance of the night.

Leaving the house at once, he went to the scene of the fire, arriving there in time to hear the rector making an arrangement with a certain number of men to watch the spot till morning. The ashes were still red-hot and flaming. Manston found that nothing could be done towards searching them at that hour of the night. He turned homeward again, in the company of the rector, who had considerately persuaded him to retire from the scene for a while, and promised that as soon as a man could live amid the embers of the Three Tranters Inn, they should be carefully searched for the remains of his unfortunate wife.

Manston then went indoors to wait for morning.

CHAPTER ELEVEN

The Events of Five Days

1. November the Twenty-Ninth

The search began at dawn, but a quarter past nine o'clock came without bringing any result. Manston ate a little breakfast, and crossed the hollow of the park which intervened between the old and modern manor-houses, to ask for an interview with Miss Aldclyffe.

He met her midway. She was about to pay him a visit of condolence, and to place every man on the estate at his disposal, that the search for any relic of his dead and destroyed wife might not be delayed an instant.

He accompanied her back to the house. At first they conversed as if the death of the poor woman was an event which the husband must of necessity deeply lament; and when all under this head that social form seemed to require had been uttered, they spoke of the material damage done, and of the steps which had better be taken to remedy it.

It was not until both were shut inside her private room that she spoke to him in her blunt and cynical manner. A certain newness of bearing in him, peculiar to the present morning, had hitherto forbidden her this tone; the demeanour of the subject of her favouritism had altered, she could not tell in what way. He was entirely a changed man.

'Are you really sorry for your poor wife, Mr Manston?' she said.

'Well, I am,' he answered shortly.

'But only as for any human being who has met with a violent death?'

He confessed it – 'For she was not a good woman,' he added.

'I should be sorry to say such a thing now the poor creature is dead,' Miss Aldclyffe returned reproachfully.

'Why?' he asked. 'Why should I praise her if she doesn't deserve it? I say exactly what I have often admired Sterne for saying in one of his letters – that neither reason nor Scripture asks us to speak nothing but good of the dead.* And now, madam,' he continued, after a short interval of thought, 'I may, perhaps, hope that you will assist me, or rather not thwart me, in endeavouring to win the love of a young lady living about you, one in whom I am much interested already.'

'Cytherea!'

'Yes, Cytherea.'

'You have been loving Cytherea all the while?'

'Yes.'

Surprise was a preface to much agitation in her, which caused her to rise from her seat, and pace to the side of the room. The steward quietly looked on and added, 'I have been loving and still love her.'

She came close up to him, wistfully contemplating his face, one hand moving indecisively at her side.

'And your secret marriage was, then, the true and only reason for that backwardness regarding the courtship of Cytherea, which, they tell me, has been the talk of the village; not your indifference to her attractions.' Her voice had a tone of conviction in it, as well as of inquiry; but none of jealousy.

'Yes,' he said; 'and not a dishonourable one. What held me back was just that one thing – a sense of morality that perhaps, madam, you did not give me credit for.' The latter words were spoken with a mien and tone of pride.

Miss Aldclyffe preserved silence.

'And now,' he went on, 'I may as well say a word in vindication of my conduct lately, at the risk, too, of offending you. My actual motive in submitting to your order that I should send for my late wife, and live with her, was not the mercenary policy of wishing to retain an office which brings me greater comforts than any I have enjoyed before, but this unquenchable passion for Cytherea. Though I saw the weakness, folly, and even wickedness of it continually, it still forced me to try to continue near her, even as the husband of another woman.'

He waited for her to speak: she did not.

'There's a great obstacle to my making any way in winning Miss Graye's love,' he went on.

'Yes, Edward Springrove,' she said quietly. 'I know it, I did once want to see them married; they have had a slight quarrel, and it will soon be made up again, unless –' she spoke as if she had only half attended to Manston's last statement.

'He is already engaged to be married to somebody else,' said the steward.

'Pooh!' said she, 'you mean to his cousin at Peakhill; that's nothing to help us; he's now come home to break it off.'

'He must not break it off,' said Manston, firmly and calmly.

His tone attracted her, startled her. Recovering herself, she said haughtily, 'Well, that's your affair, not mine. Though my wish has been to see her *your* wife, I can't do anything dishonourable to bring about such a result.'

'But it must be *made* your affair,' he said in a hard, steady voice, looking into her eyes, as if he saw there the whole panorama of her past.

One of the most difficult things to portray by written words is that peculiar mixture of moods expressed in a woman's countenance when, after having been sedulously engaged in establishing another person's position, she suddenly suspects him of undermining her own. It was thus that Miss Aldclyffe looked at the steward.

'You – know – something – of me?' she faltered.

'I know all,' he said.

'Then curse that wife of yours! She wrote and said she wouldn't tell you!' she burst out. 'Couldn't she keep her word for a day?' She reflected and then said, but no more as to a stranger, 'I will not yield. I have committed no crime. I yielded to her threats in a moment of weakness, though I felt inclined to defy her at the time: it was chiefly because I was mystified as to how she got to know of it. Pooh! I will put up with threats no more. O, can *you* threaten me?' she added softly, as if she had for the moment forgotten to whom she had been speaking.

'My love must be made your affair,' he repeated, without taking his eyes from her.

An agony, which was not the agony of being discovered in a secret, obstructed her utterance for a time. 'How can you turn upon me so when I schemed to get you here – schemed that you might win her till I found you were married. O, how can you! O! . . . O!' She wept; and the weeping of such a nature was as harrowing as the weeping of a man.

'Your getting me here was bad policy as to your secret – the most absurd thing in the world,' he said, not heeding her distress. 'I knew all, except the identity of the individual, long ago. Directly I found that my coming here was a contrived thing, and not a matter of chance, it fixed my attention upon you at once. All that was required was the mere spark of life, to make of a bundle of perceptions an organic whole.'

'Policy! – how can you talk of policy? Think, do think! And how can you threaten me when you know – you know – that I would befriend you readily without a threat!'

'Yes, yes, I think you would,' he said more kindly; 'but your indifference for so many, many years has made me doubt it.'

'No, not indifference – 'twas enforced silence: my father lived.'

He took her hand, and held it gently.

'Now listen,' he said, more quietly and humanly, when she had become calmer: 'Springrove must marry the woman he's engaged to. You may make him, but only in one way.'

'Well: but don't speak sternly, Æneas!'

'Do you know that his father has not been particularly thriving for the last two or three years?'

'I have heard something of it, once or twice, though his rents have been promptly paid, haven't they?'

'O yes; and do you know the terms of the leases of the houses which are burnt?' he said, explaining to her that by those terms she might compel him even to rebuild every house. 'The case is the clearest case of fire by negligence that I have ever known, in addition to that,' he continued.

'I don't want them rebuilt; you know it was intended by my father, directly they fell in, to clear the site for a new entrance to the park?'

'Yes, but that doesn't affect the position, which is that Farmer Springrove is in your power to an extent which is very serious for him.'

'I won't do it – 'tis a conspiracy.'

'Won't you for me?' he said eagerly.

Miss Aldclyffe changed colour.

'I don't threaten now, I implore,' he said.

'Because you might threaten if you chose,' she mournfully answered. 'But why be so – when your marriage with her was my own pet idea long before it was yours? What must I do?'

'Scarcely anything: simply this. When I have seen old Mr Springrove, which I shall do in a day or two, and told him that he will be expected to rebuild the houses, do you see the young man. See him yourself, in order that the proposals made may not appear to be anything more than an impulse of your own. You or he will bring up the subject of the houses. To rebuild them would be a matter of at least six hundred pounds, and he will almost surely say that we are hard in insisting upon the extreme letter of the leases. Then tell him that scarcely can you yourself think of compelling an old tenant like his father to any such painful extreme – there shall be no compulsion to build, simply a surrender of the leases. Then speak feelingly of his cousin, as a woman whom you respect and love, and whose secret you have learnt to be that she is heart-sick with hope deferred. Beg him to marry her, his betrothed and your friend, as some return for your consideration towards his father. Don't suggest too early a day for their marriage, or he will suspect you of some motive beyond womanly sympathy. Coax him to make a promise to her that she shall be his wife at the end of a twelve-month, and get him on assenting to this, to write to Cytherea, entirely renouncing her.'

'She has already asked him to do that.'

'So much the better – and telling her, too, that he is about to fulfil his long-standing promise to marry his cousin. If you think it worth while, you may say Cytherea was not indisposed to think of me before she knew I was married. I have at home a note she wrote me the first evening I saw her, which looks rather warm, and which I could show you. Trust me, he will give her up. When he is married to Adelaide Hinton, Cytherea will be induced to marry me – perhaps before; a woman's pride is soon wounded.'

'And hadn't I better write to Mr Nyttleton, and inquire more particularly what's the law upon the houses?'

'O no, there's no hurry for that. We know well enough how the case stands – quite well enough to talk in general terms about it. And I want the pressure to be put upon young Springrove before he goes away from home again.'

She looked at him furtively, long, and sadly, as after speaking he became lost in thought, his eyes listlessly tracing the pattern of the carpet. 'Yes,yes, she will be mine,' he whispered, careless of Cytherea Aldclyffe's presence. At last he raised his eyes inquiringly.

'I will do my best, Æneas,' she answered.

*Talibus incusat.** Manston then left the house, and again went towards the blackened ruins, where men were still raking and probing.

2. From November the Twenty-Ninth to December the Second

The smouldering remnants of the Three Tranters Inn seemed to promise that, even when the searchers should light upon the remains of the unfortunate Mrs Manston, very little would be discoverable.

Consisting so largely of the charcoal and ashes of hard dry oak and chestnut, intermingled with thatch, the interior of the heap was one glowing mass of embers, which on being stirred about, emitted sparks and flame long after it was dead and black on the outside. It was persistently hoped, however, that some traces of the body would survive the effect of the hot coals, and after a search pursued uninterruptedly for thirty hours, under the direction of Manston himself, enough was found to set at rest any doubts of her fate.

The melancholy gleanings consisted of her watch, bunch of keys, a few coins, and two charred and blackened bones.

Two days later the official inquiry into the cause of her death was held at the Rising Sun Inn, before Mr Floy, the coroner, and a jury of the chief inhabitants of the district. The little tavern – the only remaining one in the village – was crowded to excess by the neighbouring peasantry as well as their richer employers: all who could by any possibility obtain an hour's release from their duties being present as listeners.

The jury viewed the sad and infinitesimal remains, which were folded in a white cambric cloth, and laid in the middle of a well-finished coffin lined with white silk (by Manston's order), which stood in an adjoining room, the bulk of the coffin being completely filled in with carefully arranged flowers and evergreens – also the steward's own doing.

Abraham Brown, of Hoxton, London – an old white-headed man, without the ruddiness which makes white hairs so pleasing – was sworn, and deposed that he kept a lodging-house at an address he named. On a Saturday evening less than a month before the fire, a lady came to him, with very little luggage, and took the front room on the second floor. He did not inquire where she came from, as she paid a week in advance, but she gave her name as Mrs Manston, referring him, if he wished for any guarantee of her respectability, to Mr Manston, Knapwater Park. Here she lived for three weeks, rarely going out. She slept away from her lodgings one night during the time. At the end of that time, on the twenty-eighth of November, she left his house in a four-wheeled cab, about twelve o'clock in the day, telling the driver to take her to the Waterloo Station. She paid all her lodging expenses, and not having given notice the full week previous to her going away, offered to pay for the next, but he only took half. She wore a thick black veil, and grey waterproof cloak, when she left him, and her luggage was two boxes, one of plain deal, with black japanned* clamps, the other sewn up in canvas.

Joseph Chinney, porter at the Carriford Road Station, deposed that he saw Mrs Manston, dressed as the last witness had described, get out of a second-class carriage on the night of the twenty-eighth. She stood beside him whilst her luggage was taken from the van. The luggage, consisting of the clamped deal box and another covered with canvas, was placed in the cloakroom. She seemed at a loss at finding nobody there to meet her. She asked him for some person to accompany her, and carry her bag to Mr Manston's house, Knapwater Park. He was just off duty at that time, and offered to go himself. The witness here repeated the conversation he had had with Mrs Manston during their walk, and testified to having left her at the door of the Three Tranters Inn, Mr Manston's house being closed.

Next, Farmer Springrove was called. A murmur of surprise and commiseration passed round the crowded room when he stepped forward.

The events of the few preceding days had so worked upon his nervously thoughtful nature that the blue orbits of his eyes, and the mere spot of scarlet to which the ruddiness of his cheeks had contracted, seemed the result of a heavy sickness. A perfect silence pervaded the assembly when he spoke.

His statement was that he received Mrs Manston at the threshold, and asked her to enter the parlour. She would not do so, and stood in the passage whilst the maid went upstairs to see that the room was in order. The maid came down to the middle landing of the staircase, when Mrs Manston followed her up to the room. He did not speak ten words with her altogether.

Afterwards, whilst he was standing at the door listening for his son Edward's return, he saw her light extinguished, having first caught sight of her shadow moving about the room.

The Coroner: 'Did her shadow appear to be that of a woman undressing?'

Springrove: 'I cannot say, as I didn't take particular notice. It moved backwards and forwards; she might have been undressing or merely pacing up and down the room.'

Mrs Fitler, the ostler's wife, and chambermaid, said that she preceded Mrs Manston into the room, put down the candle, and went out. Mrs Manston scarcely spoke to her, except to ask her to bring a large brandy. Witness went and fetched it from the bar, brought it up, and put it on the dressing-table.

The Coroner: 'Had Mrs Manston begun to undress when you came back?'

'No, sir; she was sitting on the bed, with everything on, as when she came in.'

'Did she begin to undress before you left?'

'Not exactly before I had left; but when I had closed the door, and was on the landing, I heard her boot drop on the floor, as it does sometimes when pulled off.'

'Had her face appeared worn and sleepy?'

'I cannot say, as her bonnet and veil were still on when I left, for she seemed rather shy and ashamed to be seen at the Three Tranters at all.'

'And did you hear or see any more of her?'

'No more, sir.'

Mrs Crickett, temporary servant to Mr Manston, said that in accordance with Mr Manston's orders, everything had been made comfortable in the house for Mrs Manston's expected return on Monday night. Mr Manston told her that himself and Mrs Manston would be home late, not till between eleven and twelve o'clock, and that supper was to be ready. Not expecting Mrs Manston so early, she had gone out on a very important errand to Mrs Leat the postmistress.

Mr Manston deposed that in looking down the columns of *Bradshaw* he had mistaken the time of the train's arrival, and hence was not at the station when she came. The broken watch produced was his wife's – he knew it by a scratch on the inner plate, and by other signs. The bunch of keys belonged to her: two of them fitted the locks of her two boxes.

Mr Flooks, agent to Lord Claydonfield at Chettlewood, said that Mr Manston had pleaded as his excuse for leaving him rather early in the evening after their day's business had been settled, that he was going to meet his wife at Carriford Road Station, where she was coming by the last train that night.

The surgeon said that the remains were those of a human being. The small fragment seemed a portion of one of the lumbar vertebræ – the other the head of the os femoris* – but they were both so far gone that it was impossible to say definitely whether they belonged to the body of a male or female. There was no moral doubt that they were a woman's. He did not believe that death resulted from burning by fire. He thought she was crushed by the fall of the west gable, which being of wood, as well as the floor, burnt after it had fallen, and consumed the body with it.

Two or three additional witnesses gave unimportant testimony.

The coroner summed up, and the jury without hesitation found that the deceased Mrs Manston came by her death accidentally through the burning of the Three Tranters Inn.

When Mr Springrove came from the door of the Rising Sun at the end of the inquiry, Manston walked by his side as far as the stile to the park, a distance of about a stone's-throw.

'Ah, Mr Springrove, this is a sad affair for everybody concerned.'

'Everybody,' said the old farmer, with deep sadness, ''tis quite a misery to me. I hardly know how I shall live through each day as it breaks. I think of the words, "In the morning thou shalt say, Would God it were even! and at even thou shalt say, Would God it were morning! for the fear of thine heart wherewith thou shalt fear, and for the sight of thine eyes which thou shalt see."'* His voice became broken.

'Ah – true. I read Deuteronomy myself,' said Manston.

'But my loss is as nothing to yours,' the farmer continued.

'Nothing; but I can commiserate you. I should be worse than unfeeling if I didn't, although my own affliction is of so sad and solemn a kind. Indeed my own loss makes me more keenly alive to yours, different in nature as it is.'

'What sum do you think would be required of me to put the houses in place again?'

'I have roughly thought six or seven hundred pounds.'

'If the letter of the law is to be acted up to,' said the old man, with more agitation in his voice.

'Yes, exactly.'

'Do you know enough of Miss Aldclyffe's mind to give me an idea of how she means to treat me?'

'Well, I am afraid I must tell you that though I know very little of her mind as a rule, in this matter I believe she will be rather peremptory; she might share to the extent of a sixth or an eighth perhaps, in consideration of her getting new lamps for old, but I should hardly think more.'

The steward stepped upon the stile, and Mr Springrove went along the road with a bowed head and heavy footsteps towards his niece's cottage, in which, rather against the wish of Edward, they had temporarily taken refuge.

The additional weight of this knowledge soon made itself perceptible. Though indoors with Edward or Adelaide nearly the whole of the afternoon, nothing more than monosyllabic replies could be drawn from him. Edward continually discovered him looking fixedly at the wall or floor, quite unconscious of another's presence. At supper he ate just as usual, but quite mechanically, and with the same abstraction.

4. December the Third

The next morning he was in no better spirits. Afternoon came: his son was alarmed, and managed to draw from him an account of the conversation with the steward.

'Nonsense; he knows nothing about it,' said Edward vehemently. 'I'll see Miss Aldclyffe myself. Now promise me, father, that you'll not believe till I come back, and tell you to believe it, that Miss Aldclyffe will do any such unjust thing.'

Edward started at once for Knapwater House. He strode rapidly along the high-road, till he reached a wicket where a footpath allowed of a short cut to the mansion. Here he leant down upon the bars for a few minutes, meditating as to the best manner of opening his speech, and surveying the scene before him in that absent mood which takes cognizance of little things without being conscious of them at the time, though they appear in the eye afterwards as vivid impressions. It was a yellow, lustrous, late autumn day, one of those days of the quarter when morning and evening seem to meet together without the intervention of a noon. The clear yellow sunlight had tempted forth Miss Aldclyffe herself, who was at this same time taking a walk in the direction of the village. As Springrove lingered he heard behind the plantation a woman's dress brushing along amid the prickly husks and leaves which had fallen into the path from the boughs of the chestnut trees. In another minute she stood in front of him.

He answered her casual greeting respectfully, and was about to request a few minutes' conversation with her, when she directly addressed him on the subject of the fire. 'It is a sad misfortune for your father,' she said, 'and I hear that he has lately let his insurances expire?'

'He has, madam, and you are probably aware that either by the general terms of his holding, or the same coupled with the origin of the fire, the disaster may involve the necessity of his rebuilding the whole row of houses, or else of becoming a debtor to the estate, to the extent of some hundreds of pounds?'

She assented. 'I have been thinking of it,' she went on, and then repeated in substance the words put into her mouth by the steward. Some disturbance of thought might have been fancied as taking place in Springrove's mind during her statement, but before she had reached the end, his eyes were clear, and directed upon her.

'I don't accept your conditions of release,' he said.

'They are not conditions exactly.'

'Well, whatever they are not, they are very uncalled-for remarks.'

'Not at all – the houses have been burnt by your family's negligence.'

'I don't refer to the houses – you have of course the best of all rights to speak of that matter; but you, a stranger to me comparatively, have no right at all to volunteer opinions and wishes upon a very delicate subject, which concerns no living beings but Miss Graye, Miss Hinton, and myself.'

Miss Aldclyffe, like a good many others in her position, had plainly not realized that a son of her tenant and inferior could have become an educated man, who had learnt to feel his individuality, to view society from a Bohemian* standpoint, far outside the farming grade in Carriford parish, and that hence he had all a developed man's unorthodox opinion about the subordination of classes. And fully conscious of the labyrinth into which he had wandered between his wish to behave honourably in the dilemma of his engagement to his cousin Adelaide and the intensity of his love for Cytherea, Springrove was additionally sensitive to any allusion to the case. He had spoken to Miss Aldclyffe with considerable warmth.

And Miss Aldclyffe was not a woman likely to be far behind any second person in warming to a mood of defiance. It seemed as if she were prepared to put up with a cold refusal, but that her haughtiness resented a criticism of her conduct ending in a rebuke. By this, Manston's discreditable object, which had been made hers by compulsion only, was now adopted by choice. She flung herself into the work.

A fiery man in such a case would have relinquished persuasion and tried palpable force. A fiery woman added unscrupulousness and evolved daring strategy; and in her obstinacy, and to sustain herself as mistress, she descended to an action the meanness of which haunted her conscience to her dying hour.

'I don't quite see, Mr Springrove,' she said, 'that I am altogether what you are pleased to call a stranger. I have known your family, at any rate, for a good many years, and I know Miss Graye particularly well, and her state of mind with regard to this matter.'

Perplexed love makes us credulous and curious as old women. Edward was willing, he owned it to himself, to get at Cytherea's state of mind, even through so dangerous a medium.

'A letter I received from her,' he said, with assumed coldness, 'tells me clearly enough what Miss Graye's mind is.'

'You think she still loves you? O yes, of course you do – all men are like that.'

'I have reason to.' He could feign no further than the first speech.

'I should be interested in knowing what reason?' she said, with sarcastic archness.

Edward felt he was allowing her to do, in fractional parts, what he rebelled against when regarding it as a whole; but the fact that his antagonist had the presence of a queen, and features only in the early evening of their beauty, was not without its influence upon a keenly conscious man. Her bearing had charmed him into toleration, as Mary Stuart's charmed the indignant Puritan visitors. He again answered her honestly.

'The best of reasons – the tone of her letter.'

'Pooh, Mr Springrove!'

'Not at all, Miss Aldclyffe! Miss Graye desired that we should be strangers to each other for the simple practical reason that intimacy could only make wretched complications worse, not from lack of love – love is only suppressed.'

'Don't you know yet, that in thus putting aside a man, a woman's pity for the pain she inflicts gives her a kindness of tone which is often mistaken for suppressed love?' said Miss Aldclyffe, with soft insidiousness.

This was a translation of the ambiguity of Cytherea's tone which he had certainly never thought of; and he was too ingenuous not to own it.

'I had never thought of it,' he said.

'And don't believe it?'

'Not unless there was some other evidence to support the view.'

She paused a minute and then began hesitatingly –

'My intention was – what I did not dream of owning to you – my intention was to try to induce you to fulfil your promise to Miss Hinton not solely on her account and yours (though partly). I love Cytherea Graye with all my soul, and I want to see her happy even more than I do you. I did not mean to drag her name into the affair at all, but I am driven to say that she wrote that letter of dismissal to you – for it was a most pronounced dismissal – not on account of your engagement. She is old enough to know that engagements can be broken as easily as they can be made. She wrote it because she loved another man; very suddenly, and not with any idea or hope of marrying him, but none the less deeply.'

'Who?'

'Mr Manston.'

'Good—! I can't listen to you for an instant, madam; why, she hadn't seen him!'

'She had; he came here the day before she wrote to you; and I could prove to you, if it were worth while, that on that day she went voluntarily to his house, though not artfully or blamably; stayed for two hours playing and singing; that no sooner did she leave him than she went straight home, and wrote the letter saying she should not see you again, entirely because she had seen him and fallen desperately in love with him – a perfectly natural thing for a young girl to do, considering that he's the handsomest man in the county. Why else should she not have written to you before?'

'Because I was such a – because she did not know of the connection between me and my cousin until then.'

'I must think she did.'

'On what ground?'

'On the strong ground of my having told her so, distinctly, the very first day she came to live with me.'

'Well, what do you seek to impress upon me after all? This – that the day Miss Graye wrote to me, saying it was better that we should part, coincided with the day she had seen a certain man—'

'A remarkably handsome and talented man.'

'Yes, I admit that.'

'And that it coincided with the hour just subsequent to her seeing him.'

'Yes, just when she had seen him.'

'And been to his house alone with him.'

'It is nothing.'

'And stayed there playing and singing with him.'

'Admit that, too,' he said; 'an accident might have caused it.'

'And at the same instant that she wrote your dismissal she wrote a letter referring to a secret appointment with him.'

'Never, by God, madam! never!'

'What do you say, sir?'

'Never.'

She sneered.

'There's no accounting for beliefs, and the whole history is a very trivial matter; but I am resolved to prove that a lady's word is truthful, though upon a matter which concerns neither you nor herself. You shall learn that she *did* write him a letter concerning an assignation – that is, if Mr Manston still has it, and will be considerate enough to lend it me.'

'But besides,' continued Edward, 'a married man to do what would cause a young girl to write a note of the kind you mention!'

She flushed a little.

'That I don't know anything about,' she stammered. 'But Cytherea didn't, of course, dream any more than I did, or others in the parish, that he was married.'

'Of course she didn't.'

'And I have reason to believe that he told her of the fact directly afterwards, that she might not compromise herself, or allow him to. It is notorious that he struggled honestly and hard against her attractions, and succeeded in hiding his feelings, if not in quenching them.'

'We'll hope that he did.'

'But circumstances are changed now.'

'Very greatly changed,' he murmured abstractedly.

'You must remember,' she added more suasively, 'that Miss Graye has a perfect right to do what she likes with her own – her heart, that is to say.'

Her descent from irritation was caused by perceiving that Edward's faith was really disturbed by her strong assertions, and it gratified her.

Edward's thoughts flew to his father, and the object of his interview with her. Tongue-fencing was utterly distasteful to him.

'I will not trouble you by remaining longer, madam,' he remarked, gloomily; 'our conversation has ended sadly for me.'

'Don't think so,' she said, 'and don't be mistaken. I am older than you are, many years older, and I know many things.'

Full of miserable doubt, and bitterly regretting that he had raised his father's expectations by anticipations impossible of fulfilment, Edward slowly went his way into the village, and approached his cousin's house. The farmer was at the door looking eagerly for him. He had been waiting there for more than half-an-hour. His eye kindled quickly.

'Well, Ted, what does she say?' he asked, in the intensely sanguine tones which fall sadly upon a listener's ear, because, antecedently, they raise pictures of inevitable disappointment for the speaker, in some direction or another.

'Nothing for us to be alarmed at,' said Edward, with a forced cheerfulness.

'But must we rebuild?'

'It seems we must, father.'

The old man's eyes swept the horizon, then he turned to go in, without making another observation. All light seemed extinguished in him again. When Edward went in he found his father with the bureau open, unfolding the leases with a shaking hand, folding them up again without reading them, then putting them in their niche only to remove them again.

Adelaide was in the room. She said thoughtfully to Edward, as she watched the farmer –

'I hope it won't kill poor uncle, Edward. What should we do if anything were to happen to him? He is the only near relative you and I have in the world.' It was perfectly true, and somehow Edward felt more bound up with her after that remark.

She continued: 'And he was only saying so hopefully the day before the fire, that he wouldn't for the world let any one else give me away to you when we are married.'

For the first time a conscientious doubt arose in Edward's mind as to the justice of the course he was pursuing in resolving to refuse the alternative offered by Miss Aldclyffe. Could it be selfishness as well as independence? How much he had thought of his own heart, how little he had thought of his father's peace of mind!

The old man did not speak again till supper-time, when he began asking his son an endless number of hypothetical questions on what might induce Miss Aldclyffe to listen to kinder terms; speaking of her now not as an unfair woman, but as a Lachesis or Fate* whose course it behoved nobody to condemn. In his earnestness he once turned his eyes on Edward's face: their expression was woful: the pupils were dilated and strange in aspect.

'If she will only agree to that!' he reiterated for the hundredth time, increasing the sadness of his listeners.

An aristocratic knocking came to the door, and Jane entered with a letter, addressed –

'MR EDWARD SPRINGROVE, JUNIOR'

'Charles from Knapwater House brought it,' she said.

'Miss Aldclyffe's writing,' said Mr Springrove, before Edward had recognized it himself. 'Now 'tis all right! she's going to make an offer; she doesn't want the houses there, not she; they're going to make that the way into the park.'

Edward opened the seal and glanced at the inside. He said, with a supreme effort of self-command –

'It is only directed by Miss Aldclyffe, and refers to nothing connected with the fire. I wonder at her taking the trouble to send it to-night.'

His father looked absently at him and turned away again. Shortly

168

afterwards they retired for the night. Alone in his bedroom Edward opened and read what he had not dared to refer to in their presence.

The envelope contained another envelope in Cytherea's handwriting, addressed to '—— Manston, Esq., Old Manor House'. Inside this was the note she had written to the steward after her detention in his house by the thunderstorm –

KNAPWATER HOUSE
September 20th

I find I cannot meet you at seven o'clock by the waterfall as I promised. The emotion I felt made me forgetful of realities.

C. GRAYE

Miss Aldclyffe had not written a line, and, by the unvarying rule observable when words are not an absolute necessity, her silence seemed ten times as convincing as any expression of opinion could have been.

He then, step by step, recalled all the conversation on the subject of Cytherea's feelings that had passed between himself and Miss Aldclyffe in the afternoon, and by a confusion of thought, natural enough under the trying experience, concluded that because the lady was truthful in her portraiture of effects, she must necessarily be right in her assumption of causes. That is, he was convinced that Cytherea – the hitherto-believed faithful Cytherea – had, at any rate, looked with something more than indifference upon the extremely handsome face and form of Manston.

Did he blame her, as guilty of the impropriety of allowing herself to love the newcomer in the face of his not being free to return her love? No; never for a moment did he doubt that all had occurred in her old, innocent, impulsive way; that her heart was gone before she knew it – before she knew anything, beyond his existence, of the man to whom it had flown. Perhaps the very note enclosed to him was the result of first reflection. Manston he would unhesitatingly have called a scoundrel, but for one strikingly redeeming fact. It had been patent to the whole parish, and had come to Edward's own knowledge by that indirect channel, that Manston, as a married man, conscientiously avoided Cytherea after those first few days of his arrival during which her irresistibly beautiful and fatal glances had rested upon him – his upon her.

Taking from his coat a creased and pocket-worn envelope containing Cytherea's letter to himself, Springrove opened it and read it through.

He was upbraided therein, and he was dismissed. It bore the date of the letter sent to Manston, and by containing within it the phrase, 'All the day long I have been thinking', afforded justifiable ground for assuming that it was written subsequently to the other (and in Edward's sight far sweeter one) to the steward.

But though he accused her of fickleness, he would not doubt the genuineness, in its kind, of her partiality for him at Budmouth Regis. It was a short and shallow feeling – not perfect love:

> Love is not love
> Which alters when it alteration finds.*

But it was not flirtation; a feeling had been born in her and had died. It would be well for his peace of mind if his love for her could flit away so softly, and leave so few traces behind.

Miss Aldclyffe had shown herself desperately concerned in the whole matter by the alacrity with which she had obtained the letter from Manston, and her labours to induce himself to marry his cousin. Taken in connection with her apparent interest in, if not love for, Cytherea, her eagerness, too, could only be accounted for on the ground that Cytherea indeed loved the steward.

5. December the Fourth

Edward passed the night he scarcely knew how, tossing feverishly from side to side, the blood throbbing in his temples, and singing in his ears.

Before the day began to break he dressed himself. On going out upon the landing he found his father's bedroom door already open. Edward concluded that the farmer had risen softly, as was his wont, and gone out into the fields to start the labourers.

But neither of the outer doors was unfastened. He entered the front room, and found it empty. Then animated by a new idea, he went round to the little back parlour, in which the few wrecks saved from the fire were deposited, and looked in at the door. Here, near the window, the shutters of which had been opened half way, he saw his father, leaning on the bureau, his elbows resting on the flap, his body nearly doubled, his hands clasping his forehead. Beside him were ghostly-looking square folds of parchment – the leases of the houses destroyed.

His father looked up when Edward entered, and wearily spoke to the young man as his face came into the faint light.

'Edward, why did you get up so early?'

'I was uneasy, and could not sleep.'

The farmer turned again to the leases on the bureau, and seemed to become lost in reflection. In a minute or two, without lifting his eyes, he said –

'This is more than we can bear, Ted – more than we can bear! Ted, this will kill me. Not the loss only – the sense of my neglect about the insurance and everything. Borrow I never will. 'Tis all misery now. God help us – all misery now!'

Edward did not answer, continuing to look fixedly at the dreary daylight outside.

'Ted,' the farmer went on, 'this upset of bëen burnt out o' home makes me very nervous and doubtful about everything. There's this troubles me besides – our liven here with your cousin, and fillen up her house. It must be very awkward for her. But she says she doesn't mind. Have you said anything to her lately about when you are going to marry her?'

'Nothing at all lately.'

'Well, perhaps you may as well, now we are so mixed in together. You know, no time has ever been mentioned to her at all, first or last, and I think it right that now, since she has waited so patiently and so long – you are almost called upon to say you are ready. It would simplify matters very much, if you were to walk up to church wi' her one of these mornings, get the thing done, and go on liven here as we are. If you don't I must get a house all the sooner. It would lighten my mind, too, about the two little freeholds* over the hill – not a morsel a-piece, divided as they were between her mother and me, but a tidy bit tied together again. Just think about it, will ye, Ted?'

He stopped from exhaustion produced by the intense concentration of his mind upon the weary subject, and looked anxiously at his son.

'Yes, I will,' said Edward.

'But I am going to see her of the Great House this morning,' the farmer went on, his thoughts reverting to the old subject. 'I must know the rights of the matter, the when and the where. I don't like seeing her, but I'd rather talk to her than the steward. I wonder what she'll say to me.'

The younger man knew exactly what she would say. If his father asked her what he was to do, and when, she would simply refer him to Manston: her character was not that of a woman who shrank from a proposition she had once laid down. If his father were to say to her that his son had at last resolved to marry his cousin within the year, and had given her a promise to that effect, she would say, 'Mr Springrove, the houses are burnt: we'll let them go: trouble no more about them.'

His mind was already made up. He said calmly, 'Father, when you are talking to Miss Aldclyffe, mention to her that I have asked Adelaide if she is willing to marry me next Christmas. She is interested in my union with Adelaide, and the news will be welcome to her.'

'And yet she can be iron with reference to me and her property,' the farmer murmured. 'Very well, Ted, I'll tell her.'

6. December the Fifth

Of the many contradictory particulars constituting a woman's heart, two had shown their vigorous contrast in Cytherea's bosom just at this time.

It was a dark morning, the morning after old Mr Springrove's visit to Miss Aldclyffe, which had terminated as Edward had intended. Having risen an hour earlier than was usual with her, Cytherea sat at the window of an elegant little sitting-room on the ground floor, which had been appropriated to her by the kindness or whim of Miss Aldclyffe, that she might not be driven into that lady's presence against her will. She leant with her face on her hand, looking out into the gloomy grey air. A yellow glimmer from the flapping flame of the newly-lit fire fluttered on one side of her face and neck like a butterfly about to settle there, contrasting warmly with the other side of the same fair face, which received from the window the faint cold morning light, so weak that her shadow from the fire had a distinct outline on the window-shutter in spite of it. There the shadow danced like a demon, blue and grim.

The contradiction alluded to was that in spite of the decisive mood which two months earlier in the year had caused her to write a peremptory and final letter to Edward, she was now hoping for some answer other than the only possible one a man who, as she held, did not love her wildly, could send to such a communication. For a lover who did love wildly, she had left one little loophole in her otherwise straightforward epistle. Why she expected the letter on some morning of this particular week was, that hearing of his return to Carriford, she fondly assumed that he meant to ask for an interview before he left. Hence it was, too, that for the last few days, she had not been able to keep in bed later than the time of the postman's arrival.

The clock pointed to half-past seven. She saw the postman emerge from beneath the bare boughs of the park trees, come through the wicket, dive through the shrubbery, reappear on the lawn, stalk across it without reference to paths – as country postmen do – and come to the porch. She heard him fling the bag down on the seat, and turn away towards the village, without hindering himself for a single pace.

Then the butler opened the door, took up the bag, brought it in, and carried it up the staircase to place it on the slab by Miss Aldclyffe's dressing-room door. The whole proceeding had been depicted by sounds.

She had a presentiment that her letter was in the bag at last. She thought then in diminishing pulsations of confidence, 'He asks to see me! Perhaps he asks to see me: I hope he asks to see me.'

A quarter to eight: Miss Aldclyffe's bell – rather earlier than usual. 'She must have heard the post-bag brought,' said the maiden, as, tired of the chilly prospect outside, she turned to the fire, and drew imaginative pictures of her future therein.

A tap came to the door, and the lady's-maid entered. 'Miss Aldclyffe is awake,' she said; 'and she asked if you were moving yet, miss.'

'I'll run up to her,' said Cytherea, and flitted off with the utterance of the words. 'Very fortunate this,' she thought; 'I shall see what is in the bag this morning all the sooner.'

She took it up from the side table, went into Miss Aldclyffe's bedroom, pulled up the blinds, and looked round upon the lady in bed, calculating the minutes that must elapse before she looked at her letters.

'Well, darling, how are you? I am glad you have come in to see me,' said Miss Aldclyffe. 'You can unlock the bag this morning, child, if you like,' she continued, yawning factitiously.

'Strange!' Cytherea thought; 'it seems as if she knew there was likely to be a letter for me.'

From her bed Miss Aldclyffe watched the girl's face as she tremblingly opened the post-bag and found there an envelope addressed to her in Edward's handwriting; one he had written the day before, after the decision he had come to on an impartial, and on that account torturing, survey of his own, his father's, his cousin Adelaide's, and what he believed to be Cytherea's, position.

The haughty mistress's soul sickened remorsefully within her when she saw suddenly appear upon the speaking countenance of the young lady before her a wan desolate look of agony.

The master-sentences of Edward's letter were these: 'You speak truly. That we never meet again is the wisest and only proper course. That I regret the past as much as you do yourself, it is hardly necessary for me to say.'

173

CHAPTER TWELVE
The Events of Ten Months

1. December to April

Week after week, month after month, the time had flown by. Christmas had passed; dreary winter with dark evenings had given place to more dreary winter with light evenings. Thaws had ended in rain, rain in wind, wind in dust. Showery days had come – the period of pink dawns and white sunsets;* with the third week in April the cuckoo had appeared; with the fourth, the nightingale.

Edward Springrove was in London, attending to the duties of his new office, and it had become known throughout the neighbourhood of Carriford that the engagement between himself and Miss Adelaide Hinton would terminate in marriage at the end of the year.

The only occasion on which her lover of the idle delicious days at Budmouth watering-place had been seen by Cytherea after the time of the decisive correspondence, was once in church, when he sat in front of her, and beside Miss Hinton.

The rencounter was quite an accident. Springrove had come there in the full belief that Cytherea was away from home with Miss Aldclyffe; and he continued ignorant of her presence throughout the service.

It is at such moments as these, when a sensitive nature writhes under the conception that its most cherished emotions have been treated with contumely, that the sphere-descended Maid, Music, friend of Pleasure* at other times, becomes a positive enemy – racking, bewildering, unrelenting. The congregation sang the first Psalm and came to the verse –

> Like some fair tree which, fed by streams,
> With timely fruit doth bend,
> He still shall flourish, and success
> All his designs attend.*

Cytherea's lips did not move, nor did any sound escape her; but could she help singing the words in the depths of her being, although the man to whom she applied them sat at her rival's side?

Perhaps the moral compensation for all a woman's petty cleverness under thriving conditions is the real nobility that lies in her extreme foolishness at these other times; her sheer inability to be simply just, her exercise of an illogical power entirely denied to men in general – the power not only of kissing, but of delighting to kiss the rod by a punctilious observance of the self-immolating doctrines in the Sermon on the Mount.

As for Edward – a little like other men of his temperament, to whom, it is somewhat humiliating to think, the aberrancy of a given love is in itself a recommendation – his sentiment, as he looked over his cousin's book, was of a lower rank, Horatian rather than Psalmodic –

> O, what hast thou of her, of her
> Whose every look did love inspire;
> Whose every breathing fanned my fire,
> And stole me from myself away!*

Then, without letting him see her, Cytherea slipt out of church early, and went home, the tones of the organ still lingering in her ears as she tried bravely to kill a jealous thought that would nevertheless live: 'My nature is one capable of more, far more, intense feeling than hers! She can't appreciate all the sides of him – she never will! He is more tangible to me even now, as a thought, than his presence itself is to her!' She was less noble then.

But she continually repressed her misery and bitterness of heart till the effort to do so showed signs of lessening. At length she even tried to hope that her lost lover and her rival would love one another very dearly.

The scene and the sentiment dropped into the past. Meanwhile, Manston continued visibly before her. He, though quiet and subdued in his bearing for a long time after the calamity of November, had not simulated a grief that he did not feel. At first his loss seemed so to absorb him – though as a startling change rather than as a heavy sorrow – that he paid Cytherea no attention whatever. His conduct was uniformly kind and respectful, but little more. Then, as the date of the catastrophe grew remoter, he began to wear a different aspect towards her. He always contrived to obliterate by his manner all recollection on her side that she was comparatively more dependent than himself – making much of her womanhood, nothing of her situation. Prompt to aid her whenever occasion offered, and full of delightful *petits soins** at all times, he was not officious. In this way he irresistibly won for himself a position as her friend, and the more easily in that he allowed not the faintest symptom of the old love to be apparent.

Matters stood thus in the middle of the spring, when the next move on his behalf was made by Miss Aldclyffe.

2. The Third of May

She led Cytherea to a summer-house called the Fane, built in the private grounds about the mansion in the form of a Grecian temple;* it overlooked the lake, the island on it, the trees, and their undisturbed reflection in the smooth still water. Here the old and young maid halted; here they stood, side by side, mentally imbibing the scene.

The month was May – the time, morning. Cuckoos, thrushes, blackbirds, and sparrows gave forth a blithe* confusion of song and twitter. The road was spotted white with the fallen leaves of apple-blossoms, and the sparkling grey dew still lingered on the grass and flowers. Two swans floated into view in front of the women, and then crossed the water towards them.

'They seem to come to us without any will of their own – quite involuntarily – don't they?' said Cytherea, looking at the birds' graceful advance.

'Yes, but if you look narrowly you can see their hips just beneath the water, working with the greatest energy.'

'I'd rather not see that; it spoils the idea of proud indifference to direction which we associate with a swan.'

'It does; we'll have "involuntarily". Ah, now this reminds me of something.'

'Of what?'

'Of a human being who involuntarily comes towards yourself.'

Cytherea looked into Miss Aldclyffe's face; her eyes grew round as circles, and lines of wonderment came visibly upon her countenance. She had not once regarded Manston as a lover since his wife's sudden appearance and subsequent death. The death of a wife, and such a death, was an overwhelming matter in her ideas of things.

'Is it a man or woman?' she said, quite innocently.

'Mr Manston,' said Miss Aldclyffe quietly.

'Mr Manston attracted by me *now*?' said Cytherea, standing at gaze.

'Didn't you know it?'

'Certainly I did not. Why, his poor wife has only been dead six months.'

'Of course he knows that. But loving is not done by months, or method, or rule, or nobody would ever have invented such a phrase as "falling in love". He does not want his love to be observed just yet, on the very account you mention; but conceal it as he may from himself and us, it exists definitely – and very intensely, I assure you.'

'I suppose then, that if he can't help it, it is no harm of him,' said Cytherea naïvely, and beginning to ponder.

'Of course it isn't – you know that well enough. She was a great burden and trouble to him. This may become a great good to you both.'

A rush of feeling at remembering that the same woman, before Manston's arrival, had just as frankly advocated Edward's claims, checked Cytherea's utterance for a while.

'There, don't look at me like that, for Heaven's sake!' said Miss Aldclyffe. 'You could almost kill a person by the force of reproach you can put into those eyes of yours, I verily believe.'

Edward once in the young lady's thoughts, there was no getting rid of him. She wanted to be alone.

'Do you want me here?' she said.

'Now there, there; you want to be off, and have a good cry,' said Miss Aldclyffe, taking her hand. 'But you mustn't, my dear. There's nothing in the past for you to regret. Compare Mr Manston's honourable conduct towards his wife and yourself, with Springrove towards his betrothed and yourself, and then see which appears the more worthy of your thoughts.'

3. From the Fourth of May to the Twenty-First of June

The next stage in Manston's advances towards her hand was a clearly defined courtship. She was sadly perplexed, and some contrivance was necessary on his part in order to meet with her. But it is next to impossible for an appreciative woman to have a positive repugnance towards an unusually handsome and gifted man, even though she may not be inclined to love him. Hence Cytherea was not so alarmed at the sight of him as to render a meeting and conversation with her more than a matter of difficulty.

Coming and going from church was his grand opportunity. Manston was very religious now. It is commonly said that no man was ever converted by argument, but there is a single one which will make any Laodicean* in England, let him be once love-sick, wear prayer-books and become a zealous Episcopalian* – the argument that his sweetheart can be seen from his pew.

Manston introduced into his method a system of bewitching flattery, everywhere pervasive, yet, too, so transitory and intangible, that, as in the case of the poet Wordsworth and the Wandering Voice,* though she felt it present, she could never find it. As a foil to heighten its effect, he occasionally spoke philosophically of the evanescence of female beauty – the worthlessness of mere appearance. 'Handsome is that handsome does' he considered a proverb which should be written on the looking-glass of every woman in the land. 'Your form, your motions, your heart have won me,' he said, in a tone of playful sadness. 'They are beautiful. But I see these things, and it comes into my mind that they are doomed, they are gliding to nothing as I look. Poor eyes, poor mouth, poor face, poor maiden! "Where will her glories be in twenty years?" I say. "Where will all of her be in a hundred?" Then I think it is cruel that you should bloom a day, and fade for ever and ever. It seems hard and sad that you will die as ordinarily as I, and be buried; be food for roots and worms, be forgotten and come to earth, and grow up a mere blade of churchyard-grass and an ivy leaf. Then, Miss Graye, when I see you are a Lovely Nothing, I pity you, and the love I feel then is better and sounder, larger and more lasting than that I felt at the beginning.' Again an ardent flash of his handsome eyes.

It was by this route that he ventured on an indirect declaration and offer of his hand.

She implied in the same indirect manner that she did not love him enough to accept it.

An actual refusal was more than he had expected. Cursing himself for what he called his egregious folly in making himself the slave of a mere lady's attendant, and for having given the parish, should they know of her refusal, a chance of sneering at him – certainly a ground for thinking less of his standing than before – he went home to the Old House, and walked indecisively up and down his back-yard. Turning aside, he leant his arms upon the edge of the rainwater-butt standing in the corner, and looked into it. The reflection from the smooth stagnant surface tinged his face with the greenish shades of Correggio's* nudes. Staves of sunlight slanted down through the still pool, lighting it up with wonderful distinctness. Hundreds of thousands of minute living creatures sported and tumbled in its depth with every contortion that gaiety could suggest; perfectly happy, though consisting only of a head, or a tail, or at most a head and a tail, and all doomed to die within the twenty-four hours.

'Damn my position! Why shouldn't I be happy through my little day too? Let the parish sneer at my repulses, let it. I'll get her, if I move heaven and earth to do it!'

Indeed, the inexperienced Cytherea had, towards Edward in the first place, and Manston afterwards, unconsciously adopted bearings that would have been the very tactics of a professional fisher of men who wished to have them each successively dangling at her heels. For if any

178

rule at all can be laid down in a matter which, for men collectively, is notoriously beyond regulation, it is that to snub a petted man, and to pet a snubbed man, is the way to win in suits of both kinds. Manston with Springrove's encouragement would have become indifferent. Edward with Manston's repulses would have sheered off at the outset, as he did afterwards. Her supreme indifference added fuel to Manston's ardour – it completely disarmed his pride. The invulnerable Nobody seemed greater to him than a susceptible Princess.

4. From the Twenty-First of June to the End of July

Cytherea had in the meantime received the following letter from her brother. It was the first definite notification of the enlargement of that cloud no bigger than a man's hand* which had for nearly a twelve-month hung before them in the distance, and which was soon to give a colour to their whole sky from horizon to horizon.

BUDMOUTH REGIS,
SATURDAY

DARLING SIS, – I have delayed telling you for a long time of a little matter which, though not one to be seriously alarmed about, is sufficiently vexing, and it would be unfair in me to keep it from you any longer. It is that for some time past I have again been distressed by that lameness which I first distinctly felt when we went to Lulwind Cove, and again when I left Knapwater that morning early. It is an unusual pain in my left leg, between the knee and the ankle. I had just found fresh symptoms of it when you were here for that half-hour about a month ago – when you said in fun that I began to move like an old man. I had a good mind to tell you then, but fancying it would go off in a few days, I thought it was not worth while. Since that time it has increased, but I am still able to work in the office, sitting on the stool. My great fear is that Mr G. will have some out-door measuring work for me to do soon, and that I shall be obliged to decline it. However, we will hope for the best. How it came, what was its origin, or what it tends to, I cannot think. You shall hear again in a day or two, if it is no better. . . . – Your loving brother,

OWEN

This she answered, begging to know the worst, which she could bear, but suspense and anxiety never. In two days came another letter from him, of which the subjoined paragraph is a portion: –

I had quite decided to let you know the worst, and to assure you that it was the worst, before you wrote to ask it. And again I give you my word that I will conceal nothing – so that there will be no excuse whatever for your wearing

179

yourself out with fears that I am worse than I say. This morning then, for the first time, I have been obliged to stay away from the office. Don't be frightened at this, dear Cytherea. Rest is all that is wanted, and by nursing myself now for a week, I may avoid an illness of six months.

After a visit from her he wrote again: –

Dr Chestman has seen me. He said that the ailment was some sort of rheumatism, and I am now undergoing proper treatment for its cure. My leg and foot have been placed in hot bran, liniments have been applied, and also severe friction with a pad. He says I shall be as right as ever in a very short time. Directly I am I shall run up by the train to see you. Don't trouble to come to me if Miss Aldclyffe grumbles again about your being away, for I am going on capitally.... You shall hear again at the end of the week.

At the time mentioned came the following: –

I am sorry to tell you, because I know it will be so disheartening after my last letter, that I am not so well as I was then, and that there has been a sort of hitch in the proceedings. After I had been treated for rheumatism a few days longer (in which treatment they pricked the place with a long needle several times), I saw that Dr Chestman was in doubt about something, and I requested that he would call in a brother professional man to see me as well. They consulted together and then told me that rheumatism was not the disease after all, but erysipelas. They then began treating it differently, as became a different matter. Blisters, flour, and starch, seem to be the order of the day now – medicine, of course, besides.

Mr Gradfield has been in to inquire about me. He says he has been obliged to get a designer in my place, which grieves me very much, though, of course, it could not be avoided.

A month passed away; throughout this period, Cytherea visited him as often as the limited time at her command would allow, and wore as cheerful a countenance as the womanly determination to do nothing which might depress him could enable her to wear. Another letter from him then told her these additional facts: –

The doctors find they are again on the wrong tack. They cannot make out what the disease is. O Cytherea! how I wish they knew! This suspense is wearing me out. Could not Miss Aldclyffe spare you for a day? Do come to me. We will talk about the best course then. I am sorry to complain, but I am worn out.

Cytherea went to Miss Aldclyffe, and told her of the melancholy turn her brother's illness had taken. Miss Aldclyffe at once said that

Cytherea might go, and offered to do anything to assist her which lay in her power. Cytherea's eyes beamed gratitude as she turned to leave the room, and hasten to the station.

'O, Cytherea,' said Miss Aldclyffe, calling her back; 'just one word. Has Mr Manston spoken to you lately?'

'Yes,' said Cytherea, blushing timorously.

'He proposed?'

'Yes.'

'And you refused him?'

'Yes.'

'Tcht, tcht! Now listen to my advice,' said Miss Aldclyffe emphatically, 'and accept him before he changes his mind. The chance which he offers you of settling in life is one that may possibly, probably, not occur again. His position is good and secure, and the life of his wife would be a happy one. You may not be sure that you love him madly; but suppose you are not sure? My father used to say to me as a child when he was teaching me whist, "When in doubt win the trick!" That advice is ten times as valuable to a woman on the subject of matrimony. In refusing a man there is always the risk that you may never get another offer.'

'Why didn't you win the trick when you were a girl?' said Cytherea.

'Come, my lady Pert; I'm not the text,' said Miss Aldclyffe, her face glowing like fire.

Cytherea laughed stealthily.

'I was about to say,' resumed Miss Aldclyffe severely, 'that here is Mr Manston waiting with the tenderest solicitude for you, and you overlooking it, as if it were altogether beneath you. Think how you might benefit your sick brother if you were Mrs Manston. You will please me *very much* by giving him some encouragement. You understand me, Cythie dear?'

Cytherea was silent.

'And,' said Miss Aldclyffe, still more emphatically, 'on your promising that you will accept him some time this year, I will take especial care of your brother. You are listening, Cytherea?'

'Yes,' she whispered, leaving the room.

She went to Budmouth, passed the day with her brother, and returned to Knapwater wretched and full of foreboding. Owen had looked startlingly thin and pale – thinner and paler than ever she had seen him before. The brother and sister had that day decided that notwithstanding the drain upon their slender resources, another surgeon should see him. Time was everything.

Owen told her the result in his next letter: –

The three practitioners between them have at last hit the nail on the head, I hope. They probed the place, and discovered that the secret lay in the bone. I underwent an operation for its removal three days ago (after taking chloroform). . . . Thank God it is over. Though I am so weak, my spirits are rather better. I wonder when I shall be at work again? I asked the surgeons how long it would be first. I said a month? They shook their heads. A year? I said. Not so long, they said. Six months? I inquired. They would not, or could not, tell me. But never mind.

Run down, when you have half a day to spare, for the hours drag on so drearily. O Cytherea, you can't think how drearily!

She went. Immediately on her departure Miss Aldclyffe sent a note to the Old House, to Manston. On the maiden's return, tired and sick at heart as usual, she found Manston at the station awaiting her. He asked politely if he might accompany her to Knapwater. She tacitly acquiesced. During their walk he inquired the particulars of her brother's illness, and with an irresistible desire to pour out her trouble to some one, she told him of the length of time which must elapse before he could be strong again, and of the lack of comfort in lodgings.

Manston was silent a while. Then he said impetuously: 'Miss Graye, I will not mince matters – I love you – you know it. Stratagem they say is fair in love and I am compelled to adopt it now. Forgive me, for I cannot help it. Consent to be my wife at any time that may suit you – any remote day you may name will satisfy me – and you shall find him well provided for.'

For the first time in her life she truly dreaded the handsome man at her side who pleaded thus selfishly, and shrank from the hot voluptuous nature of his passion for her, which, disguise it as he might under a quiet and polished exterior, at times radiated forth with a scorching white heat. She perceived how animal was the love which bargained.

'I do not love you, Mr Manston,' she replied coldly.

5. From the First to the Twenty-Seventh of August

The long sunny days of the later summer-time brought only the same dreary accounts from Budmouth, and saw Cytherea paying the same sad visits.

She grew perceptibly weaker, in body and mind. Manston still persisted in his suit, but with more of his former indirectness, now that he saw how unexpectedly well she stood an open attack. His was the system of Dares at the Sicilian games –

> He, like a captain who beleaguers round
> Some strong-built castle on a rising ground,
> Views all the approaches with observing eyes,
> This and that other part again he tries,
> And more on industry than force relies.*

Miss Aldclyffe made it appear more clearly than ever that aid to Owen from herself depended entirely upon Cytherea's acceptance of her steward. Hemmed in and distressed, Cytherea's answers to his importunities grew less uniform; they were firm, or wavering, as Owen's malady fluctuated. Had a register of her pitiful oscillations* been kept, it would have rivalled in pathos the diary wherein De Quincey tabulates his combat with Opium* – perhaps as noticeable an instance as any in which a thrilling dramatic power has been given to mere numerals. Thus she wearily and monotonously lived through the month, listening on Sundays to the well-known round of chapters narrating the history of Elijah and Elisha in famine and drought;* on week-days to buzzing flies in hot sunny rooms. 'So like, so very like, was day to day.' Extreme lassitude seemed all that the world could show her.

Her state was in this wise, when one afternoon, having been with her brother, she met the surgeon, and begged him to tell the actual truth concerning Owen's condition.

The reply was that he feared that the first operation had not been thorough; that although the wound had healed, another attempt might still be necessary, unless nature were left to effect her own cure. But the time such a self-healing proceeding would occupy might be ruinous.

'How long would it be?' she said.

'It is impossible to say. A year or two, more or less.'

'And suppose he submitted to another artificial extraction?'

'Then he might be well in four or six months.'

Now the remainder of his and her possessions, together with a sum he had borrowed, would not provide him with necessary comforts for half that time. To combat the misfortune there were two courses open – her becoming betrothed to Manston, or the sending Owen to the County Hospital.

Thus terrified, driven into a corner, panting and fluttering about for some loophole of escape, yet still shrinking from the idea of being Manston's wife the poor little bird endeavoured to find out from Miss

Aldclyffe whether it was likely Owen would be well treated in the hospital.

'County Hospital!' said Miss Aldclyffe; 'why, it is only another name for slaughter-house 'in surgical cases at any rate. Certainly if anything about your body is snapt in two they do join you together in a fashion, but 'tis so askew and ugly, that you may as well be apart again.' Then she terrified the inquiring and anxious maiden by relating horrid stories of how the legs and arms of poor people were cut off at a moment's notice, especially in cases where the restorative treatment was likely to be long and tedious.

'You know how willing I am to help you, Cytherea,' she added reproachfully. 'You know it. Why are you so obstinate then? Why do you selfishly bar the clear, honourable, and only sisterly path which leads out of this difficulty? I cannot, on my conscience, countenance you; no, I cannot.'

Manston once more repeated his offer; and once more she refused, but this time weakly, and with signs of an internal struggle. Manston's eye sparkled;* he saw for the hundredth time in his life, that perseverance, if only systematic, was irresistible by womankind.

6. *The Twenty-Seventh of August*

On going to Budmouth three days later, she found to her surprise that the steward had been there, had introduced himself, and had seen her brother. A few delicacies had been brought him also by the same hand. Owen spoke in warm terms of Manston and his free and unceremonious call, as he could not have refrained from doing of any person, of any kind, whose presence had served to help away the tedious hours of a long day, and who had, moreover, shown that sort of consideration for him which the accompanying basket implied – antecedent consideration, so telling upon all invalids – and which he so seldom experienced except from the hands of his sister.

How should he perceive, amid this tithe-paying of mint, and anise, and cummin,* the weightier matters which were left undone?

Again the steward met her at Carriford Road Station on her return journey. Instead of being frigid as at the former meeting at the same place, she was embarrassed by a strife of thought, and murmured brokenly her thanks for what he had done. The same request that he might see her home was made.

He had perceived his error in making his kindness to Owen a conditional kindness, and had hastened to efface all recollection of it.

'Though I let my offer on her brother's – my friend's – behalf, seem dependent on my lady's graciousness to me,' he whispered wooingly in the course of their walk, 'I could not conscientiously adhere to my statement; it was said with all the impulsive selfishness of love. Whether you choose to have me, or whether you don't, I love you too devotedly to be anything but kind to your brother. . . . Miss Graye, Cytherea, I will do anything,' he continued earnestly, 'to give you pleasure – indeed I will.'

She saw on the one hand her poor and much-loved Owen recovering from his illness and troubles by the disinterested kindness of the man beside her, on the other she drew him dying, wholly by reason of her self-enforced poverty. To marry this man was obviously the course of common sense, to refuse him was impolitic temerity. There was reason in this. But there was more behind than a hundred reasons – a woman's gratitude and her impulse to be kind.

The wavering of her mind was visible in her tell-tale face. He noticed it, and caught at the opportunity.

They were standing by the ruinous foundations of an old mill in the midst of a meadow. Between grey and half-overgrown stone-work – the only signs of masonry remaining – the water gurgled down from the old mill-pond to a lower level, under the cloak of rank broad leaves – the sensuous natures of the vegetable world. On the right hand the sun, resting on the horizon-line, streamed across the ground from below copper-coloured and lilac clouds, stretched out in flats beneath a sky of pale soft green. All dark objects on the earth that lay towards the sun were overspread by a purple haze, against which a swarm of wailing gnats shone forth luminously, rising upward and floating away like sparks of fire.

The stillness oppressed and reduced her to mere passivity. The only wish the humidity of the place left in her was to stand motionless. The helpless flatness of the landscape gave her, as it gives all such temperaments, a sense of bare equality with, and no superiority to, a single entity under the sky.*

He came so close that their clothes touched. 'Will you try to love me? Do try to love me!' he said, in a whisper, taking her hand. He had never taken it before. She could feel his hand trembling exceedingly as it held hers in its clasp.

Considering his kindness to her brother, his love for herself, and Edward's fickleness, ought she to forbid him to do this? How truly pitiful it was to feel his hand tremble so – all for her! Should she withdraw her hand? She would think whether she would. Thinking,

185

and hesitating, she looked as far as the autumnal haze on the marshy ground would allow her to see distinctly. There was the fragment of a hedge – all that remained of a 'wet old garden' – standing in the middle of the mead, without a definite beginning or ending, purposeless and valueless. It was overgrown, and choked with mandrakes,* and she could almost fancy she heard their shrieks. . . . Should she withdraw her hand? No, she could not withdraw it now; it was too late, the act would not imply refusal. She felt as one in a boat without oars, drifting with closed eyes down a river – she knew not whither.

He gave her hand a gentle pressure, and relinquished it.

Then it seemed as if he were coming to the point again. No, he was not going to urge his suit that evening. Another respite.

7. The Early Part of September

Saturday came, and she went on some trivial errand to the village post-office. It was a little grey cottage with a luxuriant jasmine encircling the doorway, and before going in Cytherea paused to admire this pleasing feature of the exterior. Hearing a step on the gravel behind the corner of the house, she resigned the jasmine and entered. Nobody was in the room. She could hear Mrs Leat, the widow who acted as postmistress, walking about over her head. Cytherea was going to the foot of the stairs to call Mrs Leat, but before she had accomplished her object, another form stood at the half-open door. Manston came in.

'Both on the same errand,' he said gracefully.

'I will call her,' said Cytherea, moving in haste to the foot of the stairs.

'One moment.' He glided to her side. 'Don't call her for a moment,' he repeated.

But she had said, 'Mrs Leat!'

He seized Cytherea's hand, kissed it tenderly, and carefully replaced it by her side.

She had that morning determined to check his further advances, until she had thoroughly considered her position. The remonstrance was now on her tongue, but as accident would have it, before the word could be spoken, Mrs Leat was stepping from the last stair to the floor, and no remonstrance came.

With the subtlety which characterized him in all his dealings with her, he quickly concluded his own errand, bade her a good-bye, in the tones of which love was so garnished with pure politeness that it only showed its presence to herself, and left the house – putting it out of her power to refuse him her companionship homeward, or to object to his late action of kissing her hand.

The Friday of the next week brought another letter from her brother. In this he informed her that, in absolute grief lest he should distress her unnecessarily, he had some time earlier borrowed a few pounds. A week ago, he said, his creditor became importunate, but that on the day on which he wrote, the creditor had told him there was no hurry for a settlement, that 'his *sister's suitor* had guaranteed the sum'. 'Is he Mr Manston? tell me, Cytherea,' said Owen.

He also mentioned that a wheeled chair had been anonymously hired for his especial use, though as yet he was hardly far enough advanced towards convalescence to avail himself of the luxury. 'Is this Mr Manston's doing?' he inquired.

She could dally with her perplexity, evade it, trust to time for guidance, no longer. The matter had come to a crisis: she must once and for all choose between the dictates of her understanding and those of her heart. She longed, till her soul seemed nigh to bursting, for her lost mother's return to earth, but for one minute, that she might have tender counsel to guide her through this, her great difficulty.

As for her heart, she half fancied that it was not Edward's to quite the extent that it once had been; she thought him cruel in conducting himself towards her as he did at Budmouth, cruel afterwards in making so light of her. She knew he had stifled his love for her – was utterly lost to her. But for all that she could not help indulging in a woman's pleasure of re-creating defunct agonies, and lacerating herself with them now and then.

'If I were rich,' she thought, 'I would give way to the luxury of being morbidly faithful to him for ever without his knowledge.'

But she considered; in the first place she was a homeless dependent; and what did practical wisdom tell her to do under such desperate circumstances? To provide herself with some place of refuge from poverty, and with means to aid her brother Owen. This was to be Mr Manston's wife.

She did not love him.

But what was love without a home? Misery. What was a home without love? Alas, not much; but still a kind of home.

'Yes,' she thought, 'I am urged by my common sense to marry Mr Manston.'

Did anything nobler in her say so too?

With the death (to her) of Edward her heart's occupation was gone. Was it necessary or even right for her to tend it and take care of it as

187

she used to in the old time, when it was still a capable minister?

By a slight sacrifice here she could give happiness to at least two hearts whose emotional activities were still unwounded. She would do good to two men whose lives were far more important than hers.

'Yes,' she said again, 'even Christianity urges me to marry Mr Manston.'

Directly Cytherea had persuaded herself that a kind of heroic self-abnegation had to do with the matter, she became much more content in the consideration of it. A wilful indifference to the future was what really prevailed in her, ill and worn out, as she was, by the perpetual harassments of her sad fortune, and she regarded this indifference, as gushing natures will do under such circumstances, as genuine resignation and devotedness.

Manston met her again the following day: indeed, there was no escaping him now. At the end of a short conversation between them, which took place in the hollow of the park by the waterfall, obscured on the outer side by the low hanging branches of the limes, she tacitly assented to his assumption of a privilege greater than any that had preceded it. He stooped and kissed her brow.

Before going to bed she wrote to Owen explaining the whole matter. It was too late in the evening for the postman's visit, and she placed the letter on the mantelpiece to send it the next day.

The morning (Sunday) brought a hurried postscript to Owen's letter of the day before: –

September 9, 1865

DEAR CYTHEREA, – I have received a frank and friendly letter from Mr Manston explaining the position in which he stands now and also that in which he hopes to stand towards you. Can't you love him? Why not? Try, for he is a good, and not only that, but a cultured man. Think of the weary and laborious future that awaits you if you continue for life in your present position, and do you see any way of escape from it except by marriage? I don't. Don't go against your heart, Cytherea, but be wise. –
Ever affectionately yours,

OWEN

She thought that probably he had replied to Mr Manston in the same favouring mood. She had a conviction that that day would settle her doom. Yet

So true a fool is love,*

that even now she nourished a half-hope that something would happen

188

at the last moment to thwart her deliberately-formed intentions, and favour the old emotion she was using all her strength to thrust down.

8. The Tenth of September

The Sunday was the thirteenth after Trinity, and the afternoon service at Carriford was nearly over. The people were singing the Evening Hymn.*

Manston was at church as usual in his accustomed place two seats forward from the large square pew occupied by Miss Aldclyffe and Cytherea.

The ordinary sadness of an autumnal evening-service seemed, in Cytherea's eyes, to be doubled on this particular occasion. She looked at all the people as they stood and sang, waving backwards and forwards like a forest of pines swayed by a gentle breeze; then at the village children singing too, their heads inclined to one side, their eyes listlessly tracing some crack in the old walls, or following the movement of a distant bough or bird with features petrified almost to painfulness. Then she looked at Manston; he was already regarding her with some purpose in his glance.

'It is coming this evening,' she said in her mind. A minute later, at the end of the hymn, when the congregation began to move out, Manston came down the aisle. He was opposite the end of her seat as she stepped from it, the remainder of their progress to the door being in contact with each other. Miss Aldclyffe had lingered behind.

'Don't let's hurry,' he said, when Cytherea was about to enter the private path to the House as usual. 'Would you mind turning down this way for a minute till Miss Aldclyffe has passed?'

She could not very well refuse now. They turned into a secluded path on their left, leading round through a thicket of laurels to the other gate of the churchyard, walking very slowly. By the time the further gate was reached, the church was closed. They met the sexton with the keys in his hand.

'We are going inside for a minute,' said Manston to him, taking the keys unceremoniously. 'I will bring them to you when we return.'

The sexton nodded his assent, and Cytherea and Manston walked into the porch, and up the nave.

They did not speak a word during their progress or in any way interfere with the stillness and silence that prevailed everywhere around them. Everything in the place was the embodiment of decay: the fading red glare from the setting sun, which came in at the west

189

window, emphasizing the end of the day and all its cheerful doings, the mildewed walls, the uneven paving-stones, the wormy pews, the sense of recent occupation, and the dank air of death which had gathered with the evening, would have made grave a lighter mood than Cytherea's was then.

'What sensations does the place impress you with?' she said at last, very sadly.

'I feel imperatively called upon to be honest, from very despair of achieving anything by stratagem in a world where the materials are such as these.' He, too, spoke in a depressed voice, purposely or otherwise.

'I feel as if I were almost ashamed to be seen walking such a world,' she murmured; 'that's the effect it has upon me; but it does not induce me to be honest particularly.'

He took her hand in both his, and looked down upon the lids of her eyes.

'I pity you sometimes,' he said more emphatically.

'I am pitiable, perhaps; so are many people. Why do you pity me?'

'I think that you make yourself needlessly sad.'

'Not needlessly.'

'Yes, needlessly. Why should you be separated from your brother so much, when you might have him to stay with you till he is well?'

'That can't be,' she said, turning away.

He went on, 'I think the real and only good thing that can be done for him is to get him away from Budmouth a while; and I have been wondering whether it could not be managed for him to come to my house to live for a few weeks. Only a quarter of a mile from you. How pleasant it would be!'

'It would.'

He moved himself round immediately to the front of her, and held her hand more firmly, as he continued, 'Cytherea, why do you say "It would", so entirely in the tone of abstract supposition? I want him there; I want him to be my brother, too. Then make him so, and be my wife! I cannot live without you. O Cytherea, my darling, my love, come and be my wife!'

His face bent closer and closer to hers, and the last words sank to a whisper as weak as the emotion inspiring it was strong.

She said firmly and distinctly, 'Yes, I will.'

'Next month?' he said on the instant, before taking breath.

'No; not next month.'

'The next?'

'No.'

'December? Christmas Day, say?'

'I don't mind.'

'O, you darling!' He was about to imprint a kiss upon her pale, cold mouth, but she hastily covered it with her hand.

'Don't kiss me – at least where we are now!' she whispered imploringly.

'Why?'

'We are too near God.'

He gave a sudden start, and his face flushed. She had spoken so emphatically that the words 'Near God' echoed back again through the hollow building from the far end of the chancel.

'What a thing to say!' he exclaimed; 'surely a pure kiss is not inappropriate to the place!'

'No,' she replied, with a swelling heart; 'I don't know why I burst out so – I can't tell what has come over me! Will you forgive me?'

'How shall I say "Yes" without judging you? How shall I say "No" without losing the pleasure of saying "Yes"?' He was himself again.

'I don't know,' she absently murmured.

'I'll say "Yes",' he answered daintily. 'It is sweeter to fancy we are forgiven, than to think we have not sinned;* and you shall have the sweetness without the need.'

She did not reply, and they moved away. The church was nearly dark now, and melancholy in the extreme. She stood beside him while he locked the door, then took the arm he gave her, and wound her way out of the churchyard with him. Then they walked to the house together, but the great matter having been set at rest, she persisted in talking only on indifferent subjects.

'Christmas Day, then,' he said, as they were parting at the end of the shrubbery.

'I meant Old Christmas Day,'* she said evasively.

'H'm, people do not usually attach that meaning to the words.'

'No; but I should like it best if it could not be till then?' It seemed to be still her instinct to delay the marriage to the utmost.

'Very well, love,' he said gently. ''Tis a fortnight longer still; but never mind. Old Christmas Day.'

9. The Eleventh of September

'There. It will be on a Friday!'*

She sat upon a little footstool gazing intently into the fire. It was the afternoon of the day following that of the steward's successful solicitation of her hand.

'I wonder if it would be proper in me to run across the park and tell him it is a Friday?' she said to herself, rising to her feet, looking at her hat lying near, and then out of the window towards the Old House. Proper or not, she felt that she must at all hazards remove the disagreeable, though, as she herself owned, unfounded impression the coincidence had occasioned. She left the house directly, and went to search for him.

Manston was in the timber-yard, looking at the sawyers as they worked. Cytherea came up to him hesitatingly. Till within a distance of a few yards she had hurried forward with alacrity – now that the practical expression of his face became visible she wished almost she had never sought him on such an errand; in his business mood he was perhaps very stern.

'It will be on a Friday,' she said confusedly, and without any preface.

'Come this way!' said Manston, in the tone he used for workmen, not being able to alter at an instant's notice. He gave her his arm and led her back into the avenue, by which time he was lover again. 'On a Friday, will it, dearest? You do not mind Fridays, surely? That's nonsense.'

'Not seriously mind them, exactly – but if it could be any other day?'

'Well, let us say Old Christmas Eve, then. Shall it be Old Christmas Eve?'

'Yes, Old Christmas Eve.'

'Your word is solemn and irrevocable now?'

'Certainly, I have solemnly pledged my word; I should not have promised to marry you if I had not meant it. Don't think I should.' She spoke the words with a dignified impressiveness.

'You must not be vexed at my remark, dearest. Can you think the worse of an ardent man, Cytherea, for showing some anxiety in love?'

'No, no.' She could not say more. She was always ill at ease when he spoke of himself as a piece of human nature in that analytical way, and wanted to be out of his presence. The time of day, and the proximity of the house, afforded her a means of escape. 'I must be with Miss Aldclyffe now – will you excuse my hasty coming and going?' she said prettily. Before he had replied she had parted from him.

'Cytherea, was it Mr Manston I saw you scudding away from in the avenue just now?' said Miss Aldclyffe, when Cytherea joined her.

'Yes.'

'"Yes." Come, why don't you say more than that? I hate those

192

taciturn "Yesses" of yours. I tell you everything, and yet you are as close as wax with me.'

'I parted from him because I wanted to come in.'

'What a novel and important announcement! Well, is the day fixed?'

'Yes.'

Miss Aldclyffe's face kindled into intense interest at once. 'Is it indeed? When is it to be?'

'On Old Christmas Eve.'

'Old Christmas Eve.' Miss Aldclyffe drew Cytherea round to her front, and took a hand in each of her own. 'And then you will be a bride!' she said slowly, looking with critical thoughtfulness upon the maiden's delicately rounded cheeks.

The normal area of the colour upon each of them decreased perceptibly after that slow and emphatic utterance by the elder lady.

Miss Aldclyffe continued impressively, 'You did not say "Old Christmas Eve" as a *fiancée* should have said the words: and you don't receive my remark with the warm excitement that foreshadows a bright future.... How many weeks are there to the time?'

'I have not reckoned them.'

'Not? Fancy a girl not counting the weeks! I find I must take the lead in this matter – you are so childish, or frightened, or stupid, or something, about it. Bring me my diary, and we will count them at once.'

Cytherea silently fetched the book.

Miss Aldclyffe opened the diary at the page containing the almanac, and counted sixteen weeks, which brought her to the thirty-first of December – a Sunday. Cytherea stood by, looking on as if she had no appetite for the scene.

'Sixteen to the thirty-first. Then let me see, Monday will be the first of January, Tuesday the second, Wednesday third, Thursday fourth, Friday fifth – you have chosen a Friday, as I declare!'

'A Thursday, surely?' said Cytherea.

'No: Old Christmas Day comes on a Saturday.'

The perturbed little brain had reckoned wrong. 'Well, it must be a Friday,' she murmured in a reverie.

'No: have it altered, of course,' said Miss Aldclyffe cheerfully. 'There's nothing bad in Friday, but such a creature as you will be thinking about its being unlucky – in fact, I wouldn't choose a Friday myself to be married on, since all the other days are equally available.'

'I shall not have it altered,' said Cytherea firmly; 'it has been altered once already: I shall let it be.'

CHAPTER THIRTEEN
The Events of One Day

1. The Fifth of January. Before Dawn

We pass over the intervening weeks. The time of the story is thus advanced more than a quarter of a year.

On the midnight preceding the morning which would make her the wife of a man whose presence fascinated her into involuntariness of bearing, and whom in absence she almost dreaded, Cytherea lay in her little bed, vainly endeavouring to sleep.

She had been looking back amid the years of her short though varied past, and thinking of the threshold upon which she stood. Days and months had dimmed the form of Edward Springrove like the gauzes of a vanishing stage-scene, but his dying voice could still be heard faintly behind. That a soft small chord in her still vibrated true to his memory, she would not admit: that she did not approach Manston with feelings which could by any stretch of words be called hymeneal, she calmly owned.

'Why do I marry him?' she said to herself. 'Because Owen, dear Owen my brother, wishes me to marry him. Because Mr Manston is, and has been, uniformly kind to Owen, and to me. "Act in obedience to the dictates of common sense," Owen said, "and dread the sharp sting of poverty. How many thousands of women like you marry every year for the same reason, to secure a home, and mere ordinary, material comforts, which after all go far to make life endurable, even if not supremely happy."

''Tis right, I suppose, for him to say that. O, if people only knew what a timidity and melancholy upon the subject of her future grows up in the heart of a friendless woman who is blown about like a reed shaken with the wind, as I am, they would not call this resignation of one's self by the name of scheming to get a husband. Scheme to marry? I'd rather scheme to die! I know I am not pleasing my heart; I know that if I only were concerned, I should like risking a single future. But why should I please my useless self over-much, when by doing otherwise I please those who are more valuable than I?'

In the midst of desultory reflections like these, which alternated with surmises as to the inexplicable connection that appeared to exist between her intended husband and Miss Aldclyffe, she heard dull noises outside the walls of the house, which she could not quite fancy to

194

be caused by the wind. She seemed doomed to such disturbances at critical periods of her existence. 'It is strange,' she pondered, 'that this my last night in Knapwater House should be disturbed precisely as my first was, no occurrence of the kind having intervened.'

As the minutes glided by the noise increased, sounding as if some one were beating the wall below her window with a bunch of switches. She would gladly have left her room and gone to stay with one of the maids, but they were without doubt all asleep.

The only person in the house likely to be awake, or who would have brains enough to comprehend her nervousness, was Miss Aldclyffe, but Cytherea never cared to go to Miss Aldclyffe's room, though she was always welcome there, and was often almost compelled to go against her will.

The oft-repeated noise of switches grew heavier upon the wall, and was now intermingled with creaks, and a rattling like the rattling of dice. The wind blew stronger; there came first a snapping, then a crash, and some portion of the mystery was revealed. It was the breaking off and fall of a branch from one of the large trees outside. The smacking against the wall, and the intermediate rattling, ceased from that time.

Well, it was the tree which had caused the noises. The unexplained matter was that neither of the trees ever touched the walls of the house during the highest wind, and that trees could not rattle like a man playing castanets or shaking dice.

She thought, 'Is it the intention of Fate that something connected with these noises shall influence my future as in the last case of the kind?'

During the dilemma she fell into a troubled sleep, and dreamt that she was being whipped with dry bones suspended on strings, which rattled at every blow like those of a malefactor on a gibbet; that she shifted and shrank and avoided every blow, and they fell then upon the wall to which she was tied. She could not see the face of the executioner for his mask, but his form was like Manston's.

'Thank Heaven!' she said, when she awoke and saw a faint light struggling through her blind. 'Now what were those noises?' To settle that question seemed more to her than the event of the day.

She pulled the blind aside and looked out. All was plain. The evening previous had closed in with a grey drizzle, borne upon a piercing air from the north, and now its effects were visible. The hoary drizzle still continued; but the trees and shrubs were laden with icicles to an extent such as she had never before witnessed. A shoot of the diameter of a pin's head was iced as thick as her finger; all the boughs in the park were bent almost to the earth with the immense weight of the glistening incumbrance; the walks were like a looking-glass. Many boughs had snapped beneath their burden, and lay in heaps upon the icy grass. Opposite her eye, on the nearest tree, was a fresh yellow scar, showing where the branch that had terrified her had been splintered from the trunk.

'I never could have believed it possible,' she thought, surveying the bowed-down branches, 'that trees would bend so far out of their true positions without breaking.' By watching a twig she could see a drop collect upon it from the hoary fog, sink to the lowest point, and there become coagulated as the others had done.

'Or that I could so exactly have imitated them,' she continued. 'On this morning I am to be married – unless this is a scheme of the great Mother* to hinder a union of which she does not approve. Is it possible for my wedding to take place in the face of such weather as this?'

2. Morning

Her brother Owen was staying with Manston at the Old House. Contrary to the opinion of the doctors, the wound had healed after the first surgical operation, and his leg was gradually acquiring strength, though he could only as yet get about on crutches, or ride, or be dragged in a chair.

Miss Aldclyffe had arranged that Cytherea should be married from Knapwater House, and not from her brother's lodgings at Budmouth, which was Cytherea's first idea. Owen, too, seemed to prefer the plan. The capricious old maid had latterly taken to the contemplation of the wedding with even greater warmth than had at first inspired her, and appeared determined to do everything in her power, consistent with her dignity, to render the adjuncts of the ceremony pleasing and complete.

But the weather seemed in flat contradiction of the whole proceeding. At eight o'clock the coachman crept up to the House almost upon his hands and knees, entered the kitchen, and stood with his back to the fire, panting from his exertions in pedestrianism.

The kitchen was by far the pleasantest apartment in Knapwater House on such a morning as this. The vast fire was the centre of the whole system, like a sun, and threw its warm rays upon the figures of the domestics, wheeling about it in true planetary style. A nervously-feeble imitation of its flicker was continually attempted by a family of polished metallic utensils standing in rows and groups against the walls

196

opposite, the whole collection of shines nearly annihilating the weak daylight from outside. A step further in, and the nostrils were greeted by the scent of green herbs just gathered, and the eye by the plump form of the cook, wholesome, white-aproned, and floury – looking as edible as the food she manipulated – her movements being supported and assisted by her satellites, the kitchen and scullery maids. Minute recurrent sounds prevailed – the click of the smoke-jack,★ the flap of the flames, and the light touches of the women's slippers upon the stone floor.

The coachman hemmed, spread his feet more firmly upon the hearthstone, and looked hard at a small plate in the extreme corner of the dresser.

'No wedden this mornen – that's my opinion. In fact, there can't be,' he said abruptly, as if the words were the mere torso of a many-membered thought that had existed complete in his head.

The kitchen-maid was toasting a slice of bread at the end of a very long toasting-fork, which she held at arm's length towards the unapproachable fire, travestying the flanconade★ in fencing.

'Bad out of doors, isn't it?' she said, with a look of commiseration for things in general.

'Bad? Not even a liven soul, gentle or simple, can stand on level ground. As to getten up hill to the church, 'tis perfect lunacy. And I speak of foot-passengers. As to horses and carriage, 'tis murder to think of 'em. I am going to send straight as a line into the breakfast-room, and say 'tis a closer.★ ... Hullo – here's Clerk Crickett and John Day a-comen! Now just look at 'em and picture a wedden if you can.'

All eyes were turned to the window, from which the clerk and gardener were seen crossing the court, bowed and stooping like Bel and Nebo.★

'You'll have to go if it breaks all the horses' legs in the county,' said the cook, turning from the spectacle, knocking open the oven-door with the tongs, glancing critically in, and slamming it together with a clang.

'O, O; why shall I?' asked the coachman, including in his auditory by a glance the clerk and gardener who had just entered.

'Because Mr Manston is in the business. Did you ever know him to give up for weather of any kind, or for any other mortal thing in heaven or earth?'

'—Mornen so's – such as it is!' interrupted Mr Crickett cheerily, coming forward to the blaze and warming one hand without looking at the fire. 'Mr Manston gie up for anything in heaven or earth, did you say? You might ha' cut it short by sayen "to Miss Aldclyffe", and leaven out heaven and earth as trifles. But it might be put off; putten off a thing isn't getten rid of a thing, if that thing is a woman. O no, no!'

The coachman and gardener now naturally subsided into secondaries. The cook went on rather sharply, as she dribbled milk into the exact centre of a little crater of flour in a platter –

'It might be in this case; she's so indifferent.'

'Dang my old sides! and so it might be. I have a bit of news – I thought there was something upon my tongue; but 'tis a secret; not a word, mind, not a word. Why, Miss Hinton took a holiday yesterday.'

'Yes?' inquired the cook, looking up with perplexed curiosity.

'D'ye think that's all?'

'Don't be so three-cunning* – if it is all, deliver you from the evil of raising a woman's expectations wrongfully; I'll skimmer your pate* as sure as you cry Amen!'

'Well, it isn't all. When I got home last night my wife said, "Miss Adelaide took a holiday this mornen," says she (my wife, that is); "walked over to Nether Mynton, met the chosen man, and got married!" says she.'

'Got married! what, Lord-a-mercy, did Springrove come?'

'Springrove, no – no – Springrove's nothen to do wi' it – 'twas Farmer Bollens. They've been playing bo-peep for these two or three months seemingly. Whilst Master Teddy Springrove has been daddlen, and hawken, and spetten* about having her, she's quietly left him all forsook. Serve him right. I don't blame the little woman a bit.'

'Farmer Bollens is old enough to be her father!'

'Ay, quite; and rich enough to be ten fathers. They say he's so rich that he has a business in every bank, and measures his money in half-pint cups.'

'Lord, I wish it was me, don't I wish 'twas me!' said the scullery-maid.

'Yes, 'twas as neat a bit of stitching as ever I hear of,' continued the clerk, with a level eye, as if he were criticizing the process from a distance. 'Not a soul knew anything about it, and my wife is the only one in our parish who knows it yet. Miss Hinton came back from the wedden, went to Mr Manston, puffed herself out large, and said she was Mrs Bollens, but that if he wished, she had no objection to keep on the house till the regular time of giving notice had expired, or till he could get another tenant.'

'Just like her independence,' said the cook.

'Well, independent or no, she's Mrs Bollens now. Ah, I shall never forget once when I went by Farmer Bollens's garden – years ago now – years, when he was taking up ashleaf taties.* A merry feller I was at that time, a very merry feller – for 'twas before I took holy orders, and it didn't prick my conscience as 'twould now. "Farmer," says I, "little taties seem to turn out small this year, don't 'em?" "O no, Crickett" says he, "some be fair-sized." He's a dull man – Farmer Bollens is – he always was. However, that's neither here nor there; he's a-married to a sharp woman, and if I don't make a mistake she'll bring him a pretty good family, gie her time.'

'Well, it don't matter; there's a Providence in it,' said the scullery-maid. 'God A'mighty always sends bread as well as children.'

'But 'tis the bread to one house and the children to another very often. However, I think I can see my lady Hinton's reason for choosing yesterday to sickness-or-health-it.* Your young Miss, and that one, had crossed one another's path in regard to young Master Springrove; and I expect that when Addy Hinton found Miss Graye wasn't caren to have en, she thought she'd be beforehand with her old enemy in marrying somebody else too. That's maids' logic all over, and maids' malice likewise.'

Women who are bad enough to divide against themselves under a man's partiality are good enough to instantly unite in a common cause against his attack. 'I'll just tell you one thing then,' said the cook, shaking out her words to the time of a whisk she was beating eggs with. 'Whatever maids' logic is and maids' malice too, if Cytherea Graye even now knows that young Springrove is free again, she'll fling over the steward as soon as look at him.'

'No, no: not now,' the coachman broke in as a moderator. 'There's honour in that maid, if ever there was in one. No Miss Hinton's tricks in her. She'll stick to Manston.'

'Pifh!'

'Don't let a word be said till the wedden is over, for Heaven's sake,' the clerk continued. 'Miss Aldclyffe would fairly hang and quarter me, if my news broke off that there wedden at a last minute like this.'

'Then you had better get your wife to bolt you in the closet for an hour or two, for you'll chatter it yourself to the whole boiling parish if she don't! 'Tis a poor womanly feller!'

'You shouldn't ha' begun it, clerk. I knew how 'twould be,' said the gardener soothingly, in whisper to the clerk's mangled remains.

The clerk turned and smiled at the fire, and warmed his other hand.

3. Noon

The weather gave way. In half-an-hour there began a rapid thaw. By ten o'clock the roads, though still dangerous, were practicable to the extent of the half-mile required by the people of Knapwater Park. One mass of heavy leaden cloud spread over the whole sky; the air began to feel damp and mild out of doors, though still cold and frosty within.

They reached the church and passed up the nave, the deep-coloured glass of the narrow windows rendering the gloom of the morning almost night itself inside the building. Then the ceremony began. The only warmth or spirit imported into it came from the bridegroom, who retained a vigorous – even Spenserian* – bridal-mood throughout the morning.

Cytherea was as firm as he at this critical moment, but as cold as the air surrounding her. The few persons forming the wedding-party were constrained in movement and tone, and from the nave of the church came occasional coughs, emitted by those who, in spite of the weather, had assembled to see the termination of Cytherea's existence as a single woman. Many poor people loved her. They pitied her success, why, they could not tell, except that it was because she seemed to stand more like a statue than Cytherea Graye.

Yet she was prettily and carefully dressed; a strange contradiction in a man's idea of things – a saddening, perplexing contradiction. Are there any points in which a difference of sex amounts to a difference of nature? Then this is surely one. Not so much, as it is commonly put, in regard to the amount of consideration given, but in the conception of the thing considered. A man emasculated by coxcombry may spend more time upon the arrangement of his clothes than any woman, but even then there is no fetichism in his idea of them – they are still only a covering he uses for a time. But here was Cytherea, in the bottom of her heart almost indifferent to life, yet possessing an instinct with which her heart had nothing to do, the instinct to be particularly regardful of those sorry trifles, her robe, her flowers, her veil, and her gloves.

The irrevocable words were soon spoken – the indelible writing soon written – and they came out of the vestry. Candles had been necessary here to enable them to sign their names and on their return to the church the light from the candles streamed from the small open door, and across the chancel to a black chestnut screen on the south side, dividing it from a small chapel or chantry, erected for the soul's peace of some Aldclyffe of the past. Through the openwork of this screen could now be seen illuminated, inside the chantry, the reclining figures of cross-legged knights, damp and green with age, and above them a huge classic monument, also inscribed to the Aldclyffe family, heavily sculptured in cadaverous marble.

Leaning here – almost hanging to the monument – was Edward Springrove, or his spirit.

The weak daylight would never have revealed him, shaded as he was by the screen; but the unexpected rays of candle-light in the front showed him forth in startling relief to any and all of those whose eyes wandered in that direction. The sight was a sad one – sad beyond all description. His eyes were wild, their orbits leaden. His face was of a sickly paleness, his hair dry and disordered, his lips parted as if he could get no breath. His figure was spectre-thin.* His actions seemed beyond his own control.

Manston did not see him; Cytherea did. The healing effect upon her heart of a year's silence – a year and a half's separation – was undone in an instant. One of those strange revivals of passion by mere sight – commoner in women than in men, and in oppressed women common-est of all – had taken place in her – so transcendently, that even to herself it seemed more like a new creation than a revival.

Marrying for a home – what a mockery it was!

It may be said that the means most potent for rekindling old love in a maiden's heart are, to see her lover in laughter and good spirits in her despite when the breach has been owing to a slight from herself; when owing to a slight from him, to see him suffering for his own fault. If he is happy in a clear conscience, she blames him; if he is miserable because deeply to blame, she blames herself. The latter was Cytherea's case, now.

First, an agony of face told of the suppressed misery within her, which presently could be suppressed no longer. When they were coming out of the porch, there broke from her in a low, plaintive scream the words, 'He's dying – dying! O God, save us!' She began to sink down, and would have fallen had not Manston caught her. The chief bridesmaid applied her vinaigrette.

'What did she say?' inquired Manston.

Owen was the only one to whom the words were intelligible, and he was far too deeply impressed, or rather alarmed, to reply. She did not faint, and soon began to recover her self-command. Owen took advan-tage of the hindrance to step back to where the apparition had been seen. He was enraged with Springrove for what he considered an unwarrantable intrusion.

But Edward was not in the chantry. As he had come, so he had gone, nobody could tell how or whither.

It might almost have been believed that a transmutation* had taken place in Cytherea's idiosyncrasy, that her moral nature had fled.

The wedding-party returned to the house. As soon as he could find an opportunity, Owen took his sister aside to speak privately with her on what had happened. The expression of her face was hard, wild, and unreal – an expression he had never seen there before, and it disturbed him. He spoke to her severely and sadly.

'Cytherea,' he said, 'I know the cause of this emotion of yours. But remember this, there was no excuse for it. You should have been woman enough to control yourself. Remember whose wife you are, and don't think anything more of a mean-spirited fellow like Springrove; he had no business to come here as he did. You are altogether wrong, Cytherea, and I am vexed with you more than I can say – very vexed.'

'Say ashamed of me at once,' she bitterly answered.

'I am ashamed of you,' he retorted angrily; 'the mood has not left you yet, then?'

'Owen,' she said, and paused. Her lip trembled; her eye told of sensations too deep for tears. 'No, Owen, it has not left me; and I will be honest. I own now to you, without any disguise of words, what last night I did not own to myself, because I hardly knew of it. I love Edward Springrove with all my strength, and heart, and soul. You call me a wanton for it, don't you? I don't care; I have gone beyond caring for anything!' She looked stonily into his face and made the speech calmly.

'Well, poor Cytherea, don't talk like that!' he said, alarmed at her manner.

'I thought that I did not love him at all,' she went on hysterically. 'A year and a half had passed since we met. I could go by the gate of his garden without thinking of him – look at his seat in church and not care. But I saw him this morning – dying because he loves me so – I know it is that! Can I help loving him too? No, I cannot, and I will love him, and I don't care! We have been separated somehow by some contrivance – I know we have. O, if I could only die!'

He held her in his arms. 'Many a woman has gone to ruin herself,' he said, 'and brought those who love her into disgrace, by acting upon such impulses as possess you now. I have a reputation to lose as well as you. It seems that do what I will by way of remedying the stains which fell upon us, it is all doomed to be undone again.' His voice grew husky as he made the reply.

The right and only effective chord had been touched. Since she had seen Edward, she had thought only of herself and him. Owen – her name – position – future – had been as if they did not exist.

'I won't give way and become a disgrace to *you*, at any rate,' she said.

'Besides, your duty to society, and those about you, requires that you should live with (at any rate) all the appearance of a good wife, and try to love your husband.'

'Yes – my duty to society,' she murmured. 'But ah, Owen, it is difficult to adjust our outer and inner life with perfect honesty to all! Though it may be right to care more for the benefit of the many than for the indulgence of your own single self, when you consider that the many, and duty to them, only exist to you through your own existence, what can be said? What do our own acquaintances care about us? Not much. I think of mine. Mine will now (do they learn all the wicked frailty of my heart in this affair) look at me, smile sickly, and condemn me. And perhaps, far in time to come, when I am dead and gone, some other's accent, or some other's song, or thought, like an old one of mine, will carry them back to what I used to say, and hurt their hearts a little that they blamed me so soon. And they will pause just for an instant, and give a sigh to me, and think, "Poor girl!" believing they do great justice to my memory by this. But they will never, never realize that it was my single opportunity of existence, as well as of doing my duty, which they are regarding; they will not feel that what to them is but a thought, easily held in those two words of pity, "Poor girl!" was a whole life to me; as full of hours, minutes, and peculiar minutes, of hopes and dreads, smiles, whisperings, tears, as theirs: that it was my world, what is to them their world, and they in that life of mine, however much I cared for them, only as the thought I seem to them to be. Nobody can enter into another's nature truly, that's what is so grievous.'

'Well, it cannot be helped,' said Owen.

'But we must not stay here,' she continued, starting up and going. 'We shall be missed. I'll do my best, Owen – I will, indeed.'

It had been decided on account of the wretched state of the roads, the newly-married pair should not drive to the station till the latest hour in the afternoon at which they could get a train to take them to Southampton (their destination that night) by a reasonable time in the evening. They intended the next morning to cross to Havre, and thence to Paris – a place Cytherea had never visited – for their wedding tour.

The afternoon drew on. The packing was done. Cytherea was so restless that she could stay still nowhere. Miss Aldclyffe, who, though she took little part in the day's proceedings, was, as it were, instinctively conscious of all their movements, put down her charge's agitation for once as the natural result of the novel event, and Manston himself was as indulgent as could be wished.

At length Cytherea wandered alone into the conservatory. When in it, she thought she would run across to the hot-house in the outer garden, having in her heart a whimsical desire that she should also like to take a last look at the familiar flowers and luxuriant leaves collected there. She pulled on a pair of overshoes, and thither she went. Not a soul was in or around the place. The gardener was making merry on Manston's and her account.

The happiness that a generous spirit derives from the belief that it exists in others is often greater than the primary happiness itself. The gardener thought, 'How happy they are!' and the thought made him happier than they.

Coming out of the forcing-house again, she was on the point of returning indoors, when a feeling that these moments of solitude would be her last of freedom induced her to prolong them a little, and she stood still, unheeding the wintry aspect of the curly-leaved plants, the straw-covered beds, and the bare fruit-trees around her. The garden, no part of which was visible from the houe, sloped down to a narrow river at the foot, dividing it from the meadows without.

A man was lingering along the public path on the other side of the river; she fancied she knew the form. Her resolutions, taken in the presence of Owen, did not fail her now. She hoped and prayed that it might not be one who had stolen her heart away, and still kept it. Why should he have reappeared at all, when he had declared that he went out of her sight for ever?

She hastily hid herself, in the lowest corner of the garden close to the river. A large dead tree, thickly robed in ivy, had been considerably depressed by its icy load of the morning, and hung low over the stream, which here ran slow and deep. The tree screened her from the eyes of any passer on the other side.

She waited timidly and her timidity increased. She would not allow herself to see him – she would hear him pass, and then look to see if it had been Edward.

But, before she heard anything, she became aware of an object reflected in the water from under the tree which hung over the river in such a way that, though hiding the actual path, and objects upon it, it permitted their reflected images to pass beneath its boughs. The reflected form was that of the man she had seen further off, but being inverted, she could not definitely characterize him.

He was looking at the upper windows of the House – at hers – was it Edward, indeed? If so, he was probably thinking he would like to say one parting word. He came closer, gazed into the stream, and walked very slowly. She was almost certain that it was Edward. She kept more safely hidden. Conscience told her that she ought not to see him. But she suddenly asked herself a question: 'Can it be possible that he sees my reflected image, as I see his? Of course he does!'

He was looking at her in the water.

She could not help herself now. She stepped forward just as he emerged from the other side of the tree and appeared erect before her. It was Edward Springrove – till the inverted vision met his eye, dreaming no more of seeing his Cytherea there than of seeing the dead themselves.

'Cytherea!'

'Mr Springrove,' she returned, in a low voice, across the stream.

He was the first to speak again.

'Since we have met, I want to tell you something, before we become quite as strangers to each other.'

'No – not now – I did not mean to speak – it is not right, Edward.' She spoke hurriedly and turned away from him, beating the air with her hand.

'Not one common word of explanation?' he implored. 'Don't think I am bad enough to try to lead you astray. Well, go – it is better.'

Their eyes met again. She was nearly choked. O, how she longed – and dreaded – to hear his explanation!

'What is it?' she said desperately.

'It is that I did not come to the church this morning in order to distress you: I did not Cytherea. It was to try to speak to you before you were – married.'

He stepped closer, and went on, 'You know what has taken place? Surely you do? – my cousin is married, and I am free.'

'Married – and not to you?' Cytherea faltered, in a weak whisper.

'Yes, she was married yesterday! A rich man had appeared, and she jilted me. She said she never would have jilted a stranger, but that by jilting me, she only exercised the right everybody has of snubbing their own relations. But that's nothing now. I came to you to ask once more if. . . . But I was too late.'*

'But, Edward, what's that, what's that!' she cried, in an agony of reproach. 'Why did you leave me to return to her? Why did you write me that cruel, cruel letter that nearly killed me!'

'Cytherea! Why, you had grown to love – like – Mr Manston, and how could you be anything to me – or care for me? Surely I acted naturally?'

'O no – never! I loved you – only you – not him – always you! – till lately. . . . I try to love him now.'

'But that can't be correct! Miss Aldclyffe told me that you wanted to hear no more of me – proved it to me!' said Edward.

'Never! she couldn't.'

'She did, Cytherea. And she sent me a letter – a love-letter, you wrote to Mr Manston.'

'A love-letter I wrote?'

'Yes, a love-letter – you could not meet him just then, you said; you were sorry, but the emotion you had felt with him made you forgetful of realities.'

The strife of thought in the unhappy girl who listened to this distortion of her meaning could find no vent in words. And then there followed the slow revelation in return, bringing with it all the misery of an explanation which comes too late. The question whether Miss Aldclyffe were schemer or dupe was almost passed over by Cytherea, under the immediate oppressiveness of her despair in the sense that her position was irretrievable.

Not so Springrove. He saw through all the cunning half-mis-representations – worse than downright lies – which had just been sufficient to turn the scale both with him and with her; and from the bottom of his soul he cursed the woman and man who had brought all this agony upon him and his Love. But he could not add more misery to the future of the poor child by revealing too much. The whole scheme she should never know.

'I was indifferent to my own future,' Edward said, 'and was urged to promise adherence to my engagement with my cousin Adelaide by Miss Aldclyffe: now you are married I cannot tell you how, but it was on account of my father. Being forbidden to think of you, what did I care about anything? My new thought that you still loved me was first raised by what my father said in the letter announcing my cousin's marriage. He said that although you were to be married on Old Christmas Day – that is to-morrow – he had noticed your appearance with pity: he thought you loved me still. It was enough for me – I came down by the earliest morning train, thinking I could see you some time to-day, the day, as I thought, before your marriage, hoping, but hardly daring to hope, that you might be induced to marry me. I hurried from the station; when I reached the village I saw idlers about the church, and the private gate leading to the House open. I ran into the church by the small* door and saw you come out of the vestry; I was too late. I have now told you. I was compelled to tell you. O, my lost darling, now I shall live content – or die content!'

'I am to blame, Edward, I am,' she said mournfully; 'I was taught to dread pauperism; my nights were made sleepless; there was continually reiterated in my ears till I believed it –

> 'The world and its ways have a certain worth,
> And to press a point where these oppose
> Were a simple policy.*

But I will say nothing about who influenced – who persuaded. The act is mine, after all. Edward, I married to escape dependence for my bread upon the whim of Miss Aldclyffe, or others like her. It was clearly represented to me that dependence is bearable if we have another place which we call home; but to be a dependent and to have no other spot for the heart to anchor upon – O, it is mournful and harassing! . . . But that without which all persuasion would have been as air, was added by my miserable conviction that you were false; that did it, that turned me! You were to be considered as nobody to me, and Mr Manston invariably kind. Well, the deed is done – I must abide by it. I shall never let him know that I do not love him – never. If things had only remained as they seemed to be, if you had really forgotten me and married another woman, I could have borne it better. I wish I did not know the truth as I know it now! But our life, what is it? Let us be brave, Edward, and live out our few remaining years with dignity. They will not be long. O, I hope they will not be long! . . . Now, good-bye, good-bye!'

'I wish I could be near and touch you once, just once,' said Spring-rove, in a voice which he vainly endeavoured to keep firm and clear.

They looked at the river, then into it; a shoal of minnows was floating over the sandy bottom, like the black dashes on miniver;* though narrow, the stream was deep, and there was no bridge.

'Cytherea, reach out your hand that I may just touch it with mine.'

She stepped to the brink and stretched out her hand and fingers towards his, but not into them. The river was too wide.

'Never mind,' said Cytherea, her voice broken by agitation, 'I must be going. God bless and keep you, my Edward! God bless you!'

'I must touch you, I must press your hand,' he said.

They came near – nearer – nearer still – their fingers met. There was a long firm clasp, so close and still that each hand could feel the other's pulse throbbing besides its own.

'My Cytherea! my stolen pet lamb!'

She glanced a mute farewell from her large perturbed eyes, turned, and ran up the garden without looking back. All was over between them. The river flowed on as quietly and obtusely as ever, and the minnows gathered again in their favourite spot as if they had never been disturbed.

Nobody indoors guessed from her countenance and bearing that her heart was near to breaking with the intensity of the misery which gnawed there. At these times a woman does not faint, or weep, or scream, as she will in the moment of sudden shocks. When lanced by a mental agony of such refined and special torture that it is indescribable by men's words, she moves among her acquaintances much as before, and contrives so to cast her actions in the old moulds that she is only considered to be rather duller than usual.

5. Half-Past Two to Five o'Clock p.m.

Owen accompanied the newly-married couple to the railway-station, and in his anxiety to see the last of his sister, left the brougham* and stood upon his crutches whilst the train was starting.

When the husband and wife were about to enter the railway-carriage they saw one of the porters looking frequently and furtively at them. He was pale, and apparently very ill.

'Look at that poor sick man,' said Cytherea compassionately, 'surely he ought not to be here.'

'He's been very queer to-day, madam, very queer,' another porter answered. 'He do hardly hear when he's spoken to, and d' seem giddy, or as if something was on his mind. He's been like it for this month past, but nothing so bad as he is to-day.'

'Poor thing.'

She could not resist an innate desire to do some just thing on this most deceitful and wretched day of her life. Going up to him she gave him money, and told him to send to the old manor-house for wine or whatever he wanted.

The train moved off as the trembling man was murmuring his incoherent thanks. Owen waved his hand; Cytherea smiled back to him as if it were unknown to her that she wept all the while.

Owen was driven back to the Old House. But he could not rest in the lonely place. His conscience began to reproach him for having forced on the marriage of his sister with a little too much peremptoriness. Taking up his crutches he went out of doors and wandered about the muddy roads with no object in view save that of getting rid of time.

The clouds which had hung so low and densely during the day cleared from the west just now as the sun was setting, calling forth a weakly twitter from a few small birds. Owen crawled down the path to the waterfall, and lingered thereabouts till the solitude of the place oppressed him, when he turned back and into the road to the village. He was sad; he said to himself –

'If there is ever any meaning in those heavy feelings which are called presentiments – and I don't believe there is – there will be in mine to-day. . . . Poor little Cytherea!'

At that moment the last low rays of the sun touched the head and shoulders of a man who was approaching, and showed him up to Owen's view. It was old Mr Springrove. They had grown familiar with each other by reason of Owen's visits to Knapwater during the past year. The farmer inquired how Owen's foot was progressing, and was glad to see him so nimble again.

'How is your son?' said Owen mechanically.

'He is at home, sitting by the fire,' said the farmer, in a sad voice. 'This morning he slipped indoors from God knows where, and there he sits and mopes, and thinks, and thinks, and presses his head so hard, that I can't help feeling for him.'

'Is he married?' said Owen. Cytherea had feared to tell him of the interview in the garden.

'No. I can't quite understand how the matter rests. . . . Ah! Edward, too, who started with such promise; that he should now have become such a careless fellow – not a month in one place. There, Mr Graye, I know what it is mainly owing to. If it hadn't been for that heart affair, he might have done – but the less said about him the better. I don't know what we should have done if Miss Aldclyffe had insisted upon the conditions of the leases. Your brother-in-law, the steward, had a hand in making it light for us, I know, and I heartily thank him for it.' He ceased speaking, and looked round at the sky.

'Have you heard o' what's happened?' he said suddenly; 'I was just coming out to learn about it.'

'I haven't heard of anything.'

'It is something very serious, though I don't know what. All I know is what I heard a man call out by-now – that it very much concerns somebody who lives in the parish.'

It seems singular enough, even to minds who have no dim beliefs in adumbration and presentiment, that at that moment not the shadow of a thought crossed Owen's mind that the somebody whom the matter concerned might be himself, or any belonging to him. The event about to transpire was as portentous to the woman whose welfare was more dear to him than his own, as any, short of death itself, could possibly be; and ever afterwards, when he considered the effect of the knowledge the next half-hour conveyed to his brain, even his practical good sense could not refrain from wonder that he should have walked toward the village after hearing those words of the farmer, in so leisurely and unconcerned a way. 'How unutterably mean must my intelligence have appeared to the eye of a foreseeing God,' he frequently said in after-time. 'Columbus on the eve of his discovery of a world was not so contemptibly unaware.'

After a few additional words of commonplace the farmer left him, and, as has been said, Owen proceeded slowly and indifferently towards the village.

The labouring men had just left work, and passed the park gate, which opened into the street as Owen came down towards it. They went along in a drift, earnestly talking, and were finally about to turn in at their respective doorways. But upon seeing him they looked significantly at one another, and paused. He came into the road, on that side of the village-green which was opposite the row of cottages, and turned round to the right. When Owen turned, all eyes turned; one or two men went hurriedly indoors, and afterwards appeared at the doorstep with their wives, who also contemplated him, talking as they looked. They seemed uncertain how to act in some matter.

'If they want me, surely they will call me,' he thought, wondering more and more. He could no longer doubt that he was connected with the subject of their discourse.

The first who approached him was a boy.

'What has occurred?' said Owen.

'O, a man ha' got crazy-religious, and sent for the pa'son.'

'Is that all?'

'Yes, sir. He wished he was dead, he said, and he's almost out of his mind wi' wishen it so much. That was before Mr Raunham came.'

'Who is he?' said Owen.

'Joseph Chinney, one of the railway-porters; he used to be night-porter.'

'Ah – the man who was ill this afternoon; by the way, he was told to come to the Old House for something, but he hasn't been. But has anything else happened – anything that concerns the wedding to-day?'

'No, sir.'

Concluding that the connection which had seemed to be traced between himself and the event must in some way have arisen from Cytherea's friendliness towards the man, Owen turned about and went homewards in a much quieter frame of mind – yet scarcely satisfied with the solution. The route he had chosen led through the dairy-yard, and he opened the gate.

Five minutes before this point of time, Edward Springrove was looking over one of his father's fields at an outlying hamlet of three or four cottages some mile and a half distant. A turnpike-gate was close by the gate of the field.

The carrier from Casterbridge came up as Edward stepped into the road, and jumped down from the van to pay arrears of toll. He recognized Springrove. 'This is a pretty set-to in your place, sir,' he said. 'You don't know about it, I suppose?'

'What?' said Springrove.

The carrier paid his dues, came up to Edward, and spoke ten words in a confidential whisper: then sprang upon the shafts of his vehicle, gave a clinching nod of significance to Springrove, and rattled away.

Edward turned pale with the intelligence. His first thought was, 'Bring her home!'

The next – did Owen Graye know what had been discovered? He probably did by this time, but no risks of probability must be run by a woman he loved dearer than all the world besides. He would at any rate make perfectly sure that her brother was in possession of the knowledge, by telling it him with his own lips.

Off he ran in the direction of the old manor-house.

The path was across arable land, and was ploughed up with the rest of the field every autumn, after which it was trodden out afresh. The thaw had so loosened the soft earth, that lumps of stiff mud were lifted by his feet at every leap he took and flung against him by his rapid motion, as it were doggedly impeding him, and increasing tenfold the customary effort of running.

But he ran on – uphill, and downhill, the same pace alike – like the shadow of a cloud. His nearest direction, too, like Owen's, was through the dairy-barton,* and as Owen entered it he saw the figure of Edward rapidly descending the opposite hill, at a distance of two or three hundred yards. Owen advanced amid the cows.

The dairyman, who had hitherto been talking loudly on some absorbing subject to the maids and men milking around him, turned his face towards the head of the cow when Owen passed, and ceased speaking.

Owen approached him and said –

211

'A singular thing has happened, I hear. The man is not insane, I suppose?'

'Not he – he's sensible enough,' said the dairyman, and paused. He was a man noisy with his associates – stolid and taciturn with strangers.

'Is it true that he is Chinney, the railway-porter?'

'That's the man, sir.' The maids and men sitting under the cows were all attentively listening to this discourse, milking irregularly, and softly directing the jets against the sides of the pail.

Owen could contain himself no longer, much as his mind dreaded anything of the nature of ridicule. 'The people all seem to look at me, as if something seriously concerned me; is it this stupid matter, or what is it?'

'Surely, sir, you know better than anybody else if such a strange thing concerns you.'

'What strange thing?'

'Don't you know! His confessing to Parson Raunham.'

'What did he confess? Tell me.'

'If you really ha'n't heard, 'tis this. He was as usual on duty at the station on the night of the fire last year, otherwise he wouldn't ha' known it.'

'Known what? For God's sake tell, man!'

But at this instant the two opposite gates of the dairy-yard, one on the east, the other on the west side, slammed almost simultaneously.

The rector from one, Springrove from the other, came striding across the barton.

Edward was nearest, and spoke first. He said in a low voice: 'Your sister is not legally married! His first wife is still living! How it comes out I don't know!'

'O, here you are at last, Mr Graye, thank Heaven!' said the rector breathlessly. 'I have been to the Old House, and then to Miss Aldclyffe's looking for you – something very extraordinary.' He beckoned to Owen, afterwards included Springrove in his glance, and the three stepped aside together.

'A porter at the station. He was a curious nervous man. He had been in a strange state all day, but he wouldn't go home. Your sister was kind to him, it seems, this afternoon. When she and her husband had gone, he went on with his work, shifting luggage-vans. Well, he got in the way, as if he were quite lost to what was going on, and they sent him home at last. Then he wished to see me. I went directly. There was something on his mind, he said, and told it. About the time when the fire of last November twelvemonth was got under, whilst he was by himself in the porter's room, almost asleep, somebody came to the station and tried to open the door. He went out and found the person to be the lady he had accompanied to Carriford earlier in the evening, Mrs Manston. She asked, when would be another train to London? The first the next morning, he told her, was at a quarter-past six o'clock from Budmouth, but that it was express, and didn't stop at Carriford Road – it didn't stop till it got to Anglebury. "How far is it to Anglebury?" she said. He told her, and she thanked him, and went away up the line. In a short time she ran back and took out her purse. "Don't on any account say a word in the village or anywhere that I have been here, or a single breath about me – I'm ashamed ever to have come." He promised; she took out two sovereigns. "Swear it on the Testament in the waiting-room,"* she said, "and I'll pay you these." He got the book, took an oath upon it, received the money, and she left him. He was off duty at half-past five. He has kept silence all through the intervening time till now, but lately the knowledge he possessed weighed heavily upon his conscience and weak mind. Yet the nearer came the wedding-day, the more he feared to tell. The actual marriage filled him with remorse. He says your sister's kindness afterwards was like a knife going through his heart. He thought he had ruined her.'

'But whatever can be done? Why didn't he speak sooner?' cried Owen.

'He actually called at my house twice yesterday,' the rector continued, 'resolved, it seems, to unburden his mind. I was out both times – he left no message, and, they say, he looked relieved that his object was defeated. Then he says he resolved to come to you at the Old House last night – started, reached the door, and dreaded to knock – and then went home again.'

'Here will be a tale for the newsmongers of the county,' said Owen bitterly. 'The idea of his not opening his mouth sooner – the criminality of the thing!'

'Ah, that's the inconsistency of a weak nature. But now that it is put to us in this way, how much more probable it seems that she should have escaped than have been burnt—'

'You will, of course, go straight to Mr Manston, and ask him what it all means?' Edward interrupted.

'Of course I shall! Manston has no right to carry off my sister unless he's her husband,' said Owen. 'I shall go and separate them.'

'Certainly you will,' said the rector.

'Where's the man?'

'In his cottage.'

''Tis no use going to him, either. I must go off at once and overtake them – lay the case before Manston, and ask him for additional and certain proofs of his first wife's death. An up-train passes soon, I think.'

'Where have they gone?' said Edward.

'To Paris – as far as Southampton this afternoon, to proceed to-morrow morning.'

'Where in Southampton?'

'I really don't know – some hotel. I only have their Paris address. But I shall find them by making a few inquiries.'

The rector had in the meantime been taking out his pocket-book, and now opened it at the first page, whereon it was his custom every month to gum a small railway time-table – cut from the local newspaper.

'The afternoon express is just gone,' he said, holding open the page, 'and the next train to Southampton passes at ten minutes to six o'clock. Now it wants – let me see – five-and-forty minutes to that time. Mr Graye, my advice is that you come with me to the porter's cottage, where I will shortly write out the substance of what he has said, and get him to sign it. You will then have far better grounds for interfering between Mr and Mrs Manston than if you went to them with a mere hearsay story.'

The suggestion seemed a good one. 'Yes, there will be time before the train starts,' said Owen.

Edward had been musing restlessly.

'Let me go to Southampton in your place, on account of your lameness?' he said suddenly to Graye.

'I am much obliged to you, but I think I can scarcely accept the offer,' returned Owen coldly. 'Mr Manston is an honourable man, and I had much better see him myself.'

'There is no doubt,' said Mr Raunham, 'that the death of his wife was fully believed in by himself.'

'None whatever,' said Owen; 'and the news must be broken to him, and the question of other proofs asked in a friendly way. It would not do for Mr Springrove to appear in the case at all.' He still spoke rather coldly; the recollection of the attachment between his sister and Edward was not a pleasant one to him.

'You will never find them,' said Edward. 'You have never been to Southampton, and I know every house there.'

'That makes little difference,' said the rector; 'he will have a cab. Certainly Mr Graye is the proper man to go on the errand.'

'Stay; I'll telegraph to ask them to wait for me on the platform when they arrive,' said Owen; 'that is, if their train has not already arrived.'

Mr Raunham pulled out his pocket-book again. 'The two-thirty train reached Southampton a quarter of an hour ago,' he said.

It was too late to catch them at the station. Nevertheless, the rector suggested that it would be worth while to direct a message to 'all the respectable hotels in Southampton', on the chance of its finding them, and thus saving a deal of personal labour to Owen in searching about the place.

'I'll go and telegraph, whilst you return to the man,' said Edward – an offer which was accepted. Graye and the rector then turned off in the direction of the porter's cottage.

Edward, to despatch the message at once, hurriedly followed the road towards the station, still restlessly thinking. All Owen's proceedings were based on the assumption, natural under the circumstances, of Manston's good faith, and that he would readily acquiesce in any arrangement which should clear up the mystery. 'But,' thought Edward, 'suppose – and Heaven forgive me, I cannot help supposing it – that Manston is not that honourable man, what will a young and inexperienced fellow like Owen do? Will he not be hoodwinked by some specious story or another, framed to last till Manston gets tired of poor Cytherea? And then the disclosure of the truth will ruin and blacken both their futures irremediably.'

However, he proceeded to execute his commission. This he put in the form of a simple request from Owen to Manston, that Manston would come to the Southampton platform, and wait for Owen's arrival, as he valued his reputation. The message was directed as the rector had suggested, Edward guaranteeing to the clerk who sent it off that every expense connected with the search would be paid.

No sooner had the telegram been despatched than his heart sank within him at the want of foresight shown in sending it. Had Manston, all the time, a knowledge that his first wife lived, the telegram would be a forewarning which might enable him to defeat Owen still more signally.

Whilst the machine was still giving off its multitudinous series of raps, Edward heard a powerful rush under the shed outside, followed by a long sonorous creak. It was a train of some sort, stealing softly into the station, and it was an up-train. There was the ring of a bell. It was certainly a passenger train.

Yet the booking-office window was closed.

'Ho, ho, John, seventeen minutes after time and only three stations up the line. The incline again?' The voice was the station-master's, and the reply seemed to come from the guard.

'Yes, the other side of the cutting. The thaw has made it all in a perfect cloud of fog, and the rails are as slippery as glass. We had to bring them through the cutting at twice.'*

'Anybody else for the four-forty-five express?' the voice continued. The few passengers, having crossed over to the other side long before this time, had taken their places at once.

A conviction suddenly broke in upon Edward's mind; then a wish overwhelmed him. The conviction – as startling as it was sudden – was that Manston was a villain, who at some time earlier had discovered that his wife lived, and had bribed her to keep out of sight, that he might possess Cytherea. The wish was – to proceed at once by this very train that was starting, find Manston before he would expect from the words of the telegram (if he got it) that anybody from Carriford could be with him – charge him boldly with the crime, and trust to his consequent confusion (if he were guilty) for a solution of the extraordinary riddle, and the release of Cytherea!

The ticket-office had been locked up at the expiration of the time at which the train was due. Rushing out as the guard blew his whistle, Edward opened the door of a carriage and leapt in. The train moved along, and he was soon out of sight.

Springrove had long since passed that peculiar line which lies across the course of falling in love – if, indeed, it may not be called the initial itself of the complete passion – a longing to cherish; when the woman is shifted in a man's mind from the region of mere admiration to the region of warm fellowship. At this assumption of her nature, she changes to him in tone, hue, and expression. All about the loved one that said 'She' before, says 'We' now. Eyes that were to be subdued become eyes to be feared for: a brain that was to be probed by cynicism becomes a brain that is to be tenderly assisted; feet that were to be tested in the dance become feet that are not to be distressed; the once-criticized accent, manner, and dress, become the clients of a special pleader.

6. *Five to Eight o'Clock p.m.*

Now that he was fairly on the track, and had begun to cool down, Edward remembered that he had nothing to show – no legal authority whatever to question Manston or interfere between him and Cytherea as husband and wife. He now saw the wisdom of the rector in obtaining a signed confession from the porter. The document would not be a death-bed confession – perhaps not worth anything legally – but it would be held by Owen; and he alone, as Cytherea's natural guardian, could separate them on the mere ground of an unproved probability, or what might perhaps be called the hallucination of an idiot. Edward himself, however, was as firmly convinced as the rector had been of the truth of the man's story, and paced backward and forward the solitary compartment as the train wound through the dark heathery plains, the hazy woods, and moaning coppices, as resolved as ever to pounce on Manston, and charge him with the crime during the critical interval between the reception of the telegram and the hour at which Owen's train would arrive – trusting to circumstances for what he should say and do afterwards, but making up his mind to be ready second to Owen in any emergency that might arise.

At thirty-three minutes past seven he stood on the platform of the station at Southampton – a clear hour before the train containing Owen could possibly arrive.

Making a few inquiries here, but too impatient to pursue his investigation carefully and inductively, he went into the town.

At the expiration of another half-hour he had visited seven hotels and inns, large and small, asking the same questions at each, and always receiving the same reply – nobody of that name, or answering to that description, had been there. A boy from the telegraph office had called, asking for the same persons, if they recollected rightly.

He reflected awhile, struck again by a painful thought that they might possibly have decided to cross the Channel by the night-boat. Then he hastened off to another quarter of the town to pursue his inquiries among hotels of the more old-fashioned and quiet class. His stained and weary appearance obtained for him but a modicum of civility wherever he went, which made his task yet more difficult. He called at three several houses in this neighbourhood, with the same result as before. He entered the door of the fourth house whilst the clock of the nearest church was striking eight.

'Have a tall gentleman named Manston, and a young wife arrived here this evening?' he asked again, in words which had grown odd to his ears from very familiarity.

'A new-married couple, did you say?'

'They are, though I didn't say so.'

'They have taken a sitting-room and bedroom, number thirteen.'

'Are they indoors?'

'I don't know. Eliza!'

'Yes, m'm.'

'See if number thirteen is in – that gentleman and his wife.'

217

'Yes, m'm.'

'Has any telegram come for them?' said Edward, when the maid had gone on her errand.

'No – nothing that I know of.'

'Somebody did come and ask if a Mr and Mrs Masters, or some such name, were here this evening,' said another voice from the back of the bar-parlour.

'And did they get the message?'

'Of course they did not – they were not here – they didn't come till half-an-hour after that. The man who made inquiries left no message. I told them when they came that they, or a name something like theirs, had been asked for, but they didn't seem to understand why it should be, and so the matter dropped.'

The chambermaid came back. 'The gentleman is not in, but the lady is. Who shall I say?'

'Nobody,' said Edward. For it now became necessary to reflect upon his method of proceeding. His object in finding their whereabouts – apart from the wish to assist Owen – had been to see Manston, ask him flatly for an explanation, and confirm the request of the message in the presence of Cytherea – so as to prevent the possibility of the steward's palming off a story upon Cytherea, or eluding her brother when he came. But here were two important modifications of the expected condition of affairs. The telegram had not been received, and Cytherea was in the house alone.

He hesitated as to the propriety of intruding upon her in Manston's absence. Besides, the women at the bottom of the stairs would see him – his intrusion would seem odd – and Manston might return at any moment. He certainly might call, and wait for Manston with the accusation upon his tongue, as he had intended. But it was a doubtful course. That idea had been based upon the assumption that Cytherea was not married. If the first wife were really dead after all – and he felt sick at the thought – Cytherea as the steward's wife might in after-years – perhaps, at once – be subjected to indignity and cruelty on account of an old lover's interference now.

Yes, perhaps the announcement would come most properly and safely for her from her brother Owen, the time of whose arrival had almost expired.

But, on turning round, he saw that the staircase and passage were quite deserted. He and his errand had as completely died from the minds of the attendants as if they had never been. There was absolutely nothing between him and Cytherea's presence. Reason was powerless now; he must see her – right or wrong, fair or unfair to Manston – offensive to her brother or no. His lips must be the first to tell the alarming story to her. Who loved her as he! He went back lightly through the hall, up the stairs, two at a time, and followed the corridor till he came to the door numbered thirteen.

He knocked softly: nobody answered.

There was no time to lose if he would speak to Cytherea before Manston came. He turned the handle of the door and looked in. The lamp on the table burned low, and showed writing materials open beside it; the chief light came from the fire, the direct rays of which were obscured by a sweet familiar outline of head and shoulders – still as precious to him as ever.

7. A Quarter-Past Eight o'Clock p.m.

There is an attitude – approximatively called pensive – in which the soul of a human being, and especially of a woman, dominates outwardly and expresses its presence so strongly, that the intangible essence seems more apparent than the body itself. This was Cytherea's expression now. What old days and sunny eves at Budmouth Bay was she picturing? Her reverie had caused her not to notice his knock.

'Cytherea!' he said softly.

She let drop her hand, and turned her head, evidently thinking that her visitor could be no other than Manston, yet puzzled at the voice.

There was no preface on Springrove's tongue; he forgot his position – hers – that he had come to ask quietly if Manston had other proofs of being a widower – everything – and jumped to a conclusion.

'You are not his wife, Cytherea – come away, he has a wife living!' he cried in an agitated whisper. 'Owen will be here directly.'

She started up, recognized the tidings first, the bearer of them afterwards. 'Not his wife? O, what is it – what – who is living?' She awoke by degrees. 'What must I do? Edward, it is you! Why did you come? Where is Owen?'

'What has Manston shown you in proof of the death of his other wife? Tell me quick.'

'Nothing – we have never spoken of the subject. Where is my brother Owen? I want him, I want him!'

'He is coming by-and-by. Come to the station to meet him – do,' implored Springrove. 'If Mr Manston comes, he will keep you from me: I am nobody,' he added bitterly, feeling the reproach her words had faintly shadowed forth.

'Mr Manston is only gone out to post a letter he had just written,' she said, and without being distinctly cognizant of the action, she wildly looked for her bonnet and cloak, and began putting them on, but in the act of fastening them uttered a spasmodic cry.

'No, I'll not go out with you,' she said, flinging the articles down again. Running to the door she flitted along the passage, and downstairs.

'Give me a private room – quite private,' she said breathlessly to some one below.

'Number twelve is a single room, madam, and unoccupied,' said some tongue in astonishment.

Without waiting for any person to show her into it, Cytherea hurried upstairs again, brushed through the corridor, entered the room specified, and closed the door. Edward heard her sob out –

'Nobody but Owen shall speak to me – nobody!'

'He will be here directly,' said Springrove, close against the panel, and then went towards the stairs. He had seen her; it was enough.

He descended, stepped into the street, and hastened to meet Owen at the railway-station.

As for the poor maiden who had received the news, she knew not what to think. She listened till the echo of Edward's footsteps had died away, then bowed her face upon the bed. Her sudden impulse had been to escape from sight. Her weariness after the unwonted strain, mental and bodily, which had been put upon her by the scenes she had passed through during the long day, rendered her much more timid and shaken by her position than she would naturally have been. She thought and thought of that single fact which had been told her – that the first Mrs Manston was still living – till her brain seemed ready to burst its confinement with excess of throbbing. It was only natural that she should, by degrees, be unable to separate the discovery, which was matter of fact, from the suspicion of treachery on her husband's part, which was only matter of inference. And thus there arose in her a personal fear of him.

'Suppose he should come in now and seize me!' This at first mere frenzied supposition grew by degrees to a definite horror of his presence, and especially of his intense gaze. Thus she raised herself to a heat of excitement, which was none the less real for being vented in no cry of any kind. No; she could not meet Manston's eye alone, she would only see him in her brother's company.

Almost delirious with this idea, she ran and locked the door to prevent all possibility of her intentions being nullified, or a look or word being flung at her by anybody whilst she knew not what she was.

8. Half-Past Eight o'Clock p.m.

Then Cytherea felt her way amid the darkness of the room till she came to the head of the bed, where she searched for the bell-rope and gave it a pull. Her summons was speedily answered by the landlady herself, whose curiosity to know the meaning of these strange proceedings knew no bounds. The landlady attempted to turn the handle of the door. Cytherea kept the door locked. 'Please tell Mr Manston when he comes in that I am ill,' she said from the inside, 'and that I cannot see him.'

'Certainly I will, madam,' said the landlady. 'Won't you have a fire?'

'No, thank you.'

'Nor a light?'

'I don't want one, thank you.'

'Nor anything?'

'Nothing.'

The landlady withdrew, thinking her visitor half insane.

Manston came in about five minutes later, and went at once up to the sitting-room, fully expecting to find his wife there. He looked round, rang, and was told the words Cytherea had said, that she was too ill to be seen.

'She is in number twelve room,' added the maid.

Manston was alarmed, and knocked at the door. 'Cytherea!'

'I am unwell, I cannot see you,' she said.

'Are you seriously ill, dearest? Surely not.'

'No, not seriously.'

'Let me come in; I will get a doctor.'

'No, he can't see me either.'

'She won't open the door, sir, not to nobody at all!' said the chambermaid, with wonder-waiting eyes.

'Hold your tongue, and be off!' said Manston with a snap.

The maid vanished.

'Come, Cytherea, this is foolish – indeed it is – not opening the door. . . . I cannot comprehend what can be the matter with you. Nor can a doctor either, unless he sees you.'

Her voice had trembled more and more at each answer she gave, but nothing could induce her to come out and confront him. Hating scenes, Manston went back to the sitting-room, greatly irritated and perplexed.

And there Cytherea from the adjoining room could hear him pacing up and down. She thought, 'Suppose he insists upon seeing me – he probably may – and will burst open the door!' This notion increased, and she sank into a corner in a half-somnolent state, but with ears alive to the slightest sound. Reason could not overthrow the delirious fancy that outside her door stood Manston and all the people in the hotel, waiting to laugh her to scorn.

9. Half-Past Eight to Eleven p.m.

In the meantime Springrove was pacing up and down the arrival platform of the railway-station.

Half-past eight o'clock – the time at which Owen's train was due – had come, and passed, but no train appeared.

'When will the eight-thirty train be in?' he asked of a man who was sweeping the mud from the steps.

'She is not expected yet this hour.'

'How is that?'

'Christmas-time, you see, 'tis always so. People are running about to see their friends. The trains have been like it ever since Christmas Eve, and will be for another week yet.'

Edward again went on walking and waiting under the draughty roof. He found it utterly impossible to leave the spot. His mind was so intent upon the importance of meeting with Owen, and informing him of Cytherea's whereabouts, that he could not but fancy Owen might leave the station unobserved if he turned his back, and become lost to him in the streets of the town.

The hour expired. Ten o'clock struck. 'When will the train be in?' said Edward to the telegraph clerk.

'In five-and-thirty minutes. She's now at L——. They have extra passengers, and the rails are bad to-day.'

At last, at a quarter to eleven, the train came in.

The first to alight was Owen, looking pale and cold. He casually glanced round upon the nearly deserted platform, and was hurrying to the outlet, when his eyes fell upon Edward. At sight of his friend he was quite bewildered, and could not speak.

'Here I am, Mr Graye,' said Edward cheerfully. 'I have seen Cytherea, and she has been waiting for you these two or three hours.'

Owen took Edward's hand, pressed it, and looked at him in silence. Such was the concentration of his mind, that not till many minutes after did he think of inquiring how Springrove had contrived to be there before him.

On their arrival at the door of the hotel, it was arranged between Springrove and Graye that the latter only should enter, Edward waiting outside. Owen had remembered continually what his friend had frequently overlooked, that there was yet a possibility of his sister being Manston's wife, and the recollection taught him to avoid any rashness in his proceedings which might lead to bitterness hereafter.

Entering the room, he found Manston sitting in the chair which had been occupied by Cytherea on Edward's visit, three hours earlier. Before Owen had spoken, Manston arose, and stepping past him closed the door. His face appeared harassed – much more troubled than the slight circumstance which had as yet come to his knowledge seemed to account for.

Manston could form no reason for Owen's presence, but intuitively linked it with Cytherea's seclusion. 'Altogether this is most unseemly,' he said, 'whatever it may mean.'

'Don't think there is anything unfriendly by my coming here,' said Owen earnestly; 'but listen to this, and think if I could do otherwise than come.'

He took from his pocket the confession of Chinney the porter, as hastily written out by the vicar, and read it aloud. The aspects of Manston's face whilst he listened to the opening words were strange, dark, and mysterious enough to have justified suspicions that no deceit could be too complicated for the possessor of such impulses, had there not overridden them all, as the reading went on, a new and irrepressible expression – one unmistakably honest. It was that of unqualified amazement in the steward's mind at the news he heard. Owen looked up and saw it. The sight only confirmed him in the belief he had held throughout, in antagonism to Edward's suspicions.

There could no longer be any shadow of doubt that if the first Mrs Manston lived, her husband was ignorant of the fact. What he could have feared by his ghastly look at first, and now have ceased to fear, it was quite futile to conjecture.

'Now I do not for a moment doubt your complete ignorance of the whole matter; you cannot suppose for an instant that I do,' said Owen when he had finished reading. 'But is it not best for both that Cytherea should come back with me till the matter is cleared up? In fact, under the circumstances, no other course is left open to me than to request it.'

Whatever Manston's original feelings had been, all in him now gave way to irritation, and irritation to rage. He paced up and down the room till he had mastered it; then said in ordinary tones –

'Certainly, I know no more than you and others know – it was a gratuitous unpleasantness in you to say you did not doubt me. Why should you, or anybody, have doubted me?'

'Well, where is my sister?' said Owen.

'Locked in the next room.'

His own answer reminded Manston that Cytherea must, by some inscrutable means, have had an inkling of the event.

Owen had gone to the door of Cytherea's room. 'Cytherea, darling – 'tis Owen,' he said, outside the door. A rustling of clothes, soft footsteps, and a voice saying from the inside, 'Is it really you, Owen, – is it really?'

'It is.'

'O, will you take care of me?'

'Always.'

She unlocked the door and retreated again. Manston came forward from the other room with a candle in his hand, as Owen pushed open the door.

Her frightened eyes were unnaturally large, and shone like stars in the darkness of the background, as the light fell upon them. She leapt up to Owen in one bound, her small taper fingers extended like the leaves of a lupine. Then she clasped her cold and trembling hands round his neck and shivered.

The sight of her again kindled all Manston's passions into activity. 'She shall not go with you,' he said firmly, and stepping a pace or two closer, 'unless you prove that she is not my wife; and you can't do it!'

'This is proof,' said Owen, holding up the paper.

'No proof at all,' said Manston hotly. ''Tis not a death-bed confession, and those are the only things of the kind held as good evidence.'

'Send for a lawyer,' Owen returned, 'and let him tell us the proper course to adopt.'

'Never mind the law – let me go with Owen!' cried Cytherea, still holding on to him. 'You will let me go with him, won't you, sir?' she said, turning appealingly to Manston.

'We'll have it all right and square,' said Manston, with more quietness. 'I have no objection to your brother sending for a lawyer, if he wants to.'

It was getting on for twelve o'clock, but the proprietor of the hotel had not yet gone to bed on account of the mystery on the first floor, which was an occurrence unusual in the quiet family lodging. Owen looked over the banisters, and saw him standing in the hall. It struck Graye that the wisest course would be to take the landlord to a certain extent into their confidence, appeal to his honour as a gentleman, and so on, in order to acquire the information he wanted, and also to prevent the episode of the evening from becoming a public piece of news. He called the landlord up to where they stood, and told him the main facts of the story.

The landlord was fortunately a quiet, prejudiced man, and a meditative smoker.

'I know the very man you want to see – the very man,' he said, looking at the general features of the candle-flame. 'Sharp as a needle, and not over-rich. Timms will put you all straight in no time – trust Timms for that.'

'He's in bed by this time for certain,' said Owen.

'Never mind that – Timms knows me, I know him. He'll oblige me as a personal favour. Wait here a bit. Perhaps, too, he's up at some party or another – he's a nice, jovial fellow, sharp as a needle, too; mind you, sharp as a needle, too.'

He went downstairs, put on his overcoat, and left the house, the three persons most concerned entering the room, and standing motionless, awkward, and silent in the midst of it. Cytherea pictured to herself the long weary minutes she would have to stand there, whilst a sleepy man could be prepared for consultation, till the constraint between them seemed unendurable to her – she could never last out the time. Owen was annoyed that Manston had not quietly arranged with him at once; Manston at Owen's homeliness of idea in proposing to send for an attorney, as if he would be a touchstone of infallible proof.

Reflection was cut short by the approach of footsteps, and in a few moments the proprietor of the hotel entered, introducing his friend. 'Mr Timms has not been in bed,' he said; 'he had just returned from dining with a few friends, so there's no trouble given. To save time I explained the matter as we came along.'

It occurred to Owen and Manston both that they might get a misty exposition of the law from Mr Timms at that moment of concluding dinner with a few friends.

'As far as I can see,' said the lawyer, yawning, and turning his vision inward by main force, 'it is quite a matter for private arrangement between the parties, whoever the parties are – at least at present. I speak more as a father than as a lawyer, it is true, but let the young lady stay with her father, or guardian, safe out of shame's way, until the mystery is sifted, whatever the mystery is. Should the evidence prove to be false, or trumped up by anybody to get her away from you, her husband, you may sue them for the damages accruing from the delay.'

'Yes, yes,' said Manston, who had completely recovered his self-possession and common sense; 'let it all be settled by herself.' Turning to Cytherea he whispered so softly that Owen did not hear the words –

'Do you wish to go back with your brother, dearest, and leave me here miserable, and lonely, or will you stay with me, your own husband?'

'I'll go back with Owen.'

'Very well.' He relinquished his coaxing tone, and went on sternly: 'And remember this, Cytherea, I am innocent of deception in this thing as you are yourself. Do you believe me?'

'I do,' she said.

'I had no shadow of suspicion that my first wife lived. I don't think she does even now. Do you believe me?'

'I believe you,' she said.

'And now, good-evening,' he continued, opening the door and politely intimating to the three men standing by that there was no further necessity for their remaining in his room. 'In three days I shall claim her.'

The lawyer and the hotel-keeper retired first. Owen, gathering up as much of his sister's clothing as lay about the room, took her upon his arm, and followed them. Edward, to whom she owed everything, who had been left standing in the street like a dog without a home, was utterly forgotten. Owen paid the landlord and the lawyer for the trouble he had occasioned them, looked to the packing, and went to the door.

A fly, which somewhat unaccountably was seen lingering in front of the house, was called up, and Cytherea's luggage put upon it.

'Do you know of any hotel near the station that is open for night arrivals?' Owen inquired of the driver.

'A place has been bespoke for you, sir, at the White Unicorn – and the gentleman wished me to give you this.'

'Bespoken by Springrove, who ordered the fly, of course,' said Owen to himself. By the light of the street-lamp he read these lines, hurriedly traced in pencil: –

I have gone home by the mail-train. It is better for all parties that I should be out of the way. Tell Cytherea that I apologize for having caused her such unnecessary pain, as it seems I did – but it cannot be helped now.

E.S.

Owen handed his sister into the vehicle, and told the flyman to drive on.

'Poor Springrove – I think we have served him rather badly,' he said to Cytherea, repeating the words of the note to her.

A thrill of pleasure passed through her bosom as she listened to them. They were the genuine reproach of a lover to his mistress; the trifling coldness of her answer to him would have been noticed by no man who was only a friend. But, in entertaining that sweet thought, she had forgotten herself, and her position for the instant.

Was she still Manston's wife – that was the terrible supposition, and her future seemed still a possible misery to her. For, on acount of the late jarring accident, a life without Manston which would otherwise have been only a sadness, must become a burden of unutterable sorrow.

Then she thought of the misrepresentation and scandal that would ensue if she were no wife. One cause for thankfulness accompanied the reflection; Edward knew the truth.

They soon reached the quiet old inn which had been selected for them by the forethought of the man who loved her well. Here they installed themselves for the night, arranging to go to Budmouth by the first train the next day.

At this hour Edward Springrove was fast approaching his native county on the wheels of the night-mail.

CHAPTER FOURTEEN
The Events of Five Weeks

1. From the Sixth to the Thirteenth of January

Manston had evidently resolved to do nothing in a hurry.

This much was plain, that his earnest desire and intention was to raise in Cytherea's bosom no feelings of permanent aversion to him. The instant after the first burst of disappointment had escaped him in the hotel at Southampton, he had seen how far better it would be to lose her presence for a week than her respect for ever.

'She shall be mine; I will claim the young thing yet,' he insisted. And then he seemed to reason over methods for compassing that object, which, to all those who were in any degree acquainted with the recent event, appeared the least likely of possible contingencies.

He returned to Knapwater late the next day, and was preparing to call on Miss Aldclyffe, when the conclusion forced itself upon him that nothing would be gained by such a step. No; every action of his should be done openly – even religiously. At least, he called on the rector, and stated this to be his resolve.

'Certainly,' said Mr Raunham, 'it is best to proceed candidly and fairly, or undue suspicion may fall on you. You should, in my opinion, take active steps at once.'

'I will do the utmost that lies in my power to clear up the mystery, and silence the hubbub of gossip that has been set going about me. But what can I do? They say that the man who comes first in the chain of inquiry is not to be found – I mean the porter.'

'I am sorry to say that he is not. When I returned from the station last night, after seeing Owen Graye off, I went again to the cottage where he has been lodging, to get more intelligence, as I thought. He was not there. He had gone out at dusk, saying he would be back soon. But he has not come back yet.'

'I rather doubt if we shall see him again.'

'Had I known of this, I would have done what in my flurry I did not think of doing – set a watch upon him. But why not advertise for your missing wife as a preliminary, consulting your solicitor in the meantime?'

'Advertise. I'll think about it,' said Manston, lingering on the word as he pronounced it. 'Yes, that seems a right thing – quite a right thing.'

He went home and remained moodily indoors all the next day and the next – for nearly a week, in short. Then, one evening at dusk, he went out with an uncertain air as to the direction of his walk, which resulted, however, in leading him again to the rectory.

He saw Mr Raunham. 'Have you done anything yet?' the rector inquired.

'No – I have not,' said Manston absently. 'But I am going to set about it.' He hesitated, as if ashamed of some weakness he was about to betray. 'My object in calling was to ask if you had heard any tidings from Budmouth of my – Cytherea. You used to speak of her as one you were interested in.'

There was, at any rate, real sadness in Manston's tone now, and the rector paused to weigh his words ere he replied.

'I have not heard directly from her,' he said gently. 'But her brother has communicated with some people in the parish—'

'The Springroves, I suppose,' said Manston gloomily.

'Yes; and they tell me that she is very ill, and I am sorry to say, likely to be for some days.'

'Surely, surely, I must go and see her!' Manston cried.

'I would advise you not to go,' said Raunham. 'But do this instead – be as quick as you can in making a movement towards ascertaining the truth as regards the existence of your wife. You see, Mr Manston, an outstep* place like this is not like a city, and there is nobody to busy himself for the good of the community; whilst poor Cytherea and her brother are socially too dependent to be able to make much stir in the matter, which is a greater reason still why you should be disinterestedly prompt.'

The steward murmured an assent. Still there was the same indecision! – not the indecision of weakness – the indecision of conscious perplexity.

On Manston's return from this interview at the rectory, he passed the door of the Rising Sun Inn. Finding he had no light for his cigar, and it being three-quarters of a mile to his residence in the park, he entered the tavern to get one. Nobody was in the outer portion of the front room where Manston stood, but a space round the fire was screened off from the remainder, and inside the high oak settle forming a part of the screen, he heard voices conversing. The speakers had not noticed his footsteps, and continued their discourse.

One of the two he recognized as a well-known night-poacher, the man who had met him with tidings of his wife's death on the evening of the conflagration. The other seemed to be a stranger following the same mode of life. The conversation was carried on in the emphatic and confidential tone of men who are slightly intoxicated, its subject being an unaccountable experience that one of them had had on the night of the fire.

What the steward heard was enough, and more than enough, to lead him to forget or to renounce his motive in entering. The effect upon him was strange and strong. His first object seemed to be to escape from the house again without being seen or heard.

Having accomplished this, he went in at the park gate, and strode off under the trees to the Old House. There sitting down by the fire, and burying himself in reflection, he allowed the minutes to pass by unheeded. First the candle burnt down in its socket and stunk: he did not notice it. Then the fire went out: he did not see it. His feet grew cold; still he thought on.

It may be remarked that a lady, a year and a quarter before this time, had, under the same conditions – an unrestricted mental absorption – shown nearly the same peculiarities as this man evinced now. The lady was Miss Aldclyffe.

It was half-past twelve when Manston moved, as if he had come to a determination.

The first thing he did the next morning was to call at Knapwater House; where he found that Miss Aldclyffe was not well enough to see him. She had been ailing from slight internal hæmorrhage ever since the confession of the porter Chinney. Apparently not much aggrieved at the denial, he shortly afterwards went to the railway-station and took his departure for London, leaving a letter for Miss Aldclyffe, stating the reason of his journey thither – to recover traces of his missing wife.

During the remainder of the week paragraphs appeared in the local and other newspapers, drawing attention to the facts of this singular case. The writers, with scarcely an exception, dwelt forcibly upon a feature which had at first escaped the observation of the villagers, including Mr Raunham – that if the announcement of the man Chinney were true, it seemed extremely probable that Mrs Manston left her watch and keys behind on purpose to blind people as to her escape; and that therefore she would not now let herself be discovered, unless a strong pressure were put upon her. The writers added that the police were on the track of the porter, who very possibly had absconded in the fear that his reticence was criminal, and that Mr Manston, the husband, was, with praiseworthy energy, making every effort to clear the whole matter up.

2. From the Eighteenth to the End of January

Five days from the time of his departure, Manston returned from London and Liverpool, looking very fatigued and thoughtful. He explained to the rector and other of his acquaintance that all the inquiries he had made at his wife's old lodgings and his own had been totally barren of results.

But he seemed inclined to push the affair to a clear conclusion now that he had commenced. After the lapse of another day or two he proceeded to fulfil his promise to the rector and advertised for the missing woman in three of the London papers. The advertisement was a carefully considered and even attractive effusion, calculated to win the heart, or at least the understanding, of any woman who had a spark of her own nature left in her.

There was no answer.

Three days later he repeated the experiment; with the same result as before.

'I cannot try any further,' said Manston speciously to the rector, his sole auditor throughout the proceedings. 'Mr Raunham, I'll tell you the truth plainly: I don't love her; I do love Cytherea, and the whole of this

230

business of searching for the other woman goes altogether against me. I hope to God I shall never see her again.'

'But you will do your duty at least?' said Mr Raunham.

'I have done it,' said Manston. 'If ever a man on the face of this earth has done his duty towards an absent wife, I have towards her – living or dead – at least,' he added, correcting himself, 'since I have lived at Knapwater. I neglected her before that time – I own that, as I have owned it before.'

'I should, if I were you, adopt other means to get tidings of her if advertising fails, in spite of my feelings,' said the rector emphatically. 'But at any rate, try advertising once more. There's a satisfaction in having made any attempt three several times.'

When Manston had left the study, the rector stood looking at the fire for a considerable length of time, lost in profound reflection. He went to his private diary, and after many pauses, which he varied only by dipping his pen, letting it dry, wiping it on his sleeve, and then dipping it again, he took the following note of events: –

January 25. – Mr Manston has just seen me for the third time on the subject of his lost wife. There have been these peculiarities attending the three interviews: –

The first. My visitor, whilst expressing by words his great anxiety to do everything for her recovery, showed plainly by his bearing that he was convinced he should never see her again.

The second. He had left off feigning anxiety to do rightly by his first wife, and honestly asked after Cytherea's welfare.

The third (and most remarkable). He seemed to have lost all consistency. Whilst expressing his love for Cytherea (which certainly is strong) and evincing the usual indifference to the first Mrs Manston's fate, he was unable to conceal the intensity of his eagerness for me to advise him to *advertise again* for her.

A week after the second, the third advertisement was inserted. A paragraph was attached, which stated that this would be the last time the announcement would appear.

3. The First of February

At this, the eleventh hour, the postman brought a letter for Manston, directed in a woman's hand.

A bachelor friend of the steward's, Mr Dickson by name, who was somewhat of a chatterer – *plenus rimarum** – and who boasted of an endless string of acquaintances, had come over from Casterbridge the preceding day by invitation – an invitation which had been a pleasant surprise to Dickson himself, insomuch that Manston, as a rule, voted him a bore almost to his face. He had stayed over the night, and was sitting at breakfast with his host when the important missive arrived.

Manston did not attempt to conceal the subject of the letter, or the name of the writer. First glancing the pages through, he read aloud as follows: –

'MY HUSBAND, – I implore your forgiveness.

'During the last thirteen months I have repeated to myself a hundred times that you should never discover what I voluntarily tell you now, namely, that I am alive and in perfect health.

'I have seen all your advertisements. Nothing but your persistence has won me round. Surely, I thought, he *must* love me still. Why else should he try to win back a woman who, faithful unto death as she will be, can, in a social sense, aid him towards acquiring nothing? – rather the reverse, indeed.

'You yourself state my own mind – that the only grounds upon which we can meet and live together, with a reasonable hope of happiness, must be a mutual consent to bury in oblivion all past differences. I heartily and willingly forget everything – and forgive everything. You will do the same, as your actions show.

'There will be plenty of opportunity for me to explain the few facts relating to my escape on the night of the fire. I will only give the heads in this hurried note. I was grieved at your not coming to fetch me, more grieved at your absence from the station, most of all by your absence from home. On my journey to the inn I writhed under a passionate sense of wrong done me. When I had been shown to my room I waited and hoped for you till the landlord had gone upstairs to bed. I still found that you did not come, and then I finally made up my mind to leave. I had half undressed, but I put on my things again, forgetting my watch (and I suppose dropping my keys, though I am not sure where) in my hurry, and slipped out of the house. The—'

'Well, that's a rum story,' said Mr Dickson, interrupting.

'What's a rum story?' said Manston hastily, and flushing in the face.

'Forgetting her watch and dropping her keys in her hurry.'

'I don't see anything particularly wonderful in it. Any woman might do such a thing.'

'Any woman might if escaping from fire or shipwreck, or any such immediate danger. But it seems incomprehensible to me that any woman in her senses, who quietly decides to leave a house, should be so forgetful.'

'All that is required to reconcile your seeming with her facts is to assume that she was not in her senses, for that's what she did plainly, or how could the things have been found there? Besides, she's truthful enough.' He spoke eagerly and peremptorily.

'Yes, yes, I know that. I merely meant that it seemed rather odd.'
'O yes.' Manston read on: –

'—and slipped out of the house. The rubbish-heap was burning up brightly, but the thought that the house was in danger did not strike me; I did not consider that it might be thatched.

'I idled in the lane behind the wood till the last down-train had come in, not being in a mood to face strangers. Whilst I was there the fire broke out, and this perplexed me still more. However, I was still determined not to stay in the place. I went to the railway-station, which was now quiet, and inquired of the solitary man on duty there concerning the trains. It was not till I had left the man that I saw the effect the fire might have on my history. I considered also, though not in any detailed manner, that the event, by attracting the attention of the village to my former abode, might set people on my track should they doubt my death, and a sudden dread of having to go back again to Knapwater – a place which had seemed inimical to me from first to last – prompted me to run back and bribe the porter to secrecy. I then walked on to Anglebury, lingering about the outskirts of the town till the morning train came in, when I proceeded by it to London, and then took these lodgings, where I have been supporting myself ever since by needlework, endeavouring to save enough money to pay my passage home to America, but making melancholy progress in my attempt. However, all that is changed – can I be otherwise than happy at it? Of course not. I am happy. Tell me what I am to do, and believe me still to be your faithful wife,

EUNICE

'My name here is (as before)
  'MRS RONDLEY, and my address,
   79 ADDINGTON STREET,
    LAMBETH'

The name and address were written on a separate slip of paper.

'So it's to be all right at last then,' said Manston's friend. 'But after all there's another woman in the case. You don't seem very sorry for the little thing who is put to such distress by this turn of affairs? I wonder you can let her go so coolly.'

The speaker was looking out between the mullions of the window – noticing that some of the lights were glazed in lozenges, some in squares – as he said the words, otherwise he would have seen the passionate expression of agonized hopelessness that flitted across the steward's countenance when the remark was made. He did not see it, and Manston answered after a short interval. The way in which he spoke of the young girl who had believed herself his wife, whom, a few short days ago, he had openly idolized, and whom, in his secret heart, he idolized still, as far as such a form of love was compatible with his

233

nature, showed that from policy or otherwise, he meant to act up to the requirements of the position into which fate appeared determined to drive him.

'That's neither here nor there,' he said; 'it is a point of honour to do as I am doing, and there's an end of it.'

'Yes. Only I thought you used not to care over-much about your first bargain.'

'I certainly did not at one time. One is apt to feel rather weary of wives when they are so devilish civil under all aspects, as she used to be. But anything for a change – Abigail is lost, but Michal is recovered.* You would hardly believe it, but she seems in fancy to be quite another bride – in fact, almost as if she had really risen from the dead, instead of having only done so virtually.'

'You will let the young pink one know that the other has come or is coming?'

'*Cui bono?*'* The steward meditated critically, showing a portion of his intensely white and regular teeth within the ruby lips.

'I cannot say anything to her that will do any good,' he resumed. 'It would be awkward – either seeing or communicating with her again. The best plan to adopt will be to let matters take their course – she'll find it all out soon enough.'

Manston found himself alone a few minutes later. He buried his face in his hands, and murmured, 'O my lost one! O my Cytherea! That it should come to this is hard for me! 'Tis now all darkness – "a land of darkness as darkness itself; and of the shadow of death without any order, and where the light is as darkness".'*

Yes, the artificial bearing which this extraordinary man had adopted before strangers ever since he had overheard the conversation at the inn, left him now, and he mourned for Cytherea aloud.

4. The Twelfth of February

Knapwater Park is the picture – at eleven o'clock on a muddy, quiet, hazy, but bright morning – a morning without any blue sky, and without any shadows, the earth being enlivened and lit up rather by the spirit of an invisible sun than by its bodily presence.

The local Hunt had met for the day's sport on the open space of ground immediately in front of the steward's residence – called in the list of appointments, 'Old House, Knapwater' – the meet being here once every season, for the pleasure of Miss Aldclyffe and her friends.

Leaning out from one of the first-floor windows, and surveying with the keenest interest the lively picture of pink and black coats, rich-coloured horses, and sparkling bits and spurs, was the returned and long-lost woman, Mrs Manston.

The eyes of those forming the brilliant group were occasionally turned towards her, showing plainly that her adventures were the subject of conversation equally with or more than the chances of the coming day. She did not flush beneath their scrutiny; on the contrary, she seemed rather to enjoy it, her eyes being kindled with a light of contented exultation, subdued to square with the circumstances of her conjugal position.

She was, at the distance from which they surveyed her, an attractive woman – comely as the tents of Kedar.* But to a close observer it was palpable enough that God did not do all the picture. Appearing at least seven years older than Cytherea, she was probably her senior by double the number, the artificial means employed to heighten the natural good appearance of her face being very cleverly applied. Her form was full and round, its voluptuous maturity standing out in strong contrast to the memory of Cytherea's lissom girlishness.

It seems to be an almost universal rule that a woman who once has courted, or who eventually will court, the society of men on terms dangerous to her honour cannot refrain from flinging the meaning glance whenever the moment arrives in which the glance is strongly asked for, even if her life and whole future depend upon that moment's abstinence.

Had a cautious, uxorious husband seen in his wife's countenance what might now have been seen in this dark-eyed woman's as she caught a stray glance of flirtation from one or other of the red-coated gallants outside, he would have passed many days in an agony of restless jealousy and doubt. But Manston was not such a husband, and he was, moreover, calmly attending to his business at the other end of the manor.

The steward had fetched home his wife in the most matter-of-fact way a few days earlier, walking round the village with her the very next morning – at once putting an end, by this simple solution, to all the riddling inquiries and surmises that were rank in the village and its neighbourhood. Some men said that this woman was as far inferior to Cytherea as earth to heaven; others, older and sager, thought Manston better off with such a wife than he would have been with one of Cytherea's youthful impulses, and inexperience in household management. All felt their curiosity dying out of them. It was the same in Carriford as in other parts of the world – immediately circumstantial evidence became exchanged for direct, the loungers in court yawned, gave a final survey, and turned away to a subject which would afford more scope for speculation.

CHAPTER FIFTEEN
The Events of Three Weeks

1. *From the Twelfth of February to the Second of March*

Owen Graye's recovery from the illness that had incapacitated him for so long a time was, professionally, the dawn of a brighter prospect for him in every direction, though the change was at first very gradual, and his movements and efforts were little more than mechanical. With the lengthening of the days, and the revival of building operations for the forthcoming season, he saw himself, for the first time, on a road which, pursued with care, would probably lead to a comfortable income at some future day. But he was still very low down the hill as yet.

The first undertaking entrusted to him in the new year began about a month after his return from Southampton. Mr Gradfield had come back to him in the wake of his restored health, and offered him the superintendence, as clerk of works, of a church which was to be nearly rebuilt at the village of Tolchurch, fifteen or sixteen miles from Budmouth, and about half that distance from Carriford.

'I am now being paid at the rate of a hundred and fifty pounds a year,' he said to his sister in a burst of thankfulness, 'and you shall never, Cytherea, be at any tyrannous lady's beck and call again as long as I live. Never pine or think about what has happened, dear; it's no disgrace to you. Cheer up; you'll be somebody's happy wife yet.'

He did not say Edward Springrove's, for, greatly to his disappointment, a report had reached his ears that the friend to whom Cytherea owed so much had been about to pack up his things and sail for Australia. However, this was before the uncertainty concerning Mrs Manston's existence had been dispersed by her return, a phenomenon that altered the cloudy relationship in which Cytherea had lately been standing towards her old lover, to one of distinctness; which result would have been delightful but for circumstances about to be mentioned.

Cytherea was still pale from her recent illness, and still greatly dejected. Until the news of Mrs Manston's return had reached them, she had kept herself closely shut up during the day-time, never venturing forth except at night. Sleeping and waking she had been in perpetual dread lest she should still be claimed by a man whom, only a few weeks earlier, she had regarded in the light of a future husband with quiet assent, not unmixed with cheerfulness.

But the removal of the uneasiness in this direction – by Mrs Manston's arrival, and her own consequent freedom – had been the imposition of pain in another. Utterly fictitious details of the finding of Cytherea and Manston had been invented and circulated, unavoidably reaching her ears in the course of time. Thus the freedom brought no happiness, and it seemed well-nigh impossible that she could ever again show herself the sparkling creature she once had been –

> Apt to entice a deity.

On this account, and for the first time in his life, Owen made a point of concealing from her the real state of his feelings with regard to the unhappy transaction. He writhed in secret under the humiliation to which they had been subjected, till the resentment it gave rise to, and for which there was no vent, was sometimes beyond endurance; it induced a mood that did serious damage to the material and plodding perseverance necessary if he would secure permanently the comforts of a home for them.

They gave up their lodgings at Budmouth, and went to Tolchurch as soon as the work commenced.

Here they were domiciled in one half of an old farm-house standing not far from the ivy-covered church tower (which was all that was to remain of the original structure). The long steep roof of this pictur-esque dwelling sloped nearly down to the ground, the old tiles that covered it being overgrown with rich olive-hued moss. New red tiles in twos and threes had been used for patching the holes wrought by decay, lighting up the whole harmonious surface with dots of brilliant scarlet.

The chief internal features of this snug abode were a wide fireplace, enormous cupboards, a brown settle, and several sketches on the wood mantel, done in outline with the point of a hot poker – the subjects mainly consisting of old men walking painfully erect, with a curly-tailed dog behind.

After a week or two of residence in Tolchurch, and rambles amid the quaint scenery circumscribing it, a tranquillity began to spread itself through the mind of the maiden, which Graye hoped would be a preface to her complete restoration. She felt ready and willing to live the whole remainder of her days in the retirement of their present quarters: she began to sing about the house in low tremulous snatches –

' – I said, if there's peace to be found in the world,
   A heart that is humble may hope for it here.'*

2. The Third of March

Her convalescence had arrived at this point on a certain evening towards the end of the winter, when Owen had come in from the building hard by, and was changing his muddy boots for slippers, previously to sitting down to toast and tea.

A prolonged though quiet knocking came to the door.

The only person who ever knocked at their door in that way was the new vicar, the prime mover in the church-building. But he was that evening dining with the Squire.

Cytherea was uneasy at the sound – she did not know why, unless it was because her nerves were weakened by the sickness she had undergone. Instead of opening the door she ran out of the room, and upstairs.

'What nonsense, Cytherea!' said her brother, going to the door.

Edward Springrove stood in the grey light outside.

'Capital – not gone to Australia, and not going, of course!' cried Owen. 'What's the use of going to such a place as that? – I never believed that you would.'

'I am going back to London again to-morrow,' said Springrove, 'and I called to say a word before going. Where is . . .?'

'She has just run upstairs. Come in – never mind scraping your shoes – we are regular cottagers now; stone floor, yawning chimney-corner, and all, you see.'

'Mrs Manston came,' said Edward awkwardly, when he had sat down in the chimney-corner by preference.

'Yes.' At mention of one of his skeletons Owen lost his blitheness at once, and fell into a reverie.

'The history of her escape is very simple.'

'Very.'

'You know I always had wondered, when my father was telling any of the circumstances of the fire to me, how it could be that a woman could sleep so soundly as to be unaware of her horrid position till it was too late even to give shout or sound of any kind.'

238

'Well, I think that would have been possible, considering her long wearisome journey. People have often been suffocated in their beds before they awoke. But it was hardly likely a body would be completely burnt to ashes as this was assumed to be, though nobody seemed to see it at the time. And how positive the surgeon was too, about those bits of bone! Why he should have been so, nobody can tell. I cannot help saying that if it has ever been possible to find pure stupidity incarnate, it was in that jury of Carriford. There existed in the mass the stupidity of twelve and not the penetration of one.'

'Is she quite well?' said Springrove.

'Who? – O, my sister, Cytherea. Thank you, nearly well, now. I'll call her.'

'Wait one minute. I have a word to say to you.'

Owen sat down again.

'You know, without my saying it, that I love Cytherea as dearly as ever. . . . I think she loves me too, – does she really?'

There was in Owen enough of that worldly policy on the subject of matchmaking which naturally resides in the breasts of parents and guardians, to give him a certain caution in replying, and, younger as he was by five years than Edward, it had an odd effect.

'Well, she may possibly love you still,' he said, as if rather in doubt as to the truth of his words.

Springrove's countenance instantly saddened; he had expected a simple 'Yes', at the very least. He continued in a tone of greater depression –

'Supposing she does love me, would it be fair to you and to her if I made her an offer of marriage with these dreary conditions attached – that we lived for a few years on the narrowest system, till a great debt, which all honour and duty require me to pay off, shall be paid? My father, by reason of the misfortune that befell him, is under a great obligation to Miss Aldclyffe. He is getting old, and losing his energies. I am attempting to work free of the burden. This makes my prospects gloomy enough at present.

'But consider again,' he went on. 'Cytherea has been left in a nameless and unsatisfactory, though innocent state, by this unfortunate, and now void, marriage with Manston. A marriage with me, though under the – materially – untoward conditions I have mentioned, would make us happy; it would give her a *locus standi*.* If she wished to be out of the sound of her misfortunes we would go to another part of England – emigrate – do anything.'

'I'll call Cytherea,' said Owen. 'It is a matter which she alone can settle.' He did not speak warmly. His pride could not endure the pity which Edward's visit and errand tacitly implied. Yet, in the other affair, his heart went with Edward; he was on the same beat for paying off old debts himself.

'Cythie, Mr Springrove is here,' he said, at the foot of the staircase.

His sister descended the creaking old steps with a faltering tread, and stood in the firelight from the hearth. She extended her hand to Springrove, welcoming him by a mere motion of the lip, her eyes averted – a habit which had engendered itself in her since the beginning of her illness and defamation. Owen opened the door and went out – leaving the lovers alone. It was the first time they had met since the memorable night at Southampton.

'I will get a light,' she said, with a little embarrassment.

'No – don't, please, Cytherea,' said Edward softly. 'Come and sit down with me.'

'O yes. I ought to have asked *you* to,' she returned timidly. 'Everybody sits in the chimney-corner in this parish. You sit on that side. I'll sit here.'

Two recesses – one on the right, one on the left hand – were cut in the inside of the fireplace, and here they sat down facing each other, on benches fitted to the recesses, the fire glowing on the hearth between their feet. Its ruddy light shone on the underslopes of their faces, and spread out over the floor of the room with the low horizontality of the setting sun, giving to every grain of sand and tumour in the paving a long shadow towards the door.

Edward looked at his pale love through the thin azure twines of smoke that went up like ringlets between them, and invested her, as seen through its medium, with the shadowy appearance of a phantom. Nothing is so potent for coaxing back the lost eyes of a woman as a discreet silence in the man who has so lost them – and thus the patient Edward coaxed hers. After lingering on the hearth for half a minute, waiting in vain for another word from him, they were lifted into his face.

He was ready primed to receive them. 'Cytherea, will you marry me?' he said.

He could not wait in his original position till the answer came. Stepping across the front of the fire to her own side of the chimney-corner, he reclined at her feet, and searched for her hand. She continued in silence awhile.

'Edward, I can never be anybody's wife,' she then said sadly, and with firmness.

'Think of it in every light,' he pleaded; 'the light of love, first. Then, when you have done that, see how wise a step it would be. I can only offer you poverty as yet, but I want – I do so long to secure you from the intrusion of that unpleasant past, which will often and always be thrust before you as long as you live the shrinking solitary life you do now – a life which purity chooses, it may be; but to the outside world it appears like the enforced loneliness of neglect and scorn – and tongues are busy inventing a reason for it which does not exist.'

'I know all about it,' she said hastily; 'and those are the grounds of my refusal. You and Owen know the whole truth – the two I love best on earth – and I am content. But the scandal will be continually repeated, and I can never give any one the opportunity of saying to you – that – your wife. . . .' She utterly broke down and wept.

'Don't, my own darling!' he entreated. 'Don't, Cytherea!'

'Please to leave me – we will be friends, Edward – but don't press me – my mind is made up – I cannot – I will not marry you or any man under the present ambiguous circumstances – never will I – I have said it: never!'

They were both silent. He listlessly regarded the illuminated blackness overhead, where long flakes of soot floated from the sides and bars of the chimney-throat like tattered banners in ancient aisles; whilst through the square opening in the midst one or two bright stars looked down upon them from the grey March sky. The sight seemed to cheer him.

'At any rate you will love me?' he murmured to her.

'Yes – always – for ever and for ever!'

He kissed her once, twice, three times, and arose to his feet, slowly withdrawing himself from her side towards the door. Cytherea remained with her gaze fixed on the fire. Edward went out grieving, but hope was not extinguished even now.

He smelt the fragrance of a cigar, and immediately afterwards saw a small red star of fire against the darkness of the hedge. Graye was pacing up and down the lane, smoking as he walked. Springrove told him the result of the interview.

'You are a good fellow, Edward,' he said; 'but I think my sister is right.'

'I wish you would believe Manston a villain, as I do,' said Springrove.

'It would be absurd of me to say that I like him now – family feeling prevents it, but I cannot in honesty say deliberately that he is a bad man.'

Edward could keep the secret of Manston's coercion of Miss Aldclyffe in the matter of the houses a secret no longer. He told Owen the whole story.

'That's one thing,' he continued, 'but not all. What do you think of this – I have discovered that he went to Budmouth post-office for a letter the day before the first advertisement for his wife appeared in the papers. One was there for him, and it was directed in his wife's handwriting, as I can prove. This was not till after the marriage with Cytherea, it is true, but if (as it seems to show) the advertising was a farce, there is a strong presumption that the rest of the piece was.'

Owen was too astounded to speak. He dropped his cigar, and fixed his eyes upon his companion.

'Collusion!'

'Yes.'

'With his first wife?'

'Yes – with his wife. I am firmly persuaded of it.'

'What did you discover?'

'That he fetched from the post-office at Budmouth a letter from her the day *before* the first advertisement appeared.'

Graye was lost in a long consideration. 'Ah!' he said, 'it would be difficult to prove anything of that sort now. The writing could not be sworn to, and if he is guilty the letter is destroyed.'

'I have other suspicions—'

'Yes – as you said,' interrupted Owen, who had not till now been able to form the complicated set of ideas necessary for picturing the position. 'Yes, there is this to be remembered – Cytherea had been taken from him before that letter came – and his knowledge of his wife's existence could not have originated till after the wedding. I could have sworn he believed her dead then. His manner was unmistakable.'

'Well, I have other suspicions,' repeated Edward; 'and if I only had the right – if I were her husband or brother, he should be convicted of bigamy yet.'

'The reproof was not needed,' said Owen, with a little bitterness. 'What can I do – a man with neither money nor friends – whilst Manston has Miss Aldclyffe and all her fortune to back him up? God only knows what lies between the mistress and her steward, but since this has transpired – if it is true – I can believe the connection to be even an unworthy one – a thing I certainly never so much as owned to myself before.'

3. The Fifth of March

Edward's disclosure had the effect of directing Owen Graye's thoughts into an entirely new and uncommon channel.

On the Monday after Springrove's visit, Owen had walked to the top of a hill in the neighbourhood of Tolchurch – a wild hill that had no name, beside a barren down where it never looked like summer.* In the intensity of his meditations on the ever-present subject, he sat down on a weather-beaten boundary-stone gazing towards the distant valleys – seeing only Manston's imagined form.

Had his defenceless sister been trifled with? that was the question which affected him. Her refusal of Edward as a husband was, he knew, dictated solely by a humiliated sense of inadequacy to him in repute, and had not been formed till after the slanderous tale accounting for her seclusion had been circulated. Was it not true, as Edward had hinted, that he, her brother, was neglecting his duty towards her in allowing Manston to thrive unquestioned, whilst she was hiding her head for no fault at all?

Was it possible that Manston was sensuous villain enough to have contemplated, at any moment before the marriage with Cytherea, the return of his first wife, when he should have grown weary of his new toy? Had he believed that, by a skilful manipulation of such circumstances as chance would throw in his way, he could escape all suspicion of having known that she lived? Only one fact within his own direct knowledge afforded the least ground for such a supposition. It was that, possessed by a woman only in the humble and unprotected station of a lady's hired companion, his sister's beauty might scarcely have been sufficient to induce a selfish man like Manston to make her his wife, unless he had foreseen the possibility of getting rid of her again.

'But for that stratagem of Manston's in relation to the Springroves,' Owen thought, 'Cythie might now have been the happy wife of Edward. True, that he influenced Miss Aldclyffe only rests on Edward's suspicions, but the grounds are good – the probability is strong.'

He went indoors and questioned Cytherea.

'On the night of the fire, who first said that Mrs Manston was burnt?' he asked.

'I don't know who started the report.'

'Was it Manston?'

'It was certainly not he. All doubt on the subject was removed before he came to the spot – that I am certain of. Everybody knew that she did

243

not escape *after* the house was on fire, and thus all overlooked the fact that she might have left before – of course, that would have seemed such an improbable thing for anybody to do.'

'Yes, until the porter's story of her irritation and doubt as to her course made it natural.'

'What settled the matter at the inquest,' said Cytherea, 'was Mr Manston's evidence that the watch was his wife's.'

'He was sure of that, wasn't he?'

'I believe he said he was certain of it.'

'It might have been hers – left behind in her perturbation, as they say it was – impossible as that seems at first sight. Yes – on the whole, he might have believed in her death.'

'I know by several proofs that then, and at least for some time after, he had no other thought than that she was dead. I now think that before the porter's confession he knew something about her – though not that she lived.'

'Why do you?'

'From what he said to me on the evening of the wedding-day, when I had fastened myself in the room at the hotel, after Edward's visit. He must have suspected that I knew something, for he was irritated, and in a passion of uneasy doubt. He said, "You don't suppose my first wife is come to light again, madam, surely?" Directly he had let the remark slip out, he seemed anxious to withdraw it.'

'That's odd,' said Owen.

'I thought it very odd.'

'Still we must remember he might only have hit upon the thought by accident, in doubt as to your motive. Yes, the great point to discover remains the same as ever – did he doubt his first impression of her death *before* he married you. I can't help thinking he did, although he was so astounded at our news that night. Edward swears he did.'

'It was perhaps only a short time before,' said Cytherea; 'when he could hardly recede from having me.'

'Seasoning justice with mercy* as usual, Cytherea. 'Tis unfair to yourself to talk like that. If I could only bring him to ruin as a bigamist – supposing him to be one – I should die happy. That's what we must find out by fair means or foul – was he a wilful bigamist?'

'It is no use trying, Owen. You would have to employ a solicitor, and how can you do that?'

'I can't at all – I know that very well. But neither do I altogether wish to at present – a lawyer must have a case – facts to go upon, that means. Now they are scarce at present – as scarce as money is with us, and till

244

we have found more money there is no hurry for a lawyer. Perhaps by the time we have the facts we shall have the money. The only thing we lose in working alone in this way, is time – not the issue: for the fruit that one mind matures in a twelvemonth forms a more perfectly organized whole than that of twelve minds in one month, especially if the interests of the single one are vitally concerned, and those of the twelve are only hired. But there is not only my mind available – you are a shrewd woman, Cythie, and Edward is an earnest ally. Then, if we really get a sure footing for a criminal prosecution, the Crown will take up the case.'

'I don't much care to press on in the matter,' she murmured. 'What good can it do us, Owen, after all?'

'Selfishly speaking, it will do this good – that all the facts of your journey to Southampton will become known, and the scandal will die. Besides, Manston will have to suffer – it's an act of justice to you and to other women, and to Edward Springrove.'

He now thought it necessary to tell her of the real nature of the Springroves' obligation to Miss Aldclyffe – and their nearly certain knowledge that Manston was the prime mover in effecting their embarrassment. Her face flushed as she listened.

'And now,' he said, 'our first undertaking is to find out where Mrs Manston lived during the separation; next, when the first communications passed between them after the fire.'

'If we only had Miss Aldclyffe's countenance and assistance as I used to have them,' Cytherea returned, 'how strong we should be! O, what power is it that he exercises over her, swaying her just as he wishes! She loves me now. Mrs Morris in her letter said that Miss Aldclyffe prayed for me – yes, she heard her praying for me, and crying. Miss Aldclyffe did not mind an old friend like Mrs Morris knowing it, either. Yet in opposition to this, notice her dead silence and inaction throughout this proceeding.'

'It is a mystery; but never mind that now,' said Owen impressively. 'About where Mrs Manston has been living. We must get this part of it first – learn the place of her stay in the early stage of their separation, during the period of Manston's arrival here, and so on, for that was where she was first communicated with on the subject of coming to Knapwater, before the fire; and that address, too, was her point of departure when she came to her husband by stealth in the night – you know – the time I visited you in the evening and went home early in the morning, and it was found that he had been visited too. Ah! couldn't we inquire of Mrs Leat, who keeps the post-office at Carriford, if she remembers where the letters to Mrs Manston were directed?'

'He never posted his letters to her in the parish – it was remarked at the time. I was thinking if something relating to her address might not be found in the report of the inquest in the *Casterbridge Chronicle* of the date. Some facts about the inquest were given in the papers to a certainty.'

Her brother caught eagerly at the suggestion. 'Who has a file of the *Chronicles?*' he said.

'Mr Raunham used to file them,' said Cytherea. 'He was rather friendly-disposed towards me, too.'

Owen could not, on any consideration, escape from his attendance at the church-building till Saturday evening; and thus it became necessary, unless they actually wasted time, that Cytherea herself should assist. 'I act under your orders, Owen,' she said.

CHAPTER SIXTEEN
The Events of One Week

1. March the Sixth

The next morning the opening move of the game was made. Cytherea, under cover of a thick veil, hired a conveyance and drove to within a mile or so of Carriford. It was with a renewed sense of depression that she saw again the objects which had become familiar to her eye during her sojourn under Miss Aldclyffe's roof – the outline of the hills, the meadow streams, the old park trees. She hastened by a lonely path to the rectory-house, and asked if Mr Raunham was at home.

Now the rector, though a solitary bachelor, was as gallant and courteous to womankind as an ancient Iberian; and, moreover, he was Cytherea's friend in particular, to an extent far greater than she had ever surmised. Rarely visiting his relative, Miss Aldclyffe, except on parish matters, more rarely still being called upon by Miss Aldclyffe, Cytherea had learnt very little of him whilst she lived at Knapwater. The relationship was on the impecunious paternal side, and for this branch of her family the lady of the estate had never evinced much sympathy. In looking back upon our line of descent it is an instinct with us to feel that all our vitality was drawn from the richer party to any unequal marriage in the chain.

Since the death of the old captain, the rector's bearing in Knapwater House had been almost that of a stranger, a circumstance which he himself was the last man in the world to regret. This polite indifference was so frigid on both sides that the rector did not concern himself to preach at her, which was a great deal in a rector; and she did not take the trouble to think his sermons poor stuff, which in a cynical woman was a great deal more.

Though barely fifty years of age, his hair was as white as snow, contrasting strangely with the redness of his skin, which was as fresh and healthy as a lad's. Cytherea's bright eyes, mutely and demurely glancing up at him Sunday after Sunday, had been the means of driving away many of the saturnine humours that creep into an empty heart during the hours of a solitary life; in this case, however, to supplant them, when she left his parish, by those others of a more aching nature which accompany an over-full one. In short, he had been on the verge of feeling towards her that passion to which his dignified self-respect would not give its true name, even in the privacy of his own thought.

He received her kindly; but she was not disposed to be frank with him. He saw her wish to be reserved, and with genuine good taste and good nature made no comment whatever upon her request to be allowed to see the *Chronicle* for the year before the last. He placed the papers before her on his study table, with a timidity as great as her own, and then left her entirely to herself.

She turned them over till she came to the first heading connected with the subject of her search – 'Disastrous Fire and Loss of Life at Carriford'.

The sight, and its calamitous bearing upon her own life, made her so dizzy that she could, for a while, hardly decipher the letters. Stifling recollection by an effort, she nerved herself to her work, and carefully read the column. The account reminded her of no other fact than was remembered already.

She turned on to the following week's report of the inquest. After a miserable perusal she could find no more pertaining to Mrs Manston's address than this: –

ABRAHAM BROWN, of Hoxton, London, at whose house the deceased woman had been living, deposed, &c.

Nobody else from London had attended the inquest.

She arose to depart, first sending a message of thanks to Mr Raunham, who was out of doors gardening.

He stuck his spade into the ground, and accompanied her to the gate.

'Can I help you in anything, Cytherea?' he said, using her Christian name by an intuition that unpleasant memories might be revived if he called her Miss Graye after wishing her good-bye as Mrs Manston at the wedding. Cytherea saw the motive and appreciated it, nevertheless replying evasively –

'I only guess and fear.'

He earnestly looked at her again.

'Promise me that if you want assistance, and you think I can give it, you will come to me.'

'I will,' she said.

The gate closed between them.

'You don't want me to help you in anything now, Cytherea?' he repeated.

If he had spoken what he felt, 'I want very much to help you Cytherea, and have been watching Manston on your account', she would gladly have accepted his offer. As it was, she was perplexed, and raised her eyes to his, not so fearlessly as before her trouble, but as modestly, and with still enough brightness in them to do fearful execution as she said over the gate –

'No, thank you.'

She returned to Tolchurch weary with her day's work. Owen's greeting was anxious –

'Well, Cytherea?'

She gave him the words from the report of the inquest, pencilled on a slip of paper.

'Now to find out the name of the street and number,' Owen remarked.

'Owen,' she said, 'will you forgive me for what I am going to say? I don't think I can – indeed I don't think I can – take any further steps towards disentangling the mystery. I still think it a useless task, and it does not seem any duty of mine to be revenged upon Mr Manston in any way.' She added more gravely, 'It is beneath my dignity as a woman to labour for this; I have felt it so all day.'

'Very well,' he said, somewhat shortly; 'I shall work without you then. There's dignity in justice.' He caught sight of her pale tired face, and the dilated eye which always appeared in her with weariness. 'Darling,' he continued warmly, and kissing her, 'you shall not work so hard again – you are worn out quite. But you must let me do as I like.'

2. March the Tenth

On Saturday evening Graye hurried off to Casterbridge, and called at the house of the reporter to the *Chronicle*. The reporter was at home, and came out to Graye in the passage. Owen explained who and what he was, and asked the man if he would oblige him by turning to his notes of the inquest at Carriford in the December of the year preceding the last – just adding that a family entanglement, of which the reporter probably knew something, made him anxious to ascertain some additional details of the event, if any existed.

'Certainly,' said the other, without hesitation; 'though I am afraid I haven't much beyond what we printed at the time. Let me see – my old note-books are in my drawer at the office of the paper: if you will come with me I can refer to them there.' His wife and family were at tea inside the room, and with the timidity of decent poverty everywhere he seemed glad to get a stranger out of his domestic groove.

They crossed the street, entered the office, and went thence to an inner room. Here, after a short search, was found the book required. The precise address, not given in the condensed report that was printed, but written down by the reporter, was as follows: –

> ABRAHAM BROWN,
> LODGING-HOUSE KEEPER,
> 41 CHARLES SQUARE,
> HOXTON

Owen copied it, and gave the reporter a small fee. 'I want to keep this inquiry private for the present,' he said hesitatingly. 'You will perhaps understand why, and oblige me.'

The reporter promised. 'News is shop with me,' he said, 'and to escape from handling it is my greatest social enjoyment.'

It was evening, and the outer room of the publishing-office was lighted up with flaring jets of gas. After making the above remark, the reporter came out from the inner apartment in Graye's company, answering an expression of obligation from Owen with the words that it was no trouble. At the moment of his speech, he closed behind him the door between the two rooms, still holding his note-book in his hand.

Before the counter of the front room stood a tall man, who was also speaking when they emerged. He said to the youth in attendance, 'I will take my paper for this week now I am here, so that you needn't post it to me.'

The stranger then slightly turned his head, saw Owen, and recognized him. Owen passed out without recognizing the other as Manston.

Manston then looked at the reporter, who, after walking to the door with Owen, had come back again to lock up his books. Manston did not need to be told that the shabby marble-covered book which he held in his hand, opening endways and interleaved with blotting-paper, was an old reporting-book. He raised his eyes to the reporter's face, whose experience had not so schooled his features but that they betrayed a consciousness, to one half initiated as the other was, that his late proceeding had been connected with events in the life of the steward. Manston said no more, but, taking his newspaper, followed Owen from the office, and disappeared in the gloom of the street.

Edward Springrove was now in London again, and on this same evening, before leaving Casterbridge, Owen wrote a careful letter to him, stating therein all the facts that had come to his knowledge, and begging him, as he valued Cytherea, to make cautious inquiries. A tall man was standing under the lamp-post, about half-a-dozen yards above the post-office, when he dropped the letter into the box.

That same night, too, for a reason connected with the rencounter with Owen Graye, the steward entertained the idea of rushing off suddenly to London by the mail-train, which left Casterbridge at ten o'clock. But remembering that letters posted after the hour at which Owen had obtained his information – whatever that was – could not be delivered in London till Monday morning, he changed his mind and went home to Knapwater. Making a confidential explanation to his wife, arrangements were set on foot for his departure by the mail on Sunday night.

3. March the Eleventh

Starting for church the next morning several minutes earlier than was usual with him, the steward intentionally loitered along the road from the village till old Mr Springrove overtook him. Manston spoke very civilly of the morning, and of the weather, asking how the farmer's barometer stood, and when it was probable that the wind might change. It was not in Mr Springrove's nature – going to church as he was, too – to return anything but a civil answer to such civil questions, however his feelings might have been biassed by late events. The conversation was continued on terms of greater friendliness.

'You must be feeling settled again by this time, Mr Springrove, after the rough turn-out you had on that terrible night in November.'

'Ay, but I don't know about feeling settled, either, Mr Manston. The old window in the chimney-corner of the old house I shall never forget. No window in the chimney-corner where I am now, and I had been used to it for more than fifty years. Ted says 'tis a great loss to me, and he knows exactly what I feel.'

'Your son is again in a good situation, I believe?' said Manston, imitating that inquisitiveness into the private affairs of the natives which passes for high breeding in country villages.

'Yes, sir. I hope he'll keep it, or do something else and stick to it.'

''Tis to be hoped he'll be steady now.'

'He's always been that, I assure 'ee,' said the old man tartly.

'Yes – yes – I mean intellectually steady. Intellectual wild oats will thrive in a soil of the strictest morality.'

'Intellectual gingerbread! Ted's steady enough – that's all I know about it.'

'Of course – of course. Has he respectable lodgings? My own experience has shown me that that's a great thing to a young man living alone in London.'

'Warwick Street, Charing Cross – that's where he is.'

'Well, to be sure – strange! A very dear friend of mine used to live at number fifty-two in that very same street.'

'Edward lives at number forty-nine – how very near being the same house!' said the old farmer, pleased in spite of himself.

'Very,' said Manston. 'Well, I suppose we had better step along a little quicker, Mr Springrove; the parson's bell has just begun.'

'Number forty-nine,' he murmured.

4. March the Twelfth

Edward received Owen's letter in due time, but on account of his daily engagements he could not attend to any request till the clock had struck five in the afternoon. Rushing then from his office in Westminster, he called a hansom* and proceeded to Hoxton. A few minutes later he knocked at the door of number forty-one, Charles Square, the old lodging of Mrs Manston.

A tall man who would have looked extremely handsome had he not been clumsily and closely wrapped up in garments that were much too elderly in style for his years, stood at the corner of the quiet square at the same instant, having, too, alighted from a cab that had been driven along Old Street in Edward's rear. He smiled confidently when Springrove knocked.

Nobody came to the door. Springrove knocked again.

This brought out two people – one at the door he had been knocking upon, the other from the next on the right.

'Is Mr Brown at home?' said Springrove.

'No, sir.'

'When will he be in?'

'Quite uncertain.'

'Can you tell me where I may find him?'

'No. O, here he is coming, sir. That's Mr Brown.'

Edward looked down the pavement in the direction pointed out by the woman, and saw a man approaching. He proceeded a few steps to meet him.

Edward was impatient, and to a certain extent still a countryman, who had not, after the manner of city men, subdued the natural impulse to speak out the ruling thought without preface. He said in a quiet tone to the stranger, 'One word with you – do you remember a lady lodger of yours of the name of Mrs Manston?'

Mr Brown half closed his eyes at Springrove, somewhat as if he were looking into a telescope at the wrong end.

'I have never let lodgings in my life,' he said, after his survey.

'Didn't you attend an inquest a year and a half ago, at Carriford?'

'Never knew there was such a place in the world, sir; and as to lodgings, I have taken acres first and last during the last thirty years, but I have never let an inch.'

'I suppose there is some mistake,' Edward murmured, and turned away. He and Mr Brown were now opposite the door next to the one he had knocked at. The woman who was still standing there had heard the inquiry and the result of it.

'I expect it is the other Mr Brown, who used to live there, that you want, sir,' she said. 'The Mr Brown that was inquired for the other day?'

'Very likely that is the man,' said Edward, his interest reawakening.

'He couldn't make a do of lodging-letting here, and at last he went to Cornwall, where he came from, and where his brother still lived, who had often asked him to come home again. But there was little luck in the change; for after London they say he couldn't stand the rainy west winds they get there, and he died in the December following. Will you step into the passage?'

'That's unfortunate,' said Edward, going in. 'But perhaps you remember a Mrs Manston living next door to you?'

'O yes,' said the landlady, closing the door. 'The lady who was supposed to have met with such a horrible fate, and was alive all the time. I saw her the other day.'

'Since the fire at Carriford?'

'Yes. Her husband came to ask if Mr Brown was still living here – just as you might. He seemed anxious about it; and then one evening, a week or fortnight afterwards, when he came again to make further inquiries, she was with him. But I did not speak to her – she stood back, as if she were shy. I was interested, however, for old Mr Brown had told me all about her when he came back from the inquest.'

'Did you know Mrs Manston before she called the other day?'

'No. You see she was only Mr Brown's lodger for two or three weeks, and I didn't know she was living there till she was near upon leaving again – we don't notice next-door people much here in London. I much regretted I had not known her when I heard what had happened. It led me and Mr Brown to talk about her a great deal afterwards. I little thought I should see her alive after all.'

'And when do you say they came here together?'

'I don't exactly remember the day – though I remember a very beautiful dream I had that same night – ah, I shall never forget it! Shoals of lodgers coming along the square with angels' wings and bright golden sovereigns in their hands wanting apartments at West-End prices. They would not give any less; no, not if you—'

'Yes. Did Mrs Manston leave anything, such as papers, when she left these lodgings originally?' said Edward, though his heart sank as he asked. He felt that he was outwitted. Manston and his wife had been there before him, clearing the ground of all traces.

'I have always said "No" hitherto,' replied the woman, 'considering I could say no more if put upon my oath, as I expected to be. But speaking in a common everyday way now the occurrence is past, I believe a few things of some kind (though I doubt if they were papers) were left in a workbox she had, because she talked about it to Mr Brown, and was rather angry at what occurred – you see, she had a temper by all account, and so I didn't like to remind the lady of this workbox when she came the other day with her husband.'

'And about the workbox?'

'Well, from what was casually dropped, I think Mrs Manston had a few articles of furniture she didn't want, and when she was leaving they were put in an auction just by. Amongst her things were two workboxes very much alike. One of these she intended to sell, the other she didn't, and Mr Brown, who collected the things together, took the wrong one to the sale.'

'What was in it?'

'O, nothing in particular, or of any value – some accounts, and her usual sewing materials I think – nothing more. She didn't take much trouble to get it back – she said the bills were worth nothing to her or anybody else, but that she should have liked to keep the box because her husband gave it her when they were first married, and if he found she had parted with it, he would be vexed.'

'Did Mrs Manston, when she called recently with her husband, allude to this, or inquire for it, or did Mr Manston?'

'No – and I rather wondered at it. But she seemed to have forgotten it – indeed, she didn't make any inquiry at all, only standing behind him, listening to his; and he probably had never been told anything about it.'

'Whose sale were these articles of hers taken to?'

'Who was the auctioneer? Mr Halway. His place is the third turning from the end of that street you see there. Anybody will tell you the shop – his name is written up.'

Edward went off to follow up his clue with a promptness which was dictated more by a dogged will to do his utmost than by a hope of doing much. When he was out of sight, the tall and cloaked man, who had watched him, came up to the woman's door, with an appearance of being in breathless haste.

'Has a gentleman been here inquiring about Mrs Manston?'

'Yes; he's just gone.'

'Dear me! I want him.'

'He's gone to Mr Halway's.'

'I think I can give him some information upon the subject. Does he pay pretty liberally?'

'He gave me half-a-crown.'

'That scale will do. I'm a poor man, and will see what my little contribution to his knowledge will fetch. But, by the way, perhaps you told him all I know – where she lived before coming to live here?'

'I didn't know where she lived before coming here. O no – I only said what Mr Brown had told me. He seemed a nice, gentle young man, or I shouldn't have been so open as I was.'

'I shall now about catch him at Mr Halway's,' said the man, and went away as hastily as he had come.

Edward in the meantime had reached the auction-room. He found some difficulty, on account of the inertness of those whose only inducement to an action is a mere wish from another, in getting the information he stood in need of, but it was at last accorded him. The auctioneer's book gave the name of Mrs Higgins, 3 Canley Passage, as the purchaser of the lot which had included Mrs Manston's workbox.

Thither Edward went, followed by the man. Four bell-pulls, one above the other like waistcoat-buttons, appeared on the door-post. Edward seized the first he came to.

'Who did you woant?' said a thin voice from somewhere.

Edward looked above and around him; nobody was visible.

'Who did you woant?' said the thin voice again.

He found now that the sound proceeded from below the grating covering the basement window. He dropped his glance through the bars, and saw a child's white face.

'Who did you woant?' said the voice the third time, with precisely the same languid inflection.

'Mrs Higgins,' said Edward.

'Third bell up,' said the face, and disappeared.

He pulled the third bell from the bottom, and was admitted by another child, the daughter of the woman he was in search of. He gave the little thing sixpence, and asked for her mamma. The child led him upstairs.

Mrs Higgins was the wife of a carpenter who from want of employment one winter had decided to marry. Afterwards they both took to drink, and sank into desperate circumstances. A few chairs and a table were the chief articles of furniture in the third-floor back room which they occupied. A roll of baby-linen lay on the floor; beside it a pap-clogged spoon and an overturned tin pap-cup. Against the wall a Dutch clock* was fixed out of level, and ticked wildly in longs and shorts, its entrails hanging down beneath its white face and wiry hands, like the fæces of a Harpy* ('fœdissima v entris proluvies, uncæque manus, et pallida semper ora'*). A baby was crying against every chair-leg, the whole family of six or seven being small enough to be covered by a washing tub. Mrs Higgins sat helpless, clothed in a dress which had hooks and eyes in plenty, but never one opposite the other, thereby rendering the dress almost useless as a screen to the bosom. No workbox was visible anywhere.

It was a depressing picture of married life among the very poor of a city. Only for one short hour in the whole twenty-four did husband and wife taste genuine happiness. It was in the evening, when, after the sale of some necessary article of furniture, they were under the influence of a quartern* of gin.

Of all the ingenious and cruel satires that from the beginning till now have been stuck like knives into womankind, surely there is not one so lacerating to them, and to us who love them, as the trite old fact, that the most wretched of men can, in the twinkling of an eye, find a wife ready to be more wretched still for the sake of his company.

Edward hastened to despatch his errand.

Mrs Higgins had lately pawned the workbox with other useless articles of lumber, she said. Edward bought the duplicate of her, and went downstairs to the pawnbroker's.

In the back division of a musty shop, amid the heterogeneous collection of articles and odours invariably crowding such places, he produced his ticket, and with a sense of satisfaction out of all proportion to the probable worth of his acquisition, took the box and carried it off under his arm. He attempted to lift the cover as he walked, but found it locked.

It was dusk when Springrove reached his lodging. Entering his small sitting-room, the front apartment on the ground floor, he struck a light, and proceeded to learn if any scrap or mark within or upon his purchase rendered it of moment to the business in hand. Breaking open the cover with a small chisel, and lifting the tray, he glanced eagerly beneath, and found – nothing.

He next discovered that a pocket or portfolio was formed on the underside of the cover. This he unfastened, and slipping his hand within, found that it really contained some substance. First he pulled out about a dozen tangled silk and cotton threads. Under them were a short household account, a dry moss-rosebud, and an old pair of carte-de-visite photographs.* One of these was a likeness of Mrs Manston – 'Eunice' being written under it in ink – the other of Manston himself.

He sat down dispirited. This was all the fruit of his task – not a single letter, date, or address of any kind to help him – and was it likely there would be?

However, thinking he would send the fragments, such as they were, to Graye, in order to satisfy him that he had done his best so far, he scribbled a line, and put all except the silk and cotton into an envelope. Looking at his watch, he found it was then twenty minutes to seven; by affixing an extra stamp he would be enabled to despatch them by that evening's post. He hastily directed the packet, and ran with it at once to the post-office at Charing Cross.

On his return he took up the workbox again to examine it more leisurely. He then found there was also a small cavity in the tray under the pincushion, which was movable by a bit of ribbon. Lifting this he uncovered a flattened sprig of myrtle, and a small scrap of crumpled paper. The paper contained a verse or two in a man's handwriting. He recognized it as Manston's, having seen notes and bills from him at his

256

father's house. The stanza was of a complimentary character, descriptive of the lady who was now Manston's wife.

EUNICE*
Whoso for hours or lengthy days
Shall catch her aspect's changeful rays,
Then turn away, can none recall
Beyond a galaxy of all
    In hazy portraiture;
Lit by the light of azure eyes
Like summer days by summer skies:
Her sweet transitions seem to be
A pinkly pictured melody,
    And not a set contour.
           Æ.M.

To shake, pull, and ransack the box till he had almost destroyed it was now his natural action. But it contained absolutely nothing more.

'Disappointed again,' he said, flinging down the box, the bit of paper, and the withered twig that had lain with it.

Yet valueless as the new acquisition was, on second thoughts he considered that it would be worth while to make good the statement in his late note to Graye – that he had sent everything the box contained except the sewing-thread. Thereupon he enclosed the verse and myrtle-twig in another envelope, with a remark that he had overlooked them in his first search, and put it on the table for the next day's post.

In his hurry and concentration upon the matter that occupied him, Springrove, on entering his lodging and obtaining a light, had not waited to pull down the blind or close the shutters. Consequently all that he had done had been visible from the street. But as on an average not one person a minute passed along the quiet pavement at this time of the evening, the discovery of the omission did not much concern his mind.

But the real state of the case was that a tall man had stood against the opposite wall and watched the whole of his proceeding. When Edward came out and went to the Charing Cross post-office, the man followed him and saw him drop the letter into the box. The stranger did not further trouble himself to follow Springrove back to his lodging again.

Manston now knew that there had been photographs of some kind in his wife's workbox, and though he had not been near enough to see them, he guessed whose they were. The least reflection told him to whom they had been sent.

257

He paused a minute under the portico of the post-office, looking at the two or three omnibuses stopping and starting in front of him. Then he rushed along the Strand, through Holywell Street, and on to Old Boswell Court. Kicking aside the shoeblacks who began to importune him as he passed under the colonnade, he turned up the narrow passage to the publishing-office of the Post-Office Directory. He begged to be allowed to see the Directory of the south-west counties of England for a moment.

The shopman immediately handed down the volume from a shelf, and Manston retired with it to the window-bench. He turned to the county, and then to the parish of Tolchurch. At the end of the historical and topographical description of the village he read: –

Postmistress – Mrs Hurston. Letters received at 6.30 A.M. by foot-post from Anglebury.

Returning his thanks, he handed back the book and quitted the office, thence pursuing his way to an obscure coffee-house by the Strand, where he now ordered a light dinner. But rest seemed impossible with him. Some absorbing intention kept his body continually on the move. He paid his bill, took his bag in his hand, and went out to idle about the streets and over the river till the time should have arrived at which the night-mail left the Waterloo Station, by which train he intended to return homeward.

There exists, as it were, an outer chamber to the mind,* in which, when a man is occupied centrally with the most momentous question of his life, casual and trifling thoughts are just allowed to wander softly for an interval, before being banished altogether. Thus, amid his concentration did Manston receive perceptions of the individuals about him in the lively thoroughfare of the Strand; tall men looking insignificant; little men looking great and profound; lost women of miserable repute looking as happy as the days are long; wives, happy by assumption, looking careworn and miserable. Each and all were alike in this one respect, that they followed a solitary trail like the inwoven threads which form a banner, and all were equally unconscious of the significant whole they collectively showed forth.

At ten o'clock he turned into Lancaster Place, crossed the river, and entered the railway-station, where he took his seat in the down mail-train, which bore him, and Edward Springrove's letter to Graye, far away from London.

CHAPTER SEVENTEEN
The Events of One Day

1. March the Thirteenth. Three to Six o'Clock a.m.

They entered Anglebury Station in the dead, still time of early morning, the clock over the booking-office pointing to twenty-five minutes to three. Manston lingered on the platform and saw the mail-bags brought out, noticing, as a pertinent pastime, the many shabby blotches of wax from innumerable seals that had been set upon their mouths. The guard took them into a fly, and was driven down the road to the post-office.

It was a raw, damp, uncomfortable morning, though, as yet, little rain was falling. Manston drank a mouthful from his flask and walked at once away from the station, pursuing his way through the gloom till he stood at the entrance to the town adjoining, at a distance from the last house in the street of about two hundred yards.

The station road was also the turnpike-road into the country, the first part of its course being across a heath. Having surveyed the highway up and down to make sure of its bearing, Manston methodically set himself to walk backwards and forwards a stone's throw in each direction. Although the spring was temperate, the time of day, and the condition of suspense in which the steward found himself, caused a sensation of chilliness to pervade his frame in spite of the overcoat he wore. The drizzling rain increased, and drops from the trees at the wayside fell noisily upon the hard road beneath them, which reflected from its glassy surface the faint halo of light hanging over the lamps of the adjacent town.

Here he walked and lingered for two hours, without seeing or hearing a living soul. Then he heard the market-house clock strike five, and soon afterwards, quick hard footsteps smote upon the pavement of the street leading towards him. They were those of the postman for the Tolchurch beat. He reached the bottom of the street, gave his bags a final hitch-up, stepped off the pavement, and struck out for the country with a brisk shuffle.

Manston then turned his back upon the town, and walked slowly on. In two minutes a flickering light shone upon his form, and the postman overtook him.

The new-comer was a short, stooping individual of above five-and-forty, laden on both sides with leather bags large and small, and

259

carrying a little lantern strapped to his breast, which cast a tiny patch of light upon the road ahead.

'A tryen mornen for travellers!' the postman cried, in a cheerful voice, without turning his head or slackening his trot.

'It is, indeed,' said Manston, stepping out abreast of him. 'You have a long walk every day.'

'Yes – a long walk – for though the distance is only sixteen miles on the straight – that is, eight to the furthest place and eight back, what with the ins and outs to the gentlemen's houses, it makes two-and-twenty for my legs. Two-and-twenty miles a day, how many a year? I used to reckon it, but I never do now. I don't care to think o' my wear and tear, now it do begin to tell upon me.'

Thus the conversation was begun, and the postman proceeded to narrate the different strange events that marked his experience. Manston grew very friendly.

'Postman, I don't know what your custom is,' he said after a while; 'but between you and me, I always carry a drop of something warm in my pocket when I am out on such a morning as this. Try it.' He handed the bottle of brandy.

'If you'll excuse me, please. I haven't took no stimmilents these five years.'

''Tis never too late to mend.'

'Against the regulations, I be afraid.'

'Who'll know it?'

'That's true – nobody will know it. Still, honesty's the best policy.'

'Ah – it is certainly. But, thank God, I've been able to get on without it yet. You'll surely drink with me?'

'Really, 'tis a'most too early for that sort o' thing – however, to oblige a friend, I don't object to the faintest shadder of a drop.' The postman drank, and Manston did the same to a very slight degree. Five minutes later when they came to a gate, the flask was pulled out again.

'Well done!' said the postman, beginning to feel its effect; 'but guide my soul, I be afraid 'twill hardly do!'

'Not unless 'tis well followed, like any other line you take up,' said Manston. 'Besides, there's a way of liking a drop of liquor, and of being good – even religious – at the same time.'

'Ay, for some thimble-and-button* in-an-out fellers; but I could never get into the knack o' it; not I.'

'Well, you needn't be troubled; it isn't necessary for the higher class of mind to be religious – they have so much common-sense that they can risk playing with fire.'

'That hits me exactly.'

'In fact, a man I know, who always had no other god but "Me"; and devoutly loved his neighbour's wife,* says now that believing is a mistake.'

'Well, to be sure! However, believing in God is a mistake made by very few people, after all.'

'A true remark.'

'Not one Christian in our parish would walk half a mile in a rain like this to know whether the Scripture had concluded him under sin or grace.'

'Nor in mine.'

'Ah, you may depend upon it they'll do away wi' Goda'mighty altogether before long, although we've had him over us so many years.'

'There's no knowing.'

'And I suppose the Queen 'ill be done away wi' then. A pretty concern that'll be! Nobody's head to put on your letters; an then your honest man who do pay his penny will never be known from your scamp who don't. O, 'tis a nation!'

'Warm the cockles of your heart, however. Here's the bottle waiting.'

'I'll oblige you, my friend.'

The drinking was repeated. The postman grew livelier as he went on, and at length favoured the steward with a song, Manston himself joining in the chorus.

> He flung his mallet against the wall,
> Said, 'The Lord make churches and chapels to fall,
> And there'll be work for tradesmen all!'
>> When Joan's ale was new,
>>> My boys,
>> When Joan's ale was new.*

'You understand, friend,' the postman added, 'I was originally a mason by trade: no offence to you if you be a parson?'

'None at all,' said Manston.

The rain now came down heavily, but they pursued their path with alacrity, the produce of the several fields between which the lane wound its way being indicated by the peculiar character of the sound emitted by the falling drops. Sometimes a soaking hiss proclaimed that they were passing by a pasture, then a patter would show that the rain fell upon some large-leafed root crop, then a paddling plash announced the naked arable, the low sound of the wind in their ears rising and falling with each pace they took.

Besides the small private bags of the county families,* which were all locked, the postman bore the large general budget* for the remaining inhabitants along his beat. At each village or hamlet they came to, the postman searched for the packet of letters destined for that place, and thrust it into an ordinary letter-hole cut in the door of the receiver's cottage – the village post-offices being mostly kept by old women who had not yet risen, though lights moving in other cottage windows showed that such people as carters, woodmen, and stablemen, had long been stirring.

The postman had by this time become markedly unsteady, but he still continued to be too conscious of his duties to suffer the steward to search the bag. Manston was perplexed, and at lonely points in the road cast his eyes keenly upon the short bowed figure of the man trotting through the mud by his side, as if he were half inclined to run a very great risk indeed.

It frequently happened that the houses of farmers, clergymen, &c., lay a short distance up or down a lane or path branching from the direct track of the postman's journey. To save time and distance, at the point of junction of some of these paths with the main road the gate-post was hollowed out to form a letter-box, in which the postman deposited his missives in the morning, looking in the box again in the evening to collect those placed there for the return post. Tolchurch Dairy and Farmstead, lying back from the village street, were served on this principle. This fact the steward now learnt by conversing with the postman, and the discovery relieved Manston greatly, making his intentions much clearer to himself than they had been in the earlier stages of his journey.

They had reached the outskirts of the village. Manston insisted upon the flask being emptied before they proceeded further. This was done, and they approached the lane to the dairy, and the farmhouse in which Owen and Cytherea were living.

The postman paused, fumbled in his bag, took out by the light of his lantern some half-dozen letters, and tried to sort them. He could not perform the task.

'We be crippled disciples a b'lieve,' he said, with a sigh and a stagger.

'Not drunk, but market-merry,' said Manston cheerfully.

'Well done! If I bain't so weak that I can't see the clouds – much less letters. Guide my soul, if so be anybody should tell the Queen's postmaster-general of me! The whole story will have to go through Parliament House, and I shall be high-treasoned – as safe as houses – and be fined, and who'll pay for a poor martel!* O, 'tis a world!'

'Trust in the Lord – he'll pay.'

'He pay a b'lieve! why should he when he didn't drink the drink? He pay a b'lieve! D'ye think the man's a fool?'

'Well, well, I had no intention of hurting your feelings – but how was I to know you were so sensitive?'

'True – you were not to know I was so sensitive. Here's a caddle⋆ wi' these letters! Guide my soul, what will Billy do!'

Manston offered his services.

'They are to be divided,' the man said.

'How?' said Manston.

'These, for the village, to be carried on into it: any for the lower farm and dairy must be left in the box of the gate-post just here. There's none for the dairy-house this mornen, but I saw when I started there was one for the clerk o' works at the new church. This is it, isn't it?'

He held up a large envelope, directed in Edward Springrove's handwriting: –

Mr Owen Graye,
Clerk of Works,
Tolchurch,
Near Anglebury

The letter-box was scooped in an oak gate-post about a foot square. There was no slit for inserting the letters, by reason of the opportunity such a lonely spot would have afforded mischievous peasant-boys of doing damage had such been the case; but at the side was a small iron door, kept close by an iron reversible strap locked across it. One side of this strap was painted black, the other white, and white or black outwards implied respectively that there were letters inside, or none.

The postman had taken the key from his pocket and was attempting to insert it in the keyhole of the box. He touched one side, the other, above, below, but never made a straight hit.

'Let me unlock it,' said Manston, taking the key from the postman. He opened the box and reached out with his other hand for Owen's letter.

'No, no. O no – no,' the postman said. 'As – one of – Majesty's servants – care – Majesty's mails – duty – put letters – own hands.' He slowly and solemnly placed the letter in the small cavity.

'Now lock it,' he said, closing the door.

The steward placed the bar across, with the black side outwards, signifying 'empty', and turned the key.

'You've put the wrong side outwards!' said the postman. ''Tisn't empty.'

'And dropped the key in the mud, so that I can't alter it,' said the steward, letting something fall.

'What an awkward thing!'

'It is an awkward thing.'

They both went searching in the mud, which their own trampling had reduced to the consistency of pap, the postman unstrapping his little lantern from his breast, and thrusting it about, close to the ground, the rain still drizzling down, and the dawn so tardy on account of the heavy clouds that daylight seemed delayed indefinitely. The rays of the lantern were rendered individually visible upon the thick mist and seemed almost tangible as they passed off into it after illuminating the faces and knees of the two stooping figures dripping with wet; the postman's cape and private bags, and the steward's valise, glistening as if they had been varnished.

'It fell on the grass,' said the postman.

'No; it fell in the mud,' said Manston. They searched again.

'I'm afraid we shan't find it by this light,' said the steward at length, washing his muddy fingers in the wet grass of the bank.

'I'm afraid we shan't,' said the other, standing up.

'I'll tell you what we had better do,' said Manston. 'I shall be back this way in an hour or so, and since it was all my fault, I'll look again, and shall be sure to find it in the daylight. And I'll hide the key here for you.' He pointed to a spot behind the post. 'It will be too late to turn the index then, as the people will have been here, so that the box had better stay as it is. The letter will only be delayed a day, and that will not be noticed; if it is, you can say you placed the iron the wrong way without knowing it, and all will be well.'

This was agreed to by the postman as the best thing to be done under the circumstances, and the pair went on. They had passed the village and come to a cross-road, when the steward, telling his companion that their paths now diverged, turned off to the left towards Carriford.

No sooner was the postman out of sight and hearing than Manston stalked back to the farmstead letter-box by keeping inside a fence, and thus avoiding the village; arrived here, he took the key from his pocket, where it had been concealed all the time, and abstracted Owen's letter. This done, he turned towards home, by the help of what he carried in his valise adjusting himself to his ordinary appearance as he neared the quarter in which he was known.

An hour and half's sharp walking brought him to his own door in Knapwater Park.

2. *Eight o'Clock a.m.*

Seated in his private office he wetted the flap of the stolen letter, and waited patiently till the adhesive gum could be loosened. He took out Edward's note, the accounts, the rosebud, and the photographs, regarding them with the keenest interest and anxiety.

The note, the accounts, the rosebud, and his own photograph, he restored to their places again. The other photograph he took between his finger and thumb, and held it towards the bars of the grate. There he held it for half-a-minute or more, meditating.

'It is a great risk to run, even for such an end,' he muttered.

Suddenly, impregnated with a bright idea, he jumped up and left the office for the front parlour. Taking up an album of portraits, which lay on the table, he searched for three or four likenesses of the lady who had so lately displaced Cytherea, which were interspersed among the rest of the collection, and carefully regarded them. They were taken in different attitudes and styles, and he compared each singly with that he held in his hand. One of them, the one most resembling that abstracted from the letter in general tone, size, and attitude, he selected from the rest, and returned with it to his office.

Pouring some water into a plate, he set the two portraits afloat upon it, and sitting down tried to read.

At the end of a quarter of an hour, after several ineffectual attempts, he found that each photograph would peel from the card on which it was mounted. This done, he threw into the fire the original likeness and the recent card, stuck upon the original card the recent likeness from the album, dried it before the fire, and placed it in the envelope with the other scraps.

The result he had obtained, then, was this: in the envelope were now two photographs, both having the same photographer's name on the back and consecutive numbers attached. At the bottom of the one which showed his own likeness, his own name was written down; on the other his wife's name was written; whilst the central feature, and whole matter to which this latter card and writing referred, the likeness of a lady mounted upon it, had been changed.

Mrs Manston entered the room, and begged him to come to breakfast. He followed her and they sat down. During the meal he told her what he had done, with scrupulous regard to every detail, and showed her the result.

'It is indeed a great risk to run,' she said, sipping her tea.

'But it would be a greater not to do it.'

'Yes.'

The envelope was again fastened up as before, and Manston put it in his pocket and went out. Shortly afterwards he was seen, on horseback, riding in a direction towards Tolchurch. Keeping to the fields, as well as he could, for the greater part of the way, he dropped into the road by the farmhouse letter-box, and looking carefully about, to ascertain that no person was near, he restored the letter to its nook, placed the key in its hiding-place, as he had promised the postman, and again rode homewards by a roundabout way.

3. Afternoon

The letter was brought to Owen Graye, the same afternoon, by one of the vicar's servants who had been to the box with a duplicate key, as usual, to leave letters for the evening post. The man found that the index had told falsely that morning for the first time within his recollection; but no particular attention was paid to the mistake, as it was considered. The contents of the envelope were scrutinized by Owen and flung aside as useless.

The next morning brought Springrove's second letter, the existence of which was unknown to Manston. The sight of Edward's handwriting again raised the expectations of brother and sister, till Owen had opened the envelope and pulled out the twig and verse.

'Nothing that's of the slightest use, after all,' he said to her; 'we are as far as ever from the merest shadow of legal proof that would convict him of what I am morally certain he did, marry you, suspecting, if not knowing, her to be alive all the time.'

'What has Edward sent?' said Cytherea.

'An old amatory verse in Manston's writing. Fancy,' he said bitterly, 'this is the strain he addressed her in when they were courting – as he did you, I suppose.'

He handed her the verse and she read –

EUNICE

Whoso for hours or lengthy days
Shall catch her aspect's changeful rays,
Then turn away, can none recall

266

Beyond a galaxy of all
  In hazy portraiture;
Lit by the light of azure eyes
Like summer days by summer skies:
Her sweet transitions seem to be
A pinkly pictured melody,

  And not a set contour.
     Æ.M.

A strange expression had overspread Cytherea's countenance. It rapidly increased to the most death-like anguish. She flung down the paper, seized Owen's hand trembling, and covered her face.

'Cytherea! What is it, for Heaven's sake?'

'Owen – suppose – O, you don't know what I think.'

'What?'

'"*The light of azure eyes*",' she repeated with ashy lips.

'Well, "the light of azure eyes"?' he said, astounded at her manner.

'Mrs Morris said in her letter to me that her eyes are *black*!'

'H'm. Mrs Morris must have made a mistake – nothing likelier.'

'She didn't.'

'They might be either in this photograph,' said Owen, looking at the card bearing Mrs Manston's name.

'Blue eyes would scarcely photograph so deep in tone as that,' said Cytherea. 'No, they seem black here, certainly.'

'Well, then, Manston must have blundered in writing his verses.'

'But could he? Say a man in love may forget his own name, but not that he forgets the colour of his mistress's eyes. Besides she would have seen the mistake when she read them, and have had it corrected.'

'That's true, she would,' mused Owen. 'Then, Cytherea, it comes to this – you must have been misinformed by Mrs Morris, since there is no other alternative.'

'I suppose I must.'

Her looks belied her words.

'What makes you so strange – ill?' said Owen again.

'I can't believe Mrs Morris wrong.'

'But look at this, Cytherea. If it is clear to us that the woman had blue eyes two years ago, she *must* have blue eyes now, whatever Mrs Morris or anybody else may fancy. Any one would think that Manston could change the colour of a woman's eyes to hear you.'

'Yes,' she said, and paused.

'You say yes, as if he could,' said Owen impatiently.

'By changing the woman herself,' she exclaimed. 'Owen, don't you see the horrid – what I dread? – that the woman he lives with is not Mrs Manston – that she was burnt after all – and that I am HIS WIFE!'

She tried to support a stoicism under the weight of this new trouble, but no! The unexpected revulsion of ideas was so overwhelming that she crept to him and leant against his breast.

Before reflecting any further upon the subject Graye led her upstairs and got her to lie down. Then he went to the window and stared out of it up the lane, vainly endeavouring to come to some conclusion upon the fantastic enigma that confronted him. Cytherea's new view seemed incredible, yet it had such a hold upon her that it would be necessary to clear it away by positive proof before contemplation of her fear should have preyed too deeply upon her.

'Cytherea,' he said, 'this will not do. You must stay here alone all the afternoon whilst I go to Carriford. I shall know all when I return.'

'No, no, don't go!' she implored.

'Soon, then, not directly.' He saw her subtle reasoning – that it was folly to be wise.

Reflection still convinced him that good would come of persevering in his intention and dispelling his sister's idle fears. Anything was better than this absurd doubt in her mind. But he resolved to wait till Sunday, the first day on which he might reckon upon seeing Mrs Manston without suspicion. In the meantime he wrote to Edward Springrove, requesting him to go again to Mrs Manston's former lodgings.

CHAPTER EIGHTEEN
The Events of Three Days

1. March the Eighteenth

Sunday morning had come, and Owen was trudging over the six miles of hill and dale that lay between Tolchurch and Carriford.

Edward Springrove's answer to the last letter, after expressing his amazement at the strange contradiction between the verses and Mrs Morris's letter, had been to the effect that he had again visited the neighbour of the dead Mr Brown, and had received as near a description of Mrs Manston as it was possible to get at second-hand, and by hearsay. She was a tall woman, wide at the shoulders, and full-chested, and she had a straight and rather large nose. The colour of her eyes the informant did not know, for she had only seen the lady in the street as she went in or out. This confusing remark was added. The woman had almost recognized Mrs Manston when she had called with her husband lately, but she had kept her veil down. Her residence, before she came to Hoxton, was quite unknown to this next-door neighbour, and Edward could get no manner of clue to it from any other source.

Owen reached the church-door a few minutes before the bells began chiming. Nobody was yet in the church, and he walked round the aisles. From Cytherea's frequent description of how and where herself and others used to sit, he knew where to look for Manston's seat; and after two or three errors of examination he took up a prayer-book in which was written 'Eunice Manston'. The book was nearly new, and the date of the writing about a month earlier. One point was at any rate established: that the woman living with Manston was presented to the world as no other than his lawful wife.

The quiet villagers of Carriford required no pew-opener* in their place of worship: natives and in-dwellers had their own seats, and strangers sat where they could. Graye took a seat in the nave, on the north side, close behind a pillar dividing it from the north aisle, which was completely allotted to Miss Aldclyffe, her farmers and her retainers, Manston's pew being in the midst of them. Owen's position on the other side of the passage was a little in advance of Manston's seat, and so situated that by leaning forward he could look directly into the face of any person sitting there, though, if he sat upright, he was wholly hidden from such a one by the intervening pillar.

Aiming to keep his presence unknown to Manston if possible, Owen sat, without once turning his head, during the entrance of the congregation. A rustling of silk round by the north passage and into Manston's seat, told him that some woman had entered there, and as it seemed from the accompaniment of heavier footsteps, that Manston was with her.

Immediately upon rising up, he looked intently in that direction, and saw a lady standing at the end of the seat nearest himself. Portions of Manston's figure appeared on the other side of her. In two glances Graye read thus many of her characteristics, and in the following order: –

She was a tall woman.

She was broad at the shoulders.

She was full-bosomed.

She was easily recognizable from the photograph; but nothing could be discerned of the colour of her eyes.

With a preoccupied mind he withdrew into his nook, and heard the service continued – only conscious of the fact that in opposition to the suspicion which one odd circumstance had bred in his sister concerning this woman, all ostensible and ordinary proofs and probabilities tended to the opposite conclusion. There sat the genuine original of the portrait – could he wish for more? Cytherea wished for more. Eunice Manston's eyes were blue, and it was necessary that this woman's eyes should be blue also.

Unskilled labour wastes in beating against the bars ten times the energy exerted by the practised hand in the effective direction. Owen felt this to be the case in his own and Edward's attempts to follow up the clue afforded them. Think as he might, he could not think of a crucial test in the matter absorbing him, which should possess the indispensable attribute – a capability of being applied privately; that in the event of its proving the lady to be the rightful owner of the name she used, he might recede without obloquy from an untenable position.

But to see Mrs Manston's eyes from where he sat was impossible, and he could do nothing in the shape of a direct examination at present. Miss Aldclyffe had possibly recognized him, but Manston had not, and feeling that it was indispensable to keep the purport of his visit a secret from the steward, he thought it would be as well, too, to keep his presence in the village a secret from him; at any rate till the day was over.

At the first opening of the doors, Graye left the church and wandered away into the fields to ponder on another scheme. He could not call on Farmer Springrove, as he had intended, until this matter was set at rest. Two hours intervened between the morning and afternoon services.

This time had nearly expired before Owen had struck out any method of proceeding, or could decide to run the risk of calling at the Old House and asking to see Mrs Manston point-blank. But he had drawn near the place, and was standing still in the public path, from which a partial view of the front of the building could be obtained, when the bells began chiming for afternoon service. Whilst Graye paused, two persons came from the front door of the half-hidden dwelling, whom he presently saw to be Manston and his wife. Manston was wearing his old garden-hat, and carried one of the monthly magazines under his arm. Immediately they had passed the gateway he branched off and went over the hill in a direction away from the church, evidently intending to ramble along, and read as the humour moved

270

him. The lady meanwhile turned in the other direction, and went into the church path.

Owen resolved to make something of this opportunity. He hurried along towards the church, doubled round a sharp angle, and came back upon the other path, by which Mrs Manston must arrive.

In about three minutes she appeared in sight without a veil. He discovered, as she drew nearer, a difficulty which had not struck him at first – that it is not an easy matter to particularize the colour of a stranger's eyes in a merely casual encounter on a path out of doors. That Mrs Manston must be brought close to him, and not only so, but to look closely at him, if his purpose were to be accomplished.

He shaped a plan. It might by chance be effectual; if otherwise, it would not reveal his intention to her. When Mrs Manston was within speaking distance, he went up to her and said –

'Will you kindly tell me which turning will take me to Casterbridge?'

'The second on the right,' said Mrs Manston.

Owen put on a blank look: he held his hand to his ear – conveying to the lady the idea that he was deaf.

She came closer and said more distinctly –

'The second turning on the right.'

Owen flushed a little. He fancied he had beheld the revelation he was in search of. But had his eyes deceived him?

Once more he used the ruse, still drawing nearer, and intimating by a glance that the trouble he gave her was very distressing to him.

'How very deaf!' she murmured. She exclaimed loudly –

The second turning to the right.'

She had advanced her face to within a foot of his own, and in speaking mouthed very emphatically, fixing her eyes intently upon his. And now his first suspicion was indubitably confirmed. Her eyes were as black as midnight.

All this feigning was most distasteful to Graye. The riddle having been solved, he unconsciously assumed his natural look before she had withdrawn her face. She found him to be peering at her as if he would read her very soul – expressing with his eyes the notification of which, apart from emotion, the eyes are more capable than any other – inquiry.

Her face changed its expression – then its colour. The natural tint of the lighter portions sank to an ashy gray; the pink of her cheeks grew purpler. It was the precise result which would remain after blood had left the face of one whose skin was dark, and artificially coated with pearl-powder* and carmine.

She turned her head and moved away, murmuring a hasty reply to

Owen's farewell remark of 'Good-day', and with a kind of nervous twitch lifting her hand and smoothing her hair which was of a light-brown colour.

'She wears false hair,' he thought, 'or has changed its colour artificially. Her true hair matched her eyes.'

And now, in spite of what Mr Brown's neighbours had said about nearly recognizing Mrs Manston on her recent visit – which might have meant anything or nothing; in spite of the photograph, and in spite of his previous incredulity; in consequence of the verse, of her silence and backwardness at the visit to Hoxton with Manston, and of her appearance and distress at the present moment, Graye had a conviction that the woman was an impostor.

What could be Manston's reason for such an astounding trick he could by no stretch of imagination divine.

He changed his direction as soon as the woman was out of sight, and plodded along the lanes homeward to Tolchurch.

One new idea was suggested to him by his desire to allay Cytherea's dread of being claimed, and by the difficulty of believing that the first Mrs Manston lost her life as supposed, notwithstanding the inquest and verdict. Was it possible that the real Mrs Manston, who was known to be a Philadelphian by birth, had returned by the train to London, as the porter had said, and then left the country under an assumed name, to escape that worst kind of widowhood – the misery of being wedded to a fickle, faithless, and truant husband?

In her complicated distress at the news brought by her brother, Cytherea's thoughts at length reverted to her friend, the Rector of Carriford. She told Owen of Mr Raunham's warm-hearted behaviour towards herself, and of his strongly expressed wish to aid her.

'He is not only a good, but a sensible man. We seem to want an old head on our side.'

'And he is a magistrate,'* said Owen in a tone of concurrence. He thought, too, that no harm could come of confiding in the rector, but there was a difficulty in bringing about the confidence. He wished that his sister and himself might both be present at an interview with Mr Raunham, yet it would be unwise for them to call on him together, in the sight of all the servants and parish of Carriford.

There could be no objection to their writing him a letter.

No sooner was the thought born than it was carried out. They wrote to him at once, asking him to have the goodness to give them some advice they sadly needed, and begging that he would accept their assurance that there was a real justification for the additional request they made – that instead of their calling upon him, he would any evening of the week come to their cottage at Tolchurch.

2. March the Twentieth. Six to Nine o'Clock p.m.

Two evenings later, to the total disarrangement of his dinner-hour, Mr Raunham appeared at Owen's door. His arrival was hailed with genuine gratitude. The horse was tied to the palings, and the rector ushered indoors and put into the easy-chair.

Then Graye told him the whole story, reminding him that their first suspicions had been of a totally different nature, and that in endeavouring to obtain proof of their truth they had stumbled upon marks which had surprised them into these new uncertainties, thrice as marvellous as the first, yet more prominent.

Cytherea's heart was so full of anxiety that it superinduced a manner of confidence which was a death-blow to all formality. Mr Raunham took her hand pityingly.

'It is a serious charge,' he said, as a sort of original twig on which his thoughts might precipitate themselves.

'Assuming for a moment that such a substitution was rendered an easy matter by fortuitous events,' he continued, 'there is this consideration to be placed beside it – what earthly motive can Mr Manston have had which would be sufficiently powerful to lead him to run such a very great risk? The most abandoned *roué*★ could not, at that particular crisis, have taken such a reckless step for the mere pleasure of a new companion.'

Owen had seen that difficulty about the motive; Cytherea had not.

'Unfortunately for us,' the rector resumed, 'no more evidence is to be obtained from the porter, Chinney. I suppose you know what became of him? He got to Liverpool and embarked, intending to work his way to America, but on the passage he fell overboard and was drowned. But there is no doubt of the truth of his confession – in fact, his conduct tends to prove it true – and no moral doubt of the fact that the real Mrs Manston left here to go back by that morning's train. This being the case, then, why, if this woman is not she, did she take no notice of the advertisement – I mean not necessarily a friendly notice, but from the information it afforded her have rendered it impossible that she should be personified without her own connivance?'

'I think that argument is overthrown,' Graye said, 'by my earliest assumption of her hatred of him, weariness of the chain which bound her to him, and a resolve to begin the world anew. Let's suppose she has married another man – somewhere abroad, say; she would be silent for her own sake.'

'You've hit the only genuine possibility,' said Mr Raunham, tapping his finger upon his knee. 'That would decidedly dispose of the second difficulty. But his motive would be as mysterious as ever.'

Cytherea's pictured dreads would not allow her mind to follow their conversation. 'She's burnt,' she said. 'O yes; I fear – I fear she is!'

'I don't think we can seriously believe that now, after what has happened,' said the rector.

Still straining her thought towards the worst, 'Then, perhaps, the first Mrs Manston was not his wife,' she returned; 'and then I should be his wife just the same, shouldn't I?'

'They were married safely enough,' said Owen. 'There is abundance of circumstantial evidence to prove that.'

'Upon the whole,' said Mr Raunham, 'I should advise your asking in a straightforward way for legal proof from the steward that the present woman is really his original wife – a thing which, to my mind, you should have done at the outset.' He turned to Cytherea kindly, and asked her what made her give up her husband so unceremoniously.

She could not tell the rector of her aversion to Manston, and of her unquenched love for Edward.

'Your terrified state, no doubt,' he said, answering for her in the manner of those accustomed to the pulpit. 'But into such a solemn compact as marriage, all-important considerations, both legally and morally, enter; it was your duty to have seen everything clearly proved. Doubtless Mr Manston is prepared with proofs, but as it concerns nobody but yourself that her identity should be publicly established (and by your absenteeism you act as if you were satisfied) he has not troubled to exhibit them. Nobody else has taken the trouble to prove what does not affect them in the least – that's the way of the world always. You, who should have required all things to be made clear, ran away.'

'That was partly my doing,' said Owen.

The same explanation – her want of love for Manston – applied here too, but she shunned the revelation.

'But never mind,' added the rector; 'it was all the greater credit to your womanhood, perhaps. I say, then, get your brother to write a line to Mr Manston, saying you wish to be satisfied that all is legally clear (in case you should want to marry again, for instance), and I have no doubt that you will be. Or, if you would rather, I'll write myself?'

'O no, sir, no,' pleaded Cytherea, beginning to blanch, and breathing quickly. 'Please don't say anything. Let me live here with Owen. I am so afraid it will turn out that I shall have to go to Knapwater and be his wife, and I don't want to go. Do conceal what we have told you. Let him continue his deception – it is much the best for me.'

Mr Raunham at length divined that her love for Manston, if it had ever existed, had transmuted itself into a very different feeling now.

'At any rate,' he said, as he took his leave and mounted his mare, 'I will see about it. Rest content, Miss Graye, and depend upon it that I will not lead you into difficulty.'

'Conceal it,' she still pleaded.

'We'll see – but of course I must do my duty.'

'No – don't do your duty!' She looked up at him through the gloom, illuminating her own face and eyes with the candle she held.

'I will consider, then,' said Mr Raunham, sensibly moved. He turned his horse's head, bade them a warm adieu, and left the door.

The rector of Carriford trotted homewards under the cold and clear March sky, its countless stars fluttering like bright birds. He was unconscious of the scene. Recovering from the effect of Cytherea's voice and glance of entreaty, he laid the subject of the interview clearly before himself.

The suspicions of Cytherea and Owen were honest, and had foundation – that he must own. Was he – a clergyman, magistrate, and conscientious man – justified in yielding to Cytherea's importunities to keep silence, because she dreaded the possibility of a return to Manston? Was she wise in her request? Holding her present belief, and with no definite evidence either way, she could, for one thing, never conscientiously marry any one else. Suppose that Cytherea were Manston's wife – *i.e.*, that the first wife was really burnt? The adultery of Manston would be proved, and, Mr Raunham thought, cruelty sufficient to bring the case within the meaning of the statute. Suppose the new woman was, as stated, Mr Manston's restored wife? Cytherea was perfectly safe as a single woman whose marriage had been void. And if it turned out that, though this woman was not Manston's wife, his wife was still living, as Owen had suggested, in America or elsewhere, Cytherea was safe.

The first supposition opened up the worst contingency. Was she really safe as Manston's wife? Doubtful. But, however that might be, the gentle, defenceless girl, whom it seemed nobody's business to help or guard, should be put in a track to proceed against this man. She had but one life, and the superciliousness with which all the world now regarded her should be compensated in some measure by the man whose carelessness – to set him in the best light – had caused it.

Mr Raunham felt more and more positively that his duty must be done. An inquiry must be made into the matter. Immediately on reaching home, he sat down and wrote a plain and friendly letter to Mr Manston, and despatched it at once to him by hand. Then he flung himself back in his chair, and went on with his meditation. Was there anything in the suspicion? There could be nothing, surely. Nothing is done by a clever man without a motive, and what conceivable motive could Manston have for such abnormal conduct? Corinthian* that he might be, who had preyed on virginity like St George's dragon, he would never have been absurd enough to venture on such a course for the possession alone of the woman – there was no reason for it – she was inferior to Cytherea in every respect, physical and mental.

On the other hand, it seemed rather odd, when he analyzed the action, that a woman who deliberately hid herself from her husband for more than a twelve-month should be brought back by a mere advertisement. In fact, the whole business had worked almost too smoothly and effectually for unpremeditated sequence. It was too much like the indiscriminate righting of everything at the end of an old play. And there was that curious business of the keys and watch. Her way of accounting for their being left behind by forgetfulness had always seemed to him rather forced. The only unforced explanation was that suggested by the newspaper writers – that she left them behind on purpose to blind people as to her escape, a motive which would have clashed with the possibility of her being fished back by an advertisement, as the present woman had been. Again, there were the two charred bones. He shuffled the books and papers in his study, and walked about the room, restlessly musing on the same subject. The parlour-maid entered.

'Can young Mr Springrove from London see you to-night, sir?'

'Young Mr Springrove?' said the rector, surprised.

'Yes, sir.'

'Yes, of course he can see me. Tell him to come in.'

Edward came so impatiently into the room, as to show that the few short moments his announcement had occupied had been irksome to him. He stood in the doorway with the same black bag in his hand, and the same old gray cloak on his shoulders, that he had worn fifteen months earlier when returning on the night of the fire. This appearance of his conveyed a true impression; he had become a stagnant man. But he was excited now.

'I have this moment come from London,' he said, as the door was closed behind him.

The prophetic insight, which so strangely accompanies critical experiences, prompted Mr Raunham's reply.

'About the Grayes and Manston?'

'Yes. That woman is not Mrs Manston.'

'Prove it.'

'I can prove that she is somebody else – that her name is Anne Seaway.'

'And are their suspicions true indeed!'

'And I can do what's more to the purpose at present.'

'Suggest Manston's motive?'

'Only suggest it, remember. But my assumption fits so perfectly with the facts that have been secretly unearthed and conveyed to me, that I can hardly conceive of another.'

There was in Edward's bearing that entire unconsciousness of himself which, natural to wild animals, only prevails in a sensitive man at moments of extreme intentness. The rector saw that he had no trivial story to communicate, whatever the story was.

'Sit down,' said Mr Raunham. 'My mind has been on the stretch all the evening to form the slightest guess at such an object, and all to no purpose – entirely to no purpose. Have you said anything to Owen Graye?'

'Nothing – nor to anybody. I could not trust to the effect a letter might have upon yourself, either; the intricacy of the case brings me to this interview.'

Whilst Springrove had been speaking the two had sat down together. The conversation, hitherto distinct to every corner of the room, was carried on now in tones so low as to be scarcely audible to the interlocutors, and in phrases which hesitated to complete themselves. Three-quarters of an hour passed. Then Edward arose, came out of the rector's study and again flung his cloak around him. Instead of going thence homeward, he went first to the Carriford Road Station with a telegram, having despatched which he proceeded to his father's house for the first time since his arrival in the village.

3. From Nine to Ten o'Clock p.m.

The next presentation is the interior of the Old House on the evening of the preceding section. The steward was sitting by his parlour fire, and had been reading the letter arrived from the rectory. Opposite to him sat the woman known to the village and neighbourhood as Mrs Manston.

'Things are looking desperate with us,' he said gloomily. His gloom was not that of the hypochondriac, but the legitimate gloom which has its origin in a syllogism. As he uttered the words he handed the letter to her.

'I almost expected some such news as this,' she replied in a tone of much greater indifference. 'I knew suspicion lurked in the eyes of that young man who stared at me so in the church path: I could have sworn it.'

Manston did not answer for some time. His face was worn and haggard; latterly his head had not been carried so uprightly as of old. 'If they prove you to be – who you are. . . . Yes, if they do,' he murmured.

'They must not find that out,' she said, in a positive voice, and looking at him. 'But supposing they do, the trick does not seem to me to be so serious as to justify that wretched, miserable, horrible look of yours. It makes my flesh creep; it is perfectly deathlike.'

He did not reply, and she continued, 'If they say and prove that Eunice is indeed living – and dear, you know she is – she is sure to come back.'

This remark seemed to awaken and irritate him to speech. Again, as he had done a hundred times during their residence together, he categorized the events connected with the fire at the Three Tranters. He dwelt on every incident of that night's history, and endeavoured, with an anxiety which was extraordinary in the apparent circumstances, to prove that his wife must, by the very nature of things, have perished in the flames. She arose from her seat, crossed the hearth-rug, and set herself to soothe him; then she whispered that she was still as unbelieving as ever. 'Come, supposing she escaped – just supposing she escaped – where is she?' coaxed the lady.

'Why are you so curious continually?' said Manston.

'Because I am a woman and want to know. Now where is she?'

'In the Flying Isle of San Borandan.'*

'Witty cruelty is the cruellest of any. Ah, well – if she is in England, she will come back.'

'She is not in England.'

'But she will come back?'

'No, she won't. . . . Come, madam,' he said, arousing himself, 'I shall not answer any more questions.'

'Ah – ah – ah – she is not dead,' the woman murmured again poutingly.

'She is, I tell you.'

'I don't think so, love.'

'She was burnt, I tell you!' he exclaimed.

'Now to please me, admit the bare possibility of her being alive – just the possibility.'

'O yes – to please you I will admit that,' he said quickly. 'Yes, I admit the possibility of her being alive, to please you.'

She looked at him in utter perplexity. The words could only have been said in jest, and yet they seemed to savour of a tone the furthest remove from jesting. There was his face plain to her eyes, but no information of any kind was to be read there.

'It is only natural that I should be curious.' she murmured pettishly, 'if I resemble her as much as you say I do.'

'You are handsomer,' he said, 'though you are about her own height and size. But don't worry yourself. You must know that you are body and soul united with me, though you are but my housekeeper.'

She bridled a little at the remark. 'Wife,' she said, 'most certainly wife, since you cannot dismiss me without losing your character and position, and incurring heavy penalties.'

'I own it – it was well said, though mistakenly – very mistakenly.'

'Don't riddle to me about mistakenly and such dark things. Now what was your motive, dearest, in running the risk of having me here?'

'Your beauty,' he said.

'She thanks you much for the compliment, but will not take it. Come, what was your motive?'

'Your wit.'

'No, no; not my wit. Wit would have made a wife of me by this time instead of what I am.'

'Your virtue.'

'Or virtue either.'

'I tell you it was your beauty – really.'

'But I cannot help seeing and hearing, and if what people say is true, I am not nearly so good-looking as Cytherea, and several years older.'

The aspect of Manston's face at these words from her was so confirmatory of her hint, that his forced reply of 'O no', tended to develop her chagrin.

'Mere liking or love for me,' she resumed, 'would not have sprung up all of a sudden, as your pretended passion did. You had been to London several times between the time of the fire and your marriage with Cytherea – you had never visited me or thought of my existence or cared that I was out of a situation and poor. But the week after you married her and were separated from her, off you rush to make love to me – not first to me either, for you went to several places—'

'No, not several places.'

'Yes, you told me so yourself – that you went first to the only lodging in which your wife had been known as Mrs Manston, and when you found that the lodging-house-keeper had gone away and died, and that nobody else in the street had any definite ideas as to your wife's personal appearance, you came and proposed the arrangement we carried out – that I should personate her. Your taking all this trouble shows that something more serious than love had to do with the matter.'

'Humbug – what trouble after all did I take? When I found Cytherea would not stay with me after the wedding I was much put out at being left alone again. Was that unnatural?'

'No.'

'And those favouring accidents you mention – that nobody knew my first wife – seemed an arrangement of Providence for our mutual benefit, and merely perfected a half-formed impulse – that I should call you my first wife to escape the scandal that would have arisen if you had come here as anything else.'

'My love, that story won't do. If Mrs Manston was burnt, Cytherea, whom you love better than me, could have been compelled to live with you as your lawful wife. If she was not burnt, why should you run the risk of her turning up again at any moment and exposing your substitution of me, and ruining your name and prospects?'

'Why – because I might have loved you well enough to run the risk (assuming her not to be burnt, which I deny).'

'No – you would have run the risk the other way. You would rather have risked her finding you with Cytherea as a second wife, than with me as a personator of herself – the first one.'

'You came easiest to hand – remember that.'

'Not so very easy either, considering the labour you took to teach me your first wife's history. All about how she was a native of Philadelphia. Then making me read up the guide-book to Philadelphia, and details of American life and manners, in case the birthplace and history of your wife, Eunice, should ever become known in this neighbourhood – unlikely as it was. Ah! and then about the handwriting of hers that I had to imitate, and the dyeing my hair, and rouging, to make the transformation complete? You mean to say that that was taking less trouble than there would have been in arranging events to make Cytherea believe herself your wife, and live with you?'

'You were a needy adventuress, who would dare anything for a new pleasure and an easy life – and I was fool enough to give in to you—'

'Good heavens above! – did I ask you to insert those advertisements for your old wife, and to make me answer one as if I was she? Did I ask you to send me the letter for me to copy and send back to you when the third advertisement appeared – purporting to come from the long-lost wife and giving a detailed history of her escape and subsequent life – all which you had invented yourself? You deluded me into loving you, and then enticed me here! Ah, and this is another thing. How did you know the real wife wouldn't answer it, and upset all your plans?'

'Because I knew she was burnt.'

'Why didn't you force Cytherea to come back, then? Now, my love, I have caught you, and you may just as well tell first as last, *what was your motive in having me here as your first wife?*'

'Silence!' he exclaimed.

She was silent for the space of two minutes, and then persisted in going on to mutter, 'And why was it that Miss Aldclyffe allowed her favourite young lady, Cythie, to be overthrown and supplanted without an expostulation or any show of sympathy? Do you know I often think you exercise a secret power over Miss Aldclyffe. And she always shuns me as if I shared the power. A poor, ill-used creature like me sharing power, indeed!'

'She thinks you are Mrs Manston.'

'That wouldn't make her avoid me.'

'Yes it would,' he exclaimed impatiently. 'I wish I was dead – dead!' He had jumped up from his seat in uttering the words, and now walked wearily to the end of the room. Coming back more decisively, he looked in her face.

'We must leave this place if Raunham suspects what I think he does,' he said. 'The request of Cytherea and her brother may simply be for a satisfactory proof, to make her feel legally free – but it may mean more.'

'What may it mean?'

'How should I know?'

'Well, well, never mind, old boy,' she said, approaching him to make up the quarrel. 'Don't be so alarmed – anybody would think that you were the woman and I the man. Suppose they do find out what I am – we can go away from here and keep house as usual. People will say of you, "His first wife was burnt to death" (or "ran away to the Colonies", as the case may be); "he married a second, and deserted her for Anne Seaway". A very everyday case – nothing so horrible, after all.'

He made an impatient movement. 'Whichever way we do it, *nobody must know that you are not my wife Eunice.* And now I must think about arranging matters.'

Manston then retired to his office, and shut himself up for the remainder of the evening.

CHAPTER NINETEEN
The Events of a Day and Night

1. March the Twenty-First. Morning

Next morning the steward went out as usual. He shortly told his companion, Anne, that he had almost matured their scheme, and that they would enter upon the details of it when he came home at night. The fortunate fact that the rector's letter did not require an immediate answer would give him time to consider.

Anne Seaway then began her duties in the house. Besides daily superintending the cook and housemaid one of these duties was, at rare intervals, to dust Manston's office with her own hands, a servant being supposed to disturb the books and papers unnecessarily. She softly wandered from table to shelf with the duster in her hand, afterwards standing in the middle of the room, and glancing around to discover if any noteworthy collection of dust had still escaped her.

Her eye fell upon a faint layer which rested upon the ledge of an old-fashioned chestnut cabinet of French Renaissance workmanship, placed in a recess by the fireplace. At a height of about four feet from the floor the upper portion of the front receded, forming the ledge alluded to, on which opened at each end two small doors, the centre space between them being filled out by a panel of similar size, making the third of three squares. The dust on the ledge was nearly on a level with the woman's eye, and, though insignificant in quantity, showed itself distinctly on account of this obliquity of vision. Now opposite the central panel, concentric quarter-circles were traced in the deposited film, expressing to her that this panel, too, was a door like the others; that it had lately been opened, and had skimmed the dust with its lower edge.

At last, then, her curiosity was slightly rewarded. For the right of the matter was that Anne had been incited to this exploration of Manston's office rather by a wish to know the reason of his long seclusion here, after the arrival of the rector's letter, and their subsequent discourse, than by any immediate desire for cleanliness. Still, there would have been nothing remarkable to Anne in this sight but for one recollection. Manston had once casually told her that each of the two side-lockers included half the middle space, the panel of which did not open, and was only put in for symmetry. It was possible that he had opened this compartment by candlelight the preceding night, or he would have seen the marks in the dust, and effaced them, that he might not be proved guilty of telling her an untruth. She balanced herself on one foot and stood pondering. She considered that it was very vexing and unfair in him to refuse her all knowledge of his remaining secrets, in the peculiar circumstances of her connection with him. She went close to the cabinet. As there was no keyhole, the door must be capable of being opened by the unassisted hand. The circles in the dust told her at which edge to apply her force. Here she pulled with the tips of her fingers, but the panel would not come forward. She fetched a chair and looked over the top of the cabinet, but no bolt, knob, or spring was to be seen.

'O, never mind,' she said, with indifference; 'I'll ask him about it, and he will tell me.' Down she came and turned away. Then looking back again she thought it was absurd such a trifle should puzzle her. She retraced her steps, and opened a drawer beneath the ledge of the cabinet, pushing in her hand and feeling about on the underside of the board.

Here she found a small round sinking, and pressed her finger into it. Nothing came of the pressure. She withdrew her hand and looked at the tip of her finger: it was marked with the impress of the circle, and, in addition, a line ran across it diametrically.

'How stupid of me; it is the head of a screw.' Whatever mysterious contrivance had originally existed for opening the puny cupboard of the cabinet, it had at some time been broken, and this rough substitute provided. Stimulated curiosity would not allow her to recede now. She fetched a screwdriver, withdrew the screw, pulled the door open with a penknife, and found inside a cavity about ten inches square. The cavity contained –

Letters from different women, with unknown signatures, Christian names only (surnames being despised in Paphos*). Letters from his wife Eunice. Letters from Anne herself, including that she wrote in answer to his advertisement. A small pocket-book. Sundry scraps of paper.

The letters from the strange women with pet names she glanced carelessly through, and then put them aside. They were too similar to her own regretted delusion, and curiosity requires contrast to excite it.

The letters from his wife were next examined. They were dated back as far as Eunice's first meeting with Manston, and the early ones before their marriage contained the usual pretty effusions of women at such a period of their existence. Some little time after he had made her his wife, and when he had come to Knapwater, the series began again, and now their contents arrested her attention more forcibly. She closed the cabinet, carried the letters into the parlour, reclined herself on the sofa, and carefully perused them in the order of their dates.

JOHN STREET,
October 17, 1864

MY DEAREST HUSBAND, – I received your hurried line of yesterday, and was of course content with it. But why don't you tell me your exact address instead of that 'Post-Office, Budmouth'? This matter is all a mystery to me, and I ought to be told every detail. I cannot fancy it is the same kind of occupation you have been used to hitherto. Your command that I am to stay here awhile until you can 'see how things look' and can arrange to send for me, I must necessarily abide by. But if, as you say, a married man would have been rejected by the person who engaged you, and that hence my existence must be kept a secret until you have secured your position, why did you think of going at all?

The truth is, this keeping our marriage a secret is troublesome, vexing, and wearisome to me. I see the poorest woman in the street bearing her husband's name openly – living with him in the most matter-of-fact ease, and why shouldn't I? I wish I was back again in Liverpool.

To-day I bought a grey waterproof cloak. I think it is a little too long for me, but it was cheap for one of such a quality. The weather is gusty and dreary, and till this morning I had hardly set foot outside the door since you left. Please do tell me when I am to come. – Very affectionately yours,

EUNICE

JOHN STREET,
October 25, 1864

MY DEAR HUSBAND, – Why don't you write? Do you hate me? I have not had the heart to do anything this last wek. That I, your wife, should be in this strait, and my husband well to do! I have been obliged to leave my first lodging for debt – among other things, they charged me for a lot of brandy which I am quite sure I did not taste. Then I went to Camberwell and was found out by them. I went away privately from thence, and changed my name the second time. I am now Mrs Rondley. But the new lodging was the wretchedest and dearest I ever set foot in, and I left it after being there only a day. I am now at No. 20 in the same street that you left me in originally. All last night the sash of my window rattled so dreadfully that I could not sleep, but I had not energy enough to get out of bed to stop it. This morning I have been walking – I don't know how far – but far enough to make my feet ache. I have been looking at the outside of two or three of the theatres, but they seem forbidding if I regard them with the eye of an actress in search of an engagement. Though you said I was to think no more of the stage, I believe you would not care if you found me there. But I am not an actress by nature, and art will never make me one. I am too timid and retiring; I was intended for a cottager's wife. I certainly shall not try to go on the boards again whilst I am in this strange place. The idea of being brought on as far as London and then left here alone! Why didn't you leave me in Liverpool? Perhaps you thought I might have told somebody that my real name was Mrs Manston. As if I had a living friend to whom I could impart it – no such good fortune! In fact, my nearest friend is no nearer than what most people would call a stranger. But perhaps I ought to tell you that a week before I wrote my last letter to you, after wishing that my uncle and aunt in Philadelphia (the only near relatives I had) were still alive, I suddenly resolved to send a line to my cousin James, who, I believe, is still living in that neighbourhood. He has never seen me since we were babies together. I did not tell him of my marriage, because I thought you might not like it, and I gave my real maiden name, and an address at the post-office here. But God knows if the letter will ever reach him.

Do write me an answer, and send something. – Your affectionate wife,

EUNICE

Friday, October 28

MY DEAR HUSBAND, – The order for ten pounds has just come, and I am truly glad to get it. But why will you write so bitterly? Ah – well, if I had only had the money I should have been on my way to America by this time, so don't think I want to bore you of my own free-will. Who can you have met with at that new place? Remember I say this in no malignant tone, but certainly the facts go to prove that you have deserted me! You are inconstant – I know it. O, why are you so? Now I have lost you, I love you in spite of your neglect. I am weakly fond – that's my nature. I fear that upon the whole my life has been wasted. I know there is another woman supplanting me in your heart – yes, I know it. Come to me – do come.

EUNICE

---

41 CHARLES SQUARE, HOXTON,
November 19

DEAR ÆNEAS, – Here I am back again after my visit. Why should you have been so enraged at my finding your exact address? Any woman would have tried to do it – you know she would have. And no woman would have lived under assumed names so long as I did. I repeat that I did not call myself Mrs Manston until I came to this lodging at the beginning of this month – what could you expect?

A helpless creature I, had not fortune favoured me unexpectedly. Banished as I was from your house at dawn, I did not suppose the indignity was about to lead to important results. But in crossing the park I overheard the conversation of a young man and woman who had also risen early. I believe her to be the girl who has won you away from me. Well, their conversation concerned you and Miss Aldclyffe, *very peculiarly*. The remarkable thing is that you yourself, without knowing it, told me of what, added to their conversation, completely reveals a secret to me that neither of you understand. Two negatives never made such a telling positive before. One clue more, and you would see it. A single consideration prevents me revealing it – just one doubt as to whether your ignorance was real, and was not feigned to deceive me. Civility now, please.

EUNICE

41 CHARLES SQUARE,
Tuesday, November 22

MY DARLING HUSBAND, – Monday will suit me excellently for coming. I have acted exactly up to your instructions, and have sold my rubbish at the broker's in the next street. All this movement and bustle is delightful to me after the weeks of monotony I have endured. It is a relief to wish the place good-bye – London always has seemed so much more foreign to me than Liverpool. The mid-day train on Monday will do nicely for me. I shall be anxiously looking out for you on Sunday night.

I hope so much that you are not angry with me for writing to Miss Aldclyffe. You are not, dear, are you? Forgive me. – Your loving wife,

EUNICE

This was the last of the letters from the wife to the husband. One other, in Mrs Manston's handwriting, and in the same packet, was differently addressed.

THREE TRANTERS INN, CARRIFORD,
November 28, 1864

DEAR COUSIN JAMES, – Thank you indeed for answering my letter so promptly. When I called at the post-office yesterday I did not in the least think there would be one. But I must leave this subject. I write again at once under the strangest and saddest conditions it is possible to conceive.

I did not tell you in my last that I was a married woman. Don't blame me – it was my husband's influence. I hardly know where to begin my story. I had been living apart from him for a time – then he sent for me (this was last week) and I was glad to go to him. Then this is what he did. He promised to fetch me, and did not – leaving me to do the journey alone. He promised to meet me at the station here – he did not. I went on through the darkness to his house, and found his door locked and himself away from home. I have been obliged to come here, and I write to you in a strange room in a strange village inn! I choose the present moment to write to drive away my misery. Sorrow seems a sort of pleasure when you detail it on paper – poor pleasure though.

But this is what I want to know – and I am ashamed to tell it. I would gladly do as you say, and come to you as a housekeeper, but I have not the money even for a steerage passage. James, do you want me badly enough – do you pity me enough to send it? I could manage to subsist in London upon the proceeds of my sale for another month or six weeks. Will you send it to the same address at the post-office? But how do I know that you. . . .

Thus the letter ended. From creases in the paper it was plain that the writer, having got so far, had become dissatisfied with her production, and had crumpled it in her hand. Was it to write another, or not to write at all?

The next thing Anne Seaway perceived was that the fragmentary story she had coaxed out of Manston, to the effect that his wife had left England for America, might be truthful, according to two of these letters, corroborated by the evidence of the railway-porter. And yet, at first, he had sworn in a passion that his wife was most certainly consumed in the fire.

If she had been burnt, this letter, written in her bedroom, and probably thrust into her pocket when she relinquished it, would have been burnt with her. Nothing was surer than that. Why, then, did he say she was burnt, and never show Anne herself this letter?

The question suddenly raised a new and much stranger one – kindling a burst of amazement in her. How did Manston become possessed of this letter?

That fact of possession was certainly the most remarkable revelation of all in connection with this epistle, and perhaps had something to do with his reason for never showing it to her.

She knew by several proofs, that from the fire to his marriage with Cytherea, and up to the time of the porter's confession, Manston believed – honestly believed – that Cytherea would be his lawful wife, and hence, of course, that his wife Eunice was dead. So that no communication could possibly have passed between his wife and himself from the first moment that he believed her dead on the night of the fire, to the day of his wedding. And yet he had that letter. How soon afterwards could they have communicated with each other?

The existence of the letter – as much as, or more than its contents – implying that Mrs Manston was not burnt, his belief in that calamity must have terminated at the moment he obtained possession of the letter, if no earlier. Was, then, the only solution to the riddle that Anne could discern, the true one? – that he had communicated with his wife somewhere about the commencement of Anne's residence with him, or at any time since?

It was the most unlikely thing on earth that a woman who had forsaken her husband should countenance his scheme to personify her – whether she were in America, in London, or in the neighbourhood of Knapwater.

Then came the old and harassing question, what was Manston's real motive in risking his name on the deception he was practising as regarded Anne. It could not be, as he had always pretended, mere passion. Her thoughts had reverted to Mr Raunham's letter, asking for proofs of her identity with the original Mrs Manston. She could see no loophole of escape for the man who supported her. True, in her own estimation, his worst alternative was not so very bad after all – the getting the name of libertine, a possible appearance in the divorce or some other court of law, and a question of damages. Such an exposure might hinder his worldly progress for some time. Yet to him this alternative was, apparently, terrible as death itself.

She restored the letters to their hiding-place, scanned anew the other letters and memoranda, from which she could gain no fresh information, fastened up the cabinet, and left everything in its former condition.

Her mind was ill at ease. More than ever she wished that she had never seen Manston. Where the person suspected of mysterious moral obliquity is the possessor of great physical and intellectual attractions, the mere sense of incongruity adds an extra shudder to dread. The man's strange bearing terrified Anne as it had terrified Cytherea; for with all the woman Anne's faults, she had not descended to such depths of depravity as to willingly participate in crime. She had not even known that a living wife was being displaced till her arrival at Knapwater put retreat out of the question, and had looked upon personation simply as a mode of subsistence a degree better than toiling in poverty and alone, after a bustling and somewhat pampered life as housekeeper in a gay mansion.

> Non illa colo calathisve Minervæ
> Fœmineas assueta manus.*

2. Afternoon

Mr Raunham and Edward Springrove had by this time set in motion a machinery which they hoped to find working out important results.

The rector was restless and full of meditation all the following morning. It was plain, even to the servants about him, that Springrove's communication wore a deeper complexion than any that had been made to the old magistrate for many months or years past. The fact was that, having arrived at the stage of existence in which the difficult intellectual feat of suspending one's judgment becomes possible, he was now putting it in practice, though not without the penalty of watchful effort.

It was not till the afternoon that he determined to call on his relative, Miss Aldclyffe, and cautiously probe her knowledge of the subject occupying him so thoroughly. Cytherea, he knew, was still beloved by this solitary woman. Miss Aldclyffe had made several private inquiries concerning her former companion, and there was ever a sadness in her tone when the young lady's name was mentioned, which showed that from whatever cause the elder Cytherea's renunciation of her favourite and namesake proceeded, it was not from indifference to her fate.

'Have you ever had any reason for supposing your steward anything but an upright man?' he said to the old maid.

'Never the slightest. Have you?' said she reservedly.

'Well – I have.'

'What is it?'

'I can say nothing plainly, because nothing is proved. But my suspicions are very strong.'

'Do you mean that he was rather cool towards his wife when they were first married, and that it was unfair in him to leave her? I know he was; but I think his recent conduct towards her has amply atoned for the neglect.'

He looked Miss Aldclyffe full in the face. It was plain that she spoke honestly. She had not the slightest notion that the woman who lived with the steward might be other than Mrs Manston – much less that a greater matter might be behind.

'That's not it – I wish it was no more. My suspicion is, first, that the woman living at the Old House is not Mr Manston's wife.'

'Not – Mr Manston's wife?'

'That is it.'

Miss Aldclyffe looked blankly at the rector. 'Not Mr Manston's wife – who else can she be?' she said simply.

'An improper woman of the name of Anne Seaway.'

Mr Raunham had, in common with other people, noticed the extraordinary interest of Miss Aldclyffe in the well-being of her steward, and had endeavoured to account for it in various ways. The extent to which she was shaken by his information, whilst it proved that the understanding between herself and Manston did not make her a sharer of his secrets, also showed that the tie which bound her to him

289

was still unbroken. Mr Raunham had lately begun to doubt the latter fact, and now, on finding himself mistaken, regretted that he had not kept his own counsel in the matter. This it was too late to do, and he pushed on with his proofs. He gave Miss Aldclyffe in detail the grounds of his belief.

Before he had done, she recovered the cloak of reserve that she had adopted on his opening the subject.

'I might possibly be convinced that you were in the right, after such an elaborate argument,' she replied, 'were it not for one fact, which bears in the contrary direction so pointedly, that nothing but absolute proof can turn it. It is that there is no conceivable motive which could induce any sane man – leaving alone a man of Mr Manston's clear-headedness and integrity – to venture upon such an extraordinary course of conduct – no motive on earth.'

'That was my opinion till after the visit of a friend last night – a friend of mine and poor little Cytherea's.'

'Ah – and Cytherea,' said Miss Aldclyffe, catching at the idea raised by the name. 'That he loved Cytherea – yes and loves her now, wildly and devotedly, I am as positive as that I breathe. Cytherea is years younger than Mrs Manston – as I shall call her – twice as sweet in disposition, three times as beautiful. Would he have given her up quietly and suddenly for a common— Mr Raunham, your story is monstrous, and I don't believe it!' She glowed in her earnestness.

The rector might now have advanced his second proposition – the possible motive – but for reasons of his own he did not.

'Very well, madam. I only hope that facts will sustain you in your belief. Ask him the question to his face, whether the woman is his wife or no, and see how he receives it.'

'I will to-morrow, most certainly,' she said. 'I always let these things die of wholesome ventilation, as every fungus does.'

But no sooner had the rector left her presence, than the grain of mustard-seed* he had sown grew to a tree. Her impatience to set her mind at rest could not brook a night's delay. It was with the utmost difficulty that she could wait till evening arrived to screen her movements. Immediately the sun had dropped behind the horizon, and before it was quite dark, she wrapped her cloak around her, softly left the house, and walked erect through the gloomy park in the direction of the old manor-house.

The same minute saw two persons sit down in the rectory-house to share the rector's usually solitary dinner. One was a man of official appearance, commonplace in all except his eyes. The other was Edward Springrove.

The discovery of the carefully-concealed letters rankled in the mind of Anne Seaway. Her woman's nature insisted that Manston had no right to keep all matters connected with his lost wife a secret from herself. Perplexity had bred vexation; vexation, resentment; curiosity had been continuous. The whole morning this resentment and curiosity increased.

The steward said very little to his companion during their luncheon at mid-day. He seemed reckless of appearances – almost indifferent to whatever fate awaited him. All his actions betrayed that something portentous was impending, and still he explained nothing. By carefully observing every trifling action, as only a woman can observe them, the thought at length dawned upon her that he was going to run away secretly. She feared for herself; her knowledge of law and justice was vague, and she fancied she might in some way be made responsible for him.

In the afternoon he went out of the house again, and she watched him drive away in the direction of the county-town. She felt a desire to go there herself, and, after an interval of half-an-hour, followed him on foot notwithstanding the distance – ostensibly to do some shopping.

One among her several trivial errands was to make a small purchase at the druggist's. Near the druggist's stood the County Bank. Looking out of the shop window, between the coloured bottles, she saw Manston come down the steps of the bank, in the act of withdrawing his hand from his pocket, and pulling his coat close over its mouth.

It is an almost universal habit with people, when leaving a bank, to be carefully adjusting their pockets if they have been receiving money; if they have been paying it in, their hands swing laxly. The steward had in all likelihood been taking money – possibly on Miss Aldclyffe's account – that was continual with him. And he might have been removing his own, as a man would do who was intending to leave the country.

3. From Five to Eight o'Clock p.m.

Anne reached home again in time to preside over preparations for dinner. Manston came in half-an-hour later. The lamp was lighted, the shutters were closed, and they sat down together. He was pale and worn – almost haggard.

The meal passed off in almost unbroken silence. When preoccupation withstands the influence of a social meal with one pleasant companion, the mental scene must be surpassingly vivid. Just as she was rising a tap came to the door.

Before a maid could attend to the knock, Manston crossed the room and answered it himself. The visitor was Miss Aldclyffe.

Manston instantly came back and spoke to Anne in an undertone. 'I should be glad if you could retire to your room for a short time.'

'It is a dry, starlight evening,' she replied. 'I will go for a little walk if your object is merely a private conversation with Miss Aldclyffe.'

'Very well, do; there's no accounting for tastes,' he said. A few commonplaces then passed between her and Miss Aldclyffe, and Anne went upstairs to bonnet and cloak herself. She came down, opened the front door, and went out.

She looked around to realize the night. It was dark, mournful, and quiet. Then she stood still. From the moment that Manston had requested her absence, a strong and burning desire had prevailed in her to know the subject of Miss Aldclyffe's conversation with him. Simple curiosity was not entirely what inspired her. Her suspicions had been thoroughly aroused by the discovery of the morning. A conviction that her future depended on her power to combat a man who, in desperate circumstances, would be far from a friend to her, prompted a strategic movement to acquire the important secret that was in handling now. The woman thought and thought, and regarded the dull dark trees, anxiously debating how the thing could be done.

Stealthily re-opening the front door she entered the hall, and advancing and pausing alternately, came close to the door of the room in which Miss Aldclyffe and Manston conversed. Nothing could be heard through the keyhole or panels. At a great risk she softly turned the knob and opened the door to a width of about half-an-inch, performing the act so delicately that three minutes, at least, were occupied in completing it. At that instant Miss Aldclyffe said –

'There's a draught somewhere. The door is ajar, I think.'

Anne glided back under the staircase. Manston came forward and closed the door. This chance was now cut off, and she considered again. The parlour, or sitting-room, in which the conference took place, had the window-shutters fixed on the outside of the window, as is usual in the back portions of old country-houses. The shutters were hinged one on each side of the opening, and met in the middle, where they were fastened by a bolt passing continuously through them and the wood mullion within, the bolt being secured on the inside by a pin, which was

292

seldom inserted till Manston and herself were about to retire for the night; sometimes not at all.

If she returned to the door of the room she might be discovered at any moment, but could she listen at the window, which overlooked a part of the garden never visited after nightfall, she would be safe from disturbance. The idea was worth a trial.

She glided round to the window, took the head of the bolt between her finger and thumb, and softly screwed it round until it was entirely withdrawn from its position. The shutters remained as before, whilst, where the bolt had come out, was now a shining hole three-quarters of an inch in diameter, through which one might see into the middle of the room. She applied her eye to the orifice.

Miss Aldclyffe and Manston were both standing; Manston with his back to the window, his companion facing it. The lady's demeanour was severe, condemnatory, and haughty. No more was to be seen; Anne then turned sideways, leant with her shoulder against the shutters and placed her ear upon the hole.

'You know where,' said Miss Aldclyffe. 'And how could you, a man, act a double deceit like this?'

'Men do strange things sometimes.'

'What was your reason – come?'

'A mere whim.'

'I might even believe that, if the woman were handsomer than Cytherea, or if you had been married some time to Cytherea and had grown tired of her.'

'And can't you believe it, too, under these conditions; that I married Cytherea, gave her up because I heard that my wife was alive, found that my wife would not come to live with me, and then, not to let any woman I love so well as Cytherea run any risk of being displaced and ruined in reputation, should my wife ever think fit to return, induced this woman to come to me, as being better than no companion at all?'

'I cannot believe it. Your love for Cytherea was not of such a kind as that excuse would imply. It was Cytherea or nobody with you. As an object of passion, you did not desire the company of this Anne Seaway at all, and certainly not so much as to madly risk your reputation by bringing her here in the way you have done. I am sure you didn't, Æneas.'

'So am I,' he said bluntly.

Miss Aldclyffe uttered an exclamation of astonishment; the confession was like a blow in its suddenness. She began to reproach him bitterly, and with tears.

'How could you overthrow my plans, disgrace the only girl I ever had any respect for, by such inexplicable doings! ... That woman must leave this place – the country perhaps. Heavens! the truth will leak out in a day or two!'

'She must do no such thing, and the truth must be stifled somehow – nobody knows how. It I stay here, or on any spot of the civilized globe, as Æneas Manston, this woman must live with me as my wife, or I am damned past redemption!'

'I will not countenance your keeping her, whatever your motive may be.'

'You must do something,' he murmured. 'You must. Yes, you must.'

'I never will,' she said. 'It is a criminal act.'

He looked at her earnestly. 'Will you not support me through this deception if my very life depends upon it? Will you not?'

'Nonsense! Life! It will be a scandal to you, but she must leave this place. It will out sooner or later, and the exposure had better come now.'

Manston repeated gloomily the same words. 'My life depends upon your supporting me – my very life.'

He then came close to her, and spoke into her ear. Whilst he spoke he held her head to his mouth with both his hands. Strange expressions came over her face; the workings of her mouth were painful to observe. Still he held her and whispered on.

The only words that could be caught by Anne Seaway, confused as her hearing frequently was by the moan of the wind and the waterfall in her outer ear, were these of Miss Aldclyffe, in tones which absolutely quivered: 'They have no money. What can they prove?'

The listener tasked herself to the utmost to catch his answer, but it was in vain. Of the remainder of the colloquy one fact alone was plain to Anne, and that only inductively – that Miss Aldclyffe, from what he had revealed to her, was going to scheme body and soul on Manston's behalf.

Miss Aldclyffe seemed now to have no further reason for remaining, yet she lingered awhile as if loth to leave him. When, finally, the crestfallen and agitated lady made preparations for departure, Anne quickly inserted the bolt, ran round to the entrance archway, and down the steps into the park. Here she stood close to the trunk of a huge lime-tree, which absorbed her dark outline into its own.

In a few minutes she saw Manston, with Miss Aldclyffe leaning on his arm, cross the glade before her and proceed in the direction of the house. She watched them ascend the rise and advance, as two black spots, towards the mansion. The appearance of an oblong space of light in the dark mass of walls denoted that the door was opened. Miss Aldclyffe's outline became visible upon it; the door shut her in, and all was darkness again. The form of Manston returning alone arose from the gloom, and passed by Anne in her hiding-place.

Waiting outside a quarter of an hour longer, that no suspicion of any kind might be excited, Anne returned to the old manor-house.

4. From Eight to Eleven o'Clock p.m.

Manston was very friendly that evening. It was evident to her, now that she was behind the scenes, that he was making desperate efforts to disguise the real state of his mind.

Her terror of him did not decrease. They sat down to supper, Manston still talking cheerfully. But what is keener than the eye of a mistrustful woman? A man's cunning is to it as was the armour of Sisera to the thin tent-nail.* She found, in spite of his adroitness, that he was attempting something more than a disguise of his feeling. He was trying to distract her attention, that he might be unobserved in some special movement of his hands.

What a moment it was for her then! The whole surface of her body became attentive. She allowed him no chance whatever. We know the duplicated condition at such times – when the existence divides itself into two, and the ostensibly innocent chatterer stands in front, like another person, to hide the timorous spy.

Manston played the same game, but more palpably. The meal was nearly over when he seemed possessed of a new idea of how his object might be accomplished. He tilted back his chair with a reflective air, and looked steadily at the clock standing against the wall opposite to him. He said sententiously, 'Few faces are capable of expressing more by dumb show than the face of a clock. You may see in it every variety of incentive – from the softest seductions to negligence to the strongest hints for action.'

'Well, in what way?' she inquired. His drift was, as yet, quite unintelligible to her.

'Why, for instance: look at the cold, methodical, unromantic, business-like air of all the right-angled positions of the hands. They make a man set about work in spite of himself. Then look at the piquant shyness of its face when the two hands are over each other. Several attitudes imply "Make ready." The "make ready" of ten minutes to one differs from the "make ready" of ten minutes to twelve, as youth differs from age. "Upward and onward" says twenty-five minutes to eleven.

Mid-day or midnight expresses distinctly "It is done." You surely have noticed that?'

'Yes, I have.'

He continued with affected quaintness: –

'The easy dash of ten minutes past seven, the rakish recklessness of a quarter past, the drooping weariness of twenty-five minutes past, must have been observed by everybody.'

'Whatever amount of truth there may be, there is a good deal of imagination in your fancy,' she said.

He still contemplated the clock.

'Then, again, the general finish of the face has a great effect upon the eye. This old-fashioned brass-faced one we have here, with its arched top, half-moon slit for the day of the month, and ship rocking at the upper part, impresses me with the notion of its being an old cynic, elevating his brows, whose thoughts can be seen wavering between good and evil.'

A thought now enlightened her: the clock was behind her, and he wanted to get her back turned. She dreaded turning, yet, not to excite his suspicion, she was on her guard; she quickly looked behind her at the clock as he spoke, recovering her old position again instantly. The time had not been long enough for any action whatever on his part.

'Ah,' he casually remarked, and at the same minute began to pour her out a glass of wine. 'Speaking of the clock has reminded me that it must nearly want winding up. Remember that it is wound to-night. Suppose you do it at once, my dear.'

There was no possible way of evading the act. She resolutely turned to perform the operation: anything was better than that he should suspect her. It was an old-fashioned eight-day clock, of workmanship suited to the rest of the antique furniture that Manston had collected there, and ground heavily during winding.

Anne had given up all idea of being able to watch him during the interval, and the noise of the wheels prevented her learning anything by her ears. But, as she wound, she caught sight of his shadow on the wall at her right hand.

What was he doing? He was in the very act of pouring something into her glass of wine.

He had completed the manoeuvre before she had done winding. She methodically closed the clock-case and turned round again. When she faced him he was sitting in his chair as before she had risen.

In a familiar scene which has hitherto been pleasant it is difficult to realize that an added condition, which does not alter its aspect, can have made it terrible. The woman thought that his action must have been prompted by no other intent than that of poisoning her, and yet she could not instantly put on a fear of her position.

And before she had grasped these consequences, another supposition served to make her regard the first as unlikely, if not absurd. It was the act of a madman to take her life in a manner so easy of discovery, unless there were far more reason for the crime than any that Manston could possibly have.

Was it not merely his intention, in tampering with her wine, to make her sleep soundly that night? This was in harmony with her original suspicion, that he intended secretly to abscond. At any rate, he was going to set about some stealthy proceeding, as to which she was to be kept in utter darkness. The difficulty now was to avoid drinking the wine.

By means of one pretext and another she put off taking her glass for nearly five minutes, but he eyed her too frequently to allow her to throw the potion under the grate. It became necessary to take one sip. This she did, and found an opportunity of absorbing it in her handkerchief.

Plainly he had no idea of her countermoves. The scheme seemed to him in proper train, and he turned to poke out the fire. She instantly seized the glass, and poured its contents down her bosom. When he faced round again she was holding the glass to her lips, empty.

In due course he locked the doors and saw that the shutters were fastened. She attended to a few closing details of housewifery, and a few minutes later they retired for the night.

5. *From Eleven o'Clock to Midnight*

When Manston was persuaded, by the feigned heaviness of her breathing, that Ann Seaway was asleep, he softly arose, and dressed himself in the gloom. With ears strained to their utmost she heard him complete this operation; then he took something from his pocket, put it in the drawer of the dressing-table, went to the door, and down the stairs. She glided out of bed and looked in the drawer. He had only restored to its place a small phial she had seen there before. It was labelled 'Battley's Solution of Opium'.* She felt relieved that her life had not been attempted. That was to have been her sleeping-draught. No time was to be lost if she meant to be a match for him. She followed him in her nightdress. When she reached the foot of the staircase he was in the office and had closed the door, under which a faint gleam showed that he had obtained a light. She crept to the door, but could not venture to open it, however slightly. Placing her ear to the panel, she could hear him tearing up papers of some sort and a brighter and quivering ray of light coming from the threshold an instant later, implied that he was burning them. By the slight noise of his footsteps on the uncarpeted floor, she at length imagined that he was approaching the door. She flitted upstairs again and crept into bed.

Manston returned to the bedroom close upon her heels, and entered it – again without a light. Standing motionless for an instant to assure himself that she still slept, he went to the drawer in which their ready-money was kept, and removed the casket that contained it. Anne's ear distinctly caught the rustle of notes, and the chink of the gold as he handled it. Some he placed in his pocket, some he returned to its place. He stood thinking, as it were weighing a possibility. While lingering thus, he noticed the reflected image of his own face in the glass – pale and spectre-like in its indistinctness. The sight seemed to be the feather which turned the balance of indecision: he drew a heavy breath, retired from the room, and passed downstairs. She heard him unbar the back-door, and go out into the yard.

Feeling safe in a conclusion that he did not intend to return to the bedroom again, she arose, and hastily dressed herself. On going to the door of the apartment she found that he had locked it behind him. 'A precaution – it can be no more,' she muttered. Yet she was all the more perplexed and excited on this account. Had he been going to leave home immediately, he would scarcely have taken the trouble to lock her in, holding the belief that she was in a drugged sleep. The lock shot into a mortice, so that there was no possibility of her pushing back the bolt. How should she follow him? Easily. An inner closet opened from the bedroom: it was large, and had some time heretofore been used as a dressing or bath room, but had been found inconvenient from having no other outlet to the landing. The window of this little room looked out upon the roof of a porch, which was flat and covered with lead. Anne took a pillow from the bed, gently opened the casement of the inner room, and stepped forth on the flat. There, leaning over the edge of a small parapet that ornamented the porch, she dropped the pillow upon the gravel path, and let herself down over the parapet by her hands till her toes swung about two feet from the ground. From this position she adroitly alighted upon the pillow, and stood in the path.

Since she had come indoors from her walk in the early part of the evening the moon had risen. But the thick clouds overspreading the whole landscape rendered the dim light pervasive and grey: it appeared as an attribute of the air. Anne crept round to the back of the house, listening intently. The steward had had at least ten minutes' start of her. She had waited here whilst one might count fifty, when she heard a movement in the outhouse – a fragment once attached to the main building. This outhouse was partitioned into an outer and an inner room, which had been a kitchen and a scullery before the connecting erections were pulled down, but they were now used respectively as a brewhouse and workshop, the only means of access to the latter being through the brewhouse. The outer door of this first apartment was usually fastened by a padlock on the exterior. It was now closed, but not fastened. Manston was evidently in the outhouse.

She slightly moved the door. The interior of the brewhouse was wrapped in gloom, but a streak of light fell towards her in a line across the floor from the inner or workshop door, which was not quite closed. This light was unexpected, none having been visible through hole or crevice. Glancing in, the woman found that he had placed cloths and mats at the various apertures, and hung a sack at the window to prevent the egress of a single ray. She could also perceive from where she stood that the bar of light fell across the brewing-copper just outside the inner door, and that upon it lay the key of her bedroom. The illuminated interior of the workshop was also partly visible from her position through the two half-open doors. Manston was engaged in emptying a large cupboard of the tools, gallipots,* and old iron it contained. When it was quite cleared he took a chisel, and with it began to withdraw the hooks and shoulder-nails holding the cupboard to the wall. All these being loosened, he extended his arms, lifted the cupboard bodily from the brackets under it, and deposited it on the floor beside him.

That portion of the wall which had been screened by the cupboard was now laid bare. This, it appeared, had been plastered more recently than the bulk of the outhouse. Manston loosened the plaster with some kind of tool, flinging the pieces into a basket as they fell. Having now stripped clear about two feet area of wall, he inserted a crowbar between the joints of the bricks beneath, softly wriggling it until several were loosened. There was now disclosed the mouth of an old oven, which was apparently contrived in the thickness of the wall, and having fallen into disuse, had been closed up with bricks in this manner. It was formed after the simple old-fashioned plan of oven-building – a mere oblate* cavity without a flue.

Manston now stretched his arm into the oven, dragged forth a heavy weight of great bulk, and let it slide to the ground. The woman who watched him could see the object plainly. It was a common cornsack, nearly full, and was tied at the mouth in the usual way.

The steward had once or twice started up, as if he had heard sounds, and his motions now became more cat-like still. On a sudden he put out the light. Anne had made no noise, yet a foreign noise of some kind had certainly been made in the intervening portion of the house. She heard it. 'One of the rats,' she thought.

He seemed soon to recover from his alarm, but changed his tactics completely. He did not light his candle – going on with his work in the dark. She had only sounds to go by now, and, judging as well as she could from these, he was piling up the bricks which closed the oven's mouth as they had been before he disturbed them. The query that had not left her brain all the interval of her inspection – how should she get back into her bedroom again? – now received a solution. Whilst he was replacing the cupboard, she would glide across the brewhouse, take the key from the top of the copper, run upstairs, unlock the door, and bring back the key again: if he returned to bed, which was unlikely, he would think the lock had failed to catch the staple. This thought and intention, occupying such length of words, flashed upon her in an instant, and hardly disturbed her strong curiosity to stay and learn the meaning of his actions in the workshop.

Slipping sideways through the first door and closing it behind her, she advanced into the darkness towards the second, making every individual footfall with the greatest care, lest the fragments of rubbish on the floor should crackle beneath her tread. She soon stood close by the copper, and not more than a foot from the door of the room occupied by Manston himself, from which position she could distinctly hear him breathe between each exertion, although it was far too dark to discern anything of him.

To secure the key of her chamber was her first anxiety, and accordingly she cautiously reached out with her hand to where it lay. Instead of touching it, her fingers came in contact with the boot of a human being.

She drooped faint in a cold sweat. It was the foot either of a man or woman, standing on the brewing-copper where the key had lain. A warm foot, covered with a polished boot.

The startling discovery so terrified her that she could hardly repress a sound. She withdrew her hand with a motion like the flight of an arrow. Her touch was so light that the leather seemed to have been thick enough to keep the owner of the foot in entire ignorance of it, and the noise of Manston's scraping might have been quite sufficient to drown the slight rustle of her dress.

The person was obviously not the steward: he was still busy. It was somebody who, since the light had been extinguished, had taken advantage of the gloom to come from some dark recess in the brew-house and stand upon the brickwork of the copper. The fear which had at first paralyzed her lessened with the birth of a sense that fear now was utter failure: she was in a desperate position and must abide by the consequences. The motionless person on the copper was, equally with Manston, quite unconscious of her proximity, and she ventured to advance her hand again, feeling behind the feet, till she found the key. On its return to her side her finger-tip skimmed the lower verge of a trousers-leg.

It was a man, then, who stood there. To go to the door just at this time was impolitic, and she shrank back into an inner corner to wait. The comparative security from discovery that her new position ensured resuscitated reason a little, and empowered her to form some logical inferences: –

1. The man who stood on the copper had taken advantage of the darkness to get there, as she had to enter.

2. The man must have been hidden in the outhouse before she had reached the door.

3. He must be watching Manston with much calculation and system, and for purposes of his own.

She could now tell by the noises that Manston had completed his re-erection of the cupboard. She heard him replacing the articles it had contained – bottle by bottle, tool by tool – after which he came into the brewhouse, went to the window, and pulled down the cloths covering it; but the window being rather small, this unveiling scarcely relieved the darkness of the interior. He returned to the workshop, hoisted something to his back by a jerk, and felt about the room for some other article. Having found it, he emerged from the inner door, crossed the brewhouse, and went into the yard. Directly he stepped out she could see his outline by the light of the clouded and weakly moon. The sack was slung at his back, and in his hand he carried a spade.

Anne now waited in her corner in breathless suspense for the proceedings of the other man. In about half-a-minute she heard him descend from the copper and then the square opening of the door-way showed the outline of this other watcher passing through it likewise. The form was that of a broad-shouldered man enveloped in a long coat. He vanished after the steward.

The woman vented a sigh of relief, and moved forward to follow. Simultaneously, she discovered that the watcher whose foot she had touched was, in his turn, watched and followed also.

It was by one of her own sex. Anne Seaway shrank backward again.

The unknown woman came forward from the further side of the yard, and pondered awhile in hesitation. Tall, dark, and closely wrapped, she stood up from the earth like a cypress. She moved, crossed the yard without producing the slightest disturbance by her footsteps, and went in the direction the others had taken.

Anne waited yet another minute – then in her turn noiselessly followed the last woman.

But so impressed was she with the sensation of people in hiding, that in coming out of the yard she turned her head to see if any person were following her in the same way. Nobody was visible, but she discerned, standing behind the angle of the stable, Manston's horse and gig, ready harnessed.

He did intend to fly after all, then, she thought. He must have placed the horse in readiness, in the interval between his leaving the house and her exit by the window. However, there was not time to weigh this branch of the night's events. She turned about again, and continued on the trail of the other three.

6. *From Midnight to Half-Past One a.m.*

Intentness pervaded everything; Night herself seemed to have become a watcher.

The four persons proceeded across the glade, and into the park plantation, at equi-distances of about seventy yards. Here the ground, completely overhung by the foliage, was coated with a thick moss which was as soft as velvet beneath their feet. The first watcher, that is, the man walking immediately behind Manston, now fell back, when Manston's housekeeper, knowing the ground pretty well, dived circuitously among the trees and got directly behind the steward, who, encumbered with his load, had proceeded but slowly. The other woman seemed now to be about opposite to Anne, or a little in advance, but on Manston's other hand.

He reached a pit, midway between the waterfall and the engine-house. There he stopped, wiped his face, and listened.

Into this pit had drifted uncounted generations of withered leaves, half filling it. Oak, beech, and chestnut, rotten and brown alike, mingled themselves in one fibrous mass. Manston descended into the midst of them, placed his sack on the ground, and raking the leaves aside into a large heap, began digging. Anne softly drew nearer, crept into a bush, and turning her head to survey the rest, missed the man who had dropped behind, and whom we have called the first watcher.

Concluding that he, too, had hidden himself, she turned her attention to the second watcher, the other woman, who had meanwhile advanced near to where Anne lay in hiding, and now seated herself behind a tree, still closer to the steward than was Anne Seaway.

Here and thus Anne remained concealed. The crunch of the steward's spade, as it cut into the soft vegetable mould, was plainly perceptible to her ears, when the periodic cessations between the creaks of the engine concurred with a lull in the breeze, which otherwise brought the subdued roar of the cascade from the further side of the bank that screened it. A large hole – some four or five feet deep – had been excavated by Manston in about twenty minutes. Into this he immediately placed the sack, and then began filling in the earth, and treading it down. Lastly he carefully raked the whole mass of dead and dry leaves into the middle of the pit, burying the ground with them as they had buried it before.

For a hiding-place the spot was unequalled. The thick accumulation of leaves, which had not been disturbed for centuries, might not be disturbed again for centuries to come, whilst their lower layers still decayed and added to the mould beneath.

By the time this work was ended the sky had grown clearer, and Anne could now see distinctly the face of the other woman, stretching from behind the tree, seemingly forgetful of her position in her intense comtemplation of the actions of the steward. Her countenance was white and motionless.

It was impossible that Manston should not soon notice her. At the completion of his labour he turned, and did so.

'Ho – you here!' he exclaimed.

'Don't think I am a spy upon you,' she said, in an imploring whisper. Anne recognized the voice as Miss Aldclyffe's.

The trembling lady added hastily another remark, which was drowned in the recurring creak of the engine close at hand. The first watcher, if he had come no nearer than his original position, was too far off to hear any part of this dialogue, on account of the roar of the falling water, which could reach him unimpeded by the bank.

The remark of Miss Aldclyffe to Manston had plainly been concerning the first watcher, for Manston, with his spade in his hand, instantly rushed to where the man was concealed, and, before the latter could disengage himself from the boughs, the steward struck him on the head with the blade of the instrument. The man fell to the ground.

'Fly!' said Miss Aldclyffe to Manston. Manston vanished amidst the trees. Miss Aldclyffe went off in a contrary direction.

Anne Seaway was about to run away likewise, when she turned and looked at the fallen man. He lay on his face, motionless.

Many of these women who own to no moral code show considerable magnanimity when they see people in trouble. To act right simply because it is one's duty is proper; but a good action which is the result of no law of reflection shines more than any. She went up to him and gently turned him over, upon which he began to show signs of life. By her assistance he was soon able to stand upright.

He looked about him with a bewildered air, endeavouring to collect his ideas. 'Who are you?' he said to the woman, mechanically.

It was bad policy now to attempt disguise. 'I am the supposed Mrs Manston,' she said. 'Who are you?'

'I am the officer employed by Mr Raunham to sift this mystery – which may be criminal.' He stretched his limbs, pressed his head, and seemed gradually to awake to a sense of having been incautious in his utterance. 'Never you mind who I am,' he continued. 'Well, it doesn't matter now, either – it will no longer be a secret.'

He stooped for his hat and ran in the direction the steward had taken – coming back again after the lapse of a minute.

'It's only an aggravated assault, after all,' he said hastily, 'until we have found out for certain what's buried here. It may be only a bag of building rubbish; but it may be more. Come and help me dig.' He seized the spade with the awkwardness of a town man, and went into the pit, continuing a muttered discourse. 'It's no use my running after him single-handed,' he said. 'He's ever so far off by this time. The best step is to see what is here.'

It was far easier for the detective to re-open the hole than it had been for Manston to form it. The leaves were raked away, the loam thrown out, and the sack dragged forth.

'Hold this,' he said to Anne, whose curiosity still kept her standing near. He turned on the light of a dark lantern he had brought, and gave it into her hand.

The string which bound the mouth of the sack was now cut. The officer laid the bag on its side, seized it by the bottom, and jerked forth the contents. A large package was disclosed, carefully wrapped up in impervious tarpaulin, also well tied. He was on the point of pulling open the folds at one end, when a light-coloured thread of something, hanging on the outside, arrested his eye. He put his hand upon it; it fell stringy, and adhered to his fingers. 'Hold the light close,' he said.

She held it close. He raised his hand to the glass, and they both peered at an almost intangible filament he held between his finger and thumb. It was a long hair; the hair of a woman.

'God! I couldn't believe it – no, I couldn't believe it!' the detective whispered, horror-struck. 'And I have lost the man for the present through my unbelief. Let's get into a sheltered place . . . Now wait a minute whilst I prove it.'

He thrust his hand into his waistcoat pocket, and withdrew thence a minute packet of brown paper. Spreading it out he disclosed, coiled in the middle, another long hair. It was the hair the clerk's wife had found on Manston's pillow nine days before the Carriford fire. He held the two hairs to the light: they were both of a pale-brown hue. He laid them parallel and stretched out his arms: they were of the same length to a nicety. The detective turned to Anne.

'It is the body of his first wife,' he said quietly. 'He murdered her, as Mr Springrove and the rector suspected – but how and when, God only knows.'

'And I!' exclaimed Anne Seaway, a probable and natural sequence of events and motives explanatory of the whole crime – events and motives shadowed forth by the letter, Manston's possession of it, his renunciation of Cytherea, and instalment of herself – flashing upon her mind with the rapidity of lightning.

'Ah – I see,' said the detective, standing unusually close to her: and a handcuff was on her wrist. 'You must come with me, madam. Knowing as much about a secret murder as God knows is a very suspicious thing: it doesn't make you a goddess – far from it.' He directed the bull's-eye* into her face.

'Pooh – lead on,' she said scornfully, 'and don't lose your principal actor for the sake of torturing a poor subordinate like me.'

He loosened her hand, gave her his arm, and dragged her out of the grove – making her run beside him till they had reached the rectory. A light was burning here, and an auxiliary of the detective's awaiting him: a horse ready harnessed to a spring-cart was standing outside.

'You have come – I wish I had known that,' the detective said to his assistant, hurriedly and angrily. 'Well, we've blundered – he's gone – you should have been here, as I said! I was sold by that woman, Miss Aldclyffe – she watched me.' He hastily gave directions in an undertone to this man. The concluding words were, 'Go in to the rector – he's up. Detain Miss Aldclyffe. I, in the meantime, am driving to Casterbridge with this one, and for help. We shall be sure to have him when it gets light.'

He assisted Anne into the vehicle, and drove off with her. As they went, the clear, dry road showed before them, between the grassy quarters at each side, like a white riband, and made their progress easy. They came to a spot where the highway was overhung by dense firs for some distance on both sides. It was totally dark here.

There was a smash; and a rude shock. In the very midst of its length, at the point where the road began to drop down a hill, the detective drove against something with a jerk which nearly flung them both to the ground.

The man recovered himself, placed Anne on the seat, and reached out his hand. He found that the off-wheel of his gig was locked in that of another conveyance of some kind.

'Hoy!' said the officer.

Nobody answered.

'Hoy, you man asleep there!' he said again.

No reply.

'Well, that's odd – this comes of the folly of travelling without gig-lamps because you expect the dawn.' He jumped to the ground and turned on his lantern.

There was the gig which had obstructed him, standing in the middle of the road; a jaded horse harnessed to it, but no human being in or near the vehicle.

'Do you know whose gig this is?' he said to the woman.

'No,' she said sullenly. But she did recognize it as the steward's.

'I'll swear it's Manston's! Come, I can hear it by your tone. However, you needn't say anything which may criminate you. What forethought the man must have had – how carefully he must have considered possible contingencies! Why, he must have got the horse and gig ready before he began shifting the body.'

He listened for a sound among the trees. None was to be heard but the occasional scamper of a rabbit over the withered leaves. He threw the light of his lantern through a gap in the hedge, but could see nothing beyond an impenetrable thicket. It was clear that Manston was not many yards off, but the question was how to find him. Nothing could be done by the detective just then, encumbered as he was by the horse and Anne. If he had entered the thicket on a search unaided, Manston might have stepped unobserved from behind a bush and murdered him with the greatest ease. Indeed, there were such strong reasons for the exploit in Manston's circumstances at that moment that, without showing cowardice, his pursuer felt it hazardous to remain any longer where he stood.

He hastily tied the head of Manston's horse to the back of his own vehicle, that the steward might be deprived of the use of any means of

306

escape other than his own legs, and drove on thus with his prisoner to the county-town. Arrived there, he lodged her in the police-station, and then took immediate steps for the capture of Manston.

CHAPTER TWENTY
The Events of Three Hours

1. March the Twenty-Third Mid-day

Thirty-six hours had elapsed since Manston's escape.

It was market-day at the county-town. The farmers outside and inside the corn-exchange looked at their samples of wheat, and poured them critically as usual from one palm to another, but they thought and spoke of Manston. Grocers serving behind their counters, instead of using their constant phrase, 'The next article, please?' substituted, 'Have you heard if he's caught?' Dairymen and drovers standing beside the sheep and cattle pens, spread their legs firmly, readjusted their hats, thrust their hands into the lowest depths of their pockets, regarded the animals with the utmost keenness of which the eye was capable, and said, 'Ay, ay, so's: they'll have him avore night.'

Later in the day Edward Springrove passed along the street hurriedly and anxiously. 'Well, have you heard any more?' he said to an acquaintance who accosted him.

'They tracked him in this way,' said the other young man. 'A vagrant first told them that Manston had passed a rick at daybreak, under which this man was lying. They followed the track he pointed out and ultimately came to a stile. On the other side was a heap of half-hardened mud, scraped from the road. On the surface of the heap, where it had been smoothed by the shovel, was distinctly imprinted the form of a man's hand, the buttons of his waistcoat, and his watch-chain showing that he had stumbled in hurrying over the stile, and fallen there. The pattern of the chain proved the man to have been Manston. They followed on till they reached a ford crossed by stepping-stones – on the further bank were the same footmarks that had shown themselves beside the stile. The whole of this course had been in the direction of Budmouth. On they went, and the next clue was furnished them by a shepherd. He said that wherever a clear space three or four yards wide ran in a line through a flock of sheep lying about a ewe-lease,* it was proof that somebody had passed there not more than half-an-hour

307

earlier. At twelve o'clock that day he had noticed such a feature in his flock. Nothing more could be heard of him, and they got into Budmouth. The steam-packet* to the Channel Islands was to start at eleven last night, and they at once concluded that his hope was to get to France by way of Jersey and St Malo – his only chance, all the railway-stations being watched.

'Well, they went to the boat: he was not on board then. They went again at half-past ten: he had not come. Two men now placed themselves under the lamp immediately beside the gangway. Another stayed by the office door, and one or two more up Mary Street – the straight cut to the quay. At a quarter to eleven the mail-bags were put on board. Whilst the attention of the idlers was directed to the mails, down Mary Street came a man as boldly as possible. The gait was Manston's but not the clothes. He passed over to the shaded part of the street: heads were turned. I suppose this warned him, for he never emerged from the shadow. They watched and waited, but the steward did not reappear. The alarm was raised – they searched the town high and low – no Manston. All this morning they have been searching, but there's not a sign of him anywhere. However, he has lost his chance of getting across the Channel. It is reported that he has since changed his clothes with a labourer.'

During this narration, Edward, lost in thought, had let his eyes follow a shabby man in a smock-frock, but wearing light boots – who was stalking down the street under a bundle of straw which overhung and concealed his head. It was a very ordinary circumstance for a man with a bundle of straw on his shoulders and overhanging his head to go down the High Street. Edward saw him cross the bridge which divided the town from the country, place his shaggy encumbrance by the side of the road, and leave it there.

Springrove now parted from his acquaintance, and went also in the direction of the bridge, and some way beyond it. As far as he could see stretched the turnpike road, and, while he was looking, he noticed a man to leap from the hedge at a point two hundred, or two hundred and fifty yards ahead, cross the road, and go through a wicket on the other side. This figure seemed like that of the man who had been carrying the bundle of straw. He looked at the straw: it still stood alone.

The subjoined facts sprang, as it were, into juxtaposition in his brain: –

Manston had been seen wearing the clothes of a labouring man – a brown smock-frock. So had this man, who seemed other than a labourer, on second thoughts: and he had concealed his face by his bundle of straw with the greatest ease and naturalness.

The path the man had taken led, among other places, to Tolchurch, where Cytherea was living.

If Mrs Manston was murdered, as some said, on the night of the fire, Cytherea was the steward's lawful wife. Manston at bay, and reckless of results, might rush to his wife and harm her.

It was a horrible supposition for a man who loved Cytherea to entertain; but Springrove could not resist its influence. He started off for Tolchurch.

2. One to Two o'Clock p.m.

On that self-same mid-day, whilst Edward was proceeding to Tolchurch by the footpath across the fields, Owen Graye had left the village and was riding along the turnpike road to the county-town, that he might ascertain the exact truth of the strange rumour which had reached him concerning Manston. Not to disquiet his sister, he had said nothing to her of the matter.

She sat by the window reading. From her position she could see up the lane for a distance of at least a hundred yards. Passers-by were so rare in this retired nook, that the eyes of those who dwelt by the wayside were invariably lifted to every one on the road, great and small, as to a novelty.

A man in a brown smock-frock turned the corner and came towards the house. It being market-day at Casterbridge, the village was nearly deserted, and more than this, the old farm-house in which Owen and his sister were staying, stood, as had been stated, apart from the body of cottages. The man did not look respectable; Cytherea arose and bolted the door.

Unfortunately he was near enough to see her cross the room. He advanced to the door, knocked, and, receiving no answer, came to the window; he next pressed his face against the glass, peering in.

Cytherea's experience at that moment was probably as trying a one as ever fell to the lot of a gentle woman to endure. She recognized in the peering face that of the man she had married.

But not a movement was made by her, not a sound escaped her. Her fear was great; but had she known the truth – that the man outside, feeling he had nothing on earth to lose by any act, was in the last stage of recklessness, terrified nature must have given way.

'Cytherea,' he said, 'let me come in: I am your husband.'

'No,' she replied, still not realizing the magnitude of her peril. 'If you want to speak to us, wait till my brother comes.'

'O, he's not at home? Cytherea, I can't live without you! All my sin has been because I love you so! Will you fly with me? I have money enough for us both – only come with me.'

'Not now – not now.'

'I am your husband, I tell you, and I must come in.'

'You cannot,' she said faintly. His words began to terrify her.

'I will, I say!' he exclaimed. 'Will you let me in, I ask once more?'

'No – I will not,' said Cytherea.

'Then I will let myself in!' he answered resolutely. 'I will, if I die for it!'

The windows were glazed in lattice panes of leadwork, hung in casements. He broke one of the panes with a stone, thrust his hand through the hole, unfastened the latch which held the casement close, and began opening the window.

Instantly the shutters flew together with a slam, and were barred with desperate quickness by Cytherea on the inside.

'Damn you!' he exclaimed.

He ran round to the back of the house. His impatience was greater now: he thrust his fist through the pantry window at one blow, and opened it in the same way as the former one had been opened, before the terror-stricken girl was aware that he had gone round. In an instant he stood in the pantry, advanced to the front room where she was, flung back the shutters, and held out his arms to embrace her.

In extremely trying moments of bodily or mental pain, Cytherea either flushed hot or faded pale, according to the state of her constitution at the moment. Now she burned like fire from head to foot, and preserved her consciousness.

Never before had the poor child's natural agility served her in such good stead as now. A heavy oblong table stood in the middle of the room. Round this table she flew, keeping it between herself and Manston, her large eyes wide open with terror, their dilated pupils constantly fixed upon Manston's, to read by his expression whether his next intention was to dart to the right or the left.

Even he, at that heated moment, could not endure the expression of unutterable agony which shone from that extraordinary gaze of hers. It had surely been given her by God as a means of defence. Manston continued his pursuit with a lowered eye.

The panting and maddened desperado* – blind to everything but the capture of his wife – went with a rush under the table: she went over it like a bird. He went heavily over it: she flew under it, and was out at the other side.

310

> One on her youth and pliant limbs relies,
> One on his sinews and his giant size.*

But his superior strength was sure to tire her down in the long-run. She felt her weakness increasing with the quickness of her breath; she uttered a wild scream, which in its heartrending intensity seemed to echo for miles.

At the same juncture her hair became unfastened, and rolled down about her shoulders. The least accident at such critical periods is sufficient to confuse the over-wrought intelligence. She lost sight of his intended direction for one instant, and he immediately outmanoeuvred her.

'At last! my Cytherea!' he cried, overturning the table, springing over it, seizing one of the long brown tresses, pulling her towards him, and clasping her round. She writhed downwards between his arms and breast, and fell fainting on the floor. For the first time his action was leisurely. He lifted her upon the sofa, exclaiming, 'Rest there for a while, my frightened little bird!'

And then there was an end of his triumph. He felt himself clutched by the collar, and whizzed backwards with the force of a battering-ram against the fireplace. Springrove, wild, red, and breathless, had sprung in at the open window, and stood once more between man and wife.

Manston was on his legs again in an instant. A fiery glance on the one side, a glance of pitiless justice on the other, passed between them. It was again the meeting in the vineyard of Naboth the Jezreelite: 'Hast thou found me, O mine enemy? And he answered, I have found thee: because thou hast sold thyself to work evil in the sight of the Lord.'*

A desperate wrestle now began between the two men. Manston was the taller, but there was in Edward much hard tough muscle which the delicate flesh of the steward lacked. They flew together like the jaws of a gin. In a minute they were both on the floor, rolling over and over, locked in each other's grasp as tightly as if they had been one organic being at war with itself – Edward trying to secure Manston's arms with a small thong he had drawn from his pocket, Manston trying to reach his knife.

Two characteristic noises pervaded the apartment through this momentous space of time. One was the sharp panting of the two combatants, so similar in each as to be undistinguishable; the other was the stroke of their heels and toes, as they smote the floor at every contortion of body or limbs.

Cytherea had not lost consciousness for more than half-a-minute.

She had then leapt up without recognizing that Edward was her deliverer, unfastened the door, and rushed out, screaming wildly, 'Come! Help! O, help!'

Three men stood not twenty yards off, looking perplexed. They dashed forward at her words. 'Have you seen a shabby man with a smock-frock on lately?' they inquired. She pointed to the door, and ran on the same as before.

Manston, who had just loosened himself from Edward's grasp, seemed at this moment to renounce his intention of pushing the conflict to a desperate end. 'I give it all up for life – dear life!' he cried, with a hoarse laugh. 'A reckless man has a dozen lives – see how I'll baffle you all yet!'

He rushed out of the house, but no further. The boast was his last. In one half-minute more he was helpless in the hands of his pursuers.

Edward staggered to his feet, and paused to recover breath. His thoughts had never forsaken Cytherea, and his first act now was to hasten up the lane after her. She had not gone far. He found her leaning upon a bank by the roadside, where she had flung herself down in sheer exhaustion. He ran up and lifted her in his arms, and thus aided she was enabled to stand upright – clinging to him. What would Springrove have given to imprint a kiss upon her lips then!

They walked slowly towards the house. The distressing sensation of whose wife she was could not entirely quench the resuscitated pleasure he felt at her grateful recognition of him, and her confiding seizure of his arm for support. He conveyed her carefully into the house.

A quarter of an hour later, whilst she was sitting in a partially recovered, half-dozing state in an arm-chair, Edward beside her waiting anxiously till Graye should arrive, they saw a spring-cart pass the door. Old and dry mud-splashes from long-forgotten rains disfigured its wheels and sides; the varnish and paint had been scratched and dimmed; ornament had long been forgotten in a restless contemplation of use. Three men sat on the seat, the middle one being Manston. His hands were bound in front of him, his eyes were set directly forward, his countenance pallid, hard, and fixed.

Springrove had told Cytherea of Manston's crime in a few short words. He now said solemnly, 'He is to die.'

'And I cannot mourn for him,' she replied with a shudder, leaning back and covering her face with her hands.

In the silence that followed the two short remarks, Springrove watched the cart round the corner, and heard the rattle of its wheels gradually dying away as it rolled in the direction of the county-town.

312

CHAPTER TWENTY-ONE
The Events of Eighteen Hours

1. March the Twenty-Ninth. Noon

Exactly seven days after Edward Springrove had seen the man with the bundle of straw walking down the streets of Casterbridge, old Farmer Springrove was standing on the edge of the same pavement, talking to his friend, Farmer Baker.

There was a pause in their discourse. Mr Springrove was looking down the street at some object which had attracted his attention. 'Ah, 'tis what we shall all come to!' he murmured.

The other looked in the same direction. 'True, neighbour Springrove; true.'

Two men, advancing one behind the other in the middle of the road, were what the farmers referred to. They were carpenters, and bore on their shoulders an empty coffin, covered by a thin black cloth.

'I always feel a satisfaction at being breasted by such a sight as that,' said Springrove, still regarding the men's sad burden. 'I call it a sort of medicine.'

'And it is medicine. . . . I have not heard of any body being ill up this way lately? D'seem as if the person died suddenly.'

'May be so. Ah, Baker, we say sudden death, don't we? But there's no difference in their nature between sudden death and death of any other sort. There's no such thing as a random snapping off of what was laid down to last longer. We only suddenly light upon an end – thoughtfully formed as any other – which has been existing at that very same point from the beginning, though unseen by us to be so soon.'

'It is just a discovery to your own mind, and not alteration in the Lord's.'

'That's it. Unexpected is not as to the thing, but as to our sight.'

'Now you'll hardly believe me, neighbour, but this little scene in front of us makes me feel less anxious about pushing on wi' that threshing and winnowing next week, that I was speaking about. Why should we not stand still, says I to myself, and fling a quiet eye upon the Whys and the Wherefores, before the end o' it all, and we go down into the mouldering-place, and are forgotten?'

''Tis a feeling that will come. But 'twon't bear looking into. There's a back'ard current in the world, and we must do our utmost to advance in

313

order just to bide where we be. But, Baker, they are turning in here with the coffin, look.'

The two carpenters had borne their load into a narrow way close at hand. The farmers, in common with others, turned and watched them along the way.

''Tis a man's coffin, and a tall man's, too,' continued Farmer Springrove. 'His was a fine frame, whoever he was.'

'A very plain box for the poor soul – just the rough elm, you see.' The corner of the cloth had blown aside.

'Yes, for a very poor man. Well, death's all the less insult to him. I have often thought how much smaller the richer class are made to look than the poor at last pinches like this. Perhaps the greatest of all the reconcilers of a thoughtful man to poverty – and I speak from experience – is the grand quiet it fills him with when the uncertainty of his life shows itself more than usual.'

As Springrove finished speaking, the bearers of the coffin went across a gravelled square facing the two men and approached a grim and heavy archway. They paused beneath it, rang a bell, and waited.

Over the archway was written in Egyptian capitals,

'COUNTY GAOL'

The small rectangular wicket, which was constructed in one of the two iron-studded doors, was opened from the inside. The men severally stepped over the threshold, the coffin dragged its melancholy length through the aperture, and both entered the court, and were covered from sight.

'Somebody in the gaol, then?'

'Yes, one of the prisoners,' said a boy scudding by at the moment, who passed on whistling.

'Do you know the name of the man who is dead?' inquired Baker of a third bystander.

'Yes, 'tis all over town – surely you know, Mr Springrove? Why, Manston, Miss Aldclyffe's steward. He was found dead the first thing this morning. He had hung himself behind the door of his cell, in some way, by a handkerchief and some strips of his clothes. The turnkey says his features were scarcely changed, as he looked at 'em with the early sun a-shining in at the grating upon him. He has left a full account of the murder, and all that led to it. So there's an end of him.'

It was perfectly true: Manston was dead.

The previous day he had been allowed the use of writing-materials,

314

and had occupied himself for nearly seven hours in preparing the following confession: –

LAST WORDS

Having found man's life to be a wretchedly conceived scheme, I renounce it, and, to cause no further trouble, I write down the facts connected with my past proceedings.

After thanking God, on first entering my house, on the night of the fire at Carriford, for my release from bondage to a woman I detested, I went, a second time, to the scene of the disaster, and, finding that nothing could be done by remaining there, shortly afterwards I returned home again in the company of Mr Raunham.

He parted from me at the steps of my porch, and went back towards the rectory. Whilst I stood at the door, musing on my strange deliverance, I saw the figure advance from beneath the shadow of the park trees. It was the figure of a woman.

When she came near, the twilight was sufficient to show me her attire: it was a cloak reaching to the bottom of her dress, and a thick veil covering her face. These features, together with her size and gait, aided also by a flash of perception as to the chain of events which had saved her life, told me that she was my wife Eunice.

I gnashed my teeth in a frenzy of despair; I had lost Cytherea; I had gained one whose beauty had departed, whose utterance was complaint, whose mind was shallow, and who drank brandy every day. The revulsion of feeling was terrible. Providence, whom I had just thanked, seemed a mocking tormentor laughing at me. I felt like a madman.

She came close – started at seeing me outside – then spoke to me. Her first words were reproof for what I had unintentionally done, and sounded as an earnest of what I was to be cursed with as long as we both lived. I answered angrily; this tone of mine changed her complaints to irritation. She taunted me with a secret she had discovered, which concerned Miss Aldclyffe and myself. I was surprised to learn it – more surprised that she knew it, but concealed my feeling.

'How could you serve me so?' she said, her breath smelling of spirits even then. 'You love another woman – yes, you do. See how you drive me about! I have been to the station, intending to leave you for ever, and yet I come to try you once more.'

An indescribable exasperation had sprung up in me as she talked – rage and regret were all in all. Scarcely knowing what I did, I furiously raised my hand and swung it round with my whole force to strike her. She turned quickly – and it was the poor creature's end. By her movement my hand came edgewise exactly in the nape of the neck – as men strike a hare to kill it. The effect staggered me with amazement. The blow must have disturbed the vertebræ; she fell at my feet, made a few movements, and uttered one low sound.

I ran indoors for water and some wine, I came out and lanced her arm

315

with my penknife. But she lay still, and I found that she was dead.

It was a long time before I could realize my horrible position. For several minutes I had no idea of attempting to escape the consequences of my deed. Then a light broke upon me. Had anybody seen her since she left the Three Tranters? Had they not, she was already believed by the parishioners to be dust and ashes. I should never be found out.

Upon this I acted.

The first question was how to dispose of the body. The impulse of the moment was to bury her at once in the pit between the engine-house and waterfall; but it struck me that I should not have time. It was now four o'clock, and the working-men would soon be stirring about the place. I would put off burying her till the next night. I carried her indoors.

In turning the outhouse into a workshop, earlier in the season, I found, when driving a nail into the wall for fixing a cupboard, that the wall sounded hollow. I examined it, and discovered behind the plaster an old oven which had long been disused, and was bricked up when the house was prepared for me.

To unfix this cupboard and pull out the bricks was the work of a few minutes. Then, bearing in mind that I should have to remove the body again the next night, I placed it in a sack, pushed it into the oven, packed in the bricks, and replaced the cupboard.

I then went to bed. In bed, I thought whether there were any very remote possibilities that might lead to the supposition that my wife was not consumed by the flames of the burning house. The thing which struck me most forcibly was this, that the searchers might think it odd that no remains whatever should be found.

The clinching and triumphant deed would be to take the body and place it among the ruins of the destroyed house. But I could not do this, on account of the men who were watching against an outbreak of the fire. One remedy remained.

I arose again, dressed myself, and went down to the outhouse. I must take down the cupboard again. I did take it down. I pulled out the bricks, pulled out the sack, pulled out the corpse, and took her keys from her pocket and the watch from her side.

I then replaced everything as before.

With these articles in my pocket I went out of the yard, and took my way through the withy copse to the churchyard, entering it from the back. Here I felt my way carefully along till I came to the nook where pieces of bones from newly-dug graves are sometimes piled behind the laurel bushes. I had been earnestly hoping to find a skull among these old bones; but though I had frequently seen one or two in the rubbish here, there was not one now. I then groped in the other corner with the same result – nowhere could I find a skull. Three or four fragments of leg and back-bones were all I could collect, and with these I was forced to be content.

Taking them in my hand, I crossed the road, and got round behind the inn, where the couch heap was still smouldering. Keeping behind the hedge, I could see the heads of the three or four men who watched the spot.

Standing in this place I took the bones and threw them one by one over the hedge and over the men's head into the smoking embers. When the bones had all been thrown, I threw the keys; last of all I threw the watch.

I then returned home as I had gone, and went to bed once more, just as the dawn began to break. I exulted – 'Cytherea is mine again!'

At breakfast-time I thought, 'Suppose the cupboard should by some unlikely chance get moved to-day!'

I went to the mason's yard hard by, while the men were at breakfast, and brought away a shovelful of mortar. I took it into the outhouse, again shifted the cupboard, and plastered over the mouth of the oven behind. Simply pushing the cupboard back into its place, I waited for the next night that I might bury the body, though upon the while it was in a tolerably safe hiding-place.

When the night came, my nerves were in some way weaker than they had been on the previous night. I felt reluctant to touch the body. I went to the outhouse, but instead of opening the oven, I firmly drove in the shoulder-nails that held the cupboard to the wall. 'I will bury her to-morrow night, however,' I thought.

But the next night I was still more reluctant to touch her. And my reluctance increased, and there the body remained. The oven was, after all, never likely to be opened in my time.

I married Cytherea Graye, and never did a bridegroom leave the church with a heart more full of love and happiness, and a brain more fixed on good intentions, than I did that morning.

When Cytherea's brother made his appearance at the hotel in Southampton, bearing his strange evidence of the porter's disclosure, I was staggered beyond expression. I thought they had found the body. 'Am I to be apprehended and to lose her even now?' I mourned. I saw my error, and instantly saw, too, that I must act externally like an honourable man. So at his request I yielded her up to him, and meditated on several schemes for enabling me to claim the woman I had a legal right to claim as my wife, without disclosing the reason why I knew myself to have it.

I went home to Knapwater the next day, and for nearly a week lived in a state of indecision. I could not hit upon a scheme for proving my wife dead without compromising myself.

Mr Raunham hinted that I should take steps to discover her whereabouts by advertising. I had no energy for the farce. But one evening I chanced to enter the Rising Sun Inn. Two notorious poachers were sitting in the settle, which screened my entrance. They were half-drunk – their conversation was carried on in the solemn and emphatic tone common to that stage of intoxication, and I myself was the subject of it.

The following was the substance of their disjointed remarks: On the night of the great fire at Carriford, one of them was sent to meet me, and break the news of the death of my wife to me. This he did; but because I would not pay him for the news, he left me in a mood of vindictiveness. When the fire was over, he joined his comrade. The favourable hour of the night suggested to them the possibility of some unlawful gain before daylight came. My fowl-house stood in a tempting position, and still resenting his repulse during the evening, one of

317

them proposed to operate upon my birds. I was believed to have gone to the rectory with Mr Raunham. The other was disinclined to go, and the first went off alone.

It was now about three o'clock. He had advanced as far as the shrubbery, which grows near the north wall of the house, when he fancied he heard, above the rush of the waterfall, noises on the other side of the building. He described them in these words, 'The ghost of a wife nagging her man – then a fall – then a groan – then the rush of the water and the creak of the engine as before.' Only one explanation occurred to him; the house was haunted. And, whether those of the living or the dead, voices of any kind were inimical to one who had come on such an errand. He stealthily crept home.

His unlawful purpose in being behind the house led him to conceal his adventure. No suspicion of the truth entered his mind until the railway-porter had startled everybody by his strange announcement. Then he asked himself, had the horrifying sounds of that night been really an enactment in the flesh between me and my wife?

The words of the other man were:

'Why don't he try to find her if she's alive?'

'True,' said the first. 'Well, I don't forget what I heard, and if she don't turn up alive my mind will be as sure as a Bible upon her murder, and the parson shall know it though I do get six months on the treadmill for being where I was.'

'And if she should turn up alive?'

'Then I shall know that I am wrong, and believing myself a fool as well as a rogue, hold my tongue.'

I glided out of the house in a cold sweat. The only pressure in heaven or earth which could have forced me to renounce Cytherea was now put upon me – the dread of a death upon the gallows.

I sat all that night weaving strategy of various kinds. The only effectual remedy for my hazardous standing that I could see was a simple one. It was to substitute another woman for my wife before the suspicions of that one easily-hoodwinked man extended further.

The only difficulty was to find a practicable substitute.

The one woman at all available for the purpose was a friendless, innocent creature, named Anne Seaway, whom I had known in my youth, and who had for some time been the housekeeper of a lady in London. On account of this lady's sudden death, Anne stood in rather a precarious position, as regarded her future subsistence. She was not the best kind of woman for the scheme; but there was no alternative. One quality of hers was valuable; she was not a talker. I went to London the very next day, called at the Hoxton lodging of my wife (the only place at which she had been known as Mrs Manston), and found that no great difficulties stood in the way of a personation. And thus favouring circumstances determined my course. I visited Anne Seaway, made love to her, and propounded my plan.

We lived quietly enough until the Sunday before my apprehension. Anne came home from church that morning, and told me of the suspicious way in which a young man had looked at her there. Nothing could be done beyond waiting the issue of events. Then the letter came from Raunham. For the first time in my life I was half indifferent as to what fate awaited me. During the succeeding day I thought once or twice of running away, but could not quite make up my mind. At any rate it would be best to bury the body of my wife, I thought, for the oven might be opened at any time. I went to Casterbridge and made some arrangements. In the evening Miss Aldclyffe (who is united to me by a common secret which I have no right or wish to disclose) came to my house and alarmed me still more. She said that she could tell by Mr Raunham's manner that evening, that he kept back from her a suspicion of more importance even than the one he spoke of, and that strangers were in his house even then.

I guessed what this further suspicion was, and resolved to enlighten her to a certain extent, and so secure her assistance. I said that I killed my wife by an accident on the night of the fire, dwelling upon the advantage to her of the death of the only woman who knew her secret.

Her terror, and fears for my fate, led her to watch the rectory that evening. She saw the detective leave it, and followed him to my residence. This she told me hurriedly when I perceived her after digging my wife's grave in the plantation. She did not suspect what the sack contained.

I am now about to enter on my normal condition. For people are almost always in their graves. When we survey the long race of men, it is strange and still more strange to find that they are mainly dead men, who have scarcely ever been otherwise.

ÆNEAS MANSTON

The steward's confession, aided by circumstantial evidence of various kinds, was the means of freeing both Anne Seaway and Miss Aldclyffe from all suspicion of complicity with the murderer.

2. Six o'Clock p.m.

It was evening – just at sunset – on the day of Manston's death.

In the cottage at Tolchurch was gathered a group consisting of Cytherea, her brother, Edward Springrove, and his father. They sat by the window conversing of the strange events which had just taken place. In Cytherea's eye there beamed a hopeful ray, though her face was as white as a lily.

Whilst they talked, looking out at the yellow evening light that coated the hedges, trees, and church tower, a brougham rolled round the corner of the lane, and came in full view. It reflected the rays of the sun in a flash from its polished panels as it turned the angle, the spokes of the wheels bristling in the same light like bayonets. The vehicle came nearer, and arrived opposite Owen's door, then the driver pulled the rein and gave a shout, and the panting and sweating horses stopped.

'Miss Aldclyffe's carriage!' they all exclaimed.

Owen went out. 'Is Miss Graye at home?' said the man. 'A note for her, and I am to wait for an answer.'

Cytherea read in the handwriting of the Rector of Carriford: –

DEAR MISS GRAYE, – Miss Aldclyffe is ill, though not dangerously. She continually repeats your name, and now wishes very much to see you. If you possibly can, come in the carriage. – Very sincerely yours,

JOHN RAUNHAM

'How comes she ill?' Owen inquired of the coachman.

'She caught a violent cold by standing out of doors in the damp, on the night the steward ran away. Ever since, till this morning, she complained of fulness and heat in the chest. This morning the maid ran in and told her suddenly that Manston had killed himself in gaol – she shrieked – broke a blood-vessel – and fell upon the floor. Severe internal hæmorrhage continued for some time and then stopped. They say she is sure to get over it; but she herself says no. She has suffered from it before.'*

Cytherea was ready in a few moments, and entered the carriage.

3. Seven o'Clock p.m.

Soft as was Cytherea's motion along the corridors of Knapwater House, the preternaturally keen intelligence of the suffering woman caught the maiden's well-known footfall. She entered the sick-chamber with suspended breath.

In the room everything was so still, and sensation was as it were so rarefied by solicitude, that thinking seemed acting, and the lady's weak act of trying to live a silent wrestling with all the powers of the universe. Nobody was present but Mr Raunham, the nurse having left the room on Cytherea's entry, and the physician and surgeon being engaged in a whispered conversation in a side-chamber. Their patient had been pronounced out of danger.

Cytherea went to the bedside, and was instantly recognized. O, what a change – Miss Aldclyffe dependent upon pillows! And yet not a forbidding change. With weakness had come softness of aspect: the haughtiness was extracted from the frail thin countenance, and a sweeter mild placidity had taken its place.

Miss Aldclyffe signified to Mr Raunham that she would like to be alone with Cytherea.

'Cytherea?' she faintly whispered the instant the door was closed.

Cytherea clasped the lady's weak hand, and sank beside her.

Miss Aldclyffe whispered again. 'They say I am certain to live; but I know that I am certainly going to die.'

'They know, I think and hope.'

'I know best, but we'll leave that. Cytherea – O Cytherea, can you forgive me!'

Her companion pressed her hand.

'But you don't know yet – you don't know yet,' the invalid murmured. 'It is forgiveness for that misrepresentation to Edward Springrove that I implore, and for putting such force upon him – that which caused all the train of your innumerable ills!'

'I know all – all. And I do forgive you. Not in a hasty impulse that is revoked when coolness comes, but deliberately and sincerely: as I myself hope to be forgiven, I accord you my forgiveness now.'

Tears streamed from Miss Aldclyffe's eyes, and mingled with those of her young companion, who could not restrain hers for sympathy. Expressions of strong attachment, interrupted by emotion, burst again and again from the broken-spirited woman.

'But you don't know my motive. O, if you only knew it, how you would pity me then!'

Cytherea did not break the pause which ensued, and the elder woman appeared now to nerve herself by a superhuman effort. She spoke on in a voice weak as a summer breeze, and full of intermission, and yet there pervaded it a steadiness of intention that seemed to demand firm tones to bear it out worthily.

'Cytherea,' she said, 'listen to me before I die.

'A long time ago – more than thirty years ago – a young girl of seventeen was cruelly betrayed by her cousin, a wild officer of six-and-twenty. . . . He went to India, and died.

'One night when that miserable girl had just arrived home with her parents from Germany, where her baby had been born, she took all the money she possessed, pinned it on her infant's bosom, together with a letter, stating, among other things, what she wished the child's Christian name to be; wrapped up the little thing, and walked with it to Clapham. Here, in a retired street, she selected a house. She placed the child on the doorstep and knocked at the door, then ran away and watched. They took it up and carried it indoors.

'Now that her poor baby was gone, the girl blamed herself bitterly for cruelty towards it, and wished she had adopted her parents' counsel to secretly hire a nurse. She longed to see it. She didn't know what to do.

She wrote in an assumed name to the woman who had taken it in, and asked her to meet the writer with the infant at certain places she named. These were hotels or coffee-houses in Chelsea, Pimlico, or Hammersmith. The woman, being well paid, always came, and asked no questions. At one meeting – at an inn in Hammersmith – she made her appearance without the child, and told the girl it was so ill that it would not live through the night. The news, and fatigue, brought on a fainting-fit. . . .'

Miss Aldclyffe's sobs choked her utterance, and she became painfully agitated. Cytherea, pale and amazed at what she heard, wept for her, bent over her, and begged her not to go on speaking.

'Yes – I must,' she cried, between her sobs. 'I will– I must go on! And I must tell yet more plainly! . . . you must hear it before I am gone, Cytherea.' The sympathizing and astonished girl sat down again.

'The name of the woman who had taken the child was *Manston*. She was the widow of a schoolmaster. She said she had adopted the child of a relation.

'Only one man ever found out who the mother was. He was the keeper of the inn in which she fainted, and his silence she has purchased ever since.

'A twelvemonth passed – fifteen months – and the saddened girl met a man at her father's house named Graye – your father, Cytherea, then unmarried. Ah, such a man! Inexperience now perceived what it was to be loved in spirit and in truth! But it was too late. Had he known her secret he would have cast her out. She withdrew from him by an effort, and pined.

'Years and years afterwards, when she became mistress of a fortune and estates by her father's death, she formed the weak scheme of having near her the son whom, in her father's life-time, she had been forbidden to recognize. Cytherea, you know who that weak woman is.

'By such toilsome labour as this I got him here as my steward. And I wanted to see him *your husband*, Cytherea! – the husband of my true lover's child. It was a sweet dream to me. . . . Pity me – O, pity me! To die unloved is more than I can bear! I loved your father, and I love him now.'

That was the burden of Cytherea Aldclyffe.

'I suppose you must leave me again – you always leave me,' she said, after holding the young woman's hand a long while in silence.

'No – indeed I'll stay always. Do you like me to stay?'

Miss Aldclyffe in the jaws of death was Miss Aldclyffe still, though the old fire had degenerated to mere phosphorescence now. 'But you are your brother's housekeeper?'

'Yes.'

'Well, of course you cannot stay with me on a sudden like this. . . . Go home, or he will be at a loss for things. And tomorrow morning come again, won't you, dearest, come again – we'll fetch you. But you mustn't stay now, and put Owen out. O no – it would be absurd.' The absorbing concern about trifles of daily routine, which is so often seen in very sick people, was present here.

Cytherea promised to go home, and come the next morning to stay continuously.

'Stay till I die then, will you not? Yes, till I die – I shan't die till to-morrow.'

'We hope for your recovery – all of us.'

'I know best. Come at six o'clock, darling.'

'As soon as ever I can,' returned Cytherea tenderly.

'But six is too early – you will have to think of your brother's breakfast. Leave Tolchurch at eight, will you?'

Cytherea consented to this. Miss Aldclyffe would never have known had her companion stayed in the house all night; but the honesty of Cytherea's nature rebelled against even the friendly deceit which such a proceeding would have involved.

An arrangement was come to whereby she was to be taken home in the pony-carriage instead of the brougham that fetched her; the carriage to put up at Tolchurch farm for the night, and on that account to be in readiness to bring her back earlier.

4. March the Thirtieth. Daybreak

The third and last instance of Cytherea's subjection to those periodic terrors of the night which had emphasized her connection with the Aldclyffe name and blood occurred at the present date.

It was about four o'clock in the morning when Cytherea, though most probably dreaming, seemed to awaken – and instantly was transfixed by a sort of spell, that had in it more of awe than of affright. At the foot of her bed, looking her in the face with an expression of entreaty beyond the power of words to portray, was the form of Miss Aldclyffe* – wan and distinct. No motion was perceptible in her; but longing – earnest longing – was written in every feature.

Cytherea believed she exercised her waking judgment as usual in thinking, without a shadow of doubt, that Miss Aldclyffe stood before her in flesh and blood. Reason was not sufficiently alert to lead Cytherea to ask herself how such a thing could have occurred.

'I would have remained with you – why would you not allow me to stay!' Cytherea exclaimed. The spell was broken: she became broadly awake; and the figure vanished.

It was in the grey time of dawn. She trembled in a sweat of disquiet, and not being able to endure the thought of her brother being asleep, she went and tapped at his door.

'Owen!'

He was not a heavy sleeper, and it was verging upon his time to rise.

'What do you want, Cytherea?'

'I ought not to have left Knapwater last night. I wish I had not. I really think I will start at once. She wants me, I know.'

'What time is it?'

'A few minutes past four.'

'You had better not. Keep to the time agreed upon. Consider, we should have such a trouble in rousing the driver, and other things.'

Upon the whole it seemed wiser not to act on a mere fancy. She went to bed again.

An hour later, when Owen was thinking of getting up, a knocking came to the front door. The next minute something touched the glass of Owen's window. He waited – the noise was repeated. A little gravel had been thrown against it to arouse him.

He crossed the room, pulled up the blind, and looked out. A solemn white face was gazing upwards from the road, expectantly straining to catch the first glimpse of a person within the panes. It was the face of a Knapwater man sitting on horseback.

Owen saw his errand. There is an unmistakable look in the face of every man who brings tidings of death. Graye opened the window.

'Miss Aldclyffe . . .' said the messenger, and paused.

'Ah – dead?'

'Yes – she is dead.'

'When did she die?'

'At ten minutes past four, after another effusion. She knew best, you see, sir. I started directly, by the rector's orders.'

Sequel

Fifteen months have passed, and we are brought on to Midsummer Night,* 1867.

The picture presented is the interior of the old belfry of Carriford Church, at ten o'clock in the evening.

Six Carriford men* and one stranger are gathered there, beneath the light of a flaring candle stuck on a piece of wood against the wall. The six Carriford men are the well-known ringers of the fine-toned old bells in the key of F, which have been music to the ears of Carriford parish and the outlying districts for the last four hundred years. The stranger is an assistant, who has appeared from nobody knows where.

The six natives – in their shirt-sleeves, and without hats – pull and catch frantically at the dancing bell-ropes, the locks of their hair waving in the breeze created by their quick motions; the stranger, who has the treble bell, does likewise, but in his right mind and coat. Their ever-changing shadows mingle on the wall in an endless variety of kaleidoscopic forms, and the eyes of all the seven are religiously fixed on a diagram like a large addition sum, which is chalked on the floor.

Vividly constrasting with the yellow light of the candle upon the four unplastered walls of the tower, and upon the faces and clothes of the men, is the scene discernible through the screen beneath the tower archway. At the extremity of the long mysterious avenue of the nave and chancel can be seen shafts of moonlight streaming in at the east window of the church – blue, phosphoric, and ghostly.

A thorough renovation of the bell-ringing machinery and accessories had taken place in anticipation of an interesting event. New ropes had been provided; every bell had been carefully shifted from its carriage, and the pivots lubricated. Bright red 'sallies'* of woollen texture – soft to the hands and easily caught – glowed on the ropes in place of the old ragged knots, all of which newness in small details only rendered more evident the irrepressible aspect of age* in the mass surrounding them.

The triple-bob-major was ended, and the ringers wiped their faces and rolled down their shirt-sleeves, previous to tucking away the ropes and leaving the place for the night.

'Piph-h-h-h! A good forty minutes,' said a man with a streaming face, and blowing out his breath – one of the pair who had taken the tenor bell.

'Our friend here pulled proper well – that 'a did – seeing he's but a stranger,' said Clerk Crickett, who had just resigned the second rope, and addressing the man in the black coat.

325

''A did,' said the rest.

'I enjoyed it much,' said the man modestly.

'What we should ha' done without you words can't tell. The man that belongs by rights to that there bell is ill o' two gallons of old cider.'

'And now so's,' remarked the fifth ringer, as pertaining to the last allusion, 'we'll finish this drop o' cider and metheglin,* and every man home-along straight as a line.'

'With all my heart,' Clerk Crickett replied. 'And the Lord send if I ha'n't done my duty by Master Teddy Springrove – that I have so.'

'And the rest of us,' they said, as the cup was handed round.

'Ay, ay – in ringen – but I was spaken in a spiritual sense o' this mornen's business o' mine up by the chancel rails there. 'Twas very convenient to lug her here and marry her instead o' doen it at that twopenny-halfpenny town o' Budm'th. Very convenient.'

'Very. There was a little fee for Master Crickett.'

'Ah – well. Money's money – very much so – very – I always have said it. But 'twas a pretty sight for the nation. He coloured up like any maid, that he did.'

'Well enough 'a mid colour up. 'Tis no small matter for a man to play wi' fire.'

'Whatever it may be to a woman,' said the clerk absently.

'Thou'rt thinken o' thy wife, clerk,' said Gad Weedy. 'She'll play wi' it again when thou hast got mildewed.'

'Well – let her, God bless her; for I'm but a poor third man, I. The Lord have mercy upon the fourth! . . . Ay, Teddy's got his own at last. What little white ears that maid has, to be sure! Choose your wife as you choose your pig – a small ear and a small tale – that was always my joke when I was a merry feller, ah – years agone now! But Teddy's got her. Poor chap, he was getten as thin as a hermit wi' grief – so was she.'

'Maybe she'll fill out now.'

'True – 'tis nater's law, which no man shall gainsay. Ah, well do I bear in mind what I said to Pa'son Raunham about thy mother's family o' seven, the very first week of his coming here, when I was just in my prime. "And how many daughters has that poor Weedy got, clerk?" he says. "Six, sir," says I, "and every one of 'em has got a brother!" "Poor woman," says he, "a dozen children! – give her this half-sovereign from me, clerk." 'A laughed a good five minutes afterwards, when he found out my merry nater – 'a did. But there, 'tis over wi' me now. Enteren the Church is the ruin of a man's wit, for wit's nothing without a faint shadow o' sin.'

'If so be Teddy and the lady had been kept apart for life, they'd both have died,' said Gad emphatically.

'But now instead o' death there'll be increase of life,' answered the clerk.

'It all went proper well,' said the fifth bell-ringer. 'They didn't flee off to Babylonish places – not they.' He struck up an attitude – 'Here's Master Springrove standen so: here's the married woman standen likewise; here they walk across to Knapwater House; and there they bide in the chimley corner, hard and fast.'

'Yes, 'twas a pretty wedden, and well attended,' added the clerk. 'Here was my lady herself – red as scarlet: here was Master Springrove, looken as if he half wished he'd never a-come – ah, poor souls! – the men always do! The women stand it best – the maid was in her glory. Though she was so shy the glory shone plain through that shy skin.'

'Ay,' said Gad, 'and there was Tim Strooden and his five journeymen carpenters, standen on tiptoe and peepen in at the chancel winders. There was Dairyman Dodman waiten in his new spring-cart to see 'em come out – whip in hand – that 'a was. Then up comes two master tailors. Then there was Christopher Runt with his pickaxe and shovel. There was womenfolk and there was men-folk traypsen up and down church'ard till they wore a path wi' traypsen so – letting the squalling children slip down through their arms and nearly skinning 'em. And these were all over and above the gentry and Sunday-clothes folk inside. Well, I seed Mr Owen Graye at last dressed up quite the dand.*
"Well, Mr Graye," says I from the top o' church'ard wall, "how's yerself?" Mr Graye never spoke – he'd prided away his hearing. Seize the man, I didn' want en to speak. Teddy hears it, and turns round: "All right, Gad!" says he, and laughed like a boy. There's more in Teddy.'

'Well,' said Clerk Crickett, turning to the man in black, 'now you've been among us so long, and know us so well, won't ye tell us what ye've come here for, and what your trade is?'

'I am no trade,' said the thin man, smiling, 'and I came to see the wickedness of the land.'

'I said thou wast one o' the devil's brood wi' thy black clothes,' replied a sturdy ringer, who had not spoken before.

'No, the truth is,' said the thin man, retracting at this horrible translation, 'I came for a walk because it is a fine evening.'

'Now let's be off, neighbours,' the clerk interrupted.

The candle was inverted in the socket, and the whole party stepped out into the churchyard. The moon was shining within a day or two of full, and just overlooked the three or four vast yews that stood on the south-east side of the church, and rose in unvaried and flat darkness against the illuminated atmosphere behind them.

'Good-night,' the clerk said to his comrades, when the door was locked. 'My nearest way is through the park.'

'I suppose mine is too?' said the stranger. 'I am going to the railway-station.'

'Of course – come on.'

The two men went over a stile to the west, the remainder of the party going into the road on the opposite side.

'And so the romance has ended well,' the clerk's companion remarked, as they brushed along through the grass. 'But what is the truth of the story about the property?'

'Now look here, neighbour,' said Clerk Crickett, 'if so be you'll tell me what your line o' life is, and your purpose in coming here today, I'll tell you the truth about the wedden particulars.'

'Very well – I will when you have done,' said the other man.

''Tis a bargain; and this is the right o' the story. When Miss Aldclyffe's will was opened, it was found to have been drawn up on the very day that Manston (her love-child)* married Miss Cytherea Graye. And this is what that deep woman did. Deep? she was as deep as the North Star. She bequeathed all her property, real and personal, to "*the wife of Æneas Manston*" (with one exception): failen her life, to her husband: failen his life to the heirs of his head – body I would say: failen them to her absolutely and her heirs for ever: failen these to Pa'son Raunham, and so on to the end of the human race. Now do you see the depth of her scheme? Why, although upon the surface it appeared her whole property was for Miss Cytherea, by the word "*wife*" being used, and not Cytherea's name, whoever was the wife o' Manston would come in for't. Wasn't that real depth? It was done, of course, that her son Æneas, under any circumstances, should be master o' the property, without folk knowen it was her son or suspecting anything, as they would if it had been left to him straightway.'

'A clever arrangement! And what was the exception?'

'The payment of a legacy to her relative, Pa'son Raunham.'

'And Miss Cytherea was now Manston's widow and only relative, and inherited all absolutely.'

'True, she did. "Well," says she, "I shan't have it" (she didn't like the notion o' getten anything through Manston, naturally enough,

328

pretty dear). She waived her right in favour o' Mr Raunham. Now, if there's a man in the world that cares nothen about land – I don't say there is, but if there is – 'tis our pa'son. He's like a snail. He's a-growed so to the shape o' that there rectory that 'a wouldn' think o' leaven it even in name. "'Tis yours, Miss Graye," says he. "No, 'tis yours," says she. "'Tisn't mine," says he. The Crown had cast his eyes upon the case, thinken o' forfeiture by felony – but 'twas no such thing, and the Crown gied it up, too. Did you ever hear such a tale? – three people, a man and a woman and a Crown – neither o' 'em in a madhouse – flinging an estate backwards and forwards like an apple or nut? Well, it ended in this way. Mr Raunham took it: young Springrove was had as agent and steward, and put to live in Knapwater House, close here at hand – just as if 'twas his own. He does just what he'd like – Mr Raunham never interferen – and hither to-day he's brought his new wife, Cytherea. And a settlement ha' been drawn up this very day, whereby their children, heirs, and cetrer, are to inherit after Mr Raunham's death. Good fortune came at last. Her brother, too, is doing well. He came in first man in some architectural competition, and is about to move to London. Here's the house, look. Step out from these bushes, and you'll get a clear sight o't.'

They emerged from the shrubbery, breaking towards the lake, and down the south slope. When they arrived exactly opposite the centre of the mansion, they halted.

It was a magnificent picture of the English country-house. The whole of the severe regular front, with its pilasters* and cornices, was built of a white smoothly-faced freestone, which appeared in the rays of the moon as pure as Pentelic marble.* The sole objects in the scene rivalling the fairness of the façade were a dozen swans* floating upon the lake.

At this moment the central door at the top of the steps was opened, and two figures advanced into the light. Two contrasting figures were they. A young lithe woman in an airy fairy dress – Cytherea Springrove: a young man in black stereotype raiment – Edward, her husband.

They stood at the top of the steps together, looking at the moon, the water, and the general loveliness of the prospect.

'That's the married man and wife – there, I've illustrated my story by real liven specimens,' the clerk whispered.

'To be sure, how close together they do stand! You couldn't slip a penny-piece between 'em – that you couldn'! Beautiful to see it, isn't it – beautiful! . . . But this is a private path, and we won't let 'em see us, as all the ringers are going there to a supper and dance to-morrow night.'

The speaker and his companion softly moved on, passed through the wicket, and into the coach-road. Arrived at the clerk's house at the further boundary of the park, they paused to part.

'Now for your half o' the bargain,' said Clerk Crickett. 'What's your line o' life, and what d'ye come here for?'

'I'm the reporter to the *Casterbridge Chronicle*, and I come to pick up the news. Good-night.'

Meanwhile Edward and Cytherea, after lingering on the steps for several minutes, slowly descended the slope to the lake. The skiff was lying alongside.

'O, Edward,' said Cytherea, 'you must do something that has just come into my head!'

'Well, dearest – I know.'

'Yes – give me one half-minute's row on the lake here now, just as you did on Budmouth Bay three years ago.'

He handed her into the boat, and almost noiselessly pulled off from shore. When they were half-way between the two margins of the lake, he paused and looked at her.

'Ah, darling, I remember exactly how I kissed you that first time,' said Springrove. 'You were there as you are now. I unshipped the sculls in this way. Then I turned round and sat beside you – in this way. Then I put my hand on the other side of your little neck—'

'I think it was just on my cheek, in this way.'

'Ah, so it was. Then you moved that soft red mouth round to mine—'

'But, dearest – you pressed it round if you remember; and of course I couldn't then help letting it come to your mouth without being unkind to you, and I wouldn't be that.'

'And then I put my cheek against that cheek, and turned my two lips round upon those two lips, and kissed them – so.'

Notes

Title-page. *'Though . . . reality.'* From the introduction to the 1830 edition of Sir Walter Scott's *The Monastery*.

xxxi *French name for them.* This would appear to refer to the 'naturalistic' novels of Emile Zola (1840–1902).

xxxi *Wessex Poems . . . later.* See pp. 351–2.

1 *Christminster.* The name was introduced by Hardy in the 1896 edition, presumably with the intention of linking his first and last novels. See his 1896 preface.

1 *Dukery Street.* Hardy's own invention, first used in the 1912 edition.

2 *a kind of moral Gaza.* This must surely refer to Samson in Judges, XVI 1 and 21.

2 *like one just awakened.* An echo of Browning's 'The Statue and the Bust'. See ch. 3, sect. 2.

5 *nullo cultu.* This Latin phrase means 'without training or culture'. Cf. Virgil's *Eclogues*, IV, ll. 18–20:

> At tibi prima, puer, nullo munuscula cultu
> errantis hederas passim cum baccare tellus
> mixtaque ridenti colocasia fundet acantho.

Dryden's translation (1697) reads (ll. 22–4):

> Unbidden earth shall wreathing Ivy bring,
> And fragrant Herbs (the promises of Spring)
> As her first Off'rings to her Infant King.

6 *The Town Hall.* In all editions previous to 1896 Hardy described it as Elizabethan, like the Old House. See p. 82.

7 *framed in by the dark margin.* This is perhaps the first example of Hardy's 'framing' technique to focus attention on an object or person. For further discussion of this topic, see my article *'Desperate Remedies* 1871', in *The Thomas Hardy Year Book, 1971*, ed. J. and G. Stevens Cox.

7 *Tarentines . . . State.* The inhabitants of the city of Tarentum, a seaport in southern Italy, sought to protect themselves against Roman expansion southwards by a treaty in which the Romans pledged themselves not to send warships into the Gulf of Otranto. This did happen, however, in 282 B.C and war ensued.

8 *escritoire.* (French) writing-desk.

9 *bottomry security*. System of lending money to a shipowner for the purposes of a voyage on the security of the ship, the lender losing his money if the ship were lost.

9 *a well-disciplined heart*. Cf. the words of Annie Strong in Dickens's *David Copperfield* (1849–50) ch. 45: 'If I were thankful to my husband for no more . . . I should be thankful to him for having saved me from the first mistaken impulse of my undisciplined heart.'

10 *Chancery*. In this case a court of equity which would decide how to distribute most fairly the assets among the many creditors.

10 *pot-wallopers*. In certain boroughs of England, before the first Reform Act of 1832, only those men walloping (boiling) their own pots – i.e., proving that they were householders by having a separate fireplace in which to cook food – were eligible to vote.

12 *the art and science of architecture*. Cf. F. E. Hardy, *The Life of Thomas Hardy 1840–1928* (1962) p. 35: 'On Thursday, April 17, 1862, Thomas Hardy started alone for London, to pursue the art and science of architecture on more advanced lines.' The rest of the paragraph in *Desperate Remedies* reads like a comment on Hardy's own progress in the architectural profession by 1862. It would appear that there was a limit to what he could usefully learn and do in Dorchester. Arthur Blomfield's was clearly 'a bustling London practice'. Hardy returned later to Dorset, and wrote *Desperate Remedies* in 1869–70 in the intervals of working for G. R. Crickmay of Weymouth. During this period he did church restoration work, notably at St Juliot, Cornwall, where he met his first wife Emma Lavinia Gifford, and at Turnworth, Dorset (see J. Newman and N. Pevsner, *Dorset*, Buildings of England series, 1972). Other work for Crickmay can be traced in *The Architectural Notebook of Thomas Hardy*, ed. C. J. P. Beatty (1966).

12 *watering-place*. Seaside resort.

16 *whosoever's*. In the first edition Hardy wrote 'whomsoever's', but was criticized by the reviewer in the *Athenaeum* (see L. Lerner and J. Holmstrom, *Thomas Hardy and His Readers* (1968) p. 13). In the 1889 edition he tried 'whosesoever's' and finally 'whosoever's' in the 1896 edition.

17 *a Grecian nose*. A straight nose continuing the line of the forehead.

17 *tout ensemble*. (French) general effect.

18 *the pap-and-daisy school*. Possibly a phrase Hardy picked up from the *Saturday Review* to describe the minor verse of the 1860s; or it may be Hardy's invention.

21 *supererogation*. Doing of more than duty requires.

22 *the age . . . noble mind*. Cf. John Milton's 'Lycidas', ll. 70–1:

> Fame is the spur that the clear spirit doth raise
> (That last infirmity of noble mind)

23 *paddle-boxes*. Casings over the upper part of the paddle-wheels.

24 *hopeless sense . . . no more*. Cf. '. . . being then in the unpractised condition of Adam at sight of the first sunset' (*The Well-Beloved*, pt I, ch. 7). See also

Samuel Johnson's *Rasselas* (1759) ch. 35 (ch. 34 in some editions).

24 *One hope . . . smother*. From Shelley's 'One word is too often profaned'.

26 *pallet*. Straw bed; mattress.

26 *luggage trains*. Goods trains.

26 *The Houses of Parliament were on fire*. See note to p. 151 below.

27 *soi-disant*. (French) self-styled, pretended.

28 *the Ancient Mariner*. Chief character in Coleridge's 'The Rime of the Ancient Mariner'.

29 *mechanics*. Handicraftsmen; skilled workmen, especially those who use or make machinery.

29 *journeymen*. Qualified mechanics or artisans who work for another.

31 *'The Statue and the Bust'*. A poem from Robert Browning's *Men and Women* (1855).

32 *Arcadian innocence*. Arcadia was a region of Greece whose inhabitants lived a simple, pastoral life of rustic innocence.

32 *cockle-shell*. A light, and often flimsy, boat.

34 *'smooth'*. An intermittent space of smooth water.

35 *Cato the Censor . . . fashion*. Cato the Censor (234–149 B.C) was famous for his opposition to the prevalent fashions of luxury.

35 *I "meditate the thankless Muse" no longer*. Springrove no longer writes poetry. See Milton's 'Lycidas', l. 66.

35 *'sporting' . . . Amaryllis*. Also from 'Lycidas', l. 68. Amaryllis was the name given to a shepherdess by Theocritus, Virgil and Ovid.

36 *Christopher Wren . . . Pudding Lane*. Sir Christopher Wren (1632–1723) was called in to rebuild St Paul's Cathedral and fifty-two of the City churches destroyed in the Great Fire of London, 1666. The fire broke out in Pudding Lane.

36 *The truly great . . . unknown*. Geraldine uses almost exactly the same words to Egbert in *An Indiscretion in the Life of an Heiress* (pt I, ch. 8): 'The truly great stand on no middling ledge: they are either famous or unknown.'

37 *The 'bloom' and the 'purple light'*. See pp. xxiv–xxv. See also R. Gittings, *Young Thomas Hardy* (1975), p. 78.

38 *'many a voice of one delight'*. From Shelley's 'Stanzas written in Dejection near Naples'.

38 *carking*. Burdensome to the spirit.

38 *tap-roots*. The tap-root is the main root which grows down vertically.

39 *captured sparrow*. See also ch. 12, sect. 5, and ch. 20, sect. 2.

39 *forgetting . . . herself*. An echo of 'Forget thyself to marble', from Milton's 'Il Penseroso' (l. 42), a poem which he wrote in praise of 'divinest Melancholy'.

39 *Love . . . life*. From Sonnet XVIII in Thomas Watson's *The Passionate Centurie of Love* (1582).

40 *the leaden-eyed despairs*. See Keats's 'Ode to a Nightingale', l. 28.

41 *Knapwater House*. See pp. xx and xxviii.

42 *well-known . . . world*. See Portia's words in Shakespeare's *The Merchant of Venice*, Act V, sc. I:

> How far that little candle throws his beams!
> So shines a good deed in a naughty world.

'Naughty' means 'wicked' in this context.

43 *embrasure*. Recess.

43 *a Roman nose*. A nose with a high bridge. Hardy once described his own nose as 'more Roman than aquiline' (*Life*, p. 174).

43 *the Cæsars*. Roman emperors from Augustus to Hadrian.

44 *Greuze's 'Head of a Girl'*. Jean-Baptiste Greuze (1725–1805), painter of the French School. A. Smart writes: 'Hardy is presumably referring to the well-known picture in the National Gallery which was acquired as a Greuze some fifteen years before Hardy came to London, but which has since been reattributed to one of Greuze's followers ...' ('Pictorial Imagery in the Novels of Thomas Hardy', *Review of English Studies*, vol. XII).

44 *fishers of men*. See Matthew, IV 19.

46 *cubit*. See Matthew, VI 27.

47 *spring-waggon*. A waggon mounted on springs.

47 *chaise*. A light, open carriage; it is called a pony-carriage elsewhere in this section.

47 *turnpike road*. Main road or highway (the upkeep of which was paid for out of tolls collected at turnpikes).

47 *manor-house*. '... the term "manor house" can conveniently ... cover the traditional English "mansion house" of lord or squire before the days when gables gave way to cornices, mullions to sashes, and the proximity of the village church was abandoned for the "prospect" afforded by some neighbouring "eminence"' (A. Oswald, *Country Houses of Dorset* (1959) p. 45). In *Desperate Remedies* the lord/lady of the manor continues to function in the eighteenth-century mansion as previously in the Elizabethan house.

49 *a neglectful party at heart*. In the two editions previous to 1889 this read: 'a Tory at heart'.

49 *flees*. (Dial.) flies.

49 *lucifer*. Lucifer was the rebel archangel who fell from Heaven.

49 *chief baker ... Pharaoh*. See Genesis, XL.

50 *offices*. Parts of a house devoted to household work, storage and the like.

50 *freestone*. Any stone that cuts well in all directions, especially fine-grained limestone or sandstone.

50 *plainer ... orders*. This read 'plainer fashion of Greek classicism' until the final revision in 1912. The removal of 'Greek' must have been an attempt to make Knapwater House at least superficially like Kingston Maurward. The last part of this passage clearly refers to the great Palladian revival begun in England in the early eighteenth century. Later Hardy was to voice a similar opinion: 'It was Palladian, and like most architecture erected since the Gothic age was a compilation rather than a design' (*The Mayor of Casterbridge*, ch. 21).

51 *Mrs Graye.* 'Mrs' was a courtesy title prefixed to the name of a woman, married or unmarried.

52 *Blessed Damozel.* 'The Blessed Damozel' is a poem by D. G. Rossetti which begins: 'The blessed damozel leaned out/From the gold bar of Heaven.'

52 *no enemy but winter and cold weather.* An echo of the song in Shakespeare's *As You Like It*, Act II, sc. v:

> Under the greenwood tree
>   Who loves to lie with me,
> And turn his merry note
>   Unto the sweet bird's throat,
> Come hither, come hither, come hither.
>   Here shall he see no enemy
> But winter and rough weather.

54 *cabinet piano.* A small upright piano.

54 *joiner.* He was named as Mr James Sparkman in the first two editions, with possible allusion to James Sparks of Puddletown (1805–74), an uncle of Hardy's who was a cabinet-maker.

56 *Brussels net.* A machine-made imitation of Brussels-lace ground.

57 *arabesque work.* Decoration in colour or low relief, with fanciful intertwining of leaves, scroll-work, etc.

59 *a jar of electricity.* Cf. *The Woodlanders*, ch. 16: 'people living insulated . . . get charged with emotive fluid like a Leyden jar with electric'.

59 *captious reviewer.* In all earlier versions Hardy wrote 'bitter reviewer'.

59 *'fuel to maintain its fires'.* From 'Disdain Returned' by Thomas Carew (?1598–?1639):

> He that loves a rosy cheek
> Or a coral lip admires,
> Or from star-like eyes doth seek
> Fuel to maintain his fires. . . .

60 *'Possest beyond the Muse's painting'.* From 'The Passions. An Ode for Music' by William Collins (1721–59).

62 *Landed Gentry. A Genealogical and Heraldic Dictionary of the Landed Gentry of Great Britain and Ireland*, first published, under the editorship of J. Burke, in 1833–8.

68 *too rank and capricious.* In the first edition this read: 'too rank, sensuous, and capricious'. The word 'sensuous' was first omitted in the 1896 edition.

69 *Love's passions . . . sky.* From Shelley's 'Lines', 'When the lamp is shattered'. The final stanza actually begins: 'Its passions will rock thee.'

71 *status quo.* (Latin) unchanged position.

72 *How . . . death.* Hardy records an actual case in the *Life*, pp. 427–8.

76 *as Hallam says of Juliet.* Henry Hallam (1777–1859), father of Tennyson's Arthur Hallam, wrote in his *Introduction to the Literature of Europe in the 15th, 16th and 17th centuries* (1837–9) vol. II, p. 392: 'Juliet is a child whose

intoxication in loving and being loved whirls away the little reason she may have possessed.'

78 *smock-frocks*. Field labourers' outer linen garment of shirtlike shape and with the upper part closely gathered.

81 *cottages, stables, homesteads*. See *The Architectural Notebook of Thomas Hardy*.

83 *mullioned and transomed*. A mullion is a vertical post dividing a window into two or more lights. A transom divides a window horizontally.

84 *the Field and Builder*. The *Field* is a magazine, established in 1853, catering for the interests of the landed gentry and other landowners. The *Builder*, a weekly illustrated magazine, first appeared in 1843.

89 *Westminster Hotel*. The Westminster Palace Hotel, Victoria Street, now Abbey House.

94 *an ungodly machinery*. 'A carnal plot' was preferred until the 1896 edition.

94 *sighing like Donna Clara*. The lines that follow are from a song sung by Clara in Act III, sc. III of *The Duenna*, a comic opera by R. B. Sheridan (1751–1816). See also *Life*, p. 219.

98 *'lived . . . year'*. From a line in Wordsworth's sonnet 'It is a beauteous evening, calm and free': 'Thou liest in Abraham's bosom all the year.'

100 *The railway had absorbed*. . . . The railway reached Dorchester on 1 June 1847. For Hardy's own connection with the railway, see my introduction to *The Architectural Notebook of Thomas Hardy*, pp. 6 and 20.

101 *pomace*. Apples crushed to pulp in cider-making.

101 *I foresee . . . thought*. From the poem 'So Long!' in 'Songs of Parting' by Walt Whitman (1819–92).

101 *parish clerk*. A layman whose job it was to assist the clergy and lead the congregation in the responses.

101 *Bowdlerized*. Thomas Bowdler (1754–1825), an English physician, published his *Family Shakespeare*, an expurgated version of the text, in 1818.

102 *vlee*. (Dial.) fly.

102 *crabs*. Crab-apples.

102 *hopper*. Inverted cone through which apples pass into the press.

103 *"Incline . . . law."* This is the end of the congregation's response to the first nine Commandments in the Communion Service. The response to the tenth Commandment ends: '. . . and write all these thy laws in our hearts, we beseech thee'.

103 *stunpoll*. (Dial.) blockhead.

103 *so's*. I suggest this means 'souls', a friendly form of address. Cf. *Under the Greenwood Tree*, pt I, ch. 3.

103 *matrimony . . . says*. This is correct; see 'The Form of Solemnization of Matrimony' in the book of Common Prayer.

104 *zid*. (Dial.) saw.

105 *rathe-ripes and griffins*. Varieties of apple. 'Rathe-ripe' means ripening early.

105 *quean*. Bold girl or woman; hussy.

107 *Livid . . . painters*. A. Smart comments: 'too early, this, to be an allusion to

338

French Impressionism: it suggests, rather, Manet and Courbet' ('Pictorial Imagery in the Novels of Thomas Hardy').

109 *a Theomachist.* (Greek *theomachos*) one who resists the divine will.

110 *Ultima Thule.* The furthest limit; Thule being the northernmost part of the habitable world according to the ancients.

111 *from their teeth.* In profession but not in reality.

112 *he did not turn or blink.* Jean Brooks comments: 'Manson ... proves to have the devil's power of staring open-eyed at lightning and, like the demonic Fiddler of the Reels, of fascinating an impressionable girl by his music' (*Thomas Hardy: the poetic structure* (1971) pp. 153–4).

113 *The varying strains ... her own life and soul.* There are several close verbal similarities at this point of the novel to Hardy's *An Indiscretion in the Life of an Heiress.*

113 *the Pastoral Symphony.* Most likely the 'Pastoral Symphony' from Handel's *Messiah*, which features in *An Indiscretion.* Another less likely possibility is Beethoven's Symphony No. 6 (The Pastoral) in F Major, Op. 68. Keyboard transcriptions of orchestral works were popular in Victorian England.

115 *Beatrice ... chariot.* A reference to canto XXX of Dante's *Purgatorio*, in which Beatrice descends from Heaven and rebukes the poet.

117 *Ingenium ... ultro.* 'I know the disposition of women: when you will, they won't; when you won't, they set their hearts upon you of their own inclination.' From Terence's comedy *Eunuchus* (*The Eunuch*), Act IV, sc. VII, l. 42.

121 *A woman shall compass a man.* See Jeremiah, XXXI 22.

122 *'The tearful ... dawn'.* See Tennyson's 'A Dream of Fair Women', l. 74

122 *Imogen ... Belarius.* See Shakespeare's *Cymbeline*, Act III, sc. VI, particularly ll. 17–27.

126 *Carlo Crivelli.* Italian painter (*c.*1430–*c.*1493).

126 *a nameless thing.* Dramatic irony in view of what happens to Cytherea later.

128 *sang-froid.* (French) coolness, composure.

132 *Quos ego.* From Virgil's *Æneid*, bk I, l. 135: '...quos ego—! sed motos praestat componere fluctus....' (Dryden's translation (1697), l. 193: 'Whom I—But first 'tis fit, the Billows to restrain.') The words are spoken by Neptune, the god of the sea, who is angry that Æolus, the god of the winds, should have raised a storm in his domain. Æolus had been bribed by the goddess Juno, Jupiter's consort, as she was hostile to Æneas and wished to prevent him from fulfilling his destiny and founding Rome. The phrase 'quos ego' is difficult to translate and has the force of a veiled threat. In *Desperate Remedies* 'the imperious ruler of Knapwater' gets little further than 'quos ego' as she finds herself too emotionally involved.

133 *the same law of natural selection.* In 1859 Charles Darwin published *The Origin of Species by Means of Natural Selection or the Preservation of Favoured Races in the Struggle for Life.*

133 *Like Curius ... farm.* Manius Curius Dentatus (d. 270 B.C), a Roman plebeian hero, renowned for his incorruptibility and frugality, retired to a

country estate; but the phrase 'Sabine Farm' is usually applied to the country retreat of the poet Horace.

135 *Bradshaw*. Short for *Bradshaw's Monthly Railway Guide*, a publication of railway timetables originally issued in 1839 and discontinued only recently.

136 *a small twist*. An accurate detail; see the definition of 'shunts' in any *Bradshaw* for 1865.

139 *couch-grass*. A kind of grass with long, creeping roots, a common weed. See Hardy's poem 'In Time of "the Breaking of Nations"', which is relevant to the novel as a whole.

142 *barge-boards*. Pieces of board, often elaborately ornamented, covering the roof timbers which project over gables.

143 *garden engine*. A portable force-pump used for watering gardens.

143 *'Ring the bells backwards!'* Cf. 'Ring the bells backwards; I am all on fire', from 'The Rebell Scot', in *The Poems of John Cleveland*, ed. B. Morris and E. Withington (1967) p. 29. The editors explain this phrase as follows: 'Bells were rung backward (i.e. a peal was begun with the bass-bell) to give alarm of fire or invasion, or to express dismay.' Prof. Harold Brooks, to whom I am indebted for this information and for the following note on D. H. Lawrence, also pointed out that the proper name for the bell with the deepest note is 'tenor' not 'bass'. In Lawrence's *Sons and Lovers* (1913) ch. 7 occurs the following:

'. . . and when they used to ring the bells backward for alarm.'
'How?' said Annie. 'A bell sounds the same whether it's rung backwards or forwards.'
'But,' he said, 'if you start with the deep bell and ring up to the high one – der – der – der – der – der – der – der – der!'

144 *tameless, and swift, and proud*. See Shelley's 'Ode to the West Wind', l. 56.

145 *chimes*. In former years many churches in the south-west of England played chimes at regular intervals during the twenty-four hours (except on Sundays). See *The Mayor of Casterbridge*, ch. 4, for Hardy's own note. One Dorset church which still carries on this custom is Beaminster, where the chimes have played 'Hanover' since 1780.

145 *the wayward air . . . Psalm*. This tune was played by the chimes of St Andrew's Church, Plymouth; see Emma Hardy's *Some Recollections*, ed. E. Hardy and R. Gittings (1961) pp. 12 and 69–71.

145 *a narrow . . . horizon*. An example of Hardy as 'the man of measuring eye'.

146 *''Tis She . . . character.'* See Richard Crashaw's 'Wishes to His Supposed Mistress', st. 35. The two previous stanzas of Crashaw's poem are quoted as an epigraph to the first part of *The Well-Beloved*. This shows that Hardy's interest in the alchemy of love and the pursuit of the ever-illusive ideal never left him or diminished.

147 *'hungry generations' . . . city*. See Keats's 'Ode to a Nightingale', l. 62.

149 *Cushi . . . David*. It was Cushi who told David of Absalom's death. See II Samuel, XVIII 21 ff.

151 *sacrilege . . . in the church.* Anybody who reads the account of the fire that burned down the Houses of Parliament on 16 October 1834 in E. W. Brayley and John Britton's *The History of the Ancient Palace and Late Houses of Parliament at Westminster* (1836) will be struck by the parallels between that account and the narrative of the Carriford fire: inflammable nature of the buildings concerned, warnings neglected, inadequacy of the fire-fighting equipment, and one further detail – the housing of such goods and valuables as were saved in a church, St Margaret's, Westminster, in the case of the real fire. (Information kindly supplied by the Librarian of the House of Commons.)

151 *'lanch' or 'lanchet'.* Another spelling Hardy uses is 'lynchet'; see *Tess of the d'Urbervilles*, ch. 43.

151 *term of lives.* This refers to the lifehold system, whereby a tenant entered into agreement with the lord of the manor to occupy a cottage or other dwelling for a term of lives. Farmer Springrove had become the sole lessee for all the cottages/houses; cf. Giles Winterborne in *The Woodlanders*, ch. 13. The Hardys of Bockhampton were themselves lifeholders, like most of their neighbours.

153 *demise.* The conveyance of an estate.

155 *Sterne . . . dead.* Laurence Sterne (1713–68), author of *Tristram Shandy*.

158 *Talibus incusat.* From Virgil's *Æneid*, bk I, l. 410. Literally 'In such [terms he] complains.' Dryden's translation runs (l. 568): 'Against the Goddess these Complaints he made.' These words come at the end of Æneas's speech to his mother Venus, the goddess of love, in which he accuses her of generally behaving falsely towards him. The situation between Miss Aldclyffe and Manston has, until now, been very similar.

159 *japanned.* Covered with 'japan', a kind of hard lacquer-like varnish.

161 *os femoris.* (Latin) thigh-bone.

162 *"In the morning . . . see."* See Deuteronomy, XXVIII 67; cf. *Two on a Tower*, ch. 2.

164 *Bohemian.* Free and easy; socially unconventional.

168 *Lachesis or Fate.* The Greeks and Romans supposed that there were three Fates, who controlled the life and death of every man – Clotho, who held the distaff; Lachesis, who spun the thread of life; and Atropos, who cut off life when it was ended.

170 *Love . . . finds.* From Shakespeare's Sonnet 116.

171 *freeholds.* A freehold property is one held in fee simple (as absolute property) or fee-tail (limited to lineal descendant heirs). Unlike the lifeholdings of which he is only the lessee, at least one of the two freeholds is Farmer Springrove's own property.

174 *Christmas . . . white sunsets.* Cf. the opening lines of ch. 23 of *The Trumpet-Major*.

174 *sphere-descended . . . Pleasure.* From William Collins's 'The Passions. An Ode for Music'.

174 *Like . . . attend.* Third verse of the first psalm in the metrical version of the Psalms by Nahum Tate and Nicholas Brady (1696).

341

175 *O, what ... away!* From Horace's Odes, bk IV, no. XIII.

175 *petits soins.* (French) little attentions.

176 *a Grecian temple.* Eighteenth-century gentlemen liked to adorn their estates with Classical buildings of this kind: e.g., Stowe, Stourhead, Castle Howard.

176 *blithe.* First used in the 1912 edition, replacing 'perfect' in all previous editions. Surely an echo of the first line of Shelley's 'To a Skylark'?

177 *Laodicean.* An inhabitant of Laodicea, especially one of its early Christian inhabitants, who were reproached for their lukewarmness (Revelation, III 14–22).

177 *Episcopalian.* i.e., adherent of the Church of England and its hierarchy.

177 *the Wandering Voice.* See the first stanza of Wordsworth's 'To the Cuckoo': 'O Cuckoo! shall I call thee Bird/Or but a wandering Voice!'

178 *Correggio's.* Antonio da Correggio (*c.* 1494–1534), Italian painter.

179 *cloud ... man's hand.* See I Kings, XVIII 44: 'Behold, there ariseth a little cloud out of the sea, like a man's hand.'

183 *He ... relies.* From Virgil's *Æneid,* bk V, ll. 439–42. The quotation in Dryden (ll. 587–91) actually begins with 'And' not 'He'. Hardy uses exactly the same lines as an epigraph to pt II, ch. 1 of *An Indiscretion in the Life of an Heiress.*

183 *Had a register ... oscillations.* See Hardy's original description of Cytherea Graye, p. 5.

183 *De Quincey ... Opium.* See Thomas De Quincey's *Confessions of an English Opium-eater* (1822; enlarged edn, 1856).

183 *Elijah ... drought.* In this section Hardy is adhering closely to the Church calendar for 1865. In that year the prescribed readings for August included the story of Elijah and Elisha as related in I and II Kings. On the ninth Sunday after Trinity (i.e., 13 August in 1865) the prescribed chapter for Evensong was I Kings, XIX, Hardy's favourite passage of Scripture; see his poem 'Quid Hic Agis?'

184 *Manston's eye sparkled.* In the first edition this phrase is immediately followed by: 'what Lavater calls the boundary line between affection and appetite, never very distinct in him, was visibly obliterated. Moreover he saw. . . .' This passage was not removed until the 1889 edition.

184 *tithe-paying ... cummin.* See Matthew, XXIII 23.

185 *On the right hand the sun ... under the sky.* Cf. *The Return of the Native,* bk III, ch. 5.

186 *mandrakes.* The mandrake (or mandragora) is a small plant of the potato family and was the subject of many superstitions, including the belief that it was instinct with feeling and shrieked when torn from the ground. See also Gittings, *Young Thomas Hardy,* p. 141.

188 *So true a fool is love.* See Shakespeare's Sonnet 57:

> So true a fool is love, that in your Will,
> Though you do anything, he thinks no ill.

189 *the Evening Hymn.* Written by Bishop Thomas Ken (1637–1711).

191 *How shall I . . . sinned.* A similar exchange occurs in *An Indiscretion in the Life of an Heiress*, pt. I, ch. 6:

'How shall I say "Yes" without assuming that there was something to forgive?'

'Say "Yes". It is sweeter to fancy I am forgiven than to think I have not sinned.'

191 *Old Christmas Day.* When the New Style calendar was adopted in England in 1752, it was necessary to cut off eleven days, which moved 6 January back to 25 December of the previous year.

191 *a Friday.* 'Friday's ill repute has been . . . accounted for as resulting from the fact that it was the day of the Crucifixion, or the day when Eve ate the fatal apple!' (Ruth Firor, *Folkways in Thomas Hardy* (1962) p. 9).

196 *the great Mother.* A translation of the Latin 'Magna Mater', the title which the Romans gave to Cybele, a goddess of Asiatic origin, personifying the fecundity of Nature.

197 *smoke-jack.* A device for turning a spit by using the flow of air up a chimney.

197 *flanconade.* A thrust in the side, in fencing.

197 *closer.* (Dial.) a finishing argument.

197 *like Bel and Nebo.* See Isaiah, XLVI 1.

198 *three-cunning.* (Dial.) secretive, knowing.

198 *skimmer your pate.* (Dial.) beat your head with a skimming ladle.

198 *daddlen, and hawken, and spetten.* (Dial.) idling; hawking, clearing the throat; spitting.

199 *ashleaf taties.* A kind of potato.

199 *to sickness-or-health-it.* i.e., to marry. A reference to a portion of the marriage vows in the Book of Common Prayer: 'Wilt thou . . . keep her/him, in sickness and in health . . .?'

200 *Spenserian.* Edmund Spenser (?1552–99), who wrote two magnificent bridal hymns.

201 *spectre-thin.* See Keats's 'Ode to a Nightingale', l. 26: 'Where youth grows pale, and spectre-thin, and dies.'

202 *a transmutation.* In the two editions previous to 1889 this read 'an impossibility'.

205 *too late.* Cf. *Tess of the d'Urbervilles*, ch. 55.

207 *small.* First used in the 1896 edition, replacing 'north' in all previous editions. I suggest that Hardy's reason for this change was that he wanted Edward to appear beside the tombs, which are on the *south* side of the church, without his entry into the building having been observed.

207 *The world . . . policy.* From Browning's 'The Statue and the Bust'. See also *Jude the Obscure*, pt VI, ch. 4.

207 *miniver.* A kind of fur used as a lining and trimming in ceremonial costume which could be artificially spotted or variegated (*OED*).

208 *brougham.* A one-horse, closed carriage.

211 *dairy-barton*. A barton is a farmyard.

213 *the Testament in the waiting-room*. The Rev. Carr J. Glyn, a Dorset rector and active supporter of the British and Foreign Bible Society, was the instigator of the placing of Testaments in railway waiting-rooms. The first stations to be provided with copies by the Society were on the South-Western Railway, 1855–6. (Information kindly supplied by the Archivist of the B.F.B.S.)

216 *through the cutting at twice*. I understand this to mean that when the rails were slippery and the engine could not pull the train up the gradient the train had to be divided. The front portion proceeded to the nearest station and another engine was sent for the remaining carriages. This was called coming through 'at twice'.

229 *outstep*. (Dial.) out-of-the-way.

231 *plenus rimarum*. (Latin) full of rhymes. See Terence's *Eunuchus*, Act I, sc. II, l. 25.

234 *Abigail . . . recovered*. Abigail and Michal were two of David's wives. See I Samuel, XXV, and II Samuel, III.

234 *'Cui bono?'* (Latin) for whose good?

234 *"a land . . . darkness"*. See Job, X 22.

235 *comely . . . Kedar*. See the Song of Solomon, I 5.

238 *'– I said . . . here.'* From 'Ballad Stanzas' by Thomas Moore (1779–1852):

> I knew by the smoke, that so gracefully curl'd
>> Above the green elms, that a cottage was near,
> And I said, 'If there's peace to be found in the world,
>> A heart that was humble might hope for it here!'

239 *locus standi*. (Latin) literally 'a place of standing': a right to be heard, or to appear in a court.

243 *a wild hill that had no name . . . summer*. In *A Pair of Blue Eyes* the cliff that nearly costs Knight his life is called 'the Cliff without a Name'. Cf. also Hardy's poem 'It Never Looks Like Summer'.

244 *Seasoning justice with mercy*. An echo of the phrase in Portia's 'mercy' speech in *The Merchant of Venice*, Act IV, sc. I.

251 *hansom*. Two-wheeled cab.

255 *Dutch clock*. The earliest usage quoted by the *Oxford Dictionary* is in Dickens's *The Old Curiosity Shop* (1840); see ch. 10, where an illustration of 'Kit at Home' shows this popular time-keeper hanging on the wall.

255 *Harpy*. In Classical mythology a rapacious monster with a woman's face and body, and a bird's wings and claws.

255 *'fœdissima . . . ora'*. From Virgil's *Æneid*, bk III, ll. 216–18. Dryden's translation (ll. 282–4): 'with Wombs obscene,/Foul Paunches, and with Ordure still unclean;/With Claws for Hands, and Looks for ever lean.'

255 *quartern*. A quarter-pint.

256 *carte-de-visite photographs*. Portrait photographs customarily 3½″ × 2¼″ in size.

257 *Eunice*. Hardy's first published poem. In all editions previous to 1912 the penultimate line read: 'A kind of pictured melody'.

258 *outer chamber to the mind*. Echoed in *The Mayor of Casterbridge*, ch. 42.

260 *thimble-and-button*. '"Thimble and bodkin", a term of contempt (first used with reference to the Parliamentarian Army during the Civil War)' (F. B. Pinion, *A Hardy Companion*, 1968).

261 *no other ... wife*. A reference to the first and tenth Commandments.

261 *He flung ... new*. See pp. 353–5.

262 *small ... families*. The mis-use of such a 'post-bag' is dramatically described by Wilkie Collins in *The Woman in White* (1860) ch. 8.

262 *budget*. A bag and its contents.

262 *martel*. (Dial.) mortal.

263 *caddle*. (Dial.) quandary, entanglement.

269 *pew-opener*. An usher in a church.

271 *pearl-powder*. A cosmetic used to impart whiteness to the skin.

272 *he is a magistrate*. The Rector of Carriford would automatically be a magistrate.

273 *roué*. (French) debauchee, rake.

276 *Corinthian*. Worldly, dissipated man.

278 *the Flying Isle of San Borandan*. Named after St Brendan or Brandan, an Irish navigator-saint of the sixth century who went in search of the 'Islands of Paradise'. Washington Irving commented that 'the garden of Armida, where Rinaldo was detained, and which Tasso places in one of the Canary Isles, has been identified with San Borandan'. Again, this is a piece of information that serves a double purpose. The reader is apparently meant to take the hint that Eunice Manston is in the Fortunate Islands, while Anne Seaway is deterred from further questioning.

283 *Paphos*. Ancient city of Cyprus with a famous temple of Aphrodite.

288 *Non ... manus*. From Virgil's *Æneid*, bk VII, ll. 805–6. Dryden's translation (ll. 1094–7):

> Last from the *Volscians* fair *Camilla* came;
> And led her warlike Troops, a Warriour Dame:
> Unbred to Spinning, in the Loom unskill'd,
> She chose the nobler *Pallas* of the Field.

Virgil presents Minerva, known also as Pallas Athene, both as goddess of handicrafts and as a goddess of war.

290 *the grain of mustard-seed*. See Matthew, XIII 31–2.

295 *armour ... tent-nail*. An allusion to Jael slaying the sleeping Sisera with a tent-nail. See Judges, IV 21.

297 *'Battley's Solution of Opium'*. Richard Battley (1770–1856), naval surgeon and later apothecary in the City of London, introduced many important improvements in pharmaceutical operations.

299 *gallipots*. Small earthen glazed pots used for ointments, etc.

299 *oblate*. In geometry, of spheres flattened at the poles.

305 *bull's-eye*. A lantern with a thick lens concentrating the rays of light.

307 *ewe-lease*. (Dial.) a sheep pasture.

308 *steam-packet*. Mail boat.

310 *desperado*. In the two editions previous to 1889 this read 'demon'. An interesting change, indicating that Hardy wishes us to think of Manston as a human being and not as a character from a Gothic novel.

311 *One . . . size*. From Dryden's translation of Virgil's *Æneid*, bk v, ll. 570–1. Line 570 actually runs: 'One on his Youth and pliant Limbs relies.'

311 *'Hast thou . . . Lord.'* See I Kings, XXI 20.

320 *broke . . . before*. There are many similarities between Miss Aldclyffe's last hours and those of Miss Allenville in the last chapter of *An Indiscretion in the Life of an Heiress*. See also Gittings, *Young Thomas Hardy*, pp. 102–3.

323 *the form of Miss Aldclyffe. . . .* We can surely find an echo here of the moving scene in Virgil's *Æneid*, bk II, ll. 1048–80 (in Dryden's translation), in which Æneas sees the pale spectre of his recently dead wife Creusa.

325 *Midsummer Night*. Not Midsummer Eve, i.e., 23 June. It is clear that Cytherea and Edward have long resolved the uncertainty represented by the rites performed on Midsummer Eve by country girls (see *The Woodlanders*, ch. 20). More especially not Midsummer Eve in 1867, which fell on a Sunday.

325 *Six Carriford men*. Hardy is at fault here, for a triple-bob-major is rung on eight bells, not six. (See P. J. Perry, 'A Note on the Bell-ringing in Hardy's *Desperate Remedies*', *The Thomas Hardy Year Book, 1972/1973*.) In all editions previous to 1896, Hardy wrote: 'Eight Carriford men'. In changing this he forgot at the same time to alter 'triple-bob-major' to a peal appropriate to six bells.

325 *'sallies'*. A 'sally' is the thick woolly grip for the hands near the lower end of a bellrope.

325 *irrepressible aspect of age*. Cf. 'the irrepressible New' in *The Return of the Native*, bk I, ch. 1.

326 *metheglin*. Spiced mead.

327 *dand*. (Slang) dandy.

328 *(her love-child)*. Changed from '(her sly-gotten)' in the 1896 edition.

329 *pilasters*. In all editions previous to 1912, this read 'columns'. This is another example of Hardy's attempt to make Knapwater House like Kingston Maurward. Cf. note to p. 50 above.

329 *Pentelic marble*. Famous white marble quarried from Mount Pentelicus, near Athens.

329 *a dozen swans*. Cf. Dryden's translation (l. 543) of a line in Virgil's *Æneid*,

bk I: 'Twelve Swans behold, in beauteous order move', in a speech by Venus.

This closing scene, where the lovers are quite alone, has an Elysian atmosphere about it. Here the English country-house, which 'approximated to a square on the ground plan, having a projection in the centre of each side, surmounted by a pediment' (see p. 50), and which was originally decorated with columns (see note to 'pilasters' just above), has become a temple of Love. In this way Hardy's ending is by no means trite and conventional but suggests that true love can only be experienced in Elysium. (Cf. my comments on 'The Blessed Damozel', p. xvi.)

Note on the Text

No manuscript of *Desperate Remedies* survives, Hardy himself having destroyed it. It never appeared in serial form, but was first published, anonymously, by Tinsley Brothers in three volumes in 1871. In March 1874 a one-volume edition was published in America by Henry Holt & Co. in their Leisure Hour series, and for this edition Hardy made one considerable change in the text which appears in no other edition. As it concerns Miss Aldclyffe's confession, it is worth quoting in full:

'A long time ago – more than thirty years ago – a young girl of seventeen was decoyed into a secret marriage with a man she desperately loved, and whom she used to meet by stealth. He professed to be an officer in the line. Two days after the marriage, the dreadful fact transpired that he was an escaped convict who had been undergoing sentence for forging a will. He fled to Canada, and was shot in resisting his recapture.

'She had never assumed her married name, and, upon confessing to her parents, it was resolved that she should not assume it now. The whole wild transaction was to be kept silent as the grave, because of the tremendous disgrace such a union would bring upon her family if the world got to know of it.

'One night when that miserable child-widow had just arrived home from Germany with her parents, she took all the money she possessed, pinned it on an infant's bosom. . . .' (pp. 391–2)

In line with this, the following change was necessary in the early part of the novel, again in the 1874 edition only:

. . . some prior flirtation between Cytherea and some mysterious officer of the line, two or three years before Graye met her, which had suddenly been terminated by the vanishing of her vague military lover. . . . (pp. 3–4)

A 'New Edition' was published in 1889 by Ward & Downey, with a frontis-piece by F. Barnard showing Cytherea and Edward 'facing each other in the graceful yellow cockle-shell',[1] and a Prefatory Note by Hardy. His correspondence with the publishers concerning this edition is discussed in *The Letters of Thomas Hardy*, ed. Carl J. Weber (Colby College Press, Waterville, Maine, 1954) pp. 24–9. Some minor changes were made in the text. Heinemann's

[1] This illustration was reproduced in *The Thomas Hardy Festival: the official handbook* (1968) p. 55.

Popular Edition of 1892 is a reprint of the 1889 text. For Osgood, McIlvaine's edition of the Wessex Novels (1895–6), Hardy made further changes in the text, most of which concern the place-names (see Glossary of Place-names), as he himself indicates in his addition to the Preface. A few further alterations in the text were made for the definitive Wessex Edition of 1912.

Certain interesting textual changes have been set out in the Notes, though modifications in the dialect have r ‧ been included. A comparison of the cider-making scene (ch. 8, sect. 3) in the first, 1896 and 1912 editions shows that in the dialect passages the tendency is generally towards clarity and simplification, as the following examples illustrate:

1st ed., 1871	1896	1912	Standard English
Why m't that be?	mid	mid	(might)
She d'pay en well	d'pay	pays	(pays)
I sid 'em die off so	zid 'em	zid 'em	(saw them)
she'd never ha' noticed ye	ye	'ee	(you)

The dialect participle ending -en is generally retained throughout in such words as 'mouldren', 'schemen', 'thinken'; but 'beën' and 'nothen' were finally changed into 'being' and 'nothing' in the 1912 edition.

Poems by Hardy Associated with Desperate Remedies

The following is a list of the poems Hardy may have had in mind when writing his 1912 Preface. The list does not claim to be complete.

Wessex Poems (1898)
'Her Dilemma', written in 1866; see p. 190.
'She, to Him', II, written in 1866; see p. 203.
'The Bride-Night Fire', written in 1866. This could almost be called a parody of *Desperate Remedies*, since all that was left of the unfortunate bridegroom after the fire was 'a bone'! In all editions of *Desperate Remedies* previous to 1912 'Tim Tankins and his five journeymen carpenters' had been present at the wedding of Edward Springrove and Cytherea, but in the 1912 edition Hardy changed the name to Tim Strooden, perhaps because the name Tim Tankins was too close to Tim Tankens, the hero-lover of 'The Bride-Night Fire'.

Poems of the Past and the Present (1902)
'The Ruined Maid', written in 1866; see p. 258.

Poems written later than *Desperate Remedies* but which echo phrases, sentiments and observations found in the novel:

Moments of Vision (1917)
'Afternoon Service at Mellstock'; see p. 189.
'In a Waiting-Room'; see p. 212.

Late Lyrics and Earlier (1922)
'Voices from Things Growing in a Churchyard', written in 1921; see p. 178.

Poems connected with Weymouth, where *Desperate Remedies* was begun in 1869:
Time's Laughingstocks (1909)
'Her Father'. 'Weymouth: 1869' deleted in MS.
'At Waking', written in Weymouth in 1869.
'The Dawn after the Dance', written in Weymouth in 1869.

Moments of Vision (1917)
'At a Seaside Town in 1869'. The town is Weymouth (see F. E. Hardy, *The Life of Thomas Hardy, 1840–1928* (1962) p. 63).

Late Lyrics and Earlier (1922)
'The Contretemps'. This is reminiscent of other verses associated with Weymouth in 1869.

Human Shows (1925)
'On the Esplanade'. This is reminiscent of other verses associated with Weymouth in 1869.

The Song 'The Seven Trades'

The one half-verse of the song the postman (and ex-mason) sings, quoted by Hardy in the novel on p. 261, is a wry comment on nineteenth-century restoration:

> He flung his mallet against the wall,
> Said, 'The Lord make churches and chapels to fall,
> And there'll be work for tradesmen all!'
>> When Joan's ale was new,
>> My boys,
>> When Joan's ale was new.

Here is the complete version of the song as kindly copied out for me by Mrs J. R. Brooks at the English Folk Dance and Song Society at Cecil Sharp House. 'Here it is; misspellings, oral corruptions, lack of punctuation and all!'[1]

Bk V, Hammond Collection of Folk-Songs from Dorset:

No. XI.   Bowditch.[2]
pp. 16–18

The Seven Trades

> Oh seven trades they had a meeting
> They all sat down a-drinking (*bis*)
> For to be jovial there
> All over a bottle of sherry, brave boys
> All over a bottle of sherry.
>
> The first come in was a soldier
> With his fire-lock on his shoulder
> No man could be any bolder
> Amongst the jovial crew
> He swore he'd fight for England's crown
> Rather than have his nation put down
> So let K – health go round
> When Joan's ale was new, my boys,
> When Joan's ale was new.

[1] Mrs Brooks introduced the song with these words.
[2] Mrs Brooks thinks that this was the name of the singer.

The second come in was a ragman
With his ragbag on his shoulder
No man could be any bolder
Amongst the jovial crew
They did call for ale in glasses
Till all the whole lot of them was drunk as jackasses
They burned the old ragbag all to ashes
When Joan's ale was new, my boys,
When Joan's ale was new.

The third come in was a tailor
With his bodkin shears and thimbles
No one could be any nimbler
Amongst the jovial crew
They did call for ale and chalk
Till this poor tailor was almost broke
He was obliged to pawn his coat,
When . . . etc.

The fourth come in was a dyer
He sat himself down by the fire
Indeed 'twas his desire
Amongst the jovial crew
He told the landlord to his face
The chimbley's corner was his place
And there he bide and paint his face
When . . . etc.

The fifth come in was a hatter
He wanted to know what was the matter
Indeed he was no statter
Amongst the jovial crew
But he flinged his hat upon the ground
Everyman spend half-a-crown
And let K – health go round
When . . . etc.

The sixth come in was a mason
Brought mortar in a bason
There's no-one there could face 'un
Amongst the jovial crew
He flung his hammer against the wall
Wishing all churches and chapels would fall[1]

---

[1] 'Slight variation, but this quite normal in oral transmission. "Lord" could easily have been picked up from following verse. Hardy must have known this song well; "*jovial crew*" is name usually given to rustic group of tradesmen at *3 Mariners* in *The Mayor*' (J. R. Brooks).

And then there'd be work for masons all
When . . . etc.

The seventh come in was a tinker
He was no small beer drinker
Indeed he was no shrinker
Amongst the jovial crew
He did call for pots and kettles
For all his brass rivets were made of best metal
Good Lord! how this hammer and pincers did rattle
When . . . etc.

General Preface to the Wessex Edition of 1912

In accepting a proposal for a definite edition of these productions in prose and verse I have found an opportunity of classifying the novels under heads that show approximately the author's aim, if not his achievement, in each book of the series at the date of its composition. Sometimes the aim was lower than at other times; sometimes, where the intention was primarily high, force of circumstances (among which the chief were the necessities of magazine publication) compelled a modification, great or slight, of the original plan. Of a few, however, of the longer novels, and of many of the shorter tales, it may be assumed that they stand to-day much as they would have stood if no accidents had obstructed the channel between the writer and the public. That many of them, if any, stand as they would stand if written *now* is not to be supposed.

In the classification of these fictitious chronicles – for which the name of 'The Wessex Novels' was adopted, and is still retained – the first group is called 'Novels of Character and Environment', and contains those which approach most nearly to uninfluenced works; also one or two which, whatever their quality in some few of their episodes, may claim a verisimilitude in general treatment and detail.

The second group is distinguished as 'Romances and Fantasies', a sufficiently descriptive definition. The third class – 'Novels of Ingenuity' – show a not infrequent disregard of the probable in the chain of events, and depend for their interest mainly on the incidents themselves. They might also be characterized as 'Experiments', and were written for the nonce simply; though despite the artificiality of their fable some of their scenes are not without fidelity to life.[1]

It will not be supposed that these differences are distinctly perceptible in every page of every volume. It was inevitable that blendings and alternations should occur in all. Moreover, as it was not thought desirable in every instance to change the arrangement of the shorter stories to which readers have grown accustomed, certain of these may be found under headings to which an acute judgment might deny appropriateness.

[1] Novels of Character and Environment: *Tess of the d'Urbervilles, Far from the Madding Crowd, Jude the Obscure, The Return of the Native, The Mayor of Casterbridge, The Woodlanders, Under the Greenwood Tree, Life's Little Ironies and A Few Crusted Characters, Wessex Tales.*

Romances and Fantasies: *A Pair of Blue Eyes, The Trumpet-Major, Two on a Tower, The Well-Beloved, A Group of Noble Dames.*

Novels of Ingenuity: *Desperate Remedies, The Hand of Ethelberta, A Laodicean.* [General Editor's note]

It has sometimes been conceived of novels that evolve their action on a circumscribed scene – as do many (though not all) of these – that they cannot be so inclusive in their exhibition of human nature as novels wherein the scenes cover large extents of country, in which events figure amid towns and cities, even wander over the quarters of the globe. I am not concerned to argue this point further than to suggest that the conception is an untrue one in respect of the elementary passions. But I would state that the geographical limits of the stage here trodden were not absolutely forced upon the writer by circumstances; he forced them upon himself from judgment. I considered that our magnificent heritage from the Greeks in dramatic literature found sufficient room for a large proportion of its action in an extent of their country not much larger than the half-dozen counties here reunited under the old name of Wessex, that the domestic emotions have throbbed in Wessex nooks with as much intensity as in the palaces of Europe, and that, anyhow, there was quite enough human nature in Wessex for one man's literary purpose. So far was I possessed by this idea that I kept within the frontiers when it would have been easier to overleap them and give more cosmopolitan features to the narrative.

Thus, though the people in most of the novels (and in much of the shorter verse) are dwellers in a province bounded on the north by the Thames, on the south by the English Channel, on the east by a line running from Hayling Island to Windsor Forest, and on the west by the Cornish coast, they were meant to be typically and essentially those of any and every place where

Thought's the slave of life, and life time's fool

– beings in whose hearts and minds that which is apparently local should be really universal.

But whatever the success of this intention, and the value of these novels as delineations of humanity, they have at least a humble supplementary quality of which I may be justified in reminding the reader, though it is one that was quite unintentional and unforeseen. At the dates represented in the various narrations things were like that in Wessex: the inhabitants lived in certain ways, engaged in certain occupations, kept alive certain customs, just as they are shown doing in these pages. And in particularizing such I have often been reminded of Boswell's remarks on the trouble to which he was put and the pilgrimages he was obliged to make to authenticate some detail, though the labour was one which would bring him no praise. Unlike his achievement, however, on which an error would as he says have brought discredit, if these country customs and vocations, obsolete and obsolescent, had been detailed wrongly, nobody would have discovered such errors to the end of Time. Yet I have instituted inquiries to correct tricks of memory, and striven against temptations to exaggerate, in order to preserve for my own satisfaction a fairly true record of a vanishing life.

It is advisable also to state here, in response to inquiries from readers interested in landscape, prehistoric antiquities, and especially old English architecture, that the description of these backgrounds has been done from the real – that is to say, has something real for its basis, however illusively treated.

Many features of the first two kinds have been given under their existing names; for instance, the Vale of Blackmoor or Blakemore, Hambledon Hill, Bulbarrow, Nettlecombe Tout, Dogbury Hill, High-Stoy, Bubb-Down Hill, The Devil's Kitchen, Cross-in-Hand, Long-Ash Lane, Benvill Lane, Giant's Hill, Crimmercrock Lane, and Stonehenge. The rivers Froom, or Frome, and Stour, are, of course, well known as such. And the further idea was that large towns and points tending to mark the outline of Wessex – such as Bath, Plymouth, The Start, Portland Bill, Southampton, etc. – should be named clearly. The scheme was not greatly elaborated, but, whatever its value, the names remain still.

In respect of places described under fictitious or ancient names in the novels – for reasons that seemed good at the time of writing them – and kept up in the poems – discerning people have affirmed in print that they clearly recognize the originals: such as Shaftesbury in 'Shaston', Sturminster Newton in 'Stourcastle', Dorchester in 'Casterbridge', Salisbury Plain in 'The Great Plain', Cranborne Chase in 'The Chase', Beaminster in 'Emminster', Bere Regis in 'Kingsbere', Woodbury Hill in 'Greenhill', Wool Bridge in 'Wellbridge', Harfoot or Harput Lane in 'Stagfoot Lane', Hazelbury in 'Nuttlebury', Bridport in 'Port Bredy', Maiden Newton in 'Chalk Newton', a farm near Nettlecombe Tout in 'Flintcomb-Ash', Sherborne in 'Sherton Abbas', Milton Abbey in 'Middleton Abbey', Cerne Abbas in 'Abbot's Cernel', Evershot in 'Evershed', Taunton in 'Toneborough', Bournemouth in 'Sandbourne', Winchester in 'Wintoncester', Oxford in 'Christminster', Reading in 'Aldbrickham', Newbury in 'Kennetbridge', Wantage in 'Alfredston', Basingstoke in 'Stoke Barehills', and so on. Subject to the qualifications above given, that no detail is guaranteed – that the portraiture of fictitiously named towns and villages was only suggested by certain real places, and wantonly wanders from inventorial descriptions of them – I do not contradict these keen hunters for the real; I am satisfied with their statements as at least an indication of their interest in the scenes.

Thus much for the novels. Turning now to the verse – to myself the more individual part of my literary fruitage – I would say that, unlike some of the fiction, nothing interfered with the writer's freedom in respect of its form or content. Several of the poems – indeed many – were produced before novel-writing had been thought of as a pursuit; but few saw the light till all the novels had been published. The limited stage to which the majority of the latter confine their exhibitions has not been adhered to here in the same proportion, the dramatic part especially having a very broad theatre of action. It may thus relieve the circumscribed areas treated in the prose, if such relief be needed. To be sure, one might argue that by surveying Europe from a celestial point of vision – as in *The Dynasts* – that continent becomes virtually a province – a Wessex, an Attica, even a mere garden – and hence is made to conform to the principle of the novels, however far it outmeasures their region. But that may be as it will.

The few volumes filled by the verse cover a producing period of some eighteen years first and last, while the seventeen or more volumes of novels represent correspondingly about four-and-twenty years. One is reminded by this dis-proportion in time and result how much more concise and quintessential expression becomes when given in rhythmic form than when shaped in the language of prose.

One word on what has been called the present writer's philosophy of life, as exhibited more particularly in this metrical section of his compositions. Positive views on the Whence and the Wherefore of things have never been advanced by this pen as a consistent philosophy. Nor is it likely, indeed, that imaginative writings extending over more than forty years would exhibit a coherent scientific theory of the universe even if it had been attempted – of that universe concerning which Spencer owns to the 'paralysing thought' that possibly there exists no comprehension of it anywhere. But such objectless consistency never has been attempted, and the sentiments in the following pages have been stated truly to be mere impressions of the moment, and not convictions or arguments.

That these impressions have been condemned as 'pessimistic' – as if that were a very wicked adjective – shows a curious muddle-mindedness. It must be obvious that there is a higher characteristic of philosophy than pessimism, or than meliorism, or even than the optimism of these critics – which is truth. Existence is either ordered in a certain way, or it is not so ordered, and conjectures which harmonize best with experience are removed above all comparison with other conjectures which do not so harmonize. So that to say one view is worse than other views without proving it erroneous implies the possibility of a false view being better or more expedient than a true view; and no pragmatic proppings can make that *idolum specus* stand on its feet, for it postulates a prescience denied to humanity.

And there is another consideration. Differing natures find their tongue in the presence of differing spectacles. Some natures become vocal at tragedy, some are made vocal by comedy, and it seems to me that to whichever of these aspects of life a writer's instinct for expression the more readily responds, to that he should allow it to respond. That before a contrasting side of things he remains undemonstrative need not be assumed to mean that he remains unperceiving.

It was my hope to add to these volumes of verse as many more as would make a fairly comprehensive cycle of the whole. I had wished that those in dramatic, ballad, and narrative form should include most of the cardinal situations which occur in social and public life, and those in lyric form a round of emotional experiences of some completeness. But

The petty done, the undone vast!

The more written the more seems to remain to be written; and the night cometh. I realize that these hopes and plans, except possibly to the extent of a volume or two, must remain unfulfilled.

October 1911   T.H.

Glossary of Place-names

This glossary attempts to serve two purposes. The first is to show the importance of Hardy's original place-names (see Introduction, p. xxix) and to trace any subsequent changes. The second is to list the 'Wessex' place-names finally inserted in the text by Hardy in 1896 (see Preface to that edition on p. xxxi).

Aldbrickham. Reading. (First used in the 1896 edition: 'Reading' in all previous editions.)

Anglebury. Wareham. (First used in the 1896 edition. It was originally three places – Galworth, Mundsbury and even Froominster/Troominster – which Hardy saw fit to make into one.)

Budmouth Regis/Budmouth. Weymouth (First used in the 1896 edition: 'Creston' in all previous editions.)

Carriford. An imaginary village; see Introduction, p. xviii. (Unchanged throughout.)

Casterbridge. Dorchester. (A complete anomaly in this novel. The name 'Casterbridge' first appears in the first edition of *Under the Greenwood Tree* (1872), so that Hardy could easily have used 'Casterbridge' in the 1874 edition of *Desperate Remedies* if he had wished. *The Mayor of Casterbridge* was first published in 1886, yet in the 1889 edition of *Desperate Remedies* he carefully changed 'Froominster' – his original choice and that of the 1874 edition – to 'Troominster' *not* to Casterbridge!)

Christminster. Oxford. (First introduced in the 1896 edition; i.e., it does not replace another name.)

Corvsgate Castle. Corfe Castle. (First used in the 1896 edition: 'Humdon Castle' in all previous editions.)

Creston Shore. Preston. (First used in the 1896 edition: 'Laystead shore' in the first and 1874 editions and 'Layning shore' in the 1889 edition.)

Hocbridge. An imaginary town in the Midlands. (Unchanged throughout.)

Lulwind Cove. Lulworth Cove. (First used in the 1912 edition: 'Lulstead Cove' in the 1896 edition, 'Darborne Chine' in the 1889 edition and 'Lewborne Bay' in the first and 1874 editions.)

Nether Mynton. Owermoigne. (First used in the 1896 edition: 'Stintham Lane' in all previous editions.)

Ringsworth Shore. Ringstead. (First used in the 1896 edition: 'Laystead shore' in the first and 1874 editions, and 'Layning shore' in the 1889 edition. See 'Creston Shore'.)

Tolchurch. Tolpuddle. (First used in the 1896 edition: 'Palchurch' in all previous editions.)